WHEN COURAGE COMES

Paul M. Fleming

Backbone Books LLC

The characters and events portrayed in this book are fictitious. Any similarity to real persons, living or dead, is coincidental and not intended by the author.

ISBN-13: 9798673656877

Cover artwork and design by: Aaron Baksa
Library of Congress Control Number: 2018675309
Printed in the United States of America

For Annie & Mike

CONTENTS

MAY 1943

* * *

CHAPTER 1
North Africa

Prisoner

A full moon, alive with boundless light, spills onto rippled sand of the Tunisian desert. It inspires private Stephan Jurgen to dream of possibilities he long ago abandoned when he was forced to join the German Army. His war is over and for the first time in thousands of days he clings to hope. How different things are from just a week ago when his 23rd birthday passed as just another desolate day. There were no cards or pictures or care packages from home. He's not even sure his parents are still alive. In a strange battle of senses, his desert-parched mouth can taste the rum-soaked punschkrapfen his mother used to bake for him, yet he despairs that he's forgotten the sound of her soft voice. There were no birthday candles. The only fireworks were provided by the advancing Americans who lit up the sky with a barrage of mortar fire that left his ears ringing long after the artillery assault was over.

Maybe someday his birthday will be enjoyable again, but the only milestone important to him is today. Because right now he is still alive. Because yesterday someone up the chain of command finally had the guts to surrender. And while the war he has known for nearly four years is far from over, Stephan is facing a different conflict further removed from the battlefield. Stephan Jurgen is now a prisoner of war. He is not afraid of what that means for his safety. He does not dwell on the warnings of how he will be treated and tortured by his captors. He is actually relieved. He never wanted to die; especially for a Nazi regime that he has quietly come to despise. He doesn't dare share his anti-Nazi feelings. Must be more careful than ever -- knowing many of the men marching to his left and to his right would kill him right now if they knew. They scare him more than the Americans.

It is a relentless fear for Stephan, ignited in basic training. First, an innocent remark to a fellow recruit about his homesickness for Vienna. Then, a decision to share his distrust of ardent Nazis within his regiment. The consequences were furious. That same night, he awoke to the full weight of a pillow pressed violently into his face, covering his eyes, no chance to see his assailant. His arms were pinned down. Somebody was sitting on his legs. *How many are there?* He finally understood terror. He was going to die. Battling to breathe, waiting for his heart to explode, then the panic, followed by the beer-infused whisper in his ear, "the next time we will kill you." *I'm going to live.* He remembers the moment the pillow released. Grabbing instinctively at his throat, sucking precious air into his lungs. Laying there, alive but crushed. No one daring to help him. Afraid to surrender to sleep.

He never knew who attacked him, but he quickly understood the reason why. They call that pillow of death the "Holy Ghost." It happened to others too. There were often variations, each equally terrifying. Sometimes a pillowcase was forced over your head and you were beaten to whatever degree the terrorists wanted to inflict suffering and deliver their message: fall in line or else. Some, like Stephan, heeded the warning and survived. Others chose to challenge the Nazis and their fate was much worse. Like another Austrian in his unit who was bludgeoned beyond recognition with a pot from the commissary. He was sent to the infirmary and Stephan never saw him again. *Was he brave or stupid? He could have been a survivor like me.*

Stephan moves along with men who need very little motive to bludgeon him too. He watches the silhouettes of Arab locals atop their camels against the brilliant moonlit horizon. Their pace feels synchronized with his -- slow, rhythmic, undisturbed. In most ways, he blends in with the soldiers who share his journey. Enlisted men wear standard-issue desert uniforms, originally olive-drab but long ago faded to khaki. Cotton tunics and shorts with built-in belts. Some wear chocolate brown overcoats. Officers wear tunics of olive, khaki, or mustard-yellow cotton. Regardless of rank, most marchers wear boots that were once despised for their knee-high design but have now been cut down to ankle length. Soft-cover, peaked hats are almost universally worn. Stephan's disheveled blond hair peaks out from below his fading olive-drab cap, lined with loosely-woven red cotton fabric for more protection from the sun. The long visor shields his hazel eyes, more green than brown. Since he left home the thing that has changed most dramatically about Stephan is his length. When he first joined the army, he was considered average for his height. Now, as he strides through the desert, it is his 6-foot, 1-inch frame that stands out among the sea of faded khaki.

Now, his survival has been lengthened by the surrender of thousands. Now, the only orders he has to follow are from his American captors. With the obvious language barrier, most "talking" is done with gentle shoves and pointed rifles. Right now, all he has to do is march. For as far as he can see, there are prisoners, stripped of their weapons, following the directions of their captors, waving their rifles like traffic batons. Stephan joins this parade of the vanquished, marching like a good soldier, pressing on to a nameless destination.

From his right, an agitated whisper, "more dreary days with these morons."

The words yank Stephan away from his mindless marching. In the middle of the column, a prisoner considerably shorter than Stephan struggles to make eye contact. The jittery man, swallowed by his tattered uniform, looks up at Stephan and laughs, "you want to beat me up too?" He whips his arms wildly, revealing stubby fingers and pudgy hands that wave at the men marching around them. "Get in line. Take a number. You'll have to wait your turn until Hitler's finest finish me off." He nervously nibbles his fingernails, eyes darting everywhere.

Stephan shakes his head emphatically, "no, no, I have no desire to hurt you."

The prisoner stops chewing his raw fingers long enough to extend his hand. "I'm Hugo and it's your lucky day. You don't have to march next to a Nazi."

Stephan is reluctant to answer, afraid his response might attract attention from fellow soldiers he already fears. He awkwardly shakes Hugo's hand in silence while staring straight ahead. His hesitance to openly acknowledge what Hugo is brazenly expressing tears away at his fragile conscience. *I don't even have the courage to tell him my name.*

He continues to march, wondering if his nightmare is over or just beginning. Praying it's not too late to see his family again, whatever price he must pay. He instinctively presses against his inside left breast pocket. There it is. The reassuring shape he has felt so many times before. His mother's small bible, still there, still comforting him. Her words carefully written in the margins next to passages she knew he would visit.

The wind is picking up. It seems to capture the murmurs of his comrades up ahead as word spreads back through the ranks that the Americans are souvenir hunting. He touches the bible again. Heart pounding. He races through a quick inventory of everything he has to offer. Money clip. Belt buckle. Canteen. Anything but his bible. The line is slowing. *Maybe they are just stopping for the night.* An American soldier younger than Stephan uses his rifle to stop his progress and force him from the line. He is frisked roughly. It doesn't take long. The American's hands stop over the bulge in his uniform, poking it with his index finger. Now he glares at Stephan and beckons with four fingers – the universal gesture for "give it to me." Stephan's heart is tearing through his chest, beating against the bible in his breast pocket. His trembling fingers unbutton his field jacket. For a second he thinks about resisting. He holds the black leather-bound book in both hands pleading "no" with tortured eyes. The American rips the bible from his grip, while Stephan's empty fingers now press against his pounding temples. *This can't be happening.*

The thief shoves Stephan back into the moving column and keeps pace alongside the marchers as he inspects his souvenir. He frowns in disappointment, glances sideways at Stephan and tosses the bible onto the hardened sand. Cold eyes defy the prisoner to make a move. Stephan almost trips as the marchers push him forward. He looks back one last time to see another American pick up his cherished connection to home and pound off the dust. He makes one last fruitless gesture, walking backwards, raising long arms to claim ownership of his plundered keepsake. Somebody spins him around and shoves him forward. Again, just another mindless marcher, emptier than before.

CHAPTER 2
North Africa

Interrogator

Captain Ralph Bauer has been questioning German prisoners for six straight hours. They are surrendering by the thousands. The POW process is supposed to separate Nazis from rank and file soldiers who profess no allegiance to Hitler, but the task is flawed. Prisoners are either lying, switching their identities, or pretending not to understand their captors because of the language barrier.

He bums a cigarette from Private Donaldson, the military police officer whom he just met this morning. Nice enough guy, escorting each prisoner to Ralph's station for routine interrogations, yet they've barely acknowledged each other all day. He taps his cigarette on the table paying close attention, of all things, to Donaldson's uniform. In this mass of humanity, guys like Donaldson stand out. The letters, "MP" on a wide white band around the helmet, white webbing Sam Browne belt, white gloves, and white gaiters. *No wonder the Brits call them snowdrops.* A black armband is on Donaldson's left arm, displaying white letters that also say "MP."

"Christ, Donaldson. Do you hate these Krauts as much as I do?"

"Depends on which day you ask me, sir. I get fed up with the balls on some of these officers. But then other days I feel sorry for the guys younger than me who probably didn't ask to be part of this mess."

"Are you serious?" Ralph points his unlit cigarette at the blank faces waiting to be processed. "A few days ago your poor friends over there were just members of the master race trying to murder our boys. Now, I have to sit here listening to their bullshit."

"Having a bad day sir?"

Ralph lights his cigarette "Every day's a bad day – as long as I'm questioning them instead of killing them."

"We all play our part, sir. At least that's what they tell us."

"Well the only reason I get to play this part is because I happen to speak their language rather well. So I get to interrogate men who make me embarrassed to acknowledge my own heritage."

Donaldson scans the row of interrogators. "Did you ever consider that your ability to speak German is really important to winning this war?"

Ralph doesn't respond. He wants to ignore the training he received at Camp Bullis back in Texas as a member of the Military Intelligence Service. Lessons that warned him to keep his hatred of the enemy in check, reminding him what makes a successful interviewer.

A natural aptitude for interacting with one's fellow man and past experience are essential to good interviewing skills...a few months of training will not make a competent interviewer out of an individual who lacks the inherent aptitude...even strong language skills will not overcome this shortcoming...individuals who are unable to repress a violent emotional approach should not be employed as interrogators.

The sun is beginning to set. Ralph flicks his cigarette aside and pours himself into a fragile chair that manages to support his medium-sized frame. He is skinny by most standards, weighing less than 120 pounds. His once-pale skin is now red from sun exposure. He scratches sand out of his thick crew-cut black hair. They are positioned outside an overcrowded tent, barely removed from the congestion and stench created by a filthy mass of tired, hungry soldiers plucked from the desert. Typically, prisoners arrive on foot, but today a constant parade of M3 personnel carriers, filled mostly with Germans and a smattering of Italians, has been kicking up dust and choking the narrow lanes since sunrise. The temperature is beginning to drop, and a gentle breeze makes the ordeal more manageable.

"Next prisoner up, sir."

Ralph's light green eyes barely makes contact with a young soldier waiting for the order to be seated. It is Stephan.

Donaldson gestures to the empty overturned 55-gallon drum that has served as a "chair" for countless POWs. In perfect German, Ralph begins his simple interrogation.

"Name and rank?"

Stephan's eyes widen a bit as he fumbles in his pocket and produces his *Soldbuch.* The best chance to establish a prisoner's identity is this 15-page Soldiers Book that carries essential information. Ralph grabs it and points the book at Donaldson. "Finally, one of these things that hasn't been ripped off." He opens the book, looking carefully at the photograph and finally peering directly at Stephan. "Private Stephan Jurgen."

"Kannst du mir bitte helfen?" "Can you please help me?"

"No, listen carefully private. I'm going to ask...."

"Please, they took my bible, my mother's bible. Stephan tugs at his empty breast pocket. Can you help me?"

Stephan's voice is rising. Donaldson takes a step closer to the exchange.

"Everything okay, Captain?"

"No, this poor guy lost his mommy's bible and I'm about to tell him to go to hell."

Stephan turns to a confused Donaldson and says, "she gave me her bible before I left Vienna."

"Save it pal. I can't understand a word you're saying."

Ralph smacks the Soldbuch in his free hand to get Stephan's attention. "Vienna? So you're Austrian?"

"Yes! Can you help me?"

Ralph rolls his eyes at Donaldson and puts up his hand. "Look private, I'm sorry that you lost your bible, but I can't help you. He tosses the Soldbuch onto the table and leans back carefully. "Besides, why would a Nazi need a bible?" *Easy does it Ralph. Just do your job.*

Stephan hangs his head, and whispers, "I am not a Nazi. I was drafted. I had no choice. Please, my bible? It is my only connection to my home."

POWs should be protected from souvenir hunters among the guard and interrogator staff...A POW who is indignant over being stripped of his personal belongings will likely be in an uncooperative mood.

Ralph forces a sympathetic nod then adds sarcastically, "so, private can you tell me what you did against your will for the Nazis?"

"I was a mechanic. I repaired mostly tanks."

"Okay, were you involved in any type of radio communications over the last few days? Anything that would..."

"I told you I repaired tanks." Stephan points inside the processing tent. "Please, we are losing time."

Ralph pounds the table. *"Genug!"* "Enough!"

He pushes himself up from the table, motions for Stephan to stand, and braces for one more plea. Instead, Stephan jerks his head to the left, looking beyond Ralph toward the sound of those all-too-familiar trucks rumbling past the tent swollen with POWs. Without warning, Stephan reaches across the narrow table, grabs a chest full of Ralph's uniform and pulls the American violently towards him. At that instant, before prisoner and interrogator both fall to the ground, nine tons of free-wheeling personnel carrier obliterates the chair where Ralph was just sitting and smashes squarely into the rear of another M3 loaded with prisoners. Ralph lands heavily on his right shoulder. Pain shoots through his neck. He struggles to move as Stephan remains on top of him. He tries to push him off but the hot pain holds him back. Ralph rolls away instead, tasting dust as Stephan releases his grip. Ralph struggles to his feet. Screams pierce the desert air. A wide-eyed Donaldson strong arms the prisoner, lifting Stephan to his feet. A crowd moves cautiously to the accident scene leaving Ralph, Stephan, and the MP standing alone. Ralph says nothing at first, silently dusting himself off with his good arm -- realizing that his life was just saved by a stranger, his prisoner, the despised enemy. Donaldson, gripping Stephan tightly and still trying to process everything that just happened, looks to Ralph -- unsure of what to say or do.

Ralph, rubbing his shoulder, ignores Stephan and looks directly at Donaldson, "Any chance you can find this man his bible?"

CHAPTER 3
Huntsville, Texas

The Secret

Ginny's wet nose brings a smile to Rose Bauer's lips before she even opens her eyes. She doesn't need to consult the alarm clock perched on the antique night table next to the sturdy iron bed she painted white last summer. Her family's 5-year old beagle follows a routine that never wavers, so Rose is confident it is around 5:00 AM. Ginny is already off to rouse the rest of the household, her nails echoing off the hardwood floors of the Huntsville, Texas farmhouse she shares with two special people: Her precious Oma -- the German name for grandmother -- and Uncle Pete, Oma's son. Rose finally opens her eyes, rolls over, stretches instinctively for the silver wire-rimmed eyeglasses she desperately needs to begin each day. They've been a permanent fixture for Rose as long as she can remember. Her farsightedness the result of her premature birth twenty-five years ago. The spectacles are already perched on her thin long nose as she shakes her short-cropped blonde curls, focuses her watery blue eyes on the clock, and grins a second time. It is 5:15 AM. *That dog never disappoints.*

Her beagle's trusted routine is about the only thing that hasn't been reshaped around here. Since Pearl Harbor it's been slowly unraveling on the farm. In just over one year, her older brothers Ralph and Henry enlisted and shipped out. Henry, the oldest, is in the Navy, awaiting orders to join a new escort carrier operating with the Pacific Fleet. Ralph's journey has been a little more mysterious. Since he enlisted in the army, Ralph's letters have been rather vague about his whereabouts, insisting he is "just following orders and keeping my nose clean." Uncle Pete thinks Ralph is somewhere in North Africa. "After all, that's where most of our boys are going these days." Rose knows Uncle Pete is barely holding things together. He is a proud man and equally proud of his nephews. But like most independent farmers in this small town 70 miles north of Houston, he feels their absence profoundly. The biggest hole is the knowledge he passed on to them to plant, cultivate, and grow cotton. The only person Uncle Pete still trusts is Clyde, the aging overseer who has worked the Bauer fields longer than forever. Before her toes touch the damp floor, Rose is already feeling guilty about Clyde – lingering once again over the secret she's kept from him for way too long.

She moves to the window and gently parts the stiff sheer curtains that long ago faded to yellow. Closing her eyes she listens. It's faint but there it is. Like every other dawn, the laborious sound of Clyde's work boots grinding fresh footsteps on the gravel service road that leads to the work yard below Rose's window. *What does he think about on these early morning walks? Does he think about her?*

She squints hard, but the grey light and Clyde's dark skin are too much for her weak eyes to manage. Still, she recognizes Clyde's deep, strong voice. *I could listen to him talk all day.* Rose hears Uncle Pete too but his soft-spoken delivery, almost a whisper, surrenders to the fruity melody of his overseer. She may not be able to hear her uncle, but Clyde's responses underscore the pecking order on this ranch. "Right away, Mr. Bauer. I'll take care of it straight away." Clyde is whistling now, sweet and soothing. But Rose has been around the man long enough to know he whistles when he is nervous. When Uncle Pete has given him a list of things to do that is far too long for the day ahead.

Rose has her responsibilities too. She grabs her favorite red plaid robe, throws it on as she heads down the hallway, elbows popping through the last remaining threads of tattered sleeves. She picks up her pace and heads down the creaky back staircase that leads to the kitchen.

It is a simple room, one of Rose's favorites. Clean, calico curtains. She washes them once a week. No clutter. There is a place for everything. There's indoor plumbing, a luxury many nearby families still don't enjoy. And, of course the handmade oak table built and finished by her daddy, whom she never knew. She imagines her father as a teenager carefully building the table. Uncle Pete says the wood he wasted building that thing could have fueled the fireplace for a year. Rose is just grateful she can touch and feel something that her father created. Most of her fondness for this room comes from every meaningful memory that centered around that table. Rubbing the smooth beveled finish as she struggled with her arithmetic assignments. That always relaxed her. To this day she's not sure why. Wrapping Christmas presents under Oma's watchful eye, parchment paper covering the precious finish her father had painstakingly applied. Standing guard, her chest pounding, while Henry notched his initials under the table with a penknife. Listening to President Roosevelt on the radio, declaring war on Japan, too naive to understand that nothing would ever be the same around this table. In this room. In their home.

Already, the kitchen is alive with the smell of fresh coffee brewed earlier by Uncle Pete -- a chore he relinquishes to no one. The coffee's aroma reminds Rose of her last letter from Ralph. He mentioned Uncle Pete's morning brew, writing how that familiar smell helps him remember home. She didn't have the heart to tell him that coffee is rationed now. One pound has to last over a month. Before the war, that was barely enough to fuel her brothers for a week. Rose savors her single cup of coffee. She goes without sugar. Everything is rationed these days. She remembers the poster hanging in the faculty lunchroom at school, "Do with less so they'll have enough." *They are the ones making the real sacrifice. Forget the self-pity and do your part, Rose.* She remembers the letters she wrote to her brothers last night. Still cradling her coffee, she slides her free hand along the surface of the kitchen table until it meets the two envelopes that she deposited there on her way up to bed. *Don't forget to get to the post office this morning. But, first Oma.*

Rose prepares a breakfast tray for her grandmother. She's done it for countless mornings, even before the war emptied their home. *How many more of these mornings will I get to make a simple bowl of oatmeal for such a special person?* Then she assembles Uncle Pete's standard burnt toast, cottage cheese and marmalade just as the rear door squeaks open, long enough to allow the morning's warm, damp air to reach the kitchen. Ginny arrives first, oblivious to rationing, tail wagging in anticipation of her morning treat. Rose instinctively pushes her palm in front of the dog who gently lifts a morsel of toast and disappears under the kitchen table.

Uncle Pete enters the kitchen and Rose smiles, pecks him on the cheek and speaks for the first time this morning. Her gravelly voice poses the same daily question, "Is Oma coming down for breakfast?"

"Her arthritis is pretty bad Rose. I think it's best if you take this up to her." Her uncle has already lifted the tray and hands it to his niece with a smile that says, "thank you." Rose may be worn down, but she never feels taken for granted. Twilight is breaking, and the first slivers of filtered sunlight pierce the gaps in the calico curtains. She looks at the permanent creases in her uncle's forehead, the deeper wrinkles etched around his steel-blue eyes. It is only 6:00 in the morning and he already looks exhausted.

At this early hour an 85-year old woman has every right to linger in bed and delay the start of another day. But not Oma. Rose knows what to expect as she taps lightly on the bedroom door and pushes it open with the breakfast tray. Her grandmother is already sitting in her chair by the window. The room is dimmer than usual thanks to a morning sun that is now retreating behind darkening clouds. It doesn't matter. This room is never gloomy. Oma wears a bold, bright house-coat, one that no doubt she made herself, before the arthritis took its toll. Her white hair is pulled back in a tight bun. Her complexion is flawless, with slight symmetrical crinkles on the edges of her powder blue eyes. At this age you would expect her to be wearing glasses, but Rose, whose eyesight weakens every year, marvels at her grandmother's perfect vision. But then she glimpses the swollen joints on her crippled hands. The fingers that point sideways in a very unnatural direction. She knows Oma is suffering. Rose feels guilty for her own self-pity about her weak eyes. She envies Oma's grit.

"Good morning sweetheart!" *How can she be so happy?* "What tasty treat are you bringing from the kitchen of Frau Bauer?" *She can always make me smile.* "Good morning Oma. I made your favorite, oatmeal with honey." "That looks delicious Rose, but you forgot my beer." *Always ready with a wink and a tease.* "Oma, there will be no beer for you until after 10:00! You know the rules." One of her grandmother's favorite traditions is the Bavarian brotzeit, or second breakfast. On a rare day off, Rose will always try to treat Oma to a small meal of bread and cheese, a pretzel, or a veal sausage and good mustard. And a beer, of course.

"I suppose I can wait. It's just that my social calendar is so full today, I don't know if I will be around later for a little beer." *God, give me one percent of her sense of humor and I will be happy.* She kisses her grandmother on the forehead and maintains eye contact as she backs her way to the bedroom door. "Enjoy your breakfast Oma, and good luck with that busy social calendar."

Rose is almost out the door when Oma shouts, "Rose, wait. I almost forgot. Were you able to find someone who can fix my watch?"

Rose steps back in and raises her palm to her forehead. "Oma, I'm so sorry. I forgot again. I'll talk to Uncle Pete this morning. I promise."

Oma winks at Rose. "That's okay. I just need my watch to keep track of my busy schedule. Now, have a good day Rosie. And don't be too hard on those boys at school. These are tough times for all of us. Tell Pete to pay attention to the weather. My joints are telling me it's going to rain."

As she leaves the tranquility of Oma's room, Rose squints at her wristwatch and realizes once again she's behind schedule. She knows it's coming. Predicts the sound before she reaches the bottom step of the narrow staircase that places her back in the kitchen. There it is, the annoying, wheezing horn of Uncle Pete's prized 1936 Ford pickup. He never leans on the horn, just politely gives it a tap to let Rose know he's waiting. *Predictable, just like Ginny.* Rose opens the back door and sees Uncle Pete already sitting in his idling truck. *I need to get up earlier. Too many things to do before I leave for work. Don't forget about the watch.* Rose bounces off the front porch and realizes immediately she should be wearing her raincoat. Oma was right. The single squeaking windshield wiper is already rejecting the steady drizzle that greets Rose as she trudges towards the truck. *Not going to try his patience. No way I'm going back for my raincoat.* Before she even pulls the door shut, he is handing Rose an umbrella. "Thought you might need this today, Rosie." *God, he knows me so well.*

"Thanks Uncle Pete. You're my guardian angel." Rose removes her glasses and retrieves a handkerchief from her bag. It is clean but frayed and worn. It belonged to her mother, so Rose will use it forever. She cleans the round lenses, pats her damp forehead for good measure and lets out a huge sigh. "Let's go, we're going to be late!" Uncle Pete smiles broadly at her dry wit. "Sorry I held you up this morning darling. Straight to school?"

"No, I want to drop off these letters at the post office." She fumbles through her bag. "Um, Uncle Pete?"

"Don't worry darling. I'll come back and get them before Clyde and me head out to New Waverly. Oma said she wanted to go to the post office again, so it won't be out of our way."

He starts the truck rolling away from the house toward the long winding driveway that separates the property from the main road. Clyde is coming off the rear porch. The perspiration already glistens on his shaved scalp. His forehead is remarkably free of wrinkles and creases that usually come with years of toiling under the wicked Texas sun. Clyde squeezes the sweat from an unruly beard flecked with patches of white that add years to his appearance. He sees Rose and smiles. *He doesn't deserve this.*

"Okay, so what's up with Clyde? I heard him whistling this morning. What's he nervous about?"

"That man can't hide his worries, can he? Oh, he's got his ox in a ditch about manpower for chopping. We're running pretty lean and he's coming up short with the bodies we need to get the job done."

"Is he okay?"

"Why are you so worried about Clyde? He'll be fine."

Rose is silent. Sheets of rain batter the windshield.

CHAPTER 4
Huntsville, Texas

Harmless

At the end of the driveway. Uncle Pete eases the Ford onto State Highway 19 and shifts into third gear as staccato blasts of rain pummel the truck. Rose watches a slow bead of water forming on the inside of the windshield. It plops straight down and settles squarely on her foot, followed almost immediately by another drop. She tucks her feet under the seat. "Oma predicted rain this morning. Told me to warn you but it looks like it got a head start on us. Oh! Her watch. She's been asking me about getting her watch repaired and I keep forgetting."

"That's odd. You never forget anything important."

"Okay, very funny. Listen, I've got a lot on my mind. But I'm remembering now. I'm reminding you so when Oma asks me again, I can tell her you have it under control."

"Fair enough Rosie, but the problem right now is that the closest watchmaker we've got is way down in Houston. This town of ours is looking like hell with everyone out to lunch. Your grandmother will have to be patient, but we'll take care of it, I promise."

Huntsville is a small town of maybe 15,000, surrounded by a patchwork of farms and ranches. Like lots of towns in this part of Walker County, the economy is dependent upon cotton, wheat, and livestock. Uncle Pete has been saying for years that cattle production is on the rise while cotton continues to decline. One of the biggest headaches when it comes to cotton is the labor shortage. After the Dust Bowl, plenty of struggling families abandoned their farms and headed north to industrial cities where factory jobs were more plentiful. Now, since the war broke out, there are fewer men to do the backbreaking work that cotton demands.

Uncle Pete's pickup carves its way through rain-slicked narrow roads, further away from the farms and fields that families and tenant farmers have been tending since well before the Civil War. The topography becomes heavily wooded as they enter the fringe of the Piney Woods, a massive forest that extends well beyond Texas into stretches of Arkansas, Louisiana, and Oklahoma. Many of the species that define this dense growth of trees will be harder to find the further west you travel into Texas. Some like dogwood, birch, persimmon, and hickory seem to have staked their western boundary right here in Walker County. Rose has lived near these woods all her life, yet the variety of trees and the wildlife they help sustain is foreign to her. She wouldn't know a black gum from a white ash. The only tree that has any meaning to her is the southern red oak. That doesn't mean she could tell you that it grows to over 100 feet with a trunk as wide as five feet. She could care less about its unique oval-shaped glossy green leaves that set it apart from other oaks that populate the Piney Woods. Even its legacy as a signature tree of the Old South barely matters to Rose. What matters is the rare connection it gives this orphan to her father. She pictures her daddy coming here with Uncle Pete to find the cherished wood he needed to build his kitchen table. She can't even call it a memory. After all, she never knew him. It's just one of the few reminders she has of him. On this morning, that simple bond will suffice. They are heading south, still a good distance away from town, about 8 miles or so, when Uncle Pete slows the Ford and turns unexpectedly down an unmarked dirt road that will be closer to mud by the end of this rainy morning. He slows down and pulls the Ford over, allowing an empty flatbed to squeeze by, spattering the wood-paneled truck with a healthy dose of Texas mud that more closely resembles red clay than the black earth she's used to seeing on the farm. The wipers barely do their job.

Rose is confused. "Is this a shortcut?"

"Nope. This is what everybody in town is talking about. The POW camp."

"Wait. Are they finished building it? Did I miss something?" She swipes at another infuriating bead of water that finds her leg.

"Aw, Rose, honey, you've got a lot of other things on your mind right now. Like the mail and Oma's watch."

"I don't know what's more annoying -- this leaky truck or your sarcasm." The rain tapers to a drizzle. "Sorry Uncle Pete. It's not your fault that I don't pay attention to what's happening in Huntsville. But another prison? What's wrong with the six jails we already have in this county? Good Lord, how many prisoners do we need around here? They already call Huntsville the 'prison city'."

"Rosie, there are so many Krauts surrendering over in North Africa they have no place to put them. The Brits can't handle the numbers, so it looks like a bunch of them are coming here."

"They are the enemy Uncle Pete, trying to kill our boys, my brothers, and they are going to send them here to Texas? Don't we have a say in this? Are we going to be protected? What if they escape?"

"There's another town meeting scheduled for Thursday night. All for show if you ask me. Still, you should come. Get up to speed on things." She can smell the damp towel as he points it toward a patrol car sitting in the middle of the road

-- blocking traffic to the site. He leans into Rose and whispers, "Besides I'm sure your friend will be there."

Rose squints hard. "Is that Bobby Ford?"

"Sure is. He's here every morning. Bobby usually has a ten-gallon mouth but nowadays he's feeling too important to let me in on what's going on down there." He winks. "But I'm sure he'd talk to us today." He starts to roll down his window.

"Don't you dare!"

"Oh too late Rose." Uncle Pete chuckles. "Here he comes."

Deputy Bobby Ford smiles and waves. His wide-brimmed hat sheds rain as he tilts his head and ambles toward them. Even through his baggy raincoat Rose can see his ample belly. "That man has given me the creeps since high school. Is that the best we can do for police work around here?"

"Yeah, he thinks the sun comes up just to hear him crow." Uncle Pete nods at the deputy, who smugly tips his hat and heads directly to Rose's side of the truck. Thick, foggy glasses magnify his stony eyes. Rose reluctantly lowers her window and forces a smile.

"Good morning Mr. Bauer. Hello Rose."

"Bobby." She wiggles away from the window.

"Came out here with your uncle to see our prison?"

Your prison? Lazy scum. "Just passing through on my way to school. Really don't have much time."

"Sure, sure. Of course. We'll be having another open house out here real soon, but any time you want a personal tour of the place just let me know. Yup, we're pretty much ready to go."

Rose swallows hard as Uncle Pete decides to dig for more. "Lots of people are pretty uptight about the place, Bobby. Say the prisoners will be getting treated way better than they deserve."

"Got that right Mr. Bauer. Folks are already calling it the 'Fritz Ritz.' It's a country club if you ask me. Hoping a few of them decide to escape so I can teach them a lesson or two."

Uncle Pete forces a laugh. "Fair warning, right Bobby?"

The deputy is distracted, paying attention to Rose. "So maybe I can stop by the next time I'm out your way. Been a while since I've seen your grandmother."

Rose hesitates, "things are pretty busy so ...."

"Hey, Bobby sorry to cut this short but I need to get Rose to work. Last thing we want is the teacher to be late for her own class."

"Oh, right, right. Lucky students if you ask me."

Rose forces one more smile and rolls up her window.

Uncle Pete checks his side view mirror and gives the steering wheel a few strong turns, made more difficult because of the wheels settling into the boggy road. He babies the clutch, grinds the stubborn gearbox into reverse and starts backing down the path. Rose exhales. "Thank you, Uncle Pete. I can't stomach that man. And he shouldn't be flirting like that. He's married for God's sake."

"Could never figure out why that sweet girl -- what's her name?"

"Sally."

"Right. Sally Ferguson. Could never figure out why she married him."

"Good Lord Uncle Pete. You know full well he got her pregnant right out of high school. Now she's stuck with him." Rose nervously folds the towel and shoves it under the seat.

"Aw come on now. He may not be your type but he's harmless."

Far from harmless. Clyde would kill him if he knew.

CHAPTER 5
North Africa

Lucky

Ralph arrives at his station early, eager to get his day started and put even more distance between himself and the M3 that nearly crushed him yesterday like a fat-tail scorpion. There's no shortage of good-natured ribbing:

"Hey Bauer, where's your private bodyguard?"

"Ralph, don't even think of sitting near me today."

"How's it feel to owe your life to the enemy?"

That last comment stings. *Not the way I wanted to survive this war. Not even close to the brave man my father was.* He drags on his first cigarette of the day and feels the burning smoke cling to his nostrils. Yesterday was not the first time he's come out of some tough situations without a scratch. The searing desert heat jogs a distant memory -- an equally hot Texas summer when he slipped backwards off a ladder and fell two stories directly into the bed of Uncle Pete's truck filled with baled cotton. His chatty uncle, plucking cotton from his nephew's ears, said, "Ralphie, you're so lucky you could sit on a fence and the birds would feed you!" Ralph thought it was funny, but he remembers Rose was hysterical, especially because she was supposed to be holding the ladder. Rose never stops worrying about him. They are very close, even their birthdays are only

14 months apart.

As they got older and closer, they experienced the impenetrable wall that Oma had built around the memory of their parents. She was upbeat, positive and smiled every day. But she didn't believe in dwelling on the past. "Life," she would always say, "is for the living." That meant the Bauer kids learned very little about their parents from their grandmother. Uncle Pete was a different story. While Oma was reserved, almost awkward in her shyness, Uncle Pete was ready with an opinion or advice – even if he wasn't asked. Which was most of the time. Ready to talk the ears off a mule, he would answer any question his niece and nephew had – especially about their father, his only sibling. He told the kids how he and their dad hitchhiked together to the armory in Houston after the United States entered the Great War in 1917. Despite Oma's objections, Hank volunteered to join the Army, leaving behind his wife Lisa, his oldest son Henry, Jr., and Ralph. He shipped out in February 1918 and three months later he was dead, struck in the temple by German machine gun fire. He was one of the first Americans killed in action after the United States Army set foot on French soil. They said he died instantly. His infantry regiment had been in the line of battle for less than a day. He also went to his death unaware that Lisa had conceived a child just one month before he left for Europe. That was the last time Ralph's parents were together and the baby his mother carried was Rose, born prematurely -- two months after the death of a father who would never hold her in his arms. Tragically, before his sister's first birthday Ralph and his siblings would also lose their mother to the deadly influenza virus that decimated the world's population, killing almost 50 million people. Ralph was two. Henry was five.

Uncle Pete, who served in the artillery and survived the Second Battle of the Marne, returned home and soon accepted responsibility for the lives of three orphans. Once, Rose asked him why he never married, and Uncle Pete told her straight up, "I promised your daddy I would take care of you if anything ever happened to him. When your mama died, that promise became even more important. So, that's what I'm doing. Easiest promise I ever made."

Uncle Pete may not have been their father, but he was a true role model. Honest, hardworking, and well respected in Huntsville. He was also the thriftiest man in Texas. Ralph swore the ranch would have gone under a long time ago if it wasn't for Uncle Pete's wisdom, sound decision making and good judgement. The first time Rose earned a dollar for babysitting, Uncle Pete admired her earnings, smoothed the bill out, folded it carefully and returned it to her, saying, "Rosie, the quickest way to double your money is to fold it over and put it back in your pocket." Ralph wondered if Rose would remember that story. Her memory was never as good as his. Often, he would recollect a funny incident and she would look at him with the same befuddled expression, pushing those glasses back up her nose and admitting she remembered nothing. "Ralph, I wish I could remember half of what you forget." He reflects on a letter from Rose he read last night. Briefer than usual. Good report on Oma's health. But plenty of labor challenges on the ranch. *I could be helping. Instead I'm stuck here.* His thoughts of home disappear when he hears Donaldson's voice.

"Captain, glad to see you back to work."

"Thanks, Donaldson, hell of an experience. Not the way I imagined getting killed over here."

Donaldson nods and adds, "Nothing surprises me anymore. Keep thinking about those Jerrys in the truck yesterday. They survive some fierce fighting and end up buying the farm right before they get assigned to POW heaven."

"Ah, there's that compassion for the enemy again. Ever think they had it coming to them?"

"No sir. I just meant...maybe some of these guys are just

good people in a bad army."

"Give me a break. Hell, even the ones who survived are already in the base hospital, receiving the exact same care wounded Americans get. POW heaven, right Donaldson?" Without being too obvious, Ralph extends his boot and smooths the wide track marks from yesterday, cautiously checks for truck traffic, and plops into the replacement for his demolished chair. "Listen, nobody understands the rules more than me. As one of the few German-speaking Americans in this place, I'm the one who gets to tell the Kraut officers about the future treatment of their men." His tone edges towards exaggeration, "reassuring them that the Americans will always respect the rules of the Geneva Convention." He smirks. "Of course, that doesn't stop our guys from doing a little souvenir shopping, which by the way is fine with me. That reminds me, any luck with that bible yesterday?"

"Well, believe it or not I was able to find *a* bible. I was shooting the shit last night with a buddy of mine who picked this up a couple days ago during one of the prisoner marches. Donaldson offers it to Ralph.

"Said the kid it belonged too was pretty upset about giving it up. But I can't promise you it's *the* bible. Besides, these prisoners are moving through here pretty fast so the chances of getting this back to your hero boy are slim and none."

Ralph takes it. "Not what I was expecting." A lot of soldiers carried pocket bibles, small enough to fit into the chest pocket of their uniform. Some even carried "heart shields" -- metal plates that were attached to the front cover of a bible to stop a bullet from reaching a soldier's heart. But this is different. More traditional in size, a regular family bible published in German. It isn't that old but the gold lettering on the black leather cover is considerably faded. The binding needs some repairs too. Delicate onion skin pages are curled at the edges. This isn't a paperweight. It's been used daily. He opens the book. Donaldson is still speaking but Ralph doesn't hear him. He is staring intently at the words jumping off the first page:

"Keep your faith and come home to me. Love, Mother."

His gut tightens. He runs his nicotine-stained fingers over the words, then pulls his hands back, afraid he will somehow rub the message away. *This has to be his.* He imagines Oma and his father sharing the same connection. *Don't even go there.* Donaldson finally breaks through.

"Sir, there's something else."

"Sorry, what's that?"

The MP pulls something out of the top pocket of his tunic. "With all the chaos yesterday, this must have gotten lost." He holds out a heavily damaged Soldbuch. "I found it outside the tent this morning. It's his sir, the prisoner who...um"

"You can say it – who saved my life." Ralph slowly takes the book and opens it. "Well a lot of good this is going to do me. Most of the front pages are missing. I don't even see his name."

"If you don't mind my asking sir what are you going to do with the bible? Are you really going to try to get it back to him?"

"It's none of your goddamn business." Ralph's immediate anger is directed at Donaldson but it's the MPs words that taunt him. *Some of these guys are just good people in a bad army.*

CHAPTER 6
Huntsville, Texas

Favor

Rose quickly erases yesterday's homework assignment from the dusty blackboard and turns to face her students already seated for first period English composition. She is late again. It's becoming a problem for the high school's principal, Dr. Leonard Roebuck. Her eyesight prevents her from driving but she can't use that as an excuse anymore since Uncle Pete is usually waiting for her in the morning. Uncle Pete has high standards and punctuality is right at the top of the list. She looks at many of the sophomore and junior boys in the room and knows they would understand. Many of them have been reluctantly recruited by Uncle Pete to work on the farm. Seems that nobody has met Peter Bauer's demanding standards. Bill Grissom, "not worth spit." The Becker twins, "both overdrawn at the memory bank." Keith Jensen? "There's a light or two burned off on his string." But Uncle Pete also gives Keith a break. Since he lost his older brother at the battle of Midway, he hasn't been right in the head. Rose has seen the difference, too. When she shared that her brother Henry's ship would be recommissioned as the USS Midway in honor of the American naval victory, young Keith perked up and now reminds her about it every day. Maybe, Rose reflects, he feels a connection to the brother he'll never see again. Her uncle tells her to be compassionate and just listen. "The Jensens are in pain, darling. That could be any of us tomorrow."

The school bell interrupts her thoughts as the class settles down without any direction. Before Rose can begin her lesson, she is interrupted.

"Miss Bauer?"

She recognizes the voice of Rachel Dawson, probably the politest student in her class. "Yes Rachel. What is it?

"Beg your pardon ma'am but...." She points toward the front door of the classroom. Rose turns and sees Roebuck's bald head through the single pane of glass. The principal is a short man so you can barely see his eyes. The class snickers. "Alright people settle down." *God why doesn't he just knock and come in?*

She opens the door. "Good morning, Miss Bauer." His monotonous voice reminds Rose why she appreciates Clyde's.

"Miss Bauer, I've asked Mrs. Garrison to stay with your class. I'm wondering if you could come with me for a few minutes."

For the first time, she notices Ellie Garrison entering the door at the rear of her classroom. She is a dear friend, so Rose understands when she sheepishly avoids eye contact, staring down at the floor. Most of the students remain quiet, but a single voice breaks the awkward silence.

"Dr. Roebuck, will our teacher be getting detention today? Maybe you should call her parents!" Rose glares at the culprit. Bill Grissom, of course. She wants to embarrass him; let him know that she's an orphan, there is no father or mother in her life. But she bites her lip. *Uncle Pete was right, he's not worth spit.*

Out in the hallway, Roebuck simply says, "follow me Rose."

He used my first name. Is that the final act of sympathy before he fires me? Rose's heart is in her throat. *I need this job.* When they arrive at his small office at the opposite end of the corridor, Roebuck opens the door for her and manages a polite smile. *Okay, now he's kind of smiling, what gives?* She enters his office. The door quietly closes behind her and Rose realizes immediately that she is alone. Dr. Roebuck is still outside in the corridor. She hears his footsteps gradually fading away.

"Miss Bauer, in here."

Rose gasps as she unexpectedly hears her name. She peers around the corner in the direction of a commanding male voice. Standing in a small conference room is a military officer of some significant rank. He is older. Rose imagines old enough to be her father's age. Every part of his uniform from tie to toe is creased and perfect. Rose's heart sinks, her hands are drawn to her lips, as she finally speaks her brothers' names. "Ralph. Henry. Oh my God, what's happened?"

"No, no, I am not here about your brothers. I am so sorry to alarm you. Please sit down."

Rose quickly slumps into the first chair she finds, a considerable distance from the conference room table where he is standing. He doesn't make her get up. Instead, he plucks a chair from around the table and slides it over to her. He sits down gently, every crease still in place.

"I'm sorry to have frightened you. That was not my intention, but your principal was rather dramatic about my request to speak with you."

Rose finally allows herself to breathe again. "Welcome to the world of Leonard Roebuck...." She hesitates, unsure how to address him.

"Forgive me. My name is Colonel Warren, United States Army. I am with the Provost Marshall General's Office in Washington."

Rose appears openly confused.

"I know that's a mouthful. Our unit is part of the War

Department and one of our responsibilities is prisoner of war camps here in the states. Of course you know that Huntsville is one of those locations."

"Well colonel, I'm not going to lie to you. I have serious reservations about the camp."

"Understandable. You and every other resident from here to Houston. That goes with the territory. But I hope you could be open-minded and set those feelings aside because we could really use your help."

Rose smooths out her dress and sits a little more erect. "I'm not. I don't. Sorry colonel, I'm confused."

"Of course. Let me explain. When the camp opens, we are going to be processing thousands of German prisoners of war who all represent a single common barrier to us. They speak German. We don't."

"You don't have interpreters?" Rose moves to the edge of her chair, hands folded on her lap.

"Think about it. Most of our soldiers who speak German are already serving as interpreters over in North Africa." *I wonder if Ralph is doing that?* "Back in the states, we need to rely on citizen volunteers who can provide a similar service here at home. Unfortunately, teaching and learning the German language has not been a priority in this country since the Great War. You are smiling Miss Bauer. Did I say something funny?"

"Ironic, not funny, colonel. I'm just thinking of my grandmother. She's the reason I speak German. She's the one who insisted my brothers and I learn. She would be delighted to know that all her persistence paid off."

"Your grandmother should be proud. Hopefully, you were a good student and paid attention in class."

"I hope so too. I have to admit I'm a little nervous about this whole thing. Overwhelmed really."

"That's understandable, Miss Bauer."

"You can call me Rose." His immediate response is stern but kind.

"No, we will maintain order and formal reporting at all times. This is first and foremost a military operation and it's imperative our enemy views it that way. They should never know you by your first name." *Enemy. Sounds so much more exciting than teaching high school!* Colonel Warren stands for the first time and begins to pace slowly around the room, his hands clasped behind his back. He never breaks eye contact with her. "Your main responsibility will be to work with our command team when they interact with the German officers. At no time will you be required to be with the general population of enlisted men."

"Why just the officers?"

"Well, despite being prisoners, these are still soldiers used to the discipline and rigor of military life. That's not going to change when they get to Huntsville. The German officers take their leadership role seriously and it will continue within our camps across the country."

"Do you trust them?" He raises his eyebrows, considers the question longer than she expects.

"We have little choice." He stands beside his unoccupied chair, brushing the armrest with his fingers, choosing his words carefully. "If they maintain discipline in their ranks, it takes a great burden off our men. We've already seen it working in the camps in North Africa and we're hopeful it will be maintained during the journey here to the states and ultimately within our prison camps."

"What about my job at the high school? Quite frankly Colonel, our family needs the paycheck."

"I understand Miss Bauer." He finally sits again, placing his palms on his knees. His upright posture never surrenders.

"You will be compensated by the Army for your time in Camp Huntsville. Our hope is that your services will be needed this Summer as we start processing prisoners through here. With any luck, you can be back in your classroom when school resumes in the Fall, maybe Spring at the latest. What do you think?"

Rose nods but offers no response.

"Look I know it's a lot to take in. We've got another town meeting."

Rose finishes the sentence, "Thursday night."

"Yes, Thursday night. Maybe you can think about our conversation and we'll speak again after the meeting.

"I'll do it!"

"You don't have to decide right now."

"Yes I do colonel and I'll do it."

"Well thank you Miss Bauer. Your country is very grateful. There's just one more thing."

"Okay?"

"You're going to have to be on time." For the first time he manages a smile.

CHAPTER 7
Huntsville, Texas

Answers

Thursday night couldn't come fast enough for the citizens of Huntsville. The corridors of the high school are jammed with residents vying for standing room inside the already sweltering gym. The crowd is boisterous, anticipation high. The rear of the school, where the gym carves its footprint into the parking lot, is equally crowded. The doors are open to let the people inside get some air, while teasing the frustrated crowd outside. Off to the side, still close to the building is a wide swath of Negro residents. Clyde is among them, sharing small talk with many of the older men who will be working side-by-side with him in the weeks ahead.

Rose works her way through the parking lot. As she gets closer to the rear of the school, she first sees Clyde then hears a familiar voice, "Move on folks. Clear out now." The stern command comes from Bobby Ford, tapping his night stick as he repeats his instructions even more emphatically. At first Rose thinks the deputy is speaking to the entire group. But then he focuses directly on Clyde and his friends. Most of the crowd, used to this kind of treatment, slowly move away. Their spots are taken by white residents who are complaining about being displaced by the coloreds. Rose separates herself from them, not wanting Clyde to think she's doing the complaining.

His only reaction to seeing her is a smile. "Good evening, Miss Rose."

"Hello Clyde, quite a crowd we've got here I see."

"I'd say so. Folks still have lots of questions."

Before she can answer, Bobby Ford is in Clyde's face. "Quit bothering this lady and move on."

"He's not bothering me Bobby. We were having a conversation."

The night stick comes into Rose's view as it prods Clyde's shoulder. "Afraid your conversation has to wait. These people need to move."

"It's okay Miss Rose. Go on inside." Clyde is speaking to her but his eyes are fixed on the baton. "I'll see you tomorrow."

Rose is glaring at the deputy. But she does the same thing she's always done since Clyde's daughter left town unexpectedly. Nothing. She turns and walks toward the gym.

Inside, the banners from the basketball team's recent championships help brighten the room but do little to diffuse Rose's temperament or the moody crowd ready for a good Texas brawl. With the exception of a single microphone perched on its stand, Colonel Warren appears alone on the stage behind the basketball net that has been drawn to the rafters. The anxious crowd has a clear view of the unwelcome messenger. He remains at-ease, his feet shoulder length apart, both hands clasped behind his back, chest out. The olive-drab tunic of his dress uniform displays the ribbons, medals, and pins that could only be earned by a career military man. Four brilliant brass buttons and a leather belt hold everything perfectly together. A large American flag has been unfurled behind the stage, creating an even more dramatic frame around the strapping officer. Rose marvels at his composure and presence. He looks just as impressive as he did a few days ago. He is no longer a stranger to Rose. *We're in this together, now.* Rose stands several rows back from the stage, unable to withstand the surge of people pressing forward. She is already saturated, her cotton dress clinging to her like a magnet to metal. Adjusting her eyeglasses on her sweaty nose, Rose tries to find Uncle Pete. She continues to turn, now on her tiptoes and sees that the room is not big enough for the teeming crowd. Every window and door are open, but the room is far too hot, far too congested. She can feel sweat escaping every pore.

Colonel Warren steps to the microphone. "Ladies and gentlemen give me your attention." *That's an order not a request.* The room responds immediately to his commanding tone, lowering their voices and focusing on the stage. "My name is Colonel Ralph Warren." *So that's his first name, just like my brother.* "I am here on behalf of the President of the United States and the Provost Marshall General's Office."

"Go home Colonel and take your Nazis with you!" *Here we go.*

He doesn't flinch. "Let me be clear. I am here as a courtesy to this fine community. But if you choose to interrupt me, then I will choose to leave, and nothing will change. We are opening this camp with or without your cooperation. The choice is yours."

His comments draw a unanimous groan of defiance. A few voices are raised but a collective "shhhhh" from the more reasonable adults in the room restores the throng to a reasonable order. Warren has them. He is already in command. *I like my new boss.* Rose's pride gets the best of her as she feels exceptional, knowing she is one step ahead of most of her neighbors here tonight. Knowing she has a special role to play in the months ahead.

The crowd around her presses hard, bringing her back to the reality of the stifling room. She realizes that someone behind her has fainted in this oven of a gym. Rose is close enough to realize it is Mrs. Jensen, Keith's mother. She squeezes backward, hearing Keith's voice before she sees him. "Give her room, please give her room." Keith is kneeling next to his mom, now sitting on the floor. Her knees drawn to her forehead, looking more embarrassed than anything. Mrs. Jensen allows her son to help her to her feet. She continues to lean on him, manages a weak smile, then whispers to her son that she wants to leave. Rose doesn't blame her. Mrs. Jensen is a Gold Star Mother. Not the kind of title any mother desires. It means she has lost a son to this ugly war. It means a gold star now appears in the window of her home, replacing the blue star that was displayed for every family member serving in the armed forces. It is supposed to be some sort of salve on a deep wound that will never fully heal. It is a sign of respect. But Rose knows that respect is the last thing Keith's mom wants. She wants her husband to stop the heavy drinking that has consumed his life since the Western Union telegram arrived after the battle of Midway. She wants to see her boy, entombed forever at the bottom of the Pacific, just one more time. She wants Keith to wrestle with his brother in their simple yard. She wants to be a family again. Rose wonders why she put herself through the torture of this evening. *Why didn't she just stay away?*

And then Keith, her distracted student who hasn't been right in the head since the loss of his brother, starts to scream. It is unprovoked and loud enough that the crowd begins to react to the shrill sounds coming from this young man. Most don't know the source, but they can hear his anguished cry. First, they get quiet. The people closest to Keith instinctively move away, giving him space. He shouts even louder. It is a pure, primal release. He is pouring his family's sadness and pain and loss into this suffocating space. Now, there is consistent murmuring as the news ripples out for all the gymnasium to know that it is the Jensen boy. The startled crowd's response is silence, all eyes riveted on Mrs. Jensen's only living son.

Even Colonel Warren keeps his gaze intently on Keith, who turns, releases his gentle grip on his mother and returns his attention to the stage. Rose is close enough to touch him. He speaks in hushed tones, directing his comments to Colonel Warren. The crowd finally responds. "We can't hear you Keith!" "Speak up son!" The teenager looks to his mother for approval to speak his mind. But Mrs. Jensen's sad eyes stare blankly ahead, the color still missing from her face. Next to his mother he now sees Rose's blazing eyes fixed on him. He returns the gaze. Rose does not hesitate. She nods her head and smiles encouragingly. *Yes Keith. Speak your mind.* There is no hesitation. He honors the crowd's request. His voice is booming. "Colonel, sir. My name is Keith Jensen. The Japs killed my brother. He's never coming back. And now you are going to let these butchers into our town?"

"These are German prisoners, son. Not Japanese."

"I don't give a shit where they are from. They are still killers. They started a war we wanted no part of. The crowd erupts in applause and Keith, feeling their approval, has the instinct to wait until their shouts subside. "A lot of our families have already lost sons and brothers." For the first time, Keith's voice begins to waver. Rose doesn't hesitate. She steps forward and places a hand gently on her student's sagging shoulder. *You're wrong Uncle Pete. There's not a light or two burned off on his string. He's just terribly lost.* Keith regains his composure, strengthened by his teacher's support. His focus again is on Colonel Warren.

"Colonel, can you give me one good reason why we should allow these prisoners into our community?" There is a sea of nods as the crowd agrees with the validity of this question. The answer is delivered without hesitation.

"I think I can son. First, let me tell you that I share the loss you are feeling at the death of your brother." The crowd groans in defiance. They will immediately regret their harsh reaction. "My wife, like your mom, is also a Gold Star Mother. We lost our son, Todd, just a few months ago in North Africa." The colonel's voice never wavers. There is a collective gasp from the crowd. Rose removes her glasses, realizing there are tears mixed with her sweat. Her eyes are stinging. Mrs. Jenson sobs softly, putting her head on Rose's shoulder.

"You're right. This is a war none of us asked for. But we have a duty to make the sacrifices necessary to win at all costs. We have a duty to match the courage and bravery from our boys overseas. Boys like your brother. And my son. And that means treating these prisoners properly under the strict guidelines of the Geneva Convention." He pulls a piece of paper from his side pocket. "Let me quote directly for you from Part I, Article 2."

'Prisoners of war are in the power of the hostile Government, but not of the individuals or formation which captured them. They shall at all times be humanely treated and protected, particularly against acts of violence, from insults and from public curiosity. Measures of reprisal against them are forbidden.'

"That may not mean anything to you, but it will mean everything to the families in this room whose loved ones may end up being captured and imprisoned by the Germans. You must believe me when I tell you that their safety and care is directly influenced by the way we treat our prisoners here in Huntsville and throughout the states. We know for a fact that since Hitler invaded Russia, the treatment of German prisoners has been rather cruel, and the Germans have reciprocated with equally harsh treatment of Russian prisoners. That is exactly what we are trying to avoid. So, we need to put our bitterness aside. It will never bring back your brother or my son. But it can make a difference for thousands of American POWs. Do you think you can do that son?"

Keith looks at his mother again and this time she doesn't hesitate, answering for both of them, "We'll do our best Colonel." The crowd, drained of all its venom, politely applauds her courage. Colonel Warren reaches into his other pocket for a crisply folded handkerchief. *He is human after all.* He dabs his brow and resumes his dialogue with the community he will serve for the foreseeable future. For now, he has their trust. Tonight, they will listen. But their patience will erode very soon.

CHAPTER 8
Camp Huntsville

Labor

Rose and Uncle Pete are the last passengers to board one of the many school buses idling in the parking lot of Huntsville High School. Before they can find seats, they are already moving. A lot of familiar faces silently acknowledge them as the bouncing bus crawls out of the lot for the roughly 8-mile journey to the one place everyone is visiting today: Camp Huntsville. They finally slide into an open seat with Rose sitting closest to the window.

"Heavy turnout, Rosie. Second visit for a lot of these folks. Guess you're curious too, now that you're gonna be working there."

"Me and half the town Uncle Pete."

He playfully jabs her shoulder. "What's that supposed to mean?"

She lowers her voice. "I guess I was feeling kind of important when Colonel Warren asked me to help. It's the biggest news to hit Huntsville in my lifetime."

"Okay, so what's the problem?"

"Well, for starters, running a camp that will handle nearly 5,000 prisoners is going to require plenty of Rose Bauers. So, I'm far from alone Uncle Pete."

"What did you expect? How do you think they are going to take care of our unwelcome guests?"

Rose manages a smile. "Apparently with every baker, barber, nurse and firefighter they can scrounge up. Do you know what Oma said to me when I told her that Colonel Warren had asked me to be a special part of his team.?"

"Something positively uplifting, I'm sure."

"She said, 'That's wonderful sweetheart. Sounds like President Roosevelt himself sent that nice Colonel down here to find you.' She was so kind to let me babble on."

"Hey, he went out of his way to recruit you. That's saying something."

"Uncle Pete, he was just desperate. He's weeks away from opening this place and discovers he short on interpreters. And then he feeds me that line about serving my country."

Uncle Pete wags a finger in her face. "Hey, it's no different than your brothers serving on the front with millions of others. Everyone is doing their part." He surveys the passengers. "Here in Texas, we're also having a conniption fit about this prison."

From a distance on State Highway 19 the prison presents a picture most envisioned. Stockade fencing. Barbed wire. Sentry towers. Floodlights. From the road Rose can barely make out the dormant smokestack of the incinerator, tucked in the southeast corner of the camp. As the bus approaches the civilian entrance, there is an audible gasp as passengers react to the footprint of this mysterious place. Rose shares the reaction. The camp is gigantic.

Seeing it all for the first time is overwhelming for her. Beyond its size the camp is releasing a mix of jumbled expectations for her and the rest of the visitors. She also senses a tangible frustration among the crowd. They expect a spartan living space. They see 400 buildings spread over 837 acres.

They expect meager housing for the enemy. They see barracks with comfortable living conditions to sunbathe and play soccer. They see everything their sons and brothers are deprived of – given freely to the enemy. "Let me get this straight," says Wallace Smith, one of the town's two pharmacists, "my boy is in a foxhole somewhere in a godforsaken desert and some kraut is gonna get this comfortable bunk with fresh sheets and a shower? This is wrong."

As the group leaves the prisoner barracks they walk northwest back toward the main gate where they first entered. The grumbling continues but Rose is focused on another section of the complex that lies outside the actual prison. On her left, running parallel to each other are two roads -- Fifth and Sixth Streets. The area between these roads remains barren and forms a kind of no-man's land that separates the POW camp from the American garrison where Rose will work. She tugs at Uncle Pete's sleeve and points, "This is where I'll be spending most of my time." Rose explains the layout. Along with offices for the administrative staff, there is a gym, fire station, and barracks for the American guards. Finally, a hospital with over 200 beds provides care for both the Americans and POWs, picking up cases that the infirmaries within the prisoner compounds can't handle. "Pretty impressive isn't it," she says proudly. Her uncle's response captures the tone of the entire visit.

"Rosie, I gotta tell you I'm pretty bowed up about this. I know you work for these people now, but you have to admit all of this is tough to swallow. All of us are making sacrifices and these prisoners get three square meals a day without scrounging for a rationing coupon. Now you show me a hospital that is probably better than any facility within 50 miles of here."

As they board the bus back to town, Rose tries to explain it to him. "The Geneva Convention requires that POWs share the same living conditions as the soldiers guarding them. It is that simple."

"I don't give a goddamn about that convention of yours. Here's what's simple. They are the enemy and they shouldn't be treated better than one of your students getting his ass kicked over there when he should be here playing baseball with his friends. So, it's going to take some time for these folks to come around to your way of thinking. Maybe some of them never will."

JUNE 1943

* * *

CHAPTER 9

Somewhere Between Hampton Roads, Virginia And Huntsville, Texas

Land of the Free

Stephan sits in the passenger seat of a comfortable Pullman railcar. Not a filthy cattle car. Not a flatbed exposed to the elements. Just the same passenger car that a typical American would ride on a long-distance journey by rail. Right now, the MPs at the front and rear of each passenger car are the only reminders that he is a prisoner of war in a foreign land. He has been traveling for a little over a day -- staring endlessly at vast open spaces, farms teeming with livestock, small towns filled with curious Americans, and so many automobiles. *When will all the bad things happen?*

They told him there would be sleep deprivation. He looks around at his fellow prisoners, most of whom are napping like babies as the train heads south to Texas. They told him there would be strict rationing. He swears he has added a pound or two since the surrender. They told him there would be beatings and torture at the hands of the Americans. Nobody has laid a finger on him.

He turns and peeks over the padded backrest. *They've even given us great medical care.* Slumped forward in his seat, snoring quietly, is Hugo. The right side of his face in swollen and purple. A sling obscures the cast protecting his broken left arm. The cocky little man he met during the march was a victim of the truck accident when Stephan saved the American's life.

The train heads deeper into the South, closer to the next unknown in Stephan's journey. The countryside unfolding outside the window fades to nothing. His mind drifts, probing the past. Heading towards the unknown has been a constant in his young life. He did not willingly join the Wehrmacht. Like most Austrians his age, he was drafted into the army, foolishly believing that his country's willingness to be annexed by Germany would lead to prosperity and peace. His parents never believed the propaganda. *They were so brave. And I was so foolish.*

Austria had been in a deep depression as Europe braced for war. Jobs and meals were scarce. His father owned a small watch repair business in Vienna that barely managed to support his family. If he was lucky, he would occasionally sell a watch he had meticulously restored. The family lived above the shop on Weiburggasse, a quiet street off the broad, chaotic Karntner Strasse shopping district. It was a simple, charming apartment within walking distance from many of his friends whose parents had businesses in the Jewish district of Vienna. The cacophony of sounds in a neighborhood teeming with merchants was often interrupted by the pealing bells of St. Stephen's Cathedral, whose steep, massive, multi-colored tile roof dominated the skyline.

After school, Stephan would obediently report to the workshop in the rear of his parent's store, sweeping floors and organizing the dwindling inventory of watch parts. Rotors, pushers, apertures, crystals, crowns, and bezels -- Stephan knew them all. Before the Depression, he would spend hours organizing them for his father. Now it took him minutes. It went unspoken, but he knew there was less and less work to support the family. Other merchants in the area were facing similar struggles. Everyone respected his father. They'd frequently assemble in his shop, arguing about the possible union of Austria and Germany.

In the Spring of 1938, Stephan, broom in hand, listened as Mr. Schreiber, the self-proclaimed "finest kosher butcher in Vienna" held his blood-stained apron in one hand and pointed at his father with the gnarled index finger of the other. Stephan still went through the motion of sweeping the floor, but he hung on every word, confused why they spoke in such hushed tones, protecting their conversation from whom?

"Hitler was in Linz last week, Karl. You've seen the photographs. They say the crowds were going crazy for him. We are not going to have a say in this. My God, the man has already announced the union between Germany and Austria."

"Nonsense Max, this is a sovereign country. He can't make an announcement and just like that our country doesn't exist anymore."

"Tell that to the German troops who have already been here for a month. I want to believe that everything will be okay, but I have to think of my family. It's different for us. The Nazis hate the Jews. Some of these fanatics in our own city are already desecrating synagogues. It's only going to get worse."

"Max, this is your home. You have to stay and protect it. We've all worked so hard. How can we turn our backs on each other?"

"Karl, my friend, please do not be offended but you are a fool. This is not going to end well for any of us." His finger swept directly to Stephan and emphatically stabbed the air. "Hitler's army needs your boy. This is the beginning of a long nightmare for Stephan and our country."

Stephan was horrified by the butcher's comment. Until that moment he'd been nothing but a curious eavesdropper. Now, he was the focus of the room. The broom slipped from his hand, rattling off the clean-swept floor. He did what any boy would do in that moment: he looked to his father, who stepped away from his outraged friend and turned to his son. He knelt down and grabbed the broom. Still crouching on both knees, he looked up at Stephan. "Son, go upstairs now and see if your mother needs help with supper."

Later that evening, Stephan and his family enjoyed a rare treat of wiener schnitzel prepared with veal – courtesy of Mr. Schreiber, who felt guilty for his harsh words to Stephan's father earlier that day. Along with the meat, he also delivered the latest newspaper he could find with news surrounding the annexation debate. While his father settled in the parlor to read the paper, Stephan helped his mother prepare his favorite meal. As long as he could remember, he had been assisting his mother in the kitchen. Now, he carefully pounded the veal to a uniform thinness. Then coated each piece in flour, eggs, and breadcrumbs. Finally, Stephan waited patiently while his mother clarified some butter then quickly fried each cutlet – her apron protecting the simple blue dress she was wearing. Stephan could have eaten all three of the cutlets – he was that hungry. They ate in silence, relishing the special meal they were sharing together. But the weight of the day hung heavily. On all of them: Father. Mother. Son. Each had their own questions to ponder, fears to suppress. Afterward, Stephan helped his mother clear the dishes and clean the small kitchen, still in relative silence. His mother smiled softly. She gave a gentle nod toward the parlor. Now a more emphatic nod. *Go talk to him.* Finally, Stephan approached his father, seated in his favorite chair by the window, overlooking the colorful shops of Weiburggasse. Wisps of pipe smoke surrounded his shoulders, disappearing into the pages of the newspaper.

"Papa, is it true what Mr. Schreiber said today? Will I be going to war?"

A massive sigh, the pipe gently placed on the side table. There was a warmth and tenderness in his eyes offset by a sternness in his voice.

"Son, Mr. Schreiber is an old friend with a flair for the dramatic. If I have my way, the next place you will be going is to the university. Our country has lost its way a bit, but we must remain faithful, hmmm?" He taps the newspaper emphatically. "It says here that a plebiscite will be held very soon, so the voice of our people will finally be heard. God willing, we will choose the right path for our country."

Stephan gently touched the newspaper and lowered it "But some of my friends in school say their parents are in favor of joining Germany. They say that food and jobs are plentiful in that country, so why not here? Since Hitler took over the German people are happy, and the farms and factories are doing well. Would it be such a bad thing to have prosperity in our city again?"

"Stephan, you are an Austrian. If you give up your soul for a piece of bread, you will regret the day you abandoned your country."

Stephan paced around his father, threw his arms in the air. "But I cannot vote. What happens if the people choose Hitler? What choice do I have?"

His father nervously folded the newspaper, more times than necessary, every crease punctuated by silence. They held each other's gaze forever. The only sound his mother scraping the dishes. *He has no answer; he is worried, too.* From outside, there came a rhythmic clop, clop, clop of the last vegetable cart leaving the local food market that anchored the corner of their little street. Usually muffled by the din of the bustling block below, it was quieter than Stephan ever remembered. Clop, clop, clop. He still remembers those lonely footsteps and how it made him feel. *Tonight, our street is empty. Soon, the shops may be vacant. Perhaps tomorrow, our country will lose its soul.*

And then it was over. The vote was taken. The Germans announced a unanimous choice for annexation. Austrians were told that 98% of their country had voted to join Germany. For three days there were celebrations everywhere. Candlelight parades. Dancing in the streets. Field kitchens were opened, and people were fed. Stephan was ashamed because he felt contentment. He liked seeing people celebrating and he was happy his belly was full. Maybe his friends were right. Maybe this wouldn't be so bad after all. Maybe his parents would come to enjoy being part of Germany. He overheard his parents talking about the vote and its outcome. About the celebrations that mocked his father's faith in his country. "Our country is not happy," he heard his father whisper to his mother. "We are terrorized by a madman and we are too afraid to stand in his way."

It didn't take long for his father's words to bring Stephan back to the reality of a different life. On the Monday following the vote, Stephan walked to school, just a few blocks from his home. It was a very good public school attended by most of his friends. He walked into his classroom and saw that the crucifix had been replaced by Hitler's picture hanging next to a Nazi flag. His teacher, a very devout woman, stood up and told the class they wouldn't pray or have religion anymore. Instead, they sang *Deutschland, Deutschland, Uber Alles*, the national anthem of Germany. Stephan ran home after school, ignored his workshop chores and instead went straight to the family's apartment, taking the steps two at a time. He tumbled into the kitchen, startling his mother. Still out of breath, he told her everything. No crucifix. No prayer. Hitler's picture. Singing allegiance to Germany. She grabbed his hand and pulled him back down the same steps, not stopping until she deposited Stephan in front of her husband, not caring that an all-too-rare customer had entered the shop from the street at the same time she came in from the back. Now she, too, was out of breath. Her voice trembling with anger, she told her son to repeat his story. What happened next is forever chiseled in his memory.

That rare customer happened to be a German officer. He listened intently to the family's passionate conversation, approached them politely, his polished boots clicking faintly on the shop floor. He placed his hands firmly on Stephan's shoulders. He still remembers the fear as the officer's grip tightened, and he addressed his parents. "Pardon my interrupting your conversation. My name is Captain Schmidt. I will be stationed here in Vienna to assist our families in any way I can. You should not be so afraid of the great plan our

Fuhrer has for you now that Austria is unified once again with Germany. I trust your son will be joining us this Sunday for National Youth Day. It is a magnificent experience with lots of wonderful activities."

"My husband and I will discuss this and decide if Stephan will attend this event."

"It is not an *event*, madam. It is a way of life. It will take place every Sunday and your son will be required to attend."

"What about church? On Sunday we close the shop and go to church."

"Please don't worry. Sunday will now be a special day for your son. He will learn how privileged he is to join Hitler's Youth. Perhaps your husband will help you understand."

"My wife meant no disrespect. This is all very new to us and we need time to understand our options."

The German strengthened his grip and pulled Stephan even closer to him. The troublesome smile never left his face. "Ah, no options to consider really. This is a privilege and his presence will be required. I'm afraid you will be fined if your son does not attend. And if you choose to continue to ignore this opportunity, he will soon be visiting you in prison. Now, I have my eye on a watch for my wife. I'm sure you can sell it to me for a very reasonable price." He released his grip. Stephan remembered Mr. Schreiber's stern warning just a few weeks earlier. *This is the beginning of a long nightmare for Stephan and our country.*

How right his parents were to mistrust the Nazis. He hopes the letters he has written since his capture will find their way home. The Red Cross promised they would try. He just wants his parents to know that he is safe. All of Stephan's letters home have been carefully written, crafted to protect himself and them. He would never put anti-Nazi sentiments in writing. It bothers him that even in the custody of the Americans, he has never been more afraid of the Nazis.

"Don't be fooled by all of this Jurgen." Stephan is startled by the comment. His shoulders tighten as he feels another unexpected grasp – this time from Corporal Hans Schroeder, a blowhard who has been seated next to him since they boarded the train in Virginia yesterday afternoon. Schroeder is a tall, muscular soldier, who stood out among the POW crowd even before Stephan met him. Now, he occupies the aisle seat next to Stephan, who presses against the window, trying to create enough space so he is not touching his seatmate. Besides being a bully, Schroeder is also a loyal-to-the-death Nazi. The Army is full of them, but he's never met anyone as obnoxious as Schroeder. Now, removed from the stress of battle, it feels even more intense living among these soldiers fiercely devoted to the Fuhrer and the Third Reich. The distractions of war have been replaced by the reality of surrender, so their fervor seems more acute, more antagonistic.

"Why so tongue-tied private? Don't you ever speak? Don't you have an opinion about this hell-hole they've sent us to?" *What place is he talking about?*

Stephan never makes eye contact. Continues to stare out the window. "I guess this is all a bit overwhelming. I'm just trying to take it all in." *Careful Stephan. You've said enough.*

"Overwhelming, ha! You are not falling for all of this are you? You don't actually think they are letting you see the real America, do you?" Stephan forces himself to turn toward Schroeder, but no words follow. It started on the ship when they left North Africa. And it hasn't let up. Men like Schroeder couldn't wait to get to America, so they could see the damage inflicted by their cherished Luftwaffe. They wanted to observe firsthand the bombed-out buildings and the mass destruction caused by the German air force. At the time, Stephan believed it too. But now, he is seeing things for himself. They've been on the train for nearly two days. Where is the damage? They've passed through Atlanta. Nothing. Maybe elsewhere? After all, America is a very large country. But his doubts are growing. It just doesn't make sense. *Why don't you have the guts to tell him how you feel?*

"You are full of shit, Schroeder." The comment is coming

from the seat directly behind them. *It's Hugo. Oh my God, shut up!* Stephan instinctively turns to the Nazi to gauge his reaction. His bulging crimson eyes are livid with rage. Schroeder leaps to his feet, now standing in the aisle facing his accuser. "Sitzen!" The command is bellowed by one of the MPs who now approaches Schroeder brandishing a black, polished wooden baton. The German prisoner complies immediately, slumping back in his seat. The guard backs away, still tapping the baton in the palm of his gloved hand and returning to his post at the end of the car. Schroeder stares ahead, speaking through clenched teeth. "How dare you speak to me like that. How dare you insult the noble efforts of our Fuhrer's forces who have taken the fight to the Americans on their own soil. I will not forget your words. You will pay for this treason!"

Stephan's heart is pounding. He wants to vanish like fog into the passing countryside. From behind, Hugo's taunts escalate. "It is not treason to speak the truth Schroeder. You are the one who is full of lies. How long have you been on this train? Where do you expect to see this damage you are speaking of? Where would our planes come from to make such an attack? How would they refuel and return safely? How could you be so stupid? *Please stop Hugo.* "You make no sense and that is why you are full of shit."

Schroeder is on his accuser quickly and violently. Stephan turns and watches in shock. He winces as Hugo, a man half the size of Schroeder, shields his face with his free arm, while Schroeder still lands several direct blows to his face. Stephan, fearing he has waited too long, finally rises to help his friend, but the two guards are already descending on Schroeder. Now, the entire car erupts, but nobody leaves their seat. They know better. The attack ends abruptly as Schroeder is subdued and lead forcefully toward the back of the train, whistles and jeers accompanying him all the way. Then the comments come quickly. "You are crazy, Hugo." "Watch your back." Finally, "Not even the Luftwaffe can protect you now." The train erupts in laughter and even Hugo chuckles as he uses his free hand to adjust his sweat soaked khaki shirt and rub the new welts on his battered face. His eyes meet Stephan's, but no words are exchanged. *He must think I'm a coward.*

Thanks to Hugo he is free of that blowhard Schroeder for a few precious miles. He takes advantage of the empty place next to him and stretches out a bit. He closes his eyes. His pulse slows. The rail car returns to its rhythmic cadence while subdued voices resume their simple conversations. Behind him, Hugo punctuates the moment with one final hushed comment. "Nazi swine."

JULY 1943

* * *

CHAPTER 10
North Africa

Trust

Victory doesn't soothe Ralph Bauer's soul. Rommel's Africa Korps has been defeated. Nearly a quarter million Germans have surrendered. The American presence in the war has begun to make a difference. But Ralph knows there is still no end in sight. Directly ahead is more of the same. The processing of POW prisoners in Tunisia has slowed considerably. Most of the interrogators in his unit have been temporarily reassigned further north where another camp has been established. That leaves his group shorthanded, which means more work and less sleep for Ralph. He moves briskly, hoping to get to his post as early as possible. Nothing escaped the sandstorm that choked the region last night. He covers his mouth as he maneuvers his way through the perpetual chaos of the camp. His throbbing shoulder reminds him of another restless night. *I should have gotten this checked out.* He sidesteps a fast-moving group of staff cars filled with the usual brass. He notices that the last open car in the caravan contains a high-ranking German officer, who is seated between two Americans. He is the prisoner, yet his bearing stands out in contrast to the others. To his right is a civilian who appears terribly uncomfortable in the heat. To his left is Colonel Tucker, the camp commander, whom Ralph has never met. That's about to change.

Ralph waits for the dust to settle behind the passing caravan and crosses the intersection, drawn directly to the white hospital tent with red crosses prominently displayed on a massive roof secured by ropes and stakes every 15 feet. *How about now.* Ralph heads to the tent that only yesterday had been teeming with arriving prisoners. He sees several doctors and nurses smoking cigarettes and laughing loudly outside the makeshift entrance. "Captain Bauer!" He is startled to hear his name but recognizes the voice. It's Private Donaldson, who snaps off a smart salute. Ralph feels the pain in his right shoulder as he delivers a sloppy one in return. "What is it private?"

"Sir, you're needed immediately at base HQ. They sent me to find you."

"They?"

"Colonel Tucker and some hotshot from AFHQ." *Allied Force Headquarters. This must be serious.* "They need your help interrogating a prisoner." Ralph feels an adrenaline rush and the pain in his shoulder becomes an afterthought. "They asked for me?"

"Well, sir, not exactly. They asked if there was an interrogator available and you happen to be the only one on base right now."

Right place. Right time. This is your chance. "Okay, Donaldson, let's get moving."

Donaldson directs Ralph to the idling jeep he left a few yards away. The base HQ is a short drive from the hospital. Ralph jumps in and Donaldson lurches into the steady flow of military traffic crisscrossing the vast compound. *Must be that German officer I saw earlier. Who is the hotshot from AFHQ?*

Donaldson pulls the jeep up to a hastily built checkpoint within 50 yards of Colonel Tucker's quarters. He recognizes his fellow MPs immediately and smiles as he downshifts the jeep to a rolling stop. "Hey Rufus, how those Cardinals doing?"

"Last time I heard they beat your Giants in extra innings, so all is good with the world."

"Don't get ahead of yourself hotshot. The season is still young. This is Captain Bauer. He has an appointment with Colonel Tucker."

"Sir, it's not that I don't trust Private Donaldson, but I have strict orders to check all credentials."

"Understood private." Ralph easily produces the necessary documents and Donaldson's friend waves them through. The jeep pulls up behind a line of parked vehicles. Ralph recognizes the staff car from earlier. "Want me to wait for you sir?"

"No, thanks Donaldson. Something tells me this day is going to be full of surprises."

He makes his way into the tent that Colonel Tucker has called home since he built this POW compound from the ground up in just two short months. Whatever Ralph imagined he would find inside he is startled by the order and cleanliness of this place. *Uncle Pete would be impressed.* There is a constant flow of people and paperwork required to complete the daunting and important task of managing an army of prisoners. For the first time, Ralph allows himself to think beyond his singular role of prisoner interrogation and imagine the whole process that plucks a soldier from the battlefield, properly identifies him, accounts for his health requirements, provides the Red Cross with necessary information to contact his family, and releases him into a rapidly-moving system that will ultimately place him in a detention facility for the duration of the war. He begins to appreciate how each small part, including his own role, contributes to the war effort in a way few people realize. He just wishes he had something to show for his own efforts. Apart from honing his German-speaking skills, there has not been a single encounter with a prisoner that has revealed anything of strategic importance. Instead, he has a busted shoulder, an equally bruised ego, and the nagging knowledge that his life was spared by one of these prisoners. *I could have thanked him.* Ralph is rescued from his guilt by a skinny, freckled private with a tangle of brilliant red hair and heavy southern drawl that reminds him of Texas. "Good morning captain. Colonel Tucker is expecting you. Please follow me." Ralph follows the young private into a secluded area of the tented compound where a separate contingent of MPs stand guard.

Colonel Peter Tucker stands to greet him. There is no one else in the area, but the setting is far from private. Ralph salutes his superior who is already motioning him to take a seat. Tucker spares all small talk and gets right to business.

"Here's the situation, captain. We are detaining a German officer who happens to be a chaplain. Until today, I didn't think the Nazis had the balls to enlist chaplains for their troops. Makes no sense to me, but what do I know? Anyway, he may have information that our intelligence folks believe could be helpful in identifying spies within the ICRC."

Ralph's confused expression says it all, so Tucker quickly explains. "The International Committee of the Red Cross. Different from the American Red Cross but they do the same thing. Supposedly neutral so they are serving both the Brits and the Krauts, but some suspect there are Nazi sympathizers within the organization. This guy apparently let down his guard with Father Kelly, one of our camp chaplains during his processing so the good Father brought it to our attention. Nothing substantiated as far as I know but it's important enough that AFHQ asked us to check it out." *Where's the hotshot?*

"Beg your pardon, sir but why the hell would the Red Cross be spying on us?"

"Beats me captain. Just another one of those head scratchers this war keeps delivering. He picks up a large brown envelope that has been reused far too many times, handing it to Ralph. "This prisoner, Major Heller is his name, has already been processed and will be heading back to the states very soon..."

"To the United States? Why?"

"Full of questions, aren't you Captain? The Provost General has been granted permission to build prison camps throughout the United States. Hell, we've got nearly a quarter of a million prisoners coming out of North Africa alone. It's all happening pretty fast. A ship comes in from the states loaded with personnel and supplies. Heads back home filled with prisoners. Most of them are heading to Texas where the first camps are already being built.

"Where in Texas, sir?"

"Seriously, captain, how the hell do you expect me to know that?"

"Sorry, sir. I'm from Texas. Just curious."

"Well your state must have the same weather because POWs are supposed to be placed in a similar climate as the place where they were captured. Can you believe this crap? Hell, send them to Alaska. Now, before you ask any more questions, let's get back to why you are here." He points to the envelope in Ralph's hand. "I need you to interrogate this prisoner and see if you can come up with anything that would substantiate this intel. I've got a guy from AFHQ cooling his heels and he wants to leave soon with more information than he's got now. So, you have a brief window before we say farewell to this Major whatever his name is."

Ralph pulls the file from the folder. "Heller."

"Right. Chaplain Heller. What are his sources? Does he have names? Any evidence he can point us to? Give it your best shot. You know the drill. You do know the drill, right captain?"

"Absolutely sir. One last question."

"Go on."

"Is the chapel available? I'd like to start off on the right foot with this guy. Put him in the most familiar setting possible before we start talking. If that makes sense?"

"Perfect sense, captain. I like your approach. Give me a few minutes to set things up." Colonel Tucker leaves briskly, and Ralph begins to reflect on his training. Put the prisoner at ease. Earn trust and confidence. Show empathy and understanding. Look for common ground *Common Ground? The bible!* Ralph's mind is racing. *He's a German man of God. I've got a German bible. Maybe I can make the connection that way. Maybe, God forgive me, I can use my heritage. Oma. Bavaria. The cherished memories.* Ralph's heart is racing now. He's in the game. He barely notices the same soldier who escorted him earlier. That now familiar southern drawl has a soothing effect. "Beg your pardon Captain, the Colonel wanted me to escort you over to the chapel and let you know that the prisoner will be ready in five minutes."

Ralph barely makes eye contact. "Your boss doesn't waste any time. Let's get moving." He is already elbow deep into his battered attaché. He finds the bible in its familiar place, well protected from the papers and bureaucratic mess jammed inside. He carefully removes it and holds it securely against his chest. They are moving quickly, Ralph double-timing his pace to keep up with the red-headed private. Outside, he squints heavily in the brilliant mid-day sun. *It does feel a lot like Texas.* Fifty yards away is another non-descript building that looks like any other structure in the camp. The only difference is a small metal cross fixed above the doorway. *The chapel. Not much time to think about my plan.* There is commotion behind him and he realizes the prisoner is already being escorted. *The inscription! He can't see the inscription at the front of the bible! He'll know it isn't mine.* "Private, tell those people to wait outside until I am ready."

"I can't tell them anything sir, they sort of out-rank me."

"Well then tell them I am praying, and I asked not to be disturbed."

Ralph is already inside the chapel when he hears, "Give it my best shot sir."

He is surprised that actual pews have been installed in the room, enough to accommodate a hundred men. *Nice touch.* A threadbare altar holds a cross that seems way too big for the space it occupies. He quickly opens to the front of the bible. He is surprisingly calm. *There it is, written in German, "Keep your faith and come home to me. Love, Mother."* He can hear mumbling outside and resistant voices that tell him he is out of time. Ralph turns his back to the chapel door as it swings open. He leans the book against his knees for leverage and carefully tears the page as close to the spine as possible. *Good enough.* He tosses the bible into a pew and holds the flimsy page carefully between his thumb and forefinger. He is focused on the prisoner and his entourage who are all business as they deposit the chaplain in the same pew where Ralph tossed the bible. The prisoner notices it and stays fixed on the bible as he slides it further down the pew before he sits. Something makes him take second notice. He leans over and retrieves the bible. Begins paging through it. Goes back to the title page and is reading intently. His eyes leave the page and focus instead on Ralph. *He's definitely curious. Don't blow this.*

"We'll be right outside the door, Captain. Colonel Tucker ordered us to return the prisoner at 1400 hours." Ralph glances at the clock above the doorway. *It's 1:30. That gives me 30 minutes. Not much time.*

He realizes that the page he ripped out is still dangling from his fingertips. Casually, he begins to fold it neatly into a square while simultaneously responding to the guards. "Understood. Please knock before you re-enter the chapel."

He places the folded page in his top left pocket. The chaplain has not taken his eyes off him. The bible is open to the missing page. The prisoner is gently rubbing the torn remnants of the page that now resides in Ralph's pocket.

"Yes sir. Again, we'll be right outside."

The guards softly close the door behind them. Ralph is grateful for the quiet. He decides to join the chaplain in the pew, forcing the prisoner to slide even further down. The German closes the bible and sets it in his lap. He remains rigid and erect.

Ralph has been in the military long enough to understand the trappings of rank and status in any army. Still he finds himself intrigued by the chaplain's uniform, which carries the appropriate embroidery to indicate he holds the rank of Major. He isn't wearing epaulets like other highly-ranked Germans, but otherwise he could pass for an officer of the SS. The only thing identifying him as a chaplain is an armband with a purple stripe in between two white stripes on which a red cross is placed.

"Major Heller, my name is Captain Ralph Bauer of the United States Army. I've been asked to speak with you before you are processed and sent to one of our internment camps back in the United States." Ralph's German is fluent and polished. The prisoner understands every word.

"Captain, I also speak English, if that would be helpful."

"No thank you Major, that won't be necessary. I trust that you have been treated fairly since your surrender?"

"For the most part I have been very satisfied with the way our men have been treated. Your souvenir hunters have been a little aggressive, but I suppose that should be the least of my concerns."

"Unfortunately, some of our men have taken the souvenir hunting to an extreme. *That bible you are holding is proof of that.*

“I hope you have not been too inconvenienced.”

The prisoner points to a spot on the front of his sweat-stained tunic. “They took my crucifix. I thought that indeed was a bit extreme.” He shrugs his shoulders but says nothing. He may be sitting erect, but he sounds deflated to Ralph.

“Perhaps we can get a replacement for you Major. I can ask our chaplain, Father Kelly if that would be possible.”

“I am confused Captain. Recovering my crucifix is not why I am here, hmm?” He finally relaxes his posture, leaning forward to grab the pew in front of him. “Is this an interrogation? Because I know I have certain rights under the Geneva...”

Ralph cuts him off, politely. “No please Major, let’s not start this conversation with any disrespect.” *He’s still clutching the bible. Might as well break the ice.*” I see you found my bible.”

“My apologies Captain.” He offers it back to Ralph.

Ralph pushes it back into his hands, continues the conversation and begins the lie. “This is actually my grandmother’s bible. She gave it to me before I left the United States. It reminds me of her and home. I read it frequently.” *Another lie.*

“Your grandmother, she is German? “

“Yes, she was born in Bavaria. She still shares many of her childhood memories about growing up in your country. “

“I hope they are fond ones, Captain.”

“Indeed, they are. But she also is ashamed of what has become of her homeland. Her son, my father, was killed during the Great War. I never really knew him.”

There is no visible reaction from the Major, who loosens his grip on the bible and begins to page through it. “And yet she remains a woman of faith. That is quite a blessing in these terrible times.”

“I’ll be honest with you Major I don’t quite understand your role as chaplain in the German army. After all, it is common knowledge that formal religion is not tolerated by the Nazis. Are you a member of the Nazi Party?"

"I am not! I am a Catholic Priest. I serve no other master!" *You hit a raw nerve there, Ralph.*

Ralph remains calm, his voice measured. "Sorry, Major, I did not mean to offend you. But surely you can understand my curiosity. Even your uniform." He points to his right arm. "With the exception of the armband, and of course your missing crucifix, you could easily pass as a member of the SS."

"That irony is not lost on me, Captain. But just like your military, there are certain rules I must abide by in order to serve the men."

"So, are you loyal to your Fuhrer or to *our* God?"

Heller resumes his rigid posture, stiffer than before. "Perhaps your grandmother would caution you not to judge so carelessly the intentions of others. I did not join the army freely. I was conscripted. I choose to serve the men in the same way I would have served my parishioners before the war. So, to answer your question, I am loyal first to the Church, then to my men, and....

Ralph finishes the response, "then to Hitler."

"You twist my words Captain. You soften me up with your grandmother's bible. You use guilt to challenge my loyalty to the Church, and you stand in judgement without any understanding of the moral and ethical dilemma we face within our country."

"I am not a Catholic, Father." It's the first time Ralph is referring to him as a priest. "But I know enough about the history of your religion to know it is full of inspirational stories of martyred saints who stood up to tyranny and oppression, remained true to their faith, and gave up their lives rather than betray their conscience. Is your conscience clear, Father?"

Beads of perspiration are visible on the major's forehead. For the first time, Ralph realizes his own armpits are soaked with sweat. *How did this happen? What am I doing? Am I interrogating or condemning this man? No, you've created a path, now follow it.*

"Father, I don't doubt for a moment your commitment to your men. That is admirable. I also don't believe you have any sense of loyalty to the Nazi state. How could you? They view religion as a convenient tool to connect with the masses. It is the only reason you are still alive. You are being used. You know it and I know it. But what is lost on your clever Nazi friends is they have allowed you to connect with soldiers who are more worried about their own souls and the welfare of their families than about the survival of the Third Reich. You provide them hope, Father."

Heller's lower lip is visibly trembling. "Many of my friends, fellow priests, have been arrested because of their opposition to this war. Or I should say they are opposed to the treatment of many German citizens, especially the Jews. Perhaps what you said is true. Perhaps I am a coward. But I love being a priest and I want to serve my men."

"Well, Father, maybe we can help each other out."

A firm knock on the door startles both men. Ralph jumps to his feet and opens the door just enough to allow a slice of sunlight and an oppressive wave of heat to invade the chapel. The glare obscures the messenger, but the message is clear.

"Sir, it's time. Colonel needs the prisoner back."

Don't blow this Ralph. You are so close. He steps outside. *No time to be hiding behind any doors.* His tone is hushed but forceful. "Soldier, you tell the colonel that I need more time. Tell him I can end it now without any helpful information for his guest or he can let me do my job. Fifteen more minutes. I promise I'll give him more than he came here with. Can you deliver that message without sounding like a petrified schoolboy?"

His question is met by a wide smile and brighter eyes. "Absolutely, sir!"

"Good, now take your good old time getting back to the colonel."

When Ralph re-enters the chapel, he notices that Heller is standing in the aisle, paging through the bible, scrutinizing the pages more closely. Ralph approaches the prisoner until he is standing close enough to see the sandblasted features of a weary man.

"Father we don't have a lot of time. So, I will be as direct as possible with you. It has come to our attention that you may have information that could be useful to us. Is it true that you have had dealings with members of the International Committee of the Red Cross?"

"Of course, I have. They have had an active presence in this camp since we arrived as prisoners. Monitoring the men's treatment. Arranging for communication with their families. They've been very helpful. Why do you ask?"

Ralph ignores the question. "Have you had any conversations with these representatives that goes beyond the normal things you would discuss regarding the men's welfare?"

"For being as direct as possible you are being rather evasive, captain. What is it you are looking for?"

"Spies, Father. I am looking for spies. I want to know if any of these ICRC representatives have asked for your assistance in gathering intelligence about our activities here."

The prisoner laughs openly and scoffs at Ralph's inquiry. "Captain, your question is absurd. How could I possibly be gathering intelligence when I am a prisoner myself?' His raised eyebrows are teasing Ralph, playing a game.

"What about before you became a prisoner, Father?"

"Ah, now that is a different question altogether."

"Would you care to elaborate?"

"Would you care to explain to me what exactly you meant when you said, 'we could help each other out'?" *Pay dirt.*

"You talked about ministering to the soldiers. I am giving you the opportunity as a chaplain to do just that. I can't promise you who those soldiers will be, and I am not at liberty to discuss where, but I can assure you this -- for the duration of this war you will be held in a POW camp in the United States where you will be treated fairly and permitted to practice your faith openly and without penalty. It could be the most fulfilling time of this war for you."

"And what must I do to earn such wonderful treatment in the land of the free?"

"Give us names."

"I do not recall a name at the moment. My experience with the ICRC representatives has been very positive. They are honorable people who remain neutral and take their relief roles very seriously. But there is always, as you say in America, 'one bad apple.' I have not encountered this person directly but know that she has been compensated by my government for sharing information of a military and economic nature about the allies in North Africa."

"She?"

Heller puts his hands to his lips in surprise, mocking Ralph. "Shocked captain? A devious woman?"

"I need more."

"I know she is a Swiss national."

"Her name?"

"Again, I am having trouble remembering, Captain. Maybe when I am in your wonderful country practicing my religion freely among my parishioners, the name will come to me. In the meantime, perhaps you can see if Fr. Kelly can get me that crucifix. Although I am not sure I can trust him. We shall see."

The prisoner moves past Ralph and walks slowly to the chapel door. He is no longer flustered. He taps on the door, which is opened immediately by the sentry who is expecting to see Ralph.

In broken English, he advises, "I am ready to see your Colonel."

The sentry looks past the German and appeals to Ralph for direction.

"Sir?"

"Wait outside private."

"Yes sir."

Ralph speaks before the door fully closes. "Father don't protect this woman. It's not worth it. Think of all the good you can do for your men, how you can serve them. Trust me." The words feel awkward as soon as Ralph says them.

"Trust is such a casualty of this war is it not, Captain Bauer? So many of us disregard it to advance our cause. We convince ourselves that we are doing the right thing, the honorable thing. We are here for different reasons but still this war has ripped us away from everything that matters, inviting our conscience to abandon us too. I will pray for you and for your dear grandmother. Oh, one more, little thing Captain. Your precious bible? Perhaps you can get it back in the hands of its rightful owner, hmm?"

Ralph is speechless. His mouth is drier than the arid wasteland outside the chapel door. *Trust is such a casualty of this war. So too, is truth.*

CHAPTER 11
Camp Huntsville

Empty

It is 5:30 AM. Stephan stares at the open wood-framed ceiling from his bunk in Barracks # 4, tormented by a familiar emptiness. Another morning and the same feeling.

"On your feet Jurgen! Get moving!"

He is awakened by Nazis. Daily activities are led by Nazis. He marches and drills every day under the direction of Nazi officers. His basic routine still feels like the regimented life he's led for years. By 5:45 AM he rises in unison with his fellow barrack mates, part of a company of 250 men. By 7:00 they've showered, shaved, and eaten a typical breakfast of milk, cornflakes, bread, and coffee. Real coffee. There are some familiar faces but most he's only gotten to know since his arrival in America. Together they are housed in six barracks, where the smell of tar paper and freshly sawed lumber lingers. Everything is new here. And other things are as old as the uniform on his back.

He rubs his baggy breast pocket and misses his bible. It still hurts. Not having that one connection to his parents. All he can think about is his mother the night before he left for basic training, pleading with him to stay safe, do as he was told, stay out of trouble. "The Nazis will try to break you. Tell you that religion has no place in your army. So, since the bible is not necessary in their ugly world, I will give you my mine." She opened it to the inside cover, plucked a fountain pen from his shirt pocket, scribbled briefly, closed it reverently and placed it in his hands. Stephan took the holy book, but she did not let go. Instead, she slid her hands over his. He remembers the gentle kiss on his forehead that followed. Then she headed downstairs. He can still hear her footsteps echo off the stairwell. They still sound sad. Stephan opened to the inscription.

"Keep your faith and come home to me. Love, Mother."

These are the times he misses his mother's bible and her gentle prayer to come home safely. Mostly, he misses the comfort of knowing it was *hers*. Sometimes, he thinks he would have been just as happy if she had scribbled words of encouragement in a book of poems. It was the messages she wrote, the hopefulness that spoke to him. *Come home to me.* Seeing her handwriting was his only connection to a mother who penned a powerful plea to her son. *Keep your faith.* Special words that brought him back to Vienna, in the kitchen, with that gentle woman who gave purpose to a nervous adolescent, returning home from school with another bad science grade. "Let me talk to your father, He'll be fine. Now go do your chores."

"You better get moving Stephan, or you'll be cleaning the latrine."

The voice brings him back. It belongs to one of the good ones. At least Stephan hopes so. His name is Franz, another Austrian. Stephan sees him hanging out with Hugo sometimes. He laughs to himself. *That's a good sign since Hugo wouldn't be caught dead with a Nazi.*

"Thanks. I'm moving." He swings his tall frame sideways on the bunk and rests his forearms on his knees. "Hey Franz, is it true you are working with the Americans?"

"Easy, easy. Choose your words carefully. *For* the Americans, not *with* them."

Stephan lowers his voice, "you mean you're not spying on us and reporting back to the Nazis?"

"Not funny. Are you trying to get me killed?" He drops the lid on a small footlocker and slides it under his lower bunk bed. "It's not my fault I speak English."

Stephan yawns, stretches his long arms and pushes himself off the top bunk. landing beside Franz. "What's it like? Working *for* them?"

"They are very kind actually. They even invite me to sit with them during lunch breaks." He gently nods sideways to one of the barracks leaders while keeping his eyes fixed on Stephan. "Honestly, it's pretty boring. But these assholes are already calling me a traitor."

Stephan sweeps the room for eavesdroppers and continues to whisper, "Seriously? Why?"

"I'm just minding my own business Stephan. Trying to survive and get home. But they've somehow turned this into an ideological struggle. It's bizarre really. I am translating menus for the mess hall and they think I am assisting the enemy. They are threatening me, telling me to refuse the work."

What are you going to do?"

"Make things up. Tell them what they want to hear. Try to survive. It's crazy." Franz pulls an envelope from his pocket. "I can't even write home and tell them how well I am being treated."

Stephan eyes the envelope and the emptiness returns. He turns away and begins tidying his bunk.

"Shit, Stephan. Sorry, I didn't mean to rub it in."

"Two years and counting."

"I know it's rough."

"That's kind of you to say Franz, but I'm not sure you really understand. I try not to be bitter, but it's tough watching these guys open their letters. Laughing and crying about anything that connects them with people who matter. A tooth lost. A meal burnt. A baby born. I don't get to feel any of that."

Franz stuffs the envelope back in his pocket. "What about the Red Cross?"

"They promised they would try to find my parents and get word to them that I was alive. But I'm not getting my hopes up. For all I've know they've been dead for years."

"Five minutes to roll call!"

He runs his fingers over the letters "PW" stenciled on his clothing. "You know Franz, being a prisoner of the Americans is the easy part. Think about it. This is the safest we've been since we were torn away from people we love."

"So we've just got to hang on. We've got to survive. You've got to find your parents. Isn't that worth it?"

" I suppose." *If you give up your soul for a piece of bread, you will regret the day you abandoned your country.* "My father was such a brave man, sometimes I wonder how he would feel if he knew I was unwilling to stand up to the Nazis."

"Stop. Now you're making me feel guilty. We're doing the best we can."

"Are we? There are days when I just get tired of the lies. I don't even know who I am anymore."

Stephan feels the energy of the barracks rise as the vibration of footsteps rattle his bunk. It's time for roll call. Most of the men are moving past Stephan and Franz as they head outside. Some peer intently at the two. The stares linger. "See what I mean. I watch these men for any sign of their loyalties and their secrets suffocate me. Are they liars like us or do they really believe in the Nazi Party?"

They are moving outside. The air is cool and damp. Stephan's emptiness remains. *It is not just my parents I miss. It is the loss of my own integrity.* He falls in line with the others. Just another coward who wants to go home.

CHAPTER 12
Huntsville, Texas

Discreet

It's the final day of the school year for Rose and she is already outside, waiting alone for Uncle Pete. Leaning against her uncle's truck in the morning shade of the work yard, deeper thoughts nibble away at this rare solitude. Lingering reflections that kept her awake most of the night. The cool steel of the truck's body is a welcome relief from the morning heat. She reaches through the opened driver-side window and presses hard on the horn. Rose hears Clyde and Uncle Pete laughing before they appear on the porch.

"Clyde, I think I'm hallucinating. That looks like Miss Rose waiting on me. Why, she got out here faster than a sneeze through a screen door."

The truck door groans as Rose uses both hands to pull it open. "Hurry up Uncle Pete or I'm going to drive."

Within minutes, they are rolling down the driveway. "So what's got you so motivated today Rosie? Practicing for your new job?"

"Nope. Just anxious to wrap up the old one. I need to get my final grades in and clean out my desk. Don't forget you need to pick me up earlier than usual. It's going to be a short day."

He brings the truck to a full stop at the end of the driveway and points to the mailbox near the edge of the road. "I won't forget. And maybe you could remember to empty that box at the end of each day. It's getting kind of crowded in there don't you think?" His request is kind and even-toned, but Rose can read between the lines. *Please remember something around here.*

"I promise. It will get emptied before it explodes."

Despite her forgetfulness, there is a prevailing thought she hasn't been able to shake. They are getting close to school. She rolls up her window and turns sideways in her seat, peering intently at Uncle Pete. He sighs and begins rolling up his window as well. Serious talk. No outside noises. He knows the routine.

"What is it Rosie?"

"Uncle Pete, does Clyde ever confide in you? I mean, you know, talk to you about things that might be bothering him."

"Now where the heck did that question come from? Clyde, confide in me? No, ma'am. Absolutely not. What in the world would Clyde talk to me about? I'm his boss."

"Oh come on now, you are more than his boss. You've done a lot for him. For them. Before Esther died. Before Barbara left. When they were all together. You and Clyde were very close."

"Hold on now." The truck slows down as Uncle Pete turns his attention to Rose. "Let's get something straight. Clyde works for me. He is not my friend. Can we roll the damn windows down? It's hot as Hades in here."

"So he never confided in you then?"

"You are not letting this go, are you? I think I like you better in the morning when you're running late." He turns the truck down the high school's street and speeds up until he reaches the front of the building.

"In a hurry to get me out of here?"

"Nah, Rosie. Just got a busy day ahead. In fact, right now I gotta go back to the farm and have a chit chat with my buddy Clyde."

Rose manages a smile as she closes the truck door. "Thanks for listening Uncle Pete, but I'm not done with you."

As the truck pulls away Rose notices a patrol car parked across the street. She has to squint to make sure she's certain. Deputy Bobby Ford smiles at her and tips his hat.

Rose hurries up the school's path to the main entrance, her heart beating as she takes the long flight of concrete steps to the front door. She scurries down the main hall, past the school office where a surprised Dr. Roebuck is just closing the door.

"Miss Bauer, why you're...."

"Early. That's right." *Don't say a word little man.* She never breaks stride until she reaches the end of the hall and the last classroom on the right. Her sanctuary. The students are gone for the summer. Roebuck has enough sense not to mess with her today. Even a few hours without Uncle Pete's sarcasm will do her good. She closes the door gently, takes a deep breath and walks to her simple pine desk. Rose slides into her chair, unlocks the lower right drawer where the remaining tests sit, waiting to be graded. They rest on a shoe box containing most of the personal items she has collected over the years. She places the tests on the desk and pushes them aside, making room for the box. She removes the lid as her chest flutters. She already knows what she's looking for. On the side of the box, wedged between a box of pencils and an old eyeglass case is a light yellow envelope with a torn flap. Rose gently shakes the envelope and its contents spill onto the desk. She peeks inside the envelope and discovers two more. She adds them to the pile. Photographs.

Each was taken by Clyde's daughter. Nothing unusual about that really. Barbara was always taking photographs. Sometimes Rose would ask her to help out at various school events and she'd pay Barbara for her work. It started one Christmas a few years back when Clyde bought his daughter a

Kodak Brownie camera. Rose remembers because Uncle Pete helped him buy it at Garvey's Photo shop. Barbara never put that camera down. She took almost all of the yearbook pictures for her high school -- the new one built for colored kids back in 1938. She loved it, talked about applying for a job at the *Huntsville Item*. Uncle Pete said it would never happen in his lifetime. "This town's just not ready for that Rose."

But nobody denied her talent. More than a talent, really. It was an instinct. Rose saw it every time she gave Barbara an assignment. Very discreet, often taking a picture when you didn't even realize she was there. Maybe too discreet for some people's liking. She spreads the photographs out -- carefully separating them into different piles. She stands and walks to the window, which faces the street in front of the school. Bobby Ford is still there. *Who else knows?*

CHAPTER 13
North Africa

Casualty

Ralph's not sure what's worse – the pain in his right shoulder or the annoying itch since they immobilized the joint and put his arm in a sling. His heavily wrapped arm strapped to his torso leaves him perspiring and scratching. The doctor told him his bruised shoulder will heal with rest. Meanwhile, the simplest task is an ordeal. Like right now. With his free hand he holds an envelope just received from Donaldson, who tracked Ralph down at the commissary. The MP was instructed to hand-deliver it at the request of Heller, the German chaplain. *Why would he still want to talk to me?* He switches the envelope to the fingertips of his right hand and with his left carefully tears the seal. Then he grabs the letter and rapidly flicks his wrist until the letter remains in his hand and the envelope floats to the floor. He expects to see a lengthy note but there are just a few words. They are written in German. *"Sie ist hier."* She is here. There is no delay in Ralph's reaction. He knows what it means. It's the only "she" they talked about. The Swiss national. The spy. He can feel his pulse quicken. *Where the hell did Donaldson go?* Ralph steps outside the commissary, shields his eyes until they adjust to the blazing sun. There, leaning against his Jeep. Donaldson's arms are folded as if he knew Ralph would be looking for him. "Ready Captain?"

"Where is he?"

"With the colonel. Won't talk to anybody but you."

"Let's go." Ralph heads toward the Jeep, then stops and backpedals, turning to the commissary. "Hold on just a minute. I'll be right back." He takes the three steps into the commissary and disappears. Donaldson starts the engine and Ralph reappears in two minutes. The sling is gone. He grimaces as he slides in next to Donaldson. "What are you waiting for, let's go see Father Heller."

Every leap and turn of the Jeep let Ralph know his shoulder is far from healed. When they reach the command center Donaldson advises Ralph he is going off duty in an hour. "No problem private, I'll survive. Thanks for the smooth ride over here."

"Sure thing, Captain. Just doing my best to help you ignore doctor's orders. Good luck in there."

Ralph knows his way around the company HQ by now and quickly finds Colonel Turner. He's hunched over a small knee-high table, deep in conversation with a burly man dressed in crumpled civilian clothes better suited to Washington, DC than Tunisia. The stranger's chubby fingers hold a manila folder stamped CLASSIFIED. He fans himself with the envelope, sweat dripping off his double chin. *This is the hotshot from AFHQ*? Ralph salutes the colonel, who remains seated. The burly man rises, nods and offers his hand to Ralph. His grip is sweaty but firm. "Hello captain."

Turner takes the introduction from there. "Captain, this is Ray Backus from Washington. He's part of the task force assigned to this investigation into Nazi infiltration of the Red Cross."

Ralph wants more. "So, you're not with AFHQ?" Backus doesn't answer, instead looks to Turner for direction. Turner nods. "It's okay Ray, Captain Bauer can be trusted."

Backus takes a deep breath, seems to relax a bit. "Sure Colonel, understood. I'm still trying to figure out protocol around these parts."

"Still getting used to North Africa, Mr. Backus?" Ralph is smiling. *Come on Ray my new friend, relax and fill me in here.*

"I'm used to sitting at a desk in Washington. This is a little out of my element. I'm sorry Captain, let me explain. I'm with the OSS. You know about us?"

"Sure, the Office of Strategic Services, the special operations guys."

Backus laughs. It sounds more like he is trying to catch his breath "Do I look like a special operations guy?" he wheezes. "Sure, that's part of what we do. But a lot of our work is collecting data, research, censorship. You know, boring stuff. I work mostly in the area of foreign nationalities. Mostly I sit at a desk. Get a lot of help from the Brits and that's how this solid tip showed up about the Nazis and the Red Cross. Most times the trail runs dry and nothing comes of these investigations, but our friend Major Heller might be one of those lucky sources that make it all worthwhile."

"I didn't think my interrogation went very well with the chaplain."

"Well, you obviously said something that struck a chord because suddenly he is willing to talk. Right now, he only wants to have that conversation with you, so here we are."

Ralph tries to seem matter of fact, but he is loving the attention. "Okay, what's next?"

"Whatever way you want to handle this captain, let me know. You can tell me what's in the note or you can meet with him first and then fill me in. Bottom line is he won't talk to anybody but you."

"Appreciate it Mr. Backus. Let me see what's on his mind." Ralph scratches his arm and asks the question that's been lingering since he read Heller's note. "Just curious, why is he still here? I mean, I thought you were shipping him out right away."

Turner answers first. "That was never our plan. We were just trying to light a fire under his ass. Figured it might make him talk faster."

"Good plan. It lit a fire under my ass, too."

Backus smiles and offers a thumbs up. "Glad to oblige, captain. Now, you can take your time in there. Just bring us something we can work with."

The first thing Ralph sees when he enters the tent is the crucifix around Heller's neck. *Looks like Father Kelly delivered.* Heller is seated at a bare table, hands folded. He is clean shaven since they last spoke and appears calm. He stands and bows his head in Ralph's direction. Waits for Ralph to speak.

"Father, I didn't think we would have the chance to see each other again. Our last meeting ended so abruptly. Why the change of heart?"

Heller sits again and refolds his hands. "Not a change of heart Captain. Just a little more time to reflect on your offer. Hopefully, you remember your offer?"

Ralph sits on the edge of the table and guides his right arm close to his chest. He misses his sling. "I remember it very clearly Father. You were going to share some information with me and I would make sure you got to a POW camp in America where you could tend to your flock without all this Nazi bullshit."

"That's a very charming description, Captain. I hope the offer still stands?"

"She is here?" Ralph produces the note from his right chest pocket. "How long have you known that?"

"Only for a day or so. After our meeting I was taken back to my original holding area and asked to continue helping the men with their transition to incarceration. Counseling them. Helping with personal effects. Translating for the Americans. Making sure their families knew they were okay. So, of course I began interacting again with the Red Cross and that is when I met her."

"The woman you told me about? The Swiss national?"

"Exactly." The chaplain changes direction. "Do you have any American cigarettes?" Ralph gets up, walks to the end of the tent and pokes his head outside, talks to the guard. When he returns a pack of cigarettes are in his left hand. He reaches the table and slides the half-opened pack over to the chaplain. He strikes a match, grimaces with the simple motion and holds the open flame out for the prisoner. Heller notices his discomfort but says nothing and lights his cigarette. He takes a very long draw, allowing the smoke to fill his lungs. He closes his eyes, tilts his head back and blows the smoke away from Ralph. "I have come to appreciate your cigarettes during my brief stay here."

Ralph continues questioning, ignoring the comment. "I thought you said you never met her before? Why all of a sudden this different story?"

Heller shakes his head vigorously in denial. "When you and I last spoke, it was still true that I had never met this woman. But our paths finally crossed a few days ago, and I became suspicious very quickly."

"How so?"

"At first, our conversations were routine, focused mainly on the men and their needs. Then, things changed. She began to ask me unusual questions. Where I had been? How long had I interacted with the Americans? Did I know how long this camp would remain open? Was there a timetable for prisoners reaching the docks in Algiers?"

"But since you never met her before, how did you know she was the one?"

"First, the obvious. I could see from her credentials that she was a Swiss national. Then, the odd questions. Based on the conversations I've had in the past with Red Cross volunteers these were, as I already said, unusual. Plus, she made me an offer.

Ralph is not expecting this comment from Heller. He approaches him and leans in. "Wait, what kind of offer?"

The tip of Heller's cigarette gets brighter. Smoke pours from his nostrils before he speaks. "She told me she could get my family out of Germany and safely to Switzerland if I could find out more details about troop movements and schedules of ship departures."

"How does she know about your family?"

"Just innocent conversation. She went to school in Munich, where my parents were teachers. We talked a great deal about the White Rose."

"Sorry Father, what is the White Rose?"

"It's a resistance movement in Munich that started among students opposed to Hitler. The Gestapo shut it down rather quickly and some of the student leaders were executed. My parents were never implicated but they taught several of the students, so life has been uncomfortable for them. That's all. I just shared this with her and she offered to get them to Switzerland, which I refused."

"Because you don't trust her?"

"Put yourself in my place, captain. Acknowledging that I would like to help my parents leave Germany only implicates them as guilty and me as a willing accomplice. Why would they need to leave if they are innocent? That's how the Gestapo thinks. So, better left alone."

Ralph despises the Germans every time he hears these stories. He wants to believe Heller but now finds himself judging the chaplain's intentions. *Why doesn't anyone in your world stand up to these demons? How can you live with yourself?* Silence reminds him that Heller is waiting for a response. "What did you tell her?"

"I said I would help gather information but declined her offer to help my parents." He pushes his chair back, takes one final draw on the cigarette and flicks it to the ground. "Then I wrote you the note."

Ralph walks around the table and steps on the smoldering cigarette. "So now I am supposed to believe that you are ready to help us?"

"No, believe that I am ready to be there for our soldiers. Many are like me. Confused and afraid and trying to do the right thing. Just spending a little bit of time with them, seeing how much I could help, made me realize what my vocation means to me. I have no interest in this woman and I certainly care more about my faith than any Nazi ideology. So, your offer came to mind, and I decided to pursue it. I want to go to America. I want to be sent to a prison camp where my only focus can be my men, not the hypocrisy of Hitler."

"What if she turns out to be nothing more than a nosy volunteer?"

"A nosy volunteer would not be bargaining with the safety of my family captain. I have done what you asked of me. What you do with this information is of no interest to me. Now I ask you to honor your end of the bargain. Send me to America. Let me be a priest."

Ralph knows this is not his decision. "Okay, Father. Let me discuss it with my team here and I will let you know." He slides the cigarettes back across the table. "I will be back soon."

The conversation with Backus and Turner doesn't take very long. The Red Cross volunteers are moving out within the next 24 hours. Backus decides to give Heller false information to pass on to the Swiss national. His surveillance team will follow her and hope she leads them to a wider network of Nazi contacts. As long as Heller is willing to comply, he will have his deal. Backus joins Ralph when he returns to update Heller.

Translating for the OSS agent, Ralph explains the details. They will supply the chaplain with meaningless information about prisoner transports from Algiers. Times of departure, shipping lanes, enough details to seem legitimate. Heller has no objection to the plan, asking only how long this will take. When he hears the time frame Heller is visibly elated. They review the false information he will pass on and agree on the time and place the exchange will take place within the camp. Backus is adamant about one thing. "We need to see the exchange. We need visible identification of this person." Once they have identified the target, Backus will take over and Heller will be released into the custody of the Americans for proper placement in a POW camp.

Two days later, Ralph and Heller are back in the chapel where they originally met. Where everything seemed to go all wrong. Now, Ralph has accomplished his mission and Heller has his deal. All that is left is to say goodbye. But Ralph still has one final question for the chaplain.

"Father, how did you know about the bible? How did you know it did not belong to me?"

"It is not very old, captain. Printed within the last ten years by a religious publisher in Austria who distributes their work almost exclusively for the Catholic Church. You said you were not Catholic?"

Embarrassed, Ralph acknowledges, "No. Lutheran."

"So, your Lutheran grandmother would probably not have that bible in her possession. It would be especially difficult for one that was just recently printed in Europe to find its way to your country, especially under the current circumstances.

"Anything else I screwed up?"

Heller hesitates.

“Oh, please. This is your last chance to embarrass me. What else?”

“Captain, the page you obviously tore from the front of the book is not the only one that contains a message meant for its owner. If you had cared to actually read the bible, you would have found more messages– as I did. More reasons for you to understand that not all of the men I serve in this army are evil. Many of us have just been thrown into a very dark place.”

Ralph stares at his feet for the longest time. *Good people in a bad army.*

“You look ashamed captain. Don’t be. You were just trying to do your job. In the end, we both got what we wanted.”

Ralph offers his hand, but part of him wants to spit in Heller’s face. He is still the enemy, but it feels like the right thing to do. “Good luck, Father. I hope the rest of this war brings you a little peace.”

“Thank you, Captain. Now I’m the one who feels a bit guilty -- getting to America before you. Please be assured I will pray for your safe return as well. Now, if you don’t mind, I think I will stay in the chapel for a little longer, until Mr. Backus is ready to leave.”

Ralph leaves the chapel, the door closing on a rare chapter in his version of the war. Almost immediately he sees Backus approaching, looking uncomfortably hot as usual.

“Captain, glad I caught up with you before we ship your friend back to the states. Listen, thanks again for your help. We’ve got Heller’s contact in our sights now and will tail her until she leads us to something bigger – I hope. You do good work and it won’t be lost on my superiors.”

Ralph extends his hand. Backus wipes his trousers first before acknowledging the gesture. “Sorry, this heat is killing me.” He shakes Ralph’s hand but the grip is still moist. “Like

I was saying, good work and let me know if I can return the favor."

"Actually, there is something."

"Well, don't be shy now." He winks at Ralph, "Make it fast or lower the temperature by 50 degrees."

Ralph reaches into his pocket and produces the remnants of Stephan's soldbuch. "Here, I'm hoping you can help me track down this guy. Not sure when he was sent to the states but it can't be too long ago. I'd like to find him if I could."

Backus takes one look and laughs. "Where's the rest of it?"

"That's all I have. Come on isn't that what you guys do? Put together pieces of the puzzle?"

"Not making any promises but I'll give it a try." He looks more closely. "There's enough of his military record here that we may be able to connect it back to original paperwork in Tunisia."

"Thanks, it's important."

"Mind if I ask why?"

"Let's just say I have something that belongs to him."

CHAPTER 14
Camp Huntsville

Bribes

Stephan has spent most of this sunny day mowing grass throughout the prison grounds. He moves freely as he performs his chores while sentries high above the camp watch all prisoner movements. By the end of his 6-hour shift he has walked most of the compound's vast footprint. The camp's simple layout is beginning to make sense. Adjacent to his barracks are showers, a mess hall, and a recreation building that round out the remaining facilities available for his company. Three other companies just like Stephan's feed into a shared canteen and infirmary. Together, these four companies are housed in one compound. All barracks throughout the sprawling camp are set up in a similar fashion within three almost-identical compounds separated only by chain link fences. Two 10-feet tall barbed wire barriers surround the entire camp. They have been warned: If escaping prisoners reach the swath of flat ground between these two fences they will be shot.

With his workday finished he spends time in the library, grabs another decent meal in the mess hall and heads to the canteen to buy a comb with the scrip money he's earned from his daily job.

One of the first familiar faces he sees is Hugo, who is assigned to another company. It's the first time they've been together since Hugo was attacked by Schroeder on the train. He joins him in a slow-moving line of prisoners gathering to cash in their daily beer coupons. Their conversation is guarded and hushed.

"Stephan, are you sure you want to be seen with me? You might get a bad reputation."

"Stop being such a hero Hugo, you've got to back off."

"It's too late for that. I'm a marked man. There are hundreds of guys like Schroeder and the word travels fast. They see me talking to the guards and that even makes them more suspicious."

"Why are you talking to the guards?"

"They are my only way out of here."

"You just got here. And what exactly are you talking to the guards about?"

Hugo looks around cautiously, grabs Stephan's arm and steps back from the men in front of him. His eyes dart nonstop. The paranoia is evident. Stephan strains his ears to hear Hugo's answer, "Right now, I'm just getting to know them," he whispers. "And I'm letting them get to know me. My parents worked in New York City before the war, so I've lived more of my life here than in Germany. I speak English like a native. I know their culture. I absolutely love jazz, even though Hitler has banned it. I even understand baseball. Played a pretty mean shortstop back in New York." Hugo senses Stephan's confusion and smiles. "Stephan, you don't even know what a shortstop does, do you?"

"I have no idea what you are talking about Hugo."

"That's okay. But the guards do, right? I'm a curiosity to them and they are a necessary connection for me."

"Connection to what Hugo? Where are you going?"

"The least you know the better Stephan." He shifts the

conversation as they reach the double doors of the canteen. "Listen, I know you don't smoke. Do you think I could have your cigarettes?"

"Not unless you tell me what's going on."

"We get plenty of cigarettes in here but the Americans have theirs rationed. So..."

"So, you want to bribe the guards with cigarettes? Is that it? Are you crazy?" Stephan pushes his friend outside of the line, and this time plenty of people notice the guarded conversation. "You've got to stop this nonsense. It's going to get you in a lot of trouble."

"Well staying here is going to get me killed." The canteen door opens and closes as more prisoners file past the two men.

"Why don't you take it to your company commander? Explain what's going on. Maybe get yourself moved to a friendlier group." They re-join the line while Stephan digs into his pocket for the beer coupon.

Hugo rolls his eyes. "This is the army Stephan, not first grade. Look, pretty soon we'll be getting assigned to work details outside the camp. Finally doing more than cutting grass and painting posts. We'll be spending most of our days out there rather than in here. I can make a little money, buy some extra cigarettes and if the opportunity comes for me, I'll be ready. In the meantime, I won't lie just to live." They reach the counter where coupons are being exchanged. "Now, if you really care about me, you'll give me your coupon for your beer. How is a man supposed to get drunk on one bottle of this piss?"

"Well it's your lucky night. I don't drink either. Just promise me you'll stay out of trouble."

Hugo laughs loudly. "That my friend is a promise I will break. Let's face it. We follow the same routine, eat the same food, and answer to the same captors. But your world is temporary and tolerable as long as you continue to look the other way and stay out of trouble. I'm not judging you Stephan but please don't judge me. Just keep those beer coupons coming my way."

Stephan leaves his friend and returns to his barracks. The short walk is a lonely one. *Why can't he do what's necessary to survive? Doesn't he want to go home? All of us lie to live. All of us ignore our conscience.*

CHAPTER 15
Huntsville, Texas

Visit

Daylight teases the Texas horizon as Rose approaches Clyde's home. Dabbing the perspiration above her lip, she surveys the simple one-floor house with its mismatched shutters and scarred gray siding shielded by a rusted tin roof. Morning dew clouds the single window that makes the homely structure feel lopsided. Uncle Pete dropped her off this morning, never asking why she wanted to visit. It would have been an appropriate question since Rose has never seen the inside of Clyde's home. She grew up on the farm playing in the fields with Barbara, bolls of cotton stuck to their hair and clothes, but not once did she ever cross the threshold of this house. *And we never invited Barbara to my home.*

Rose stands on the farm's unpaved service road, a stone's throw from the front of the house. To her left the road leads to a rusted corrugated garage resting on a concrete slab as dark as the soil supporting it. On her right she hears the warbling whistle of eastern bluebirds already gathering on a now-dormant field that long ago held the summer vegetables that she and Barbara helped Esther pick. There is no porch or path. Just a couple tentative steps from the service road and Rose is at the front door. She knocks and leans back.

Almost immediately, the door swings inward and Clyde fills the opening.

"Miss Rose, is everything okay? Are you okay?"

"Oh everything is fine Clyde. I'm sorry to surprise you like this. May I come in?"

He steps back from the doorway. "Of course, of course." He waves Rose inside. His large, calloused hands betray the decades of hard labor on the Bauer Farm, where chopping and harvesting cotton is still done manually.

The interior is spartan but clean and tidy. Standing by the front door, Rose scans the kitchen, tiny living room and a narrow hall that must lead to the bedroom. "Clyde, your home is lovely. And you keep it so neat."

"Well, now you can thank Esther for that. She'd rise up out of her grave and beat me silly if I didn't keep the place tidy, yes ma'am for certain."

"She would be proud of you Clyde, that's for sure."

"Thank you, Miss Rose. It's an honor to have you in my home but I need to..."

"Oh of course Clyde. You don't have to explain. We all know how punctual my uncle is. I don't want to make you late. Is it okay if I walk with you this morning? That is if you don't mind my company."

Clyde shuffles toward the kitchen. He walks with a permanent limp. "Mind? It would be my pleasure Miss Rose. I just need to lock up the storage shed. It's easier if we just head out the back."

He leads Rose past the modest kitchen but stops as she pauses to pick up a framed picture resting on a round table, freshly painted bright yellow. The table wobbles as the picture frame sticks briefly before surrendering to Rose's grip. "This is a nice picture of Esther. The light captures her features beautifully. Did..."

"Barbara took that photograph." He opens the door and points to a porch. "Right out here in fact. Esther never knew she took it."

"She has a gift Clyde." *Inconspicuous. Discreet.*

Rose steps onto the small porch and Clyde closes the door behind them. A canopy formed by a sturdy stand of 100-feet tall loblolly pines allows the rising sun to gently filter through bundles of small needles.

"Clyde, I love the shade out here. It's so comfortable."

He folds his arms and leans back, shields his eyes and looks skyward "Don't know what we'd do out here without these trees. In the winter, when the cotton fields are empty, they can put a stop to some mighty angry winds."

"Year round protection."

"For sure. That's why Esther loved it out here any time of the year." He smiles and points toward the house. "Course, she was happy to be any place but the kitchen."

Rose laughs. "I'm not fond of the kitchen either Clyde. I can relate to that."

He glances at his watch. Heading toward the storage shed he says, "give me a couple minutes and I'll meet you out front."

By the time Rose reaches the front, Clyde is already there, leaning against the house. He moves slowly away and Rose follows. They cross the service road where Clyde's pace quickens as they move towards a loose gravel path. To their right is the cotton crop that provides his livelihood. Nearly all of the cotton is planted on medium-high beds that rise gently above Clyde and Rose as they now walk side by side. Rose inhales slowly. "Sometimes in the morning I swear I can actually smell the dirt."

"Black gumbo. Been smelling it all my life."

Rose nods. She knows the history, too. The Bauer Cotton Farm is located in the Blackland Prairie of East Texas -- named for its rich, dark soil. The tall grasslands that welcomed settlers generations ago has been further blackened by the char from wildfires and controlled burns. The prairie also delivers a temperate climate suitable for growing cotton. The region is blessed with warm nights, plenty of rainfall, and proper drainage thanks to the rolling, gentle topography that silhouettes their morning stroll.

"How long does this walk normally take Clyde?"

"In decent weather about 45 minutes."

"Why don't you just ride the tractor?"

"Fuel is precious, Miss Rose. I want to do my part. Besides, I actually enjoy the walk. Gives me time to clear my head." The path turns sharply to the left. Clyde slows down and looks back toward the house.

"Did you forget something?'

"No just force of habit." He points toward the corner of the porch, unobscured by the pine trees but barely visible from where they are standing. "Every morning, Esther would lean over the railing and wave my way. Seems I can't stop looking back still."

"Then keep looking back Clyde."

"Not sure that's the smartest thing. Sometimes, I think it's better to put the past behind and just move on. "

"Do you feel that way about Barbara?"

Clyde stops abruptly and looks at Rose, who turns and walks back to him.

"Clyde, I'm sorry. That was inappropriate." She resumes walking but the overseer remains standing. He wipes his forehead and looks back in the direction of his house, which is no longer visible from the path. "Clyde, please. You'll be late."

He approaches Rose. "You knew her better than most people around here, Miss Rose. You grew up together. Why would she leave?" *I don't want to answer that.*

"Clyde, after she was fired by the Fords, did they give you

any explanation?"

"It was Mrs. Ford who told me that she was going to be doing the work herself from now on, even gave Barbara a few extra dollars for the final week she wouldn't be needed. It just didn't add up."

"Why, what do you mean?"

"Just a few days earlier I ran into her when me and Mr. Bauer were at the hardware store. She's such a kind lady. Went out of her way to thank me. Said Barbara was doing a fine job for them. Best help they ever had, colored or white. Their kids loved her. She told me they trusted her, Miss Rose. Didn't know what they would do without my daughter."

Clyde's pace slows, his limp more apparent as they navigate the short climb to the top of a hill, where the Bauer farmhouse is finally in sight. A dusty path briefly levels out and then gently rolls its way gradually down toward their destination.

"They trusted her but let her go. Did Barbara ever explain her side of the story?"

"I tried Miss Rose. Silence is all the explaining I got. Three months later she left for Chicago. Been almost two years since I heard from her." Sunlight is blanketing the young cotton crops as they approach the work yard. "Listen, Miss Rose I appreciate your concern but I'm confused. Is there something you want to tell me?"

"First of all, this is not a sudden concern. It's been bothering me for way too long but I haven't done enough to help you. I want to help. I want to get Barbara back home." *That's as honest as I can be for now.*

"Thanks Miss Rose, but I can't say I blame my daughter for staying away. Esther was the only reason she would have stayed in touch. Working these fields kept me away from her growing up. I know I missed a lot of things."

"Nonsense, Clyde. Barbara loves you. More than you know."

They enter the work yard and Clyde begins to whistle.

CHAPTER 16
Camp Huntsville

Work Detail

Today, Rose is finally earning her paycheck. Along with Colonel Warren, she stands at the front of a cramped meeting room within the American garrison. Standing at attention before them in a classroom-style setting are 50 or so German officers. She has no idea of ranks or pecking order. Her armpits are soaked. An invisible weight presses the square shoulders of her simple yellow dress. She removes her foggy spectacles to clean them. Her hands are trembling. *This is a bad idea.*

In an unexpected gesture, many of the officers salute Colonel Tucker with the distinctive Hitler Greeting, right arm stretched above the neck, hand straightened. A few offer "Heil Hitler" along with their salute. It unnerves Rose even more. The men take their seats. The colonel remains stoic. "Miss Bauer let's begin."

The steady voice of Colonel Warren does little to calm her. The dull thud of a pencil eraser tapping magnifies the pounding in her ears. Keeping the steady beat in front of her is a stern-looking officer who senses her nervousness like a lion sniffs out its wounded prey. Tap.Tap.Tap. His piercing eyes, no hint of compassion or mercy, are fixed on her.

He is naked, except for his shiny boots. Rose smiles. For

the first time she takes a full breath and feels her thumping heart surrender. *Thank you, Oma.*

Before she left the house this morning, she mentioned to her grandmother how nervous and intimidated she felt. Oma stood up, still holding her breakfast tray, and shouted "stille!" loud enough to interrupt Clyde's whistling outside. *Hush!* "You are a free American. They are prisoners. You will not be intimidated."

Rose walked over to the second-floor window, peered through the sheer curtains. In the driveway below, Clyde was talking to Uncle Pete inside his truck.

"But I am intimidated Oma. These men have been through so much, seen so much. I have never been outside of Texas. Why will they listen to me?"

"Would you be intimidated if Ralph or Henry were in the room?"

Rose was still fixed on the driveway below, remembering a time when her siblings would have been laughing with Uncle Pete and Clyde. "Of course not. They are my brothers...."

"Well those men are just brothers too, Rose. They may be Nazi swine, but they still miss *their* sisters and families and friends. They want to go home too. So, help them. But let them know you are in charge."

Rose let go of the curtains, turned to her grandmother, surrender in her voice. "I don't want to let Colonel Warren down."

"He picked you for a reason." Oma was back in her chair, surveying her breakfast. "You won't let him down. You are his voice, his messenger. So be strong and do your duty, just like your brothers."

"Well, I'm still nervous Oma."

"Oh, we'll fix that. She began buttering her toast then pointed the knife at Rose. "When you get to that meeting, I want you to pick out the toughest looking Kraut you can find.

Take a good look at him Rose. Then...."

A pause. That mischievous grin.

"Then, what?"

"Imagine the man is buck naked."

"Oma!" Rose giggled, covered her mouth and appreciated her sassy grandmother more than ever.

Oma waved her toast toward the door. "Now get going. You're already late. Uncle Pete is waiting."

Rose straightens her posture. Smooths the invisible wrinkles on her dress. Her hands are now clasped waist high. Her head is erect. She steps forward and begins to translate for Colonel Warren, stumbling a bit in the beginning but recovering quickly. They are attentive. Her German is fluent. She is not intimidated.

Within an hour they have accomplished their task. Rose stands at the rear of the room, near the only exit. The officers are polite. Some bow slightly. Others offer a formal "danke, fräulein." One nervous officer, cap in hand, compliments Rose on her excellent German. The naked man, now fully clothed, clicks the heels of his shiny boots and accepts the handout Rose is distributing. She is passing out information that summarizes her presentation.

The officers have been told their men will be assigned to work details that will be sent into the Huntsville community. It all makes sense. Huntsville is an agricultural area and farms are experiencing serious labor shortages. The prisoners offer an immediate solution to the problem. The Geneva Convention permits the use of prisoner labor, but they must be paid. The average wage is 80 cents an hour, the same pay an American private is receiving. Officers are not compelled to work. Part of the prisoners' wages is held back to pay for the POW program. The rest is given to them in scrip money, meaning that they are issued coupons instead to be used at the canteen. Colonel Warren explained to Rose that scrip is used instead of American currency because real money would be more helpful to prisoners if they escaped.

None of this will work if the local farms refuse to hire the enemy, especially when they find out that the prisoners are being paid the same wages as an American GI. Colonel Warren is unphased. "Profits for these farmers is what matters, Miss Bauer. Once they realize half their crops could be lost without prisoner labor maybe they'll see things differently."

The room is now empty. Rose gathers her material, feeling good about her morning. She expects a positive response from Colonel Warren, but he seems distracted. "Excuse me Colonel, are you okay with how things went this morning?"

"Of course, Miss Bauer, everything went well. Listen, this is the Army where you don't always get a compliment for doing the job you're expected to do. So, get used to it. Believe me, if I'm not happy with your work I'll let you know."

"I wasn't searching for a compliment. You just seem distracted." *Shut up Rose.* "I'll just collect my things and keep moving. I've got plenty of paperwork to finish."

"Very good. And I am not concerned with your work. There are plenty of bigger problems we're facing here in camp."

Rose hesitates, fighting her natural inclination to want more information. "Well, I'm sure you 'll figure things out Colonel. You've done such a good job of getting things running smoothly around here."

"Sometimes I don't feel like I'm in control of anything." *Just listen Rose.* "Those men in this room today are really in charge. People above me made the decision to let them maintain order within their ranks. On paper, that makes sense. We don't have the personnel to handle 5,000 prisoners any other way. But it's not working."

"I'm confused Colonel. What part of this isn't working?"

"It started back in North Africa. Prisoners should have been separated according to their Nazi loyalty. Of course, that's not as simple as it sounds because many of them lied. Now, they are arriving here in Huntsville mixed together, Nazi and anti-Nazi. And it is the Nazis who are exerting control already.

"The salute," Rose whispers.

Colonel Warren grimaces and nods in agreement. "Used by the Nazi Party since the thirties to proclaim loyalty to Hitler. Most of the officers here today are battle-hardened members of the Africa Korps. They were the first to join the German army and their allegiance to Hitler is fierce. They intend to control their men in a far different way than we imagined. We expected simple military order to rule the day. Just like it would be if Americans were imprisoned by the Germans. Here, we have a giant crack in the system, very different ideologies within the same army. And one side clearly represents the troublemakers and the thugs."

"What are we going to do?"

"*We* are not going to do anything Miss Bauer. *You* are just going to keep following orders and doing your job. I will be taking this problem to Washington. Hopefully, when I get back, I'll have an answer."

CHAPTER 17
Huntsville, Texas

Schnell

Stephan twirls the battered hoe he holds in his right hand. He inspects the tool as he stands with a dozen other POWS who have been assigned to the same work detail at a cotton farm. A caravan of buses has been depositing prisoners at area farms since it left the camp early this morning. A disinterested guard, satisfied he has the right location, steers the work detail up a curved, gravel driveway that leads from the main road. Stephan sees a typical rural mailbox stuffed with mail -- its front flap lost long ago. Stenciled on each side in faded black letters is the name BAUER. Marching single file around a bend ten yards from the road, they pass a stand of tall pine trees that remind Stephan of the dense forests in the Austrian countryside. Beyond the trees they get their first glimpse of a simple two-story house. It looks no different than the dozens of homes they passed on their commute this morning. The worn shutters could stand a coat of paint. The whitewashed clapboard siding seems well-maintained, except for the western side of the house obscured by those trees. There, a splash of green mold covers the lower part of the house that gets very little exposure to its only chance for morning sun. The most charming feature to Stephan is the home's broad porch wrapping around its side and continuing to parallel the same driveway that deposits the prisoners into a work yard. There, the marchers stop, separated from the house by a waist-high picket fence.

That's when Stephan sees her. An elderly woman in a powder blue housecoat. Sitting upright, gently moving back and forth while the porch barely creaks under her rocking chair's weight. Her eyes are riveted on the prisoners. Stephan is unable to break his gaze from her as well. There is something that draws him toward her. He feels like he wants to climb the porch stairs and introduce himself. *How odd would that be? And dangerous.* So far, his only experience with American citizens has been the day they arrived at the train station. People were gawking from the roadside as prisoners marched past them toward the camp. Always a curiosity about them. Maybe even a bit of fear. But not this woman. He knows she is not intimidated. She openly cringes, then actually smiles as the American guard butchers his command in German to the straggling prisoners to move quickly. He means to say "schnell," but it sounds more like "schale." Stephan sees the humor in it because the guard's feeble attempt means he is screaming the name of an inanimate object, "bowl." But how does the woman on the porch know? Their eye's meet, and they share more than a smile. They connect. The guard's gaffe is understood between them. *She speaks German.*

They stand at attention in the work yard. The man who appears to be in charge approaches the group. Stephan has never been this close to an American Negro before. He watches out of the corner of his eye as the overseer moves down the row of POWs. He limps slightly, stopping in front of each prisoner, sizing up their lean bodies, looking at their hands, whistling while he saunters down the line. Stephan is on the far right, nearest to the single American soldier who is guarding the group. As usual, Stephan is the tallest, towering over the others, making eye contact only briefly as the man stops in front of him, raises his head, and whistles in surprise. Stephan offers a slight smile. The man mutters to himself though Stephan cannot understand the words, "didn't know they made them this tall."

Stephan can't stop thinking about the old woman he just saw on the porch. He wants to turn back toward the house and see her one more time. Share another smile. But his work detail is on the move again, the guard prodding him with the barrel of his rifle. Stephan is now leading the way, moving further from the house and closer to the fields where they will be working. That's when the scale of this crop and the size of this farm finally settles in. All he can see for an eternity are rows of cotton shrubs that are so evenly spaced he is astonished at the symmetry of the landscape. He also thought he would see white tufts of cotton dotting the fields but all he notices are dark green clumps with speckles of yellow and red and pink. Passing clouds dampen some of the colors while the sun decides to illuminate other parts of the vast crop. He doesn't know a thing about cotton but figures out quickly that he won't be picking any today. *That's why they gave us these.* The old blade he is holding is still very sharp and heavy, while the handle is far shorter than he imagined. Whatever he's supposed to do with this, he knows he'll be doing it bent over. *Better than being in the camp, living a lie. At least I can get some fresh air, stay out of trouble and make some money.*

Standing much closer to the fields now, he can't help but feel the difference in humidity. It's as if the plants themselves are saturating the air. The wind picks up, rippling the bushy crops and kicking up dust around his feet. It cools the shirt already clinging to his back. Coming from the distant driveway is the gentle grind of slowly churning gravel and the sound of a vehicle. Several heads turn back toward the driveway and farmhouse. Stephan joins them long enough to notice the rocking chair is empty. "Eyes ahead!" The guard shouts in English, not even attempting to communicate in German. The prisoners react instinctively. They are used to taking orders, regardless of the language. The truck stops and belches as the ignition is turned off. They hear the slow squeak of the door opening, muffled conversations with the Negro, and the sound of footsteps approaching them.

An older man wearing a high-crowned, wide brimmed hat stained with sweat offers the second smile of Stephan's less than ordinary day. Then he begins to speak to the prisoners in German. *They all speak German. Who are these people?* Stephan shares nods of surprise among his fellow prisoners -- with one exception. Standing directly to Stephan's left is Werner, a corporal and a troublemaker everyone in camp knows as one of Schroeder's cronies. Even on the bus ride to the farm, he overheard Werner saying that no one could force him to work for the Americans. "They'll regret the day they put a hoe in my hand," was Werner's comment. A few heads nodded in agreement, but nobody argued with him, including Stephan, who instinctively thought of Hugo. *He would have challenged Werner.* Stephan hopes Hugo's work assignment on a livestock farm is keeping him safe and far away from the troublemakers like Werner and Schroeder. At the very least, his friend is hopefully keeping his mouth shut.

The man in the hat speaks to them while holding a hoe in his left hand. His German is flawless. "My name is Peter Bauer, and this is my family's farm. With his right thumb he gestures over his shoulder to the fields behind him. Our primary crop is cotton, which was planted earlier this Spring. The crops have been thinned out a few times since then to give them space to grow." He drops his hoe to the ground, pulls a handkerchief from his back pocket, removes his hat and dabs the back of his neck. "We call that 'chopping cotton.' You are here to make sure any new weeds are eliminated so the plants continue to grow. He points to the Negro with handkerchief still in hand. "This is Mister Clyde Turner. He oversees this farm. He'll supervise your work and he'll begin today by showing you how to use these hoes."

Werner turns to Stephan and mutters under his breath.

"Save your breath, Mr. Bauer. We're in no hurry to help you win the war." Stephan swallows hard and looks straight ahead. *Did the American hear? Does he think I said it?*

Uncle Pete understands every word whispered by Werner. He stops speaking and approaches the prisoner. The guard pulls his rifle down and reluctantly steps toward the two. In English, Uncle Pete addresses the American. "At ease soldier there ain't gonna be any trouble here." To Stephan's relief, Uncle Pete turns to Werner, speaking again in German. "Son, there's a saying around here that might be good advice for you to hear. 'Never miss a good chance to shut up.' He moves in closer, almost toe to toe. "I don't know what your problem might be, and I really don't care. All I know is I have two nephews who aren't on this farm right now because of your Goddam country and this crazy war that might get them killed. So, take your righteous Nazi attitude back to the camp and tell them to send me somebody who is willing to work for an honest day's wages. And if you do show up again tomorrow, I expect you to shut up and do your job."

Stephan can feel Werner's anger. He's been humiliated publicly by the American. *How is he going to save face and explain this one on the bus ride back to camp?* The group is instructed to follow Clyde. Werner makes sure he is the last in line. His delay is deliberate enough that Clyde must wait. None of this is lost on Uncle Pete who whispers into Clyde's ear and then prepares to translate as the group is instructed on the proper way to eliminate weeds. The lesson lasts fifteen minutes and Clyde is sweating heavily at its conclusion. Before they even began, Stephan notices that a handful of Negro workers, all about Clyde's age, have arrived. They get to work immediately, setting a pace that none of the prisoners will match for the rest of the day.

For Stephan the hard labor that comes closest to the relentless swinging of a hoe is digging ditches. There were plenty of times he was forced to do that in the North African desert, but this is tougher. His back aches already and he has only been working the hoe for less than an hour. Each time he straightens up to gauge his progress, the row of cotton he has been assigned doesn't seem to be getting any shorter. He can't even see the end, which he estimates is still a half-kilometer away. To his left and right many of the prisoners are struggling to keep up. Werner is easily twenty yards behind all of them, deliberately taking his time. Far ahead, Clyde and his friends are laughing and chopping, seldom taking a break.

One of the white farmhands, probably a local schoolboy, is directing a horse-drawn cart down a 6-foot wide path that separates the area where they are working from similar sections. He stops the cart, rings a bell and the Negro workers leave their rows to take a water break. Stephan approaches the wagon where Clyde and his friends are already gathered. He submerges his canteen in a large tub of fresh water and watches the bubbles rapidly disappear as water fills it. The Negroes suddenly stop talking and turn their attention to Stephan. Their silence is odd and misplaced. They look at one another, then at the young man driving the cart. Now, Stephan realizes they are watching him. Something is wrong. The young boy shakes his head, jumps off his cart and grabs both Stephan and his canteen. He walks him around to the other side of the cart, where a similar tub of water sits. "Your water," he says slowly and deliberately in English. Stephan doesn't understand. The boy points first at Clyde's group and then to the original urn where Stephan drew his first drink. "Colored water" he repeats again and again as he points to the Negroes. Stephan is even more confused. He thinks the prisoners are not permitted to use the workers' water supply. But he has it backwards. Clyde and the other Negro laborers are forbidden to drink Stephan's water. It is actually Werner who smugly explains it to Stephan. "See what hypocrites the Americans are? They claim to be freedom fighters, but they segregate their schools and armies and treat these men like second class citizens. Welcome to the real America."

There is still plenty of daylight remaining when the work detail finally finishes for the day. Uncle Pete advises the group that tomorrow will be much busier, with expectations that the prisoners will be able to cover more ground. "Make sure you are all ready to work. We'll have less patience for stragglers." Everyone knows his message is intended for Werner.

The group begins their journey back to the main road and the waiting bus. They double time their steps moving through the work yard toward the house. Stephan is exhausted, everything aches, but he feels grateful, with simple expectations for the hours ahead. A shower, decent meal, and then a good night's sleep free of emptiness and fear. He has one more expectation as they approach the house and the porch comes into view. He is not disappointed. The elderly woman is waiting. She is standing, her crooked hands on the porch railing. Most of the group ignores her, their eyes straight ahead as they trot by. But Stephan is fixed on his anonymous friend. As they pass, closer to the porch, Werner again is in his usual spot, well behind the group deliberately displaying his defiance. And then she is no longer the quiet old lady on the porch. "Schnell, schnell!" Her voice is loud and anything but frail. Her German is crisp, clear, and confident. The other prisoners laugh in appreciation, raise their tired arms and wave. She acknowledges them all, but she is looking at Stephan. For now, that is the extent of their unspoken relationship. Neither of them has any idea that someday they will not just be friends, but allies in a very different war.

AUGUST 1943

* * *

CHAPTER 18
Huntsville, Texas

Biscuits

Saturday morning. Rose is standing on the bottom step of the rear staircase, holding her spectacles. Rubbing her eyes with both fists. Not used to sleeping in, she is taking full advantage of a rare day off. Something else is different about this morning -- Oma is making breakfast. Instead of entering the kitchen, Rose gently sits down on the step, pulls her legs in and rests her head on her knees. She hears Uncle Pete speaking to Oma.

"Well, what have we got here? A Saturday surprise."

"Couldn't take another breakfast confined to my room Pete. Arthritis is giving me a break today so I decided to reclaim my kitchen. Could use some help with this darn apron though."

"Sure thing. I hope you're planning to make extra cause I'm fixin' to eat twice my share this morning." Rose hears the familiar routine of Uncle Pete making coffee. She jerks when he slams the coffee can on the counter. "You know it's a crime you're working so hard on this meal and we can barely manage a cup of coffee to wash it down."

"Don't let it bother you Pete. Remember we need to ration so our boys have what they need."

"That used to make sense to me, but now these prisoners

get plenty of coffee every morning without making any sacrifice. They already had their breakfast back at their fancy camp and I'm sure they had as much coffee as they wanted. It just don't make sense."

Rose's voice unexpectedly joins the conversation as she steps into the room. "It doesn't have to make sense Uncle Pete. We are just following the rules for treating prisoners."

"Well, look who just rolled out of bed still spewing her Geneva Convention hogwash."

"Peter, that's enough." Oma points her spatula at her son. "Enough."

"It's okay Oma, Uncle Pete feels the same as everyone else in this town." She kisses her uncle on the cheek. "I understand his frustration. Not much about this crazy war that does make sense. Thank you for making breakfast Oma. And Uncle Pete, thank you for your famously brewed, still delicious, rationed coffee."

He winks at her. "You get one cup and watch your sugar. Now let me get these men moving outside so I can come back and enjoy my meal." He makes his way across the narrow L-shaped kitchen floor that ends with a single step down toward the back door of the house. There is a gentle rap on the door and Ginny howls. He opens the door and looks surprised to see Clyde. Oma is already behind Uncle Pete, pushing him out the door.

"Clyde, I knew you wouldn't forget."

"Not a chance Mrs. Bauer. Not a chance."

"Fresh eggs from the Cunninghams?"

"Yes, ma'am. And bacon too, just like you asked." He inhales slowly. "I hope I'm not out of line Mrs. Bauer but I'm pretty sure I smell some of your buttermilk biscuits."

She winks at him, "made them just for you Clyde. Come back in a half hour and you can join us for breakfast."

Alone on the porch, Clyde hesitates. He turns his head toward the men assembled in the work yard.

"Mr. Turner, this is my kitchen and you are welcome here any time. Be back here in thirty minutes and you will sit down with my family to eat breakfast. Are we clear?"

"Yes, Mrs. Bauer. You're so kind." He turns to leave and Oma's crooked fingers brush his shoulder.

"Clyde, have you heard from your beautiful Barbara?"

"She's pretty busy up north you know. Making a living and hopefully finding a good man."

"I'm sure she'll get in touch. Such a sweet girl."

She watches him limp down the back steps and walk toward the prisoners and Uncle Pete, congregating in their familiar spot. Rose notices her lingering at the window.

"Oma, everything okay out there?"

"Oh fine dear. Just looking for the tall one. Such a polite young man."

"You're talking to prisoners?"

"Honey, you don't have to talk to someone to know they've been raised properly."

Rose joins her at the back door. "Oma, our boys are at war. These are enemy prisoners. There is to be no social interaction."

"Heavens no, Rose." She makes her way to the kitchen table. "Just a polite wave and a smile. Harmless."

Rose tilts her head, peers over her eyeglasses, and scolds her grandmother with her eyes. Then she shakes her head and smiles.

Oma smiles too, slides slowly into the ladderback chair at the end of the kitchen table and struggles to snap her fingers. Ginny's wet nose arrives in seconds. She takes the dog's head in her frail hands and kisses its forehead. Ginny is motionless except for her thumping tail.

"Alright, Gin Gin. That's all for now. Stick around, I'm sure there will be some breakfast treats coming your way. If I ever get this meal going."

Soon, Oma is back on her feet, moving slowly toward the oven. She removes the first batch of biscuits. She may not rule this room like she once did, but she still knows every inch of it. She instinctively reaches for the cast iron skillet, wisely using two hands to steer it toward the stove. Within minutes, the bacon is sizzling, a second batch of biscuits is in the oven, and the whisk is in her fragile hands, ready to turn those fresh eggs from the Cunningham farm into her signature omelets. She sighs and surrenders the whisk. Cradling a single egg in her hand, she looks down at the dog. "Gin Gin, looks like our guests are having fried eggs this morning." She tenderly cracks the egg on the side of the skillet and watches its contents slide smoothly onto the hot surface. She picks up the next egg and repeats the process as the kitchen door announces the return of Uncle Pete.

"Looks like I'm gonna need a fresh shirt before breakfast. Hopefully all that time in the desert got these prisoners ready for some real Texas heat." A copy of the morning paper is tucked under his arm. He pulls it out and waves it at the women. "Says here it's gonna be a little hotter for a little longer."

Rose takes the paper and starts fanning herself. "We've even gone so far as to explain to the prisoners that the hot season in East Texas is longer than anywhere else in the eastern United States. So they're not getting a break from the heat they just left."

There is a quiet knock on the door. So faint, even Ginny stays put under the kitchen table. Uncle Pete parts the curtains covering the window near the sink, where he has a clear view of the back porch. "It's Clyde. What's he doing back up here?"

Oma interrupts. "It's okay. I invited him for breakfast."

Uncle Pete lowers his hand, letting the curtains rest on the sill. He is rarely at a loss for words but struggles to respond to Oma. He is uncomfortable, and both Oma and Rose sense it. Rose sees that mischievous twinkle in her grandmother's eyes. "Well don't let the poor man standing outside. Open the door for God's sake."

Uncle Pete, closest to the door, grabs the knob, shakes his head and before he pulls it open, grumbles, "He's a good man but this just complicates things." He opens the door and in a flat tone invites Clyde inside. Oma immediately welcomes him, and Rose invites Clyde to sit next to her. He takes his place, but remains standing, waiting for Oma to sit down. Rose puts her hand gently on Clyde's shoulder, acknowledging his respectful presence at the table. Sensing Clyde's uneasiness with the gesture she quickly removes her hand, but her smile lingers. Oma removes her apron as Uncle Pete pulls her chair back then carefully guides her into her seat. She watches her son take his place at the opposite end, bows her head and waits patiently until they do the same. Her eyes are closed as she prays, "Come, Lord Jesus, be our Guest," Here, she tilts her head toward Uncle Pete, opens her eyes and emphasizes the word *guest* then finishes, "and let these gifts to us be blessed. Amen." Uncle Pete seems to soften, clears his throat, and says, "Don't be shy Clyde. Help yourself. Those biscuits aren't going to jump on your plate all by themselves."

Rose passes the bacon and breaks the ice further, "So you two, how are the prisoners working out?" Clyde defers to Uncle Pete, who is quick to respond. "Well, the real test will be when we start picking in the next few weeks. Then we'll see what these boys are made of. But so far, with the exception of a few Nazi blowhards, we've got a good crew on our hands. It sure beats lazy high school students."

Oma, sitting at the end of the table, next to Clyde, offers him the plate of eggs and asks, "Clyde, have the new workers been helpful?"

"I'm grateful for any help we can get Mrs. Bauer, but I do believe they'll be fine, just fine. They learn real fast and they work hard. Well, like Mr. Bauer said, there's a couple I could do without, but I ain't complaining. No way. I think we'll be fine."

Oma continues, "I'm curious. You know I watch those boys from the porch each day and I notice a young man who can't help but stand out. He's rather tall."

"Yes ma'am. I know exactly who you are talking about. No trouble, that one. Works real hard. Keeps his head down and does his work. Probably one of our best workers."

Uncle Pete surprises them, adding, "Well, Rose I hate to admit it, but these boys so far have been exactly what we needed around here. As long as they don't cause any trouble, I imagine we'll have an easier harvest this year. But if you ask me they still get fed too well."

Oma lowers her voice on purpose, knowing full well that her son can hear her comments directed toward Clyde, "Well Clyde, maybe you can take some of these extra biscuits for yourself and why don't you bring the rest out to those men in the field. Give them a real lesson in southern hospitality." She looks at Uncle Pete and they both laugh.

"She's the boss, Clyde." He stands up, grabs an extra biscuit for himself and heads for the back door. Clyde is on his feet immediately, bowing toward Oma and Rose. "Thanks again for your hospitality. Much obliged." Rose hands him the basket of biscuits and he hastens to the open door being held by Uncle Pete.

Rose plops herself back down into her chair. "God, almighty Oma, what is it with him and Clyde. They've worked together for years. Uncle Pete trusts him with this farm, that's fairly obvious. But he won't let that poor man into his kitchen to share a meal?"

Oma is silent, feeding Ginny pieces of brittle bacon from the palm of her hand. The dog finishes, licks her chops and hopes for more. Oma rises slowly, goes to the kitchen sink and washes her hands deliberately, as if she is trying to cleanse herself of her son's stubbornness. She dabs her fragile fingers with a dish towel that matches the same calico pattern of the curtains. "He's a good man, we all know that. And he's done more for Clyde than most of his friends have ever even imagined doing for a black man in this county. But his quiet way of doing things is not because of humility. It's because your uncle is afraid. When he says that having a black man join us for breakfast in our home complicates things it's because he's scared that some of the people in town who he relies on to service and support this farm will look the other way when he needs them the most."

"Oma, I'm not naive. I grew up around here. I get it. But I'm not a child anymore. It is 1943. Americans are dying to liberate strangers half-way around the world and we can't invite Clyde inside our house. Hasn't the poor man suffered enough?"

"Rose I want to tell you a few things about your uncle's relationship with Clyde that might surprise you."

"I doubt that. I've seen it all."

"No, you've seen the public side of their relationship. But there's a private side that would maybe change some of your opinions." Rose stands and begins circling the table.

"Like what?"

"Well first of all, excuse the history lesson but for a long time this town and this farm took advantage of sharecroppers. People like Clyde's parents who never escaped the debt and burden of renting land then borrowing against a crop that rarely delivered a profit."

"Thank God that's behind us."

"And nobody did it faster than our family. Honey, the Bauers abandoned sharecropping so far back the *other* Roosevelt was president. We hired Clyde as an overseer and paid him decent wages. Now, I understand you recently visited Clyde's home". *How does she know?* "It's not much but Pete gave that house to the Turners. No mortgage. And he supplied all the materials Clyde needed to fix it up. And the porch."

"What about the porch? So he gave him some lumber to build it. I'm sorry, but..."

"Why don't you let me finish and then you can decide how unjust your uncle might be?"

Rose stops and sits again, this time right next to Oma. "The porch."

"Clyde busted his ankle up real good jumping off a tractor. Couldn't walk. Couldn't work. Uncle Pete paid him full wages. And he went down to that house every night and built that porch for him. Never bragged about it either."

"How did you find out?"

"Rose, there's not much I don't know about. *Apparently.* I know that he paid for Esther's funeral, too. And Barbara? When Pete found out she was leaving he told Clyde he wanted to pay for the bus fare to Houston and the train tickets to Chicago. Your uncle is a good man who is trying his best to support his family and still do the right thing. His heart is in the right place. Some people just need a good kick in the ass to stand up to the real cowards who hide behind their badges and their twisted laws. Trust me, sweetheart, he'll sort this out."

"This war has opened my eyes to so many bad people, Oma. I see the evil of the Nazis up close. On one hand it makes me feel so lucky to be an American. On the other, it makes me realize that we have such a long way to go in this country while we tell the rest of the world that all men are created equal. And then bury our boys to prove it."

Oma, still seated, reaches out with both her hands, pulling Rose close to her. "Rose, I've known hardship and loss for much of my life. I'm not complaining. Those are just the facts. Yet, at this moment, I've never felt safer and more optimistic about the future. I know this country still has flaws. But I also know the capacity for change and goodness is in the hands of a whole new generation. Maybe not in my lifetime but people like you and your brothers will heal the wounds and make this country a better place."

Rose reaches over and hugs her grandmother, wrapping both arms around her neck. "Thank you, Oma. Thank you for sharing so much. Now I have something I need to share with you. Something I can't keep to myself any longer. I need your advice."

"Sounds serious. About what?"

"Well for starters, I want to hear everything you know about Bobby Ford and his family."

Oma slowly stands and leans her hands on the kitchen table. "Well, what I could tell you about his daddy alone could take a while, so I just have one request."

"Of course, what is it?"

"It is well past 10:00. Do we have time for a beer?"

CHAPTER 19
Washington, DC

Connections

Ralph sits in the rear of a taxi as it weaves its way through the bustling traffic of Washington DC and heads for the E Street Campus of the OSS. His only orders are to report for a meeting at the intelligence headquarters to discuss a new assignment. *Wherever they're sending me next, maybe I'll get a few days off to visit the family.* He checks the telegram he got from Backus, inviting him for a drink before the meeting.

Let's catch up before your meeting. Heurich Brewery Tavern. 1300 sharp -- Backus

Ralph checks his watch. Close, but he'll make it. Exhausted from his bumpy flight from Chicago, he's grateful for the chain-smoking cabbie who hasn't said a word since picking him up at the airport. He reaches down and opens his attaché, carefully removing the bible. It feels comfortable in his hands now. He knows where to turn. Tightly written in the narrow margins of Proverbs. *Stay strong and do the right thing.* He gently thumbs forward. Colossians. *Pray. Trust. Wait.* He peers out the window, barely catching a glimpse of the Washington Monument through the summer haze. He runs his hands over the mother's words to her son. One more. Before the New Testament begins. *Don't let them break you.* Ralph takes a deep breath, closes the bible and slides it back into his attaché. *Oma could have written these words to me.*

"Okay soldier. This is as close as I can get without wasting your time and mine around these one-way streets." Ralph pulls the attaché onto his lap and slides forward.

"Anywhere up here is fine, thanks."

He exits the cab and is surprised by the park-like surroundings. Tucked between the Navy Medical campus and Potomac Park, the OSS complex feels very detached from the frenzied downtown his cabbie just navigated. He easily finds the central quadrangle with its prolific display of shrubbery. The walkways are thick with pedestrians as he sees the sign ahead for the Heurich Brewery. He finds the side entrance to a small tavern attached to the building. Ralph enters and immediately locates Backus sitting at the bar.

"Captain Bauer, nice to see you again."

Ralph shakes his hand. *Dry for a change.* "Thanks for the invite."

"You bet. Yeah, hope you don't mind meeting in here but it's a lot more comfortable than my office and you get to share one of these with me." He holds up a half-empty stein. "This is Senate Beer, pretty much what this place is known for."

"Just one. I've got a meeting don't forget."

Backus drains his glass and orders two more. "Sorry I couldn't get a table but this place gets jammed. He points to the direction of the brewery. "They send us down here to the vaults when there's an air raid drill. Most of us know to bring our coffee mug and they let us enjoy a sample... or two while we're hanging out. Plus, it's nice and cool in here."

Ralph sips his beer and wipes the foam from his parched lips. "Come on, this heat doesn't come close to Tunisia."

"You're right. So speaking of Tunisia, I wanted to give you an update"

"You found the prisoner?"

"The what? Oh shit Bauer I never followed up on that. God, I'm sorry. I don't even remember what I did with the ID book you gave me. I promise. I'll find it and get back to you."

Ralph places the glass on the bar. "What the hell, Backus. You said you were going to do me a favor. I thought I could count on you."

"I said I was sorry, okay. I'll take care of it."

"Maybe before this damn war is over, if you don't mind. So then what's the update you needed to give me?"

"Oh Christ. This isn't getting any easier. It's about your chaplain friend."

"Heller? Am I going to be pissed off about this too?'

"Afraid so. He tricked us."

"What do you mean, how?"

"Well first of all the Red Cross worker never led us to anyone. We followed her for three days then finally detained and questioned her. Turns out she did have confidential talks with him but never because of the White Rose or an offer to help the Nazis or a deal to protect his family." Backus' voice turns syrupy, "that sweet girl just asked him to hear her confession."

Ralph drops his head and stares at the floor. "That doesn't make sense, what about the exchange?"

"Oh there was an exchange alright. We saw it just as we had arranged. But the info he passed on to her was nothing more than a useless address in Munich."

"That bastard."

"Yup, he used the girl because he knew there were already rumors about her. It was a smart move. And we played right into it. She was an innocent victim."

"He didn't play us. He played me. And now he gets a free ticket to the states and a cozy job tending his sheep."

"I might as well pour more salt on the wound. He's been

sent to Huntsville."

Ralph slams his glass on the bar, even startling Backus. "And I look like a fool. I could choke him to death right now!"

"Whoa. Easy now. Listen Ralph. If you're going to play the intelligence game, you've got to have thick skin. Don't take it so personal. Hey, trust me. I'm already over it."

Ralph steps away from the bar. "Good for you. Thanks for the beer."

"Slow down now. Not so fast. I haven't even gotten to the real reason I asked you here."

Ralph glances quickly at his watch and says sarcastically, "listen I'd love to share more good news but I've got to move my ass. I've got a meeting in fifteen minutes."

"Slow down. And sit down." Backus slides a barstool toward Ralph. "*This* is the meeting. And we've got a lot to discuss."

* * *

Huntsville, Texas

Rose moves quickly along a busy sidewalk in Huntsville's business district. Most of her Saturday errands are finished. For once, she'll be on time when Uncle Pete picks her up in front of Ball Brothers Market. She crosses the intersection, turns right and heads toward the market in the middle of the block. In front of Wellman's Five and Dime she sees the usual line of negro patrons lining up at a side window to pick up their orders from the store's lunch counter service. Beyond them, directly in front of the store she is surprised to see three POWs, even recognizing one of them as an officer from the camp. *What are they doing here?*

"Hey Rose." The voice belongs to Stanley Dorsett, a very good friend of Uncle Pete. He and his brother own a successful lumber operation just on the edge of Sam Houston Forest. She realizes now that he is with the prisoners.

"Well, hello, Mr. Dorsett."

"Our truck broke down, so I thought I'd take the men inside to eat lunch."

"That's very kind of you. People are not used to seeing that, I'm sure."

"Actually, I've done it before. Folks here are fine with it. These men have been a godsend. Your uncle can back me up on that. So it doesn't hurt to treat them to a little lunch now and then. Well, better keep moving. It's getting crowded inside. Say hi to Pete for me."

"Okay Mr. Dorsett. I will." As the prisoners enter Wellman's, Rose can't help but notice the stares of the Negro customers waiting for their orders. She finally looks away and sees a redheaded woman peering through the luncheonette's large picture window. Rose squints and realizes it is Sally Ford. The deputy's wife is wearing a bright yellow shirtwaist dress that's too big for her gaunt frame. Two of the large white plastic buttons in the front of her dress are missing. The V-neckline tumbles well below her collarbone. Sally enters the luncheonette. Rose sidesteps a baby carriage and hesitates. She checks her watch and follows Sally.

Inside, the clatter of dishes and utensils is constant. Servers bark their requests and the tat-tat-tat of a counter bell announces another order is ready. Hungry patrons are engaged in the typical gossip and friendly conversation that tunes out the rest of the world. The counter is L-shaped, tucked into the corner of the store, with easy access from the street. The shorter end of the counter can accommodate a dozen patrons before it turns sharply left and runs away toward the back of the building. That's where Rose sees Sally, settling into a round red-leather pedestal seat with a short backrest. She is speaking to Betty Sturgis, their high school classmate. Betty is holding a steaming pot of coffee and smiles as she sees Rose approach. "Hello Rosie Bauer."

Sally swivels around , surprised to see Rose.

"Hi girls. Looks like we have a little high school reunion going here."

Betty is already moving away. "Wish I could join you but I've got lots of faces to feed."

Sally turns back towards the counter and sips her coffee. "How are you Rose? It's been a while."

"Good thanks. Doing our best like everyone else."

The man sitting next to Sally gets up, leaves a 25-cent tip and turns his empty seat towards Rose. "Thank you, sir." She slides in and turns toward Sally. "Where's the rest of your family?"

"Oh, Bobby just came off his shift so he's home sleeping and my mom took the kids overnight, so nice break, right?"

"Good for you Sally. You deserve a break. Listen, I'm glad we have some time alone. I was wondering if I could ask you a question? It's kind of sensitive."

"Depends on the question I guess." She begins biting her lip. The waitress swings by and offers Rose a menu.

"Just coffee for me Betty, thanks." Rose waits until they are alone again. She stares at the steaming cup and then directly into Sally's eyes. "So, the question is whether you could maybe help me understand why you let Barbara Turner go?"

"Rose that was years ago. Why are you asking me now?"

"I'm kind of asking myself the same question Sally. I wish I hadn't waited. Barbara and I grew up together and she left so suddenly I was wondering if something happened to make you and Bobby decide to cut her off like that."

"It was my decision."

"Okay, well..."

"Bobby had nothing to do with it. I decided she had to go."

"That sounds serious. Why did she have to go? Didn't you and the kids love her?"

"Who told you that?"

The same person who told me you trusted her.

Sally is already standing up. "Look, a colored domestic worker didn't work out and I let her go, okay? I'm done talking about this. And you can pay for my coffee." She turns and walks quickly away. Rose fumbles through her bag and drops a crumpled dollar on the counter. By the time Rose reaches Sally she is out on the sidewalk with no intention of stopping.

Rose shouts, "Sally, how would you feel if I talked to Bobby about this?"

Sally turns away from the curb, back towards Rose then closes the gap. "Jesus, Rose, please?"

"Okay, calm down. I'm not trying to upset you but I need answers. I need you to do the right thing."

"How dare you." She is so close now that Rose can smell cheap perfume and Betty's coffee. "Don't judge me!" Through clenched teeth, "I protected that girl. I saved her...."

"Saved her? From who, Sally?"

"Rose, please. I'm barely holding things together."

Rose glares hard. "Were there others?"

A blaring horn makes both of them jump. Rose turns to see Uncle Pete's truck, holding up traffic. He bellows through the open window, "Rosie, where the hell have you been? I've been looking everywhere for you." Impatient horns are telling him to move.

"Okay. I'm coming!"

Rose turns back in Sally's direction, but she is gone. *You poor woman. I'm not done with you.*

SEPTEMBER 1943

* * *

CHAPTER 20
Huntsville, Texas

Fraulein

Rose settles into the last tattered bench seat, her chosen spot in the rear of the drab gray bus that will take her home from Camp Huntsville. Every inch of the fifteen-year old vehicle betrays its age, including Mr. Martin, who was driving this thing when Rose and her brothers used to pelt it with pinecones on summer nights during the Great Depression. She avoids eye contact with him every time she boards, quickly escaping to the back. Even now, she's panicked he'll recognize her from the stupid prank that occurred more than ten summers ago.

Henry was always the ringleader, but Rose and Ralph were willing co-conspirators, hiding impatiently in the tall pine trees with their older brother. Mr. Martin seemed to anticipate the ambush and always accelerated as he approached the stretch of road in front of the Bauer Farm. Henry was the first to leap from the trees, sprinting alongside the bus and rapidly hurling pinecones into its broad side, careful to avoid the passenger windows. He was always the instigator. Ralph was a different story. He was the competitor. It may have been Henry's idea, but Ralph was going to do it faster and better. And Rose, she was the worrier. Wanting to be included was so important to her that she went along with her brothers' capers, but secretly she was scared to death they would be caught. And when it finally happened, it was Rose who took the fall.

It was an especially muggy night, in late July, when the siblings waited for Mr. Martin. There was plenty of ammunition scattered atop the pine straw that sagged under their young feet. The pinecones came in two distinct sizes. Those from the loblolly were usually up to five inches long, ripened to a pale buff-brown. The shortleaf pine produced a reddish brown cone that was usually only two inches in length. Henry preferred the smaller shortleaf cone because it was easier to throw and more accurate. Rose just liked its color better. And Ralph was going to pick the opposite of whatever Henry chose, so the loblolly was his weapon of choice. Well-armed, they saw the approaching bus and pounced. As always, Rose was shoeless. The thick grass bordering the woods felt cool under her feet. A step behind her brothers when they targeted the bus, she paid the price. Ralph launched his last loblolly cone, but it sailed on him and found its way through an open window. Whatever happened inside that bus caused Mr. Martin to hit the brakes hard. Rose remembers being startled as the bus swerved slightly and came to an abrupt halt in the middle of the road, burnt rubber filling her nostrils. She can still hear the squeal of the folding bus door as it flew open and she stood face to face with the driver. She didn't have to look around to know that her brothers were long gone. Mr. Martin seemed more annoyed than furious. He didn't speak at first, just beckoned her with his index finger. But Rose couldn't move. It was like the cool turf had turned to quicksand. Hands on hips he walked slowly to her, squatted down to eye level, touched her trembling chin with that same index finger and said, "tell your cowardly brothers that if another pinecone ever touches my bus, I'll bury both of them under these trees and you'll never see them again." Then he walked quickly back to the idling bus and was gone. She passed the warning on to her brothers and for good measure added her own intentions to kill them both if they ever abandoned her again. As for Mr. Martin, from that night forward she avoided riding his bus until he eventually retired. Her plan had worked just fine until she landed at the POW camp and discovered Mr. Martin and his aging bus had been unretired to shuttle passengers to and from Camp Huntsville. Suddenly she's that 12-year old all over again. Stuck. She knows how silly this has become. *He probably doesn't even remember me or that night. God, he's got to be older than Oma.* She promises herself to act like an adult and resolve it soon.

As the bus turns on to State Highway 19 for the straight fifteen-minute drive to the Bauer Farm, Rose turns her attention to workers completing installation of a new billboard along the highway. The image of a prisoner behind barbed wire is accompanied by the message, "Help me get home. Buy Bonds." She is struck by the irony of the advertisement. So close to the inner workings of Camp Huntsville, Rose can't help but wonder if Americans are being treated as well as these German POWs. Peering intently at the billboard makes her realize something else -- she is squinting hard to read the large letters already past the bus. Her eyesight is faltering again.

While the bus is making its final two stops before the Bauer property, Stephan and his work crew are finishing up a relatively easy day on the farm. They were told that it will be full harvest by the weekend, so Clyde spent the last hour of the day showing them how to pick cotton. He was incredibly fast. Uncle Pete explained to the workers that speed was important, and they needed to maintain a steady pace. They each tried removing the fibers bursting from the bolls and laughed good-naturedly with Clyde's experienced crew as the prisoners timidly plucked the cotton and winced from the points on the burrs. Stephan appreciates his camaraderie with the Americans but also realizes that back-breaking work is just days away.

The crew works its way down the path from the fields

to the Bauer house. Their conversation is light-hearted and friendly. Stephan has seen a subtle shift in their interaction with one another over the last few weeks. He has a better sense of who thinks like him. Everyday conversation in the fields has identified the reluctant conscripts and unwilling participants in this war. "Where are you from?" "When did you join?" "Have you heard from family?" It has happened naturally though men like Stephan are still feeling outnumbered within the general camp population. Still, he is hopeful he can navigate the chasm and survive. They pass the porch and wave to the old woman, now a permanent fixture this time of day, who wiggles her fingers and yells, "ruhen Sie Ihr Finger aus." *Rest your fingers*. The men laugh, knowing she is referring to the hard work of picking cotton that lies ahead. They tip their caps and wave. Their laughter quickly turns to conversation about the much anticipated intra-camp football match on Friday night. Rumors are that many of the American guards have been placing bets on the outcome, offering to share their winnings for cigarettes. They are hitting their stride, adjusting to their routines as prisoners. By this time the men have arrived on the road in front of the driveway, waiting for the prisoner bus to pick them up.

Very soon, they see a bus approaching and begin gathering in single file without any instructions from the two Americans guarding them. As the bus gets closer, they realize it is not their camp transportation. They break ranks again and resume their conversations about beer and football and the terrible bread they are served at meals. Stephan can't help but recall the kinds of conversations they were having before they surrendered, back in the desert when rations were infrequent, and football never fit into the routine of an army in full retreat. He glances at Werner and some of his Nazi comrades. *They will never admit how good we have it here.*

Rose braces herself as her bus comes to a stop in front of the farm. She is seated on the opposite side, so her view of the prisoners gathered near the driveway is blocked. As she makes her way toward the front, she notices the rural mailbox stuffed with mail – a reminder that she has once again ignored her household responsibility to retrieve the mail every day. It looks like about four days-worth. She reaches the front, passes Mr. Martin, and hesitates as she considers looking him in the eye and saying "thank you" -- just like any reasonable adult would do. She says nothing then steps off the bus feeling embarrassed and childish. To her left, on the far side of the driveway, she sees the prisoners for the first time. Despite her role at Camp Huntsville, this is the closest she has ever been to enlisted POWs. The band of young men never averts its collective gaze. All eyes are on Rose. The prisoners' conversations are hushed but animated. After all, there is an attractive young woman standing in front of them. Stephan feels uncomfortable for her. He wants the others to shut up and mind their own business, but he is staring too. Stephan is certain he has not seen this woman before. He would have remembered her. Perhaps she is a visitor. The guards move toward the group holding their rifles parallel to the ground and motioning the men away from the driveway and out toward the road. Stephan lingers briefly then rejoins the group. He remains nearest to Rose, who is still separated from the group by the driveway. She reaches the mailbox and begins extracting the tangled mail from the oversized box. She wishes their bus would arrive. *Stop staring. Go back to your barbed wire.*

Rose stacks the mail on her left forearm while her right hand continues to pluck several days-worth of letters from the box. There is more in there than she thought. She knows it's her own fault for waiting so long. One more piece lodged way in the back and she'll be finished. On her tip toes, she stretches to reach inside. She is now off balance. The mail in her left arm begins to shift and then tips entirely out of her grasp. She tries using her chin to pin down the moving pile. The mail hits the road and scatters in all directions. A couple heavier parcels land at her feet. Most skip across the road, and the rest spray beyond the driveway toward the prisoners. Stephan instinctively steps on an envelope that reaches him. Then another. Now he picks them up. Cautious of the guards watching him, he moves further away from the group and continues to slowly collect the errant mail. The wind picks up and redirects escaping letters toward the road. Stephan picks up his pace too, now stepping quickly from one piece to another.

"Stop!" He knew the command would come. He obeys, gathering the dozen or so pieces he was able to retrieve, unsure of what to do next.

"Please help me, someone!" Many of the prisoners are willing to assist Rose but the guards, worried about losing control, raise their rifles and refuse to let them help. She is standing in the middle of the road, making very little progress. Her right hand is clutching just a few letters. With her left hand, she reaches down and unties her black, round-toe oxfords, then clumsily removes them as she hops around the asphalt. The men are cheering her ingenuity. Stephan looks at the guards while his body language says it all. *Let me help her.* The American closest to him finally grabs the mail Stephan is holding, nods and points toward Rose with his rifle. *Permission granted.* Stephan eyes a long narrow wooden box that holds the hoes. He grabs the box and tilts it up until the tools pour onto the parched turf bordering the driveway. Grabbing the empty box, he jumps onto the road and joins the hunt. The tall angular prisoner and the petite shoeless American work separately, but soon the toolbox is brimming with most of the mail. Stephan keeps his distance from Rose while his friends provide plenty of good-natured encouragement.

"Hurry, Stephan, your damsel is in distress."

"Get her address so you can deliver her next letter personally."

"Keep your distance or they'll have you picking cotton until Christmas!"

The guards have no idea what the men are saying but Rose understands every word. She is amused by their camaraderie and sense of humor. *His name is Stephan.*

His task completed, Stephan looks down and sees one last letter resting under the sole of his shoe. He carefully collects it and walks timidly toward Rose, offering the envelope as he approaches, still careful to maintain a dignified distance. Rose accepts the letter, immediately recognizing its importance. It is impossible not to make eye contact. *I wonder if this is the tall one Oma keeps talking about.* She speaks to Stephan in German, explaining, "This is a letter from my brother. He is on a ship in the Pacific. I haven't heard from him in months."

Stephan is unsure how to reply. It would be rude not to say anything, but improper to pursue a conversation. Instead, he chooses to respond, "Your German is very good." *What a stupid thing to say.* Before Rose can answer, she hears the familiar voice of Uncle Pete. "Well Rose, looks like you got yourself a little help out here. Better get a move on. These men are leaving." Uncle Pete points down the road to the approaching transport bus. She picks up her shoes and walks toward the driveway. Stephan turns to rejoin his group, so for a few seconds they are headed in the same direction, walking side by side. He hesitates then points to the letter in Rose's hand. "I hope your brother is safe." Uncle Pete's awkward glance tells him to shut up and keep moving.

Clyde and one of the farmhands grab the ends of the toolbox. They carry it to the driveway, transfer the mail to a sack and slide the box back toward the prisoners, who are now boarding the idling bus. Stephan hangs back on purpose, slowly returning the hoes to the box, hoping to get one more glance at the girl named Rose. *Peter Bauer is related to her. She lives here.* At this moment he just feels better about everything in his life. He likes working on the farm, enjoys the company of the farmhands, knows his connection to the lady on the porch is real and now this. *Now what? Be careful Stephan or you'll find yourself back at the camp cleaning latrines.*

Rose lingers on the driveway where she bends down, slips on her shoes and ties the laces. "Let's go Rosie. I've got a farm to run." Stephan hears Uncle Pete's voice as he loads the toolbox onto the bus and is pressed forward by the guards. On the bus he looks for an empty seat while glancing outside for a glimpse of her. She is gone. She only said a few words to him, but the distinct sound of her raspy voice stays with him. The only available seat is next to Werner, who wastes no time deflating Stephan's spirits. "Remember your duty to the Reich. You are still a soldier. You had your little dance with the American now get back to reality."

Stephan turns to Werner. "May I ask you a question?"

"Of course." Werner is surprised but curious.

Stephan leans in. He wants to ask the question in confidence and whispers, "Do you wake up every morning with a swastika up your ass?" For the first time since he has known this malcontent, Werner is silent. Seething but silent. Stephan closes his eyes. *Hugo would be proud.* He sees images of a shoeless Rose chasing mail and pushing those spectacles up her cute nose. Hears that gravelly voice. A satisfied smile lingers as he falls asleep.

Halfway up the driveway, Rose hears the fading sounds of the POW transport. It occurs to her the last time she spent so much time running shoeless around that road was the night Mr. Martin threatened to bury her brothers. She glances down at the envelope from Henry. She smiles. *Maybe it's time I bury the past with Mr. Martin.* Of all the things she could be thinking about, she finds herself dwelling on Stephan. He was so tall, especially after she removed her shoes. *Probably not the most lady-like thing to do. I'll have to tell Oma I met her friend.* She recalls how Clyde described him as one of his best workers. *And so polite.* His hazel eyes were hard to forget. *Okay, stop this.* She begins her final ascent towards the house. *I never even said thank you.*

At the bottom of the driveway, Bobby Ford's patrol car creeps slowly past the property then slowly accelerates down the now-empty highway.

CHAPTER 21
Camp Huntsville

Lilli Marleen

Stephan leans his tall frame against the barrack's rear wall. The best place to view the sunset. Remaining daylight on this unseasonably cool Friday is delivered by a brilliant sun that seems to teeter for a moment on the tall pines scraping the western horizon. The image is brief but spectacular before the orange ball begins to slide behind the trees and a phosphorous glow offers the remnants of daylight. Behind the thin barrack walls Stephan can hear muffled voices and laughter. There is heightened interest in the much anticipated football match tonight between the top two teams still standing after weeks of intense competition. Stephan will just be a spectator but doesn't mind. He loves the game. The Americans call it soccer, but to Europeans it is football. And when Stephan was growing up, Austria dominated the continent. He and his father were dedicated supporters of Rapid Vienna, one of the most successful teams in their country.

They rarely attended a game. His father's business was always the priority. Stephan would often plead with him to close his shop for just a few hours, so they could attend a match. He could always count on the watchmaker's response, "keeping time keeps us fed." But that didn't stop them from passionately following the many victories of Rapid Vienna. Each knew the roster, discussed statistics and argued often about strategy. Stephan misses those animated arguments, always good-natured and always precipitated by his father taking the opposite position just to get his son agitated. His father would chuckle every time his needling would leave Stephan frustrated. It was a special bond. The kind you never forget. And then the conversations about football stopped almost overnight.

Right after the annexation, Rapid Vienna joined the German football system and Stephan's father was finished. No Sundays poring over the sports pages. No friendly arguments. Silence. As far as his father was concerned, the team's move to the German league was an act of treason. By 1941, Stephan was already part of the newly formed Afrika Korps, preparing to leave Europe for Libya. He still followed his beloved team, which rewarded his loyalty by winning the German Championship. They defeated Schalke, the most powerful of all German clubs, which made the victory even sweeter. Rapid Vienna won the match 4-3 after falling behind 3-0. Stephan was jubilant. He hoped his father was too. After all, they defeated the supposedly superior German team. His father could take some consolation from that. That was his hope, but he had no way of knowing. Then -- just like today -- there was no word from his parents. He waits for that usual empty feeling to return but chooses instead to be hopeful. There are plenty of others who have been unable to connect with their families. The Red Cross volunteers remind him all the time that many people are displaced in Europe, so it takes time to locate them. Even fellow prisoners complain that it can take up to six months to hear from family. In the meantime, he knows things could be far worse. He has been treated fairly by the Americans. He is healthy, well fed, and working for wages. And maybe he has even discovered the courage to confront the Nazis who normally find a way to darken his day. But not tonight. Tonight, he is going to watch the football match and enjoy an activity that for just a few hours doesn't involve

Werner and his Nazi babble. He decides to head early toward the lighted recreation fields, so he can get a good view of the action.

That's when Stephan sees Hugo and holds his breath. He's dangerously close to an area of the fence where he could get his head blown off. *What is he even doing over here? His company's barracks are on the other side of the compound.* Hugo is talking to Dobbs, the American private who rotates in as a guard every few days. He is skirting the inner fence of the compound, patrolling the perimeter. Dobbs is one of Stephan's least favorites. Most American guards are very fair to the prisoners. Some even kid with them, earning their respect in a friendly way. Then, there are men like Dobbs, who consider themselves above the prisoners. Dobbs is the type who probably didn't fare well in the regular Army. Never made it to the real war, yet he holds a grudge against most of these battle-tested prisoners who long ago abandoned any fantasized notions of gallantry or bravery. Suffocating in the turret of a burning tank will do that to you. He's probably annoyed that a prisoner's living space is the same size as his bunk area over in the American garrison. Needs to prove that his war matters too – even if nobody is listening. So, bullying or threatening an unarmed enemy provides him that twisted satisfaction. Of course, he's not above taking a bribe either. He is having an animated conversation with Hugo, who casually slips something through the fence, then quickly moves away. *Cigarettes.* Hugo is at it again. Stephan knows it's none of his business but decides to follow him.

Twilight offers a small measure of cover, so he hangs back, trying to blend in with other prisoners milling about the camp. Hugo quickens his pace and disappears between the last two barracks. Stephan keeps him in view as his friend heads toward the canteen. Hugo is stopped briefly by a prisoner Stephan doesn't recognize. That's not unusual. There are thousands of prisoners here now and it's impossible to know everybody. The conversation is brief. In fact, Hugo seems impatient with the man, anxious to get somewhere else. For the first time he turns and looks back. Stephan is certain Hugo can't see him, not at this distance. *What's your hurry Hugo?* His friend maintains his pace until he reaches the canteen, bypassing the line of prisoners waiting to cash in their beer coupons. Stephan waits until Hugo enters the building. Then walks up the steps of the canteen but doesn't enter. He peers through the rectangular glass at the top of the door. For most people it would be a stretch to get a clear view. But Stephan's height easily allows him to peek inside. He sees Hugo talking to one of the prisoners working the beer line. Stephan doesn't recognize him either. *How does he know all these people?* An American guard inside is observing their conversation. The prisoner nods to Hugo and leaves the line abruptly, asking another prisoner to cover for him. The door to the canteen opens and closes continuously so Stephan finds himself stepping aside then jumping back in to keep his eye on Hugo. Finally, the man returns, then hands what looks like a full sack of potatoes to Hugo, who turns and slowly departs. Stephan's heart is racing, and he doesn't even know why. The American guard is clearly watching Hugo. *He's going to get caught. Should I warn him? It's too late.* Hugo simply slides by the guard, places something on an empty table and keeps walking toward the door. He is 20 feet away. Stephan gets one last peek just in time to see the guard approach the table and stuff a couple packs of cigarettes in his jacket. Stephan jumps off the porch and scurries to the end of the beer line just as the door swings outward and Hugo hustles down the steps. His eyes are straight ahead, the sack buried under his right arm. He walks right past Stephan and never notices him.

Stephan thinks about tracking Hugo further but decides against it. *What's the point? Let him go. I am not responsible for him. Instead of following him I could be enjoying myself.* Two prisoners, both of whom Stephan knows from the farm detail, see him and pull him into the line.

"Stephan, buy a beer and join us."

"Take your mind off your damsel in distress."

He has no interest in a beer, but they are singing, and Stephan instantly recognizes the song. He knows all the lyrics to "Lilli Marleen" one of the most popular songs among the Afrika Korps. Even Erwin Rommel favored it. The men used to say it reminded them of their girlfriends or wives, but Stephan was too embarrassed to admit that the words made him think of his mother.

Outside the barracks
By the corner light
I'll always stand and wait for you at night
We will create a world for two
I'll wait for you, the whole night through

He is singing now with passion, matching the energy of his friends, but wondering still if his mother is even alive. *Is she waiting for me? Will I ever come home to her?*

When we are marching in the mud and cold
And when my pack seems more than I can hold
My love for you renews my might
I'm warm again, my pack is light

Tonight, he will hope for the best. He will pray that somewhere she is waiting too. If not in Vienna, then somewhere safe. There is no other choice. That has to be enough for now.

Suppressing his guilt, Stephan allows himself to savor this time spent with friends. Together, they head to the match. The field is not only crowded with prisoners, but also camp personnel from the American garrison who seem equally excited about the match. The playing field separates the captors from the prisoners, but the mood is equally upbeat on both sides. For a few hours, there is something both can enjoy, even to the point of friendly wagering between the guards and prisoners.

* * *

Among the crowd is Rose, who convinced Uncle Pete to drive her to the game. She wanted to invite Clyde as well but decided not to push her luck. *Another excuse.* Once they arrived, Uncle Pete quickly mingled with many of his friends. In the brief time she stayed with him, Rose could sense the relief he shared with all of his fellow farmers. The POWs are making a big difference and his friends are willing to admit it. The plan is working, production will be up, and most importantly, the prisoners have been nothing close to the threat many feared when they first arrived. Rose is glad to see Uncle Pete a little more relaxed and enjoying himself for a few hours. The cotton harvest will come soon enough. She has no interest in the match so finds herself searching the crowd for familiar faces, realizing that many of the people in attendance are not even camp personnel. They are just local residents whose curiosity drew them in for some entertainment on a Friday night. Either way, she stands in a very different place from the empty camp she visited during the open house just a few months ago. It has really happened. Thousands of prisoners live here. They are working in the community. And so far, if you listen to the local farmers, nobody in Huntsville seems to feel threatened or unsafe. There is a loud roar, then a collective groan from the crowd. Rose has no idea why. Nor does she care. She continues to scan the crowd and stops on Sally Ford. She is standing alone, her hands tucked into the pockets of a tan windbreaker. A yellow and white polka dot scarf holds her long red hair away from her face.

"Sally?"

She shrinks into her windbreaker. "Rose, not here."

"There never seems to be a good time Sally so it has to be here."

"Please, leave me alone."

Sally breaks for the parking lot. Rose sags her head. *It has to be here!* And then her feet are moving. She closes the gap on the brilliant polka dot scarf that her weak eyes can still see moving through the crowd. *Nothing matters but the truth.* She reaches the parking lot, breathless but determined. Hears the squeak of a heavy car door opening. It is coming from the right. Rose heads in that direction. *There she is.* Siting inside a battered, maroon 1939 Chevrolet 2-door sedan with white sidewall tires that long ago lost their luster. Rose opens the passenger door and grabs Sally's hands as she fumbles with the keys.

"Sally you might as well talk because I will not let this go. I swear I will go to your mother's home if you keep ignoring me."

Sally leans her head against the steering wheel, pulls the scarf away from her head and surrenders. "Why are you doing this?"

"Sally, I know you are a good person. And I'm not judging your choices. God knows, we've all made mistakes we have to live with. But Sally, I know there's a reason you let Barbara go and it wasn't because she couldn't fold the laundry."

Sally's lips quiver. "I had to protect her."

"From Bobby?"

"It was the only way I could think to get her away from him. From what he did."

"What happened?"

Sally begins sobbing and Rose carefully holds her hands.

"It's okay Sally. It's not your fault." Rose is ready to cry, too.

"Usually, I visit my mom on Wednesdays. But she was sick

so I came home. Bobby was asleep. The kids were still at school so I went outside to work in the garden. Barbara came over like she always does and went straight in the house to start her chores. A little later I heard Barbara shouting so I ran inside. He, he.....

"It's okay, go on."

"He had her up against the wall and he was groping her. I screamed for him to stop. He let Barbara go and told me he found her looking through my jewelry. Hasn't changed his story since that day."

"What happened next?"

"Nothing. Who could I go to? The police? He *is* the law. Besides, who were they going to believe? Bobby Ford or the colored help? I got her out of there as fast as I could. And I knew sooner or later he would do it again if she came back. So I let her go. I swear, I didn't want her to leave her father."

"That's not on you. It was your husband who forced Barbara to leave, Sally."

"I don't understand."

"Barbara was doing a photo assignment for me at the school and Bobby waited outside for her. Told her if she didn't leave town, he would find a reason to put her father in jail. And if she ever came back, he would make sure he never saw the outside of a prison again."

"So, she left to protect Clyde?"

"That's right. And you were protecting Barbara. But, the only one who is still strutting their shit around here is your husband."

"Rose, you asked me before if there were others. I swear to you Barbara is the only one I know about, but...I have my suspicions. I don't trust him. Our marriage is a joke and we don't love each other. But the kids. I worry about our family."

"Listen Sally. I can't tell you what to do about your marriage. That's your business. But he is directly responsible for breaking up another family and I can't let that happen."

Sally pounds her fist on the dashboard. "Jesus, Clyde must hate me. I don't know what to do. Tell me what to do."

"Right now just answer one question for me. Your in-laws are pretty connected in New Orleans, right?"

"Yes, but how do you know that?"

"I have my connections, too."

"Rose, please don't get them involved. His daddy loves the kids. Would do anything for them. And he's always been kind to me."

"Right now I'm just listening Sally. That's all. I'm still working on the rest. In the meantime, take care of your boys and let me know if you need anything, you hear me?"

"Okay, Rose. Thank you."

"Don't thank me yet. I've got more work to do. Okay, I'm heading back to the game to find my ride home."

Sally nods and turns the ignition. The Chevy sputters and finally responds. Rose pushes mightily to open her door. A welcoming breeze sweeps across the parking lot and caresses her. *Maybe I can make this right.*

Adrenaline fuels Rose as she heads back to the soccer match. All the yelling and screaming from the onlookers feels a world away from her conversation with Sally. Searching the crowd for Uncle Pete is fruitless. Rose turns toward the field hoping to find her ride home along the sidelines. Instead, she sees Colonel Warren standing by himself behind one of the goal keepers. He sees Rose too, and nods. She walks toward him slowly.

"Good evening, Miss Bauer. Big soccer fan, are you?"

"To be perfectly honest Colonel, I know nothing about the game. How about you?"

"Well I believe they call it football over in Europe, but I much prefer the American version. Played a little bit at West Point."

Rose knows enough about Army football to be impressed. Her reaction shows it.

"Don't be too in awe. I said I played a little bit. Most of the time I sat on the bench, where quite frankly I belonged. All great memories though."

Uncomfortable talking about a game she knows nothing about, Rose decides to change the subject. "So welcome back Colonel. I hope you had a good trip."

"It was productive. We'll have much to talk about in the next few days." He hesitates. "There are going to be some changes around here."

Rose asks carefully, "staff changes?"

"No, changes among the prisoners. Let's leave it at that for now, shall we?"

Rose knows better than to pursue further, almost wishing she hadn't asked. Now she'll have to get through the weekend without knowing. "Of course, Colonel. I understand." She awkwardly turns her attention to the game, wanting to get away as soon as she can. A goal is scored right in front of her. The crowd erupts as Colonel Warren turns to her and says, "Well, enough for me. Oh, Miss Bauer, any chance you could come in tomorrow? I know it's an inconvenience, but it can't wait until Monday."

That's more like it! "Of course, Colonel."

"Thank you. Good night then." *Come on Colonel. You're allowed to smile.*

Rose watches him as he walks toward some of his military staff. As her eyes drift in that direction, she sees Stephan on the opposite side of the field. It's hard to miss him. He is clapping and whistling, clearly enjoying himself. So different than the stoic, polite prisoner who was scrambling after her mail just a few days ago. She realizes that she is smiling too. Catches herself, remembering that he is a prisoner of war, not her friend. But she keeps looking anyway, now curious that his smile has disappeared completely. He looks very serious. Something is wrong.

CHAPTER 22
Camp Huntsville

Battered

"My God, what happened?" Hugo's right eye is swollen shut. His cheek below is smeared with fresh blood. He is holding a crimson-soaked rag to his nose. Stephan, remembering his friend's recent interplay with the guards, surprises himself by asking, "did the Americans do this to you?"

Hugo removes the rag to speak. His puffed lips only exaggerate the incredulous look on his face. "Americans? Are you serious? Why would you ask that?"

Stephan doesn't want to admit he was spying on his friend earlier. He deflects Hugo's question, again asks more emphatically, "What happened to you?" He has to raise his voice to be heard over the cheering crowd.

"It wasn't the Americans so why don't you guess again?" He sounds almost angry with Stephan. Others are watching now, some giving Hugo his space. A few Nazi bystanders are enjoying his discomfort, almost laughing at him.

Stephan feels like every hopeful thought he enjoyed tonight is draining out of his body. Now, he knows. He doesn't want to think it, let alone say it. *How could I be so stupid?*

"Werner. It was Werner."

Hugo has a sick smile on his face, revealing a chipped tooth. "Ah, your friend, Werner. After he stepped on my face, he made me promise to tell you that the next time he would drive a swastika up my ass. Said you would understand."

"Come on Hugo, let's get you some help." He gently guides his friend by the elbow and carefully leads him away from the group. No one else offers to help. They make their way back toward the prisoner compounds, further away from the lights of the American garrison and the recreation fields. Stephan has to stop for a moment to get oriented. He wants to take his injured friend to the camp hospital attached to the American garrison but knows that's impossible at this hour. So, he heads to the infirmary situated closest to Hugo's barracks. Each of the four prisoner compounds, surrounded by a chain link fence is like a prison within a prison. They all look the same so it's easy to get confused, especially in the evening, when subtle landmarks disappear. Stephan is unsure where to turn. Hugo, who is resisting the infirmary idea altogether is of little help. Stephan begins counting the guard towers to his left. He remembers there are three before he will reach the area where Hugo's company is housed. Twenty feet high, the towers and the faceless guards attached to them are one of the few reminders that he is in a prison. His friend's battered face drives home a deepening reality: there is no protection despite the guards and the towers and the fences. There is evil from within. As they struggle to find their way, Stephan decides to tell Hugo the whole story. Helping Rose. Chasing the mail. Support from his friends and silence from the Nazis. Werner's stern reprimand. And Stephan's sarcastic response. It gave him immense pleasure at the time. Now, it paralyzes him with guilt. "Please forgive me Hugo. I never imagined he would take it out on you. It was a stupid thing to say."

Hugo's bruised body comes alive. He turns to face Stephan. "Wait. Let me get this straight. You actually said that to Werner? Timid little Stephan stood up to that Nazi coward? I would have lost my front teeth to hear that."

"Well, you got half your wish." They both manage to laugh. "How can I make this right? There has to be a way to stop this." They continue walking again. One more guard tower. Stephan's mind is racing. "Was Schroeder involved?"

"He is always involved, even when he's not around. But I think this was pretty much on Werner. The little twit was pretty angry."

The ebb and flow of the cheers from the match are now replaced by shouts and laughter of the men as they begin their trek from the field to their barracks. "Then why didn't he come after me? Why you? You didn't do anything."

"Come on Stephan, this was his perfect revenge. He gets to beat the crap out of me again, while sending you a message. Classic Gestapo intimidation tactics. Right here in our safe little camp." Hugo hesitates when they reach the crossroads that lead either to the infirmary or towards his barracks. "Let's just go to the canteen and get some ice. I'll be fine."

Stephan chooses the path toward the infirmary and Hugo follows. "Listen, you could have a concussion. Besides, at least I know you'll be safe overnight while we figure out what to do."

"There is no figuring out. I told you before I'm never going to be safe here. I need to get away."

Stephan feels overwhelmed. He is whispering, eyes up at the guard in the final tower, as if he could actually hear their conversation. "Escaping? Is that what you are thinking about? He tilts his head toward the tower. "Because he will shoot you if you try."

"And if I don't try? I will be suffocated while I'm sleeping. What's the difference?"

"Listen, just don't do anything stupid. Give me time to figure this out. Think of your family. You've made it this far.

Don't you want to go home to them?"

Hugo plops to the ground. Leans back and rests his palms behind him. Struggling to get comfortable, he extends his left leg. Stephan sees the gash across his knee, blood staining his denim work pants.

"Stephan, I have no home. You and me, we come from very different worlds. Your parents hate the Nazis. My parents *are* Nazis. They believe what Werner believes. They would disown me if they knew how I was behaving."

Now the returning prisoners, still far off near the first set of barracks, are singing marching songs. Stephan recognizes each distant chorus, feels the energy in the words echoing throughout the camp. He is annoyed by the distraction. His focus instead remains on his wounded friend, who pleads his case.

"Think about it Stephan, Austria is your home. You love Vienna. Me, I just lived wherever my father's job took him. And for many years that was right here in America. He had a great job and we lived a very comfortable life. New York City means more to me than Munich or Frankfurt or Berlin. I imagined staying here and pursuing a career in design. I was even accepted at the Parsons School of Design, which I can brag to you was quite an accomplishment. But when war was certain, my father didn't hesitate to take us back to Germany – away from my dreams and plans. To a place that holds no future for me. Sad, isn't it? America is where I would like to live, but it will never have me." Hugo offers an outstretched arm. He needs help getting to his feet.

Stephan steadies his friend. "So, you are an artist. I never knew that about you."

"There's still a lot you don't know about me and perhaps it's better to keep it that way my friend."

Stephan feels guilty that he was spying on Hugo but sees no point telling him. He probes further, "Where will you go?"

Hugo laughs, knowing Stephan's question requires a much deeper answer. "Not to the infirmary, Stephan. I am going back to the barracks. Werner has sent his message. He's done for tonight at least. You better get back. Lights out soon."

Stephan leaves Hugo reluctantly. His false bravado is in tatters. Tomorrow he will be back at the Bauer Farm, harvesting cotton. His stomach tightens at the thought of facing Werner. Every encounter he considers in his anxious mind does not end well. *Do I confront him? Do I defend Hugo's honor? Will I be a coward one more time?* But there is one scenario Stephan has not considered. Tomorrow, Werner will not be a problem at all. Tomorrow, Werner will be gone forever.

CHAPTER 23
Huntsville, Texas

Witnesses

The sun has already risen and Rose is anxious to get to the camp. Colonel Warren's request for her help today created a sleepless night . She yawns widely as she makes her way down the driveway toward the mailbox. *Might as well make myself useful until Uncle Pete is ready to leave.* Even though it's early she still checks for traffic as she clings to the side of the road and approaches the mailbox. Pulling the mail out, she hears a vehicle approach and slow down, tightening brakes squeal just a bit louder on this quiet morning. Her stomach sinks, hoping to hear the car continue. Instead, the window goes down -- unleashing the chatter of a police radio.

"Good morning, Rose."

Still pulling mail out she replies, "oh, Bobby. Hi. Good morning."

"Kind of early to be retrieving the mail. Don't you usually wait for your prisoner friend to help you?"

She ignores the comment and turns to face the car. "Just getting an early start this morning. Busy day ahead."

"Is that so? Anything I need to know about?"

"Bobby, you know I can't talk about those things." She starts to walk away.

"Hold on now. What's your hurry Rose?" He leans across the seat while still driving.

She continues walking. The patrol car keeps pace.

"My uncle is waiting for me. I have to go." She reaches the driveway and hears the car lurch forward and stop.

"Rose, wait!" He pushes the door open, steps out and approaches her with his palms up. "Easy now, I just want to ask you something, okay?"

Rose takes a step back. "Alright then. What is it?"

"Several witnesses told me that you were talking to my wife."

"Witnesses? What is this, a trial? Since when is it a crime to talk to someone at a public event?"

He folds his arms. They rest on his belly. "What were the two of you talking about?"

"Geez, deputy I don't know. Maybe you should ask your witnesses."

"You don't want to mess with me Rose."

She stabs his belly with the stack of mail she's holding. "Are you threatening me?"

"Me, nah, never. Just suggesting that you might want to mind your own business, that's all. Stop fraternizing with prisoners, too. And maybe keep a closer eye on your friend Clyde."

"What does Clyde have to do with this? Is there something I should know?"

He turns and walks back towards the patrol car. "Let's just say he needs to keep his nose clean, that's all. I'd hate to see your uncle lose his services just when the harvest is coming. Have a pleasant day now at your top secret job. And remember to stay away from my wife."

Too late for that, pea brain.

CHAPTER 24
Camp Huntsville

Friend

As routine as the pattern of camp life has become, changes today will upset the ordinary and send a divisive ripple towards every barrack throughout this vast complex. Life at Camp Huntsville is about to tilt in a very different direction.

By the time men are falling out for their normal Saturday morning routine, things are already peculiar. Many of the officers and company leaders are noticeably absent. It doesn't take long for word to spread that some kind of meeting is taking place at the American garrison. As the prisoners make their way to breakfast, they see an unusually large contingent of guards inside the compounds. Outside the camp, there is a noticeable increase in the number of troop transports standing by. This is anything but a lazy Saturday for the Americans, who continue to shuttle back and forth between their garrison and the newly arrived trucks that line the single road leading to the POW camp. The prevailing rumor Stephan hears is that more prisoners are coming. It seems to make the most sense.

Instead of the usual conversation you would expect after last night's football match, the mess hall is buzzing with chatter around this curious morning. Stephan arrives for breakfast and looks for Hugo, hoping he survived the night without any further attacks. He settles into line and scans the crowd. No sign of his friend. *Maybe he's in the hospital or worse.* Filling his tray and grabbing his second glass of orange juice, he recognizes some of the men from Hugo's company and decides to sit with them. His intention is to ask about Hugo's whereabouts but realizes that some of the men clustered at the end of the table are friends of Werner. He says nothing and quickly finishes his meal. In an hour he is supposed to be joining his work crew for their routine march to the gates and the waiting bus. Stephan is concerned that work crews may be held back. *This is the last place I want to be right now.* He realizes how much he needs to be on that farm because that's where he feels safe. Even though Werner will be gloating and threatening and inviting Stephan to give him another reason to assault Hugo. *The hell with him.* He thinks of Clyde and his crew. *They would protect me.* He knows that Peter Bauer is counting on the prisoners to make a difference. He doesn't want to let him down. Doesn't want to miss the lady on the porch. Then, he allows a silly thought to blossom. What if he got to see Rose again? Nothing more than that, just a chance to learn more about her from a distance. He can hear her voice so clearly in his head and his weak response. *"Your German is very good." That's the best you could do?* He drains his coffee and feels it burn a hole in his stomach. He needs to get moving.

Outside, the fresh air does little to buoy his spirits. He considers a quick trip to Hugo's barracks but doesn't want to confront any more bad news. Besides, he needs to get back to his own company and hopefully prepare for a day of work outside these fences. As he walks back, he recognizes many of the faces heading towards the same compound. Over the last week or so he has begun playing a little game. The premise is simple. He has lived with these men now for several months. Looking at their faces, especially of those in his own company, he recognizes who he can trust and who is trouble. He assigns a label to every face he sees. They are either a Nazi or a friend.

He calls it the "face game" and repeats this ideological inventory every so often.

He begins. "Nazi. Nazi. Friend. Friend. Nazi. Nazi. Nazi...." The game ends abruptly as he rounds the corner towards his company's barracks and hears a female voice speaking German on the loudspeaker. Prisoners are being instructed to return to their company immediately. He has never heard a female on the loudspeaker before, yet he feels he recognizes the voice. Raspy. Her German is excellent. *"This is a letter from my brother. He is on a ship in the Pacific. I haven't heard from him in months."* Five minutes later she repeats the message, this time with more urgency. He is certain it is her. It is Rose Bauer.

He is distracted from his thoughts as the shrill orders of German officers quickly transform his company into an impressive column of 250 or so men at attention. Chin up, chest out, shoulders back, stomach in. No one moves. No one speaks. Stephan imagines that this same exercise is being repeated this morning among nearly 5,000 prisoners throughout the camp. All listening. All waiting for the rumor to be confirmed that more prisoners are joining the ranks. Instead, they receive instructions to listen carefully for your name. If it is called out, you are to fall out and line up separately. And then the roll call begins. As the names are being called Stephan is totally confused. Should he be happy or troubled if his name is called? He can't be sure, but his loose count tells him nearly a third of the prisoners are called out of line. *What is going on?*

Then, the list is finished. Stephan is still standing at attention. He has not been called. Finally, the shocking explanation is delivered as if the men were being told to brush their teeth. All business. No drama. Just the following orders: If your name was called, you have thirty minutes to collect your gear and report back here. Red Cross volunteers will be available to assist you. *Assist with what?* You are being transferred to a different camp and will be moving out within two hours. The prisoners who have not been called will resume their usual routine, including their assigned work details for the day. *Relief.*

Confusion and tension are ripe. Stephan is trying to decide why this is happening. And then it dawns on him slowly. As he looks at the men who are being reassigned, he recognizes a common connection. He feels a growing sense of anticipation. The kind you feel when you know you've done well in a test or when you know a football match is almost over and your team is going to win. It is inevitable. There is good news to be enjoyed. But first he must play the face game. He turns to the men whose names were never called. Men like him who are remaining in Camp Huntsville. And he begins. "Friend. Friend. Friend. Friend." There are more faces to be counted, but he knows the answer will be the same. "Friend. Friend. Friend." He stops playing. *The Nazis are leaving.* Mistakes have been made. Lessons have been learned. The Americans mean business. He wants to find Hugo and share this good news. He wants to know why Rose Bauer's voice is swimming in his head.

A few hundred yards away, the American garrison is energized. Rose has been here since 6:00 AM. Last night on the drive home from the soccer match, she asked Uncle Pete to sacrifice the cotton harvest for an hour to drive her in this morning. Said that it was a matter of national security. He just rolled his eyes and told her to be ready at 5:00 sharp. Now, coffee and adrenaline are helping her keep pace with the events of this frantic morning. A few hours ago, none of it made sense. Now she sees everything falling into place and realizes this is not just an administrative shift within the camp. This is an all-out battle against an enemy who was supposed to be neutralized once they surrendered. Instead, the Nazis have threatened and bullied their way into an almost surreal control of the camp. Apparently, Camp Huntsville is not the only victim of this passive insurrection. It is plaguing other POW camps as well.

The solution for the Americans? Move the troublemakers out. Without asking anyone directly Rose is able to put the pieces together. Some of the prisoners are being transferred to other POW camps where Nazi sympathizers will be separated from the general population. In return, those camps will be transferring low-risk prisoners back to Camp Huntsville. She's read enough files and talked to enough Red Cross volunteers to see a pattern developing. There is a new camp in Oklahoma, Camp Alva, that keeps showing up on the files she is processing. One of Colonel Warren's staff members confided to Rose that this is a camp for "the hard cases." *That's what the colonel has been doing in Washington.*

Colonel Warren barks her name, "Miss Bauer?" Rose is startled and nearly spills the third cup of coffee she is preparing for herself. Her boss is standing next to her holding many of the same files they have already exchanged several times this morning. "Sorry to startle you."

"Oh no, Colonel. I've already had far too much coffee already this morning." She wipes her hands before reaching for the files.

"These are the last of the transfer files the Red Cross should see before the prisoners ship out. Let's make sure we get all the paperwork right. I don't want to see any of these men back here again."

"I'll do it right away colonel." Rose turns to leave the room, but Colonel Warren interrupts her exit.

"Thanks for all your help today. Translating for the German officers this morning. Taking over the public address for our camp announcements. Consuming all our rationed coffee."

It takes a second to register that Colonel Warren has just made a joke. She smiles but remembers her role in the chain of command. She answers politely, "Thank you, colonel."

"Please thank the staff for me. Let's get you and these folks home as soon as possible. The bus will be here shortly. Tell all the non-essentials to get out of here and enjoy the rest of their weekend. You included."

Rose flies through the paperwork with her new friends from the Red Cross. All is in order. Before long, she is standing outside with most of the staff, eager to get home. There is a dense haze of cigarette smoke surrounding the group as they gossip and laugh about the morning's events. They wonder about prisoners who will be transplanted from other camps. For now, their important work is done as they watch the loaded troop transports slowly move away from the compound. They are surprisingly quiet, watching the exodus of a cancer they helped remove. Reflecting perhaps on the important role they played in the war effort here at home. Now, they will go back to their houses and apartments, farms and families. Some sadly to gold stars in their windows. Others to young children they hope will never experience the sacrifice and toil of their older siblings scattered throughout the globe. Rose thinks of Henry and Ralph. She knows they would be proud of her. She is profoundly blessed by these thoughts.

Now the work details formed by the remaining prisoners begin to trickle down towards the outer gate, its chain-link frame capped with that familiar jumble of barbed wire. From where Rose is standing at the edge of the American garrison, she has a clear line of sight. *Look for the tall one.* He seemed so anguished last night when she caught sight of him in the crowd. He would be easy to spot, and she doesn't see him. Maybe he was one of the prisoners who was transferred. *That doesn't fit. He couldn't be one of the troublemakers.* Several more work details pass and board their buses. She thinks about Oma and how disappointed she will be if Stephan is missing today. *Is Oma the only one?* Only a few buses remain at the gate. Most of the workers have filed out. The next group comes into view and she sees him immediately. The smile is back. His conversation is animated. His group has been thinned out a bit because the troublemakers have been eliminated. The Bauers can be grateful today. Oma. Uncle Pete. *And me.*

The familiar grind of Mr. Martin's bus alerts the group. They form single file, with Rose taking her familiar spot in back of the line. Everyone eagerly moves forward as soon as the doors creak open. Rose is the last one up the steps. Mr. Martin is slumped forward in his well-worn seat. His chin rests on arms folded over the steering wheel. He is watching the final prisoner activity at the gate. She doesn't hesitate. "Good morning Mr. Martin." He never looks at her and continues staring straight ahead. But a pleasant grin crosses his face. "Good morning Rose."

Rose hesitates then takes the empty seat right behind him. She slides in next to the window, miles away from the usual seat that left her stuck in the past. The large rear view mirror, cracked long ago, is suspended high above Mr. Martin. Rose can see his reflection as the bus pulls away. He is still smiling.

CHAPTER 25
Huntsville, Texas

Auf Wiedersehen

Leaving Camp Huntsville this morning with his leaner work detail Stephan can breathe again. The noose has been loosened. The guard towers and the fences and the barbed wire still make him a prisoner of the Americans. Yet in an astonishing turn of events, he is abruptly free of the confinement and control of the Nazis. Hugo can close his eyes tonight and rest peacefully. A new freedom, however temporary, gives purpose and optimism to their daily routine. It's fitting that the day's original forecast of scattered showers has been erased. The sun has turned the Blackland Prairie into a furnace, with heat that will rise throughout the day. Stephan is determined to bask in its glow. To appreciate his new-found freedom.

He arrives at the Bauer Farm, grateful to be free from the likes of Werner. Back in familiar fields, among the Negro workers whom he now considers his friends. By now, he shares their water, offers them sandwiches from camp, and mingles with them freely. Even the guards long ago abandoned their attempts to segregate him from Clyde's group, who know him by name. They call him "Steph." These are proud men, protective of their relationships and wary of those who threaten their fragile lives. Yet, they have accepted this foreigner who has earned their respect simply by being himself and working hard. Their conversation is limited, but Stephan is picking up their expressions and they are learning bits of German. They've taught him that Clyde is his "boss" and have easily learned to say "hallo," while struggling with "auf wiedersehen," which elicits a laugh every time they attempt it. A shared bond was always their mutual dislike of Werner. Stephan taught them to call him *fauler arsch* or "lazy ass."

Arnie, the senior member of Clyde's crew, is the first to notice several fewer faces as Stephan's work detail arrives. The brief dialogue that follows reveals just how few words are needed to commune with friends.

"Hallo Steph." Arnie raises his hands in a questioning motion. "Fauler arsch?"

Stephan doesn't hesitate. He offers the universal gesture of a hand waving goodbye, adds a big smile and says, "auf wiedersehen!"

They embrace him and slap his back. Truly, he is among friends.

He appreciates their kinship but recognizes a profuse difference in their lives. He views them as prisoners, too. While his incarceration is temporary, men like Clyde and Arnie are trapped, their situation changeless. His raw fingers will eventually heal from picking cotton. Theirs will never soften -- forever layered with thickened, hardened skin. New tissue over old wounds, just like the tough lives they muddle through. And yet they seem happy. Singing and laughing while they keep a pace that seems intolerable to Stephan. Their arms move like pistons. Left. Right. Left. Right. Snatching each tuft of cotton. Their seasoned fingers immune to the pointed bolls. Stuffing their hands until they are bursting with clouds of white against dark skin. Filling a burlap sack that drags behind them, another burden that never seems to disappear. A shoulder strap keeps their hands free to keep picking, keep moving. Even as the 8-foot long sack is bursting with nearly 70 pounds of raw cotton, they just shift into a different gear to keep pace, pistons still pumping smoothly.

Clyde always arranges Negro workers among Stephan's group, hoping to encourage a better pace from prisoners by placing them next to seasoned pickers. The plan always fails miserably. Within ten minutes of a group starting a new section, the prisoners are always behind. Chatter and laughter up ahead are unintelligible to the foreigners, but on this morning, Arnie stops, turns and hollers to Stephan, "hey lazy ass," then a dozen of his buddies all chime in, "auf wiedersehen!"

Everyone is laughing, farmhands and prisoners. Except for Clyde, who interrupts, "Arnie, you better keep moving your lazy black ass." More laughter and even a reluctant roll of the eyes from Clyde.

Clyde's men always fill more sacks than the others, far exceeding the amount of cotton the prisoners pick in a day. The sacks are dragged to a wagon fitted with boards that extend so high a ladder is needed to reach the top. A nearby scale rests on a battered hand truck. Everything is designed to move cotton from the field as fast as possible. Clyde carefully hooks each sack onto the scale, records its weight and then gingerly heads up the ladder to empty its contents into the wagon. Wisps of renegade cotton float through the dense air, evading capture, coming to rest on the sleeves of Stephan's overalls, free and without purpose. At least for today, there is harmony in the fields.

OCTOBER 1943

CHAPTER 26
Virginia

P.O. Box 1142

On a crystal clear night, a nondescript convoy of three buses, their windows painted jet black, pulls away from the gates of Fort Meade, Maryland for a 40-mile journey south to a location near Alexandria, Virginia. The convoy is escorted by U.S. Military Police. It is well past midnight as the caravan makes its way along a less-traveled route that hugs the western bank of the Potomac River. A brilliant full moon illuminates the poplar and maple trees that would normally be invisible at this hour. Instead the crimson and yellow leaves provide a stunning mix of Autumn hues boldly washed by the lunar light. The breathtaking scene goes entirely unobserved by the isolated passengers. Inside the cramped buses, separate compartments keep Nazis isolated from anti-Nazis; officers segregated from enlisted men. All of them are high-value German captives who have possible information the Allies want to acquire.

Their destination is a top secret military location known only as P.O. Box 1142 where these men will be detained for questioning. The facility is so secret that not even the Red Cross has been notified of the transfer or whereabouts of these prisoners. Which makes this whole exercise a direct violation of the Geneva Convention.

P.O. Box 1142 is a strategic gold mine. Nothing like it

exists anywhere else in the United States. Successful interrogations could deliver information on any number of critical issues, saving lives or even shortening a war that has already gripped the world far too long. The breadth of information sought is so wide it might include sensitive military data such as troop movements or technical secrets around weapons or even insights into the status of civilian morale in German cities. Each prisoner provides a potential breakthrough. Or they could deliver fool's gold.

In Alexandria, the convoy reaches a remote area shielded from the George Washington Parkway. Long ago it was part of Washington's plantation estate. But most locals today know the destination as the site of a former Civil War military camp. The buses move beyond iron fence and razor wire, entering a sprawling compound of 87 buildings, mostly constructed within the last two years. They provide lodging and support for a staff of over 1,000 people sworn to secrecy. Most are the type of personnel expected to run a facility this size. But it's the roles others perform that defy the imagination of the prisoners sitting in these buses. Fake Red Cross workers. Imposter Russian agents. Decoy prisoners. Eavesdroppers. All supporting an elite team of Interrogating Officers, who are individually assigned to each POW arriving in Alexandria. Known as I/Os they are expertly trained in interrogation methods, well-schooled on counterintelligence techniques, and immersed in prisoner psychology. By the time a POW is medically cleared and processed for interrogation the I/O has a thorough file already prepared for him and is free to use his own style of questioning to gather the information he is seeking.

Some of these unknowing prisoners will match wits with the most ambitious of all I/Os at P.O. Box 1142. A young German-American who takes his role very seriously. He's been wrong only once and will never allow it to happen again. An obsession for his craft and more aggressive training by the greatest minds in interrogation have seen to that. Now, he can sniff out a lie before a dishonest word reaches his ears. His name is Captain Ralph Bauer from Huntsville, Texas.

CHAPTER 27
Camp Huntsville

Joke

Rose is stepping in to help with the influx of prisoners arriving at the camp. Some are new arrivals from North Africa, but most are here as part of the carefully planned prisoner exchange. The Americans treat the process like an assembly line, repeating the same tasks over and over with little enthusiasm. Like Rose, most are civilians. They sort through personal effects, complete paperwork for physicals, take photos and fingerprints then verify credentials for the Red Cross. Rose doesn't have an official role. She's mostly available if there are language barriers that can't be overcome. Nearby is a young dark-haired, female Red Cross worker who is handing each man a care package stenciled with a red cross. She manages a smile. It is warm and genuine.

A German officer approaches her and begins a conversation. Rose steps forward to help but then realizes he is speaking English. It is broken but understandable so she steps away and just listens.

"Thank you for your kindness. What is your name?

"My name is Mary, sir. Mary Jenkins."

"Hello Mary Jenkins. My name is Major Heller. I am a chaplain." He points to the crucifix hanging around his neck.

"I don't think I've ever met a German chaplain before. Welcome to Texas, sir."

"Thank you, Mary. You remind me of a Red Cross worker I knew before I was sent here. She was kind, like you. She trusted me." Mary looks sideways at Rose, not sure what to say. Heller is holding the care package but not moving away. Again, Rose steps in, but this time another voice interrupts, speaking German.

"If you don't want that, I'll take it." It's the prisoner standing next to Heller. Rose is close enough to notice his breath is vile. The few remaining teeth in his mouth are scattered and yellow. "With any luck there will be some extra cigarettes in there." Heller reluctantly surrenders the package. The man accepts without offering a word of thanks. Mary is staring at his nicotine-stained fingertips and a pinkie finger turned horribly wrong. The prisoner notices that she is staring. He leans in and stares hard at the young woman until she backs away. He turns and sizes up Heller then asks surprisingly, "you are a chaplain?'

"Yes. I am a priest."

"You are kidding me, right? They sent you here?" Heller looks more closely at his uniform and can see that he is a captain. Heller outranks him and yet there is no respect for the chain of command.

"I'm sorry, captain. I don't understand." He stresses the word, "captain," a weak attempt to sound like the man's superior. Rose can feel her stomach turning.

Pointing to the crucifix, the captain says, "if I were you, I would put that away, SIR." Now it's the captain's turn at sarcasm delivered far more effectively. Heller's voice wavers.

"Why would I do that? Does it offend you?"

"Our loyalty is to Adolph Hitler." His hand sweeps behind him to include the other prisoners standing in the room. "We have no time for religion and less time for the people who put

God ahead of the Reich." There is confusion on Heller's face.

The captain continues, "I don't recognize you. You weren't part of the transfer from Camp Mexia were you?"

"No. I just arrived here. In this country. I came directly from Tunisia. I have only been in America for a week."

"Well, welcome your holiness. The joke is on you." Most of the men cackle. Rose notices that one prisoner, a private, holds back. Younger than the rest, he timidly smiles but hesitates to join in at Heller's expense.

The defiant captain repeats his warning, while he teases the crucifix with his bent finger "Be careful, Father. Nobody here wants to join your congregation." They are interrupted by commands to move along, past the Red Cross volunteer who didn't understand a word of their exchange. But Rose senses trouble. She grabs a care package and moves with the small group that includes Heller.

Outside, the ranks swell as others join the line heading towards one of the prisoner compounds within the camp. Rose can see that Heller is clearly afraid. He holds back, hesitant to even join the line.

"Are you okay, Father?" It is the young private. The concern in his voice appears genuine, but Heller seems understandably cautious about responding. The private lowers his voice and adds, "they are bad news."

"What did he mean by 'the joke is on you'? Why did he say that?"

Rose is only three feet away, staring at the ground, trying hard not to be noticed..

"Most of us were transferred here this morning from Camp Mexia as part of a prisoner exchange. The best I can explain it is they tried to get rid of the troublemakers in this camp and thought they were getting anti-Nazis in return. The 'joke' that asshole was talking about is that most of these camps just unloaded their troublemakers too. And believe me, those guys are trouble. So, whatever they thought they were getting here – people like you and me – they got a lot worse in return."

He points to the American garrison as they march through the gates. "So, I guess you could say the real joke is on them." Rose's heart sinks. She knows Colonel Warren is looking forward to the return of discipline and order. He thinks his prison will get back to the kind of facility it was always meant to be. How could he know that within months, Camp Huntsville will be known as the worst Nazi-infested camp in the southern United States.

NOVEMBER 1943

* * *

CHAPTER 28
P.O. Box 1142

Fundevogel

Ralph's last forkful of overcooked bacon and dry scrambled eggs explodes from his mouth. Everyone seated around him at the narrow mess hall table instinctively leaps to their feet as if recoiling from a poisonous snake. They are roaring in laughter.

"Holy shit, Bauer, get a grip." Edmudson, a naval I/O, is wiping flecks of egg from his soiled shirt. He is still chuckling.

"Ralph are you alright?" Gene Cohen, chief storyteller and instigator of the whole event, is slapping Ralph on his back in a feeble effort to help him clear his throat. Cohen -- his friends call him Gino -- would be happier if he could get another laugh from Ralph who is covering his mouth while reaching for a glass of water. He points at Gino with glass in hand, tries to speak, hesitates, then half-laughs and half-sneezes. His friends howl again, and Ralph joins right in. Gino hands him a stiff napkin. Ralph wipes his mouth, finally gains his composure and says, "Gino, nobody would believe that story outside these walls."

"I know, I know, can you believe it? I'm gonna tell my grandchildren someday that I helped defeat Hitler at the ladies underwear counter at Lansburgh's. He glances at his watch, grabs his empty tray and separates himself from the group. "Shit, I've got an interrogation in ten minutes. Gotta go boys." As quickly as he swept in and turned breakfast upside down, Gino is gone.

Ralph cleans himself up and heads back to the barracks, still smiling. He's not even thinking about his next interrogation session later this afternoon. Every time he thinks he's heard the craziest story around here somebody tops it. Hopefully, by the time Gino has grandchildren he'll be able to share his -- because right now they are all sworn to secrecy. Nothing is shared outside P.O. Box 1142. Nothing. Nobody else knows how they've changed the rules to get information from high-value targets. Sure, the end game is still about information. But getting there can be quite an adventure. Wining and dining prisoners at the finest restaurants in Alexandria. Visiting Washington museums and gift shops. Playing chess and cards at the oddest hours, always with ample liquid refreshment. And -- in Gino's case -- taking a group of German scientists to a local department store to buy underwear for their wives.

For starters, the greatest irony is that the whole incident took place at one of Washington's finest department stores, which happens to be Jewish-owned. Ending up at the ladies underwear counter, a handful of Gino's prisoners brought out slide rules to calculate the difference between centimeters and inches. If that wasn't confusing enough to the slightly shaken salesclerk, they also demanded to see wool underwear, explaining that the winter back home was going to be hard. When they moved on to the bras and began making similar calculations, the salesclerk apparently had enough and insisted that store management call for help. The Military Police promptly arrived and arrested Gino and his cronies. Of course, Gino had the same phone number in his pocket that Ralph keeps close at hand. One call to the right person at P.O. Box 1142 and the matter disappeared from the police blotter. Ralph wonders sometimes if the President of the United States even knows what's going on here in his own backyard.

He jumps on to the wooden plankways that lead toward his barracks, holding his collar tight against a stiff wind that reminds him how the Fall arrives so defiantly here in the Northeast. So different than home in the Blackland Prairie. *They should still be getting one more cotton harvest in down there.* He misses Texas. Just turned in his request for Thanksgiving leave. His Chief I/O didn't sound too hopeful, so Ralph played the Huntsville card, suggesting that maybe he could interrogate some high-value POWs while he was visiting. That suggestion got a "nice try Bauer but no promises." He kicks at the damp, yellow leaves sticking to the wooden slats. His barrack is last in the compound, thirty yards away from a stand of bare pin oaks. Their leaves, already raked into tight piles, are smoldering unattended. Ralph hates the smell of burning leaves. Reminds him too much of the brush wood fires built by Bedouins in the desert of North Africa. A bunch of his buddies shout to him as they throw a football around, easing the stress of their daily struggle to peel secrets away from the enemy. To a man, there is a cigarette dangling from their lips. The butts ending up as useless fuel for the slowly burning compost. He thinks about joining them but decides a nap is the best use of his time. He likes to be well rested for interrogations. They are mentally draining. Each is unique, challenging the best use of his instincts, along with the instruction received at the Camp Ritchie Military Intelligence Training Center in Cascade, Maryland.

During that intense period, Ralph received an introduction to counterintelligence and prisoner psychology that far exceeded the basic techniques he learned before landing in North Africa. He reflects back on those early days and wishes he knew some of the tactics he uses today. *Maybe Heller would not have deceived me. Maybe I would have seen through the lies.* He remembers Heller was sent to Camp Huntsville. *Another reason for me to get down there, just to see him again and kick his ass.* Despite his angst over Heller's misdirection, Ralph is able to justify his own vacillation between trust and deceit every day. His own conscience is clear, not conflicted. For him, it is righteous and real. The Germans are unscrupulous. They are evil and need to be stopped. Even men like Heller. To win this war he will gladly earn the trust of a prisoner while he uses every resource available only to deceive him.

Once, he had a German officer whose greatest fear was being turned over to the Russians. So, Ralph arranged for a fake Russian agent to be brought into his interrogation session, demanding the prisoner be released to him. The prisoner gave Ralph what he needed.

It doesn't always happen that smoothly. Sometimes, all the training in the world won't deliver the information. Often, a prisoner just refuses to play the game. When that happens, Ralph uses the same tool that every successful I/O here in P.O. Box 1142 leans on without any moral reservations. Eavesdroppers. When the prisoner barracks were constructed, each was fitted with electronic listening devices built into the ceilings and walls. In a separate room, a team of eavesdroppers – they call themselves electronic monitors as if it makes their job less personal -- spends their days and nights listening to conversations among cell mates. Usually they have to endure small talk or exaggerated tales of sexual conquests. But sooner or later they will hear a prisoner share information they proudly withheld from their interrogating officer. It is a badge of honor for the inmate to believe he misled his I/O. And usually he can't wait to share that conquest with his cellmate --maybe even disclosing the true information while bragging and boasting.

Ralph stretches out on his cot. He is alone but comforted by sounds of his fellow interrogators still tossing the ball outside. Still cold from his walk, he pulls an olive-green wool blanket up to his chin. He closes his eyes but knows already that sleep will not come. Too many thoughts racing through his mind. Heller. Trusting. Lying. Cheating. Winning. Now it is Oma that dominates his wide-awake thoughts. *Would she be proud of me?* He reaches under his cot and pulls out the bible. He combs the pages, hoping to find a message he may have missed. *Why do I care so much?* He flips to the very back and realizes the last two pages are stuck together. Curious, he carefully peels away the first delicate page. It easily separates until the second page reveals several lines of writing -- the ink somewhat faded. These are familiar words. They mean something to Ralph --committed to memory. His memory:

If you will never leave me, I too will never leave you.

Words from a story that Oma read to them often. *Fundevogel* by the Grimm Brothers. She began reading the fairy tale to Ralph, Rose, and Henry because they told her how losing their parents made them worry about also losing each other. As they grew up those words became an innocent oath among siblings. Ralph also remembers Oma whispering the phrase in his ear at bedtime. He pinches the corners of his eyes but it doesn't stop the tears. He wipes them, careful not to touch the fragile words he needs to read one more time.

He carefully stores the bible and exits the barrack. A lot of things feel different now. In the distance he can hear yet another busload of prisoners arriving. Through the trees he catches a glimpse of darkened windows hiding the enemy . He picks up the football abandoned by his friends. Sends a perfect spiral into the now-dormant leaf pile. *Maybe Donaldson was right. Maybe some of them are just good people in a bad army.*

CHAPTER 29
Camp Huntsville

Hand-picked

Stephan sits alone in the mess hall. His breakfast tray is already empty. Today is final harvest day and his skeleton crew of prisoners will be leaving earlier than usual for the Bauer Farm, their ranks thinned by the absence of many of the original Nazis like Werner. He collects his tray and scans the room looking for Hugo, who is supposed to be finishing an early kitchen shift. He can't find him but sees plenty of faces he hardly knows. Stephan still can't believe how quickly this all went wrong both for the Americans and for the prisoners they were trying to protect. Like one of those Tunisian sandstorms that comes out of nowhere and leaves you blind and directionless in seconds.

Among the new arrivals there are more officers than enlisted men. And officers do not have to work. Another rule courtesy of the Geneva Convention. The officers can choose to join their men but to no one's surprise, very few make that choice. More perplexing is that most of the officers are Nazis, an insult to Colonel Warren's prisoner exchange.

Hoping to find his friend, Stephan leaves the mess hall from a seldom used rear exit that deposits him in the rear of the building near the trash bins. Sure enough, he finds Hugo picking through trash he is preparing for the incinerator. It is now an unspoken understanding: Stephan doesn't ask what the scavenger is hunting. But camp news is a different story and Hugo, who has stepped up his interplay with the guards, continues to pry loose inside information courtesy of a few extra cigarettes. Since his injuries, he has been working at odd jobs throughout the prisoner compounds. He seldom leaves the camp, giving him ample time to work his sources. It amazes Stephan that a man so battered as Hugo can cling to his sense of humor. Hugo's sarcasm is particularly sharp this morning.

"Well Stephan, it appears our American friends suffer from a severe case of chronic bureaucracy just like the morons in Berlin."

"What's that supposed to mean?"

"It means that other camps here in Texas and other places are just passing their problems down the line to our friendly little camp." He taps two empty egg cartons together. "So, my friend Werner, who I miss dearly, may have been transferred but his replacement and the rest coming with him -- God I hate to even say it, they may be a lot worse."

"Nobody can be worse than him." Stephan remembers Hugo's battered face the night of the football match. He grimaces at his hobbled friend's tortured movements while exploring another trash can. "How can you think that?"

"Well, for starters, Werner was not an officer. Many of these new guys are. Plus, it looks like some of them are SS and Gestapo, which of course we didn't have before.

"Wonderful."

"Oh, it gets better." He is searching his pockets and getting frustrated. "You wouldn't happen to have a cigarette, would you?"

"You know I don't smoke. Besides, you're supposed to be the cigarette czar."

"Please don't call me a czar. I've got enough trouble with

the Nazis. The last thing I need is for them to think I'm also a Russian."

Stephan snickers. Wishes he did have an extra cigarette to reward Hugo's unconquerable sense of humor. "Hey, I promise you'll get my next beer coupons, now go on. My work detail is leaving soon. What else?"

"Okay, okay. It seems that the mail system for a lot of the camps is controlled through Camp Hearne."

"I don't even know where that is."

"It's also in Texas, pretty close by, I think. Anyway, prisoners who work in the mail room at Camp Hearne are all Nazis and they've been using the mail system to communicate with Nazis in other camps. Can you believe it? Right under the Americans' noses. Even worse, the Nazis already knew who the troublemakers were before they got sent here. So, you know, guys like us arrived here with targets on their backs."

"Guys like *us*, or guys like *you*, Hugo. I'm trying to keep my nose clean. You're trying to get yours busted."

"Doesn't matter." He flattens the top flap of a corn starch box and places it reverently in his apron. A solid find for the scavenger. "Anybody transferring in here who isn't willing to kiss the Fuhrer's ass is a marked man. So, it looks like things are going to get nasty again. Maybe worse than before. It reminds me of some of those poor bastards in North Africa who would have surgery in a field hospital. Instead of getting better they would get an infection and end up in worse shape."

"So, the Americans are lousy surgeons."

"Looks that way." He slams a battered lid back on a trash can and wipes his hands across his kitchen apron. "And now their patient is running a fever."

Two hours later, Hugo's sad assessment is a distant memory for Stephan. He always feels better away from the prison camp, untroubled by the tough work in front of him at the

Bauer Farm. His patchwork crew hears Uncle Pete loud and clear this morning: "pick every plant clean." Today, there are remnants of bolls that just burst out of their pods within the last few days. The work will be less demanding, and the volume of cotton left to be picked will be far less, but the end result is just as important. While he has not been forced to make gunpowder or artillery shells for the Americans, it is still not lost on Stephan that much of this cotton – the result of his "enemy" labor, will eventually be spun into uniforms and tents and other material that will be consumed by a war machine that no other country is this world can match. He was taught that the Americans joined the war to conquer Europe. But he has been in a tiny sliver of this vast country long enough to understand the lies created by the Nazis The same myths his own parents refused to believe. He envies the American soldiers who want to win just so they can come home, leaving Europe behind. He wonders what will be left of his country when he returns. *Will it be barren and empty just like this cotton plant?* He pulls the last piece of fiber from a stubborn boll. His fingers are burning. His back is stiff. He looks up and acres of unfinished work are taunting him. *How will all this work get done?*

He stops to stretch and notices a group of Negro women entering the fields from the south end. Each is carrying a sack, much smaller than Stephan is used to dragging. Bonnets cover most of their heads. Ivory and checked and calico -- far from pristine or starched or pretty. None are heirlooms. Probably hand-me downs picked up from a thrift shop or tossed away by employers whose wives used them once for a few hours on an Easter Sunday. Their ragtag appearance is incompatible with Stephan's world of military order and uniformity. Everything about them fascinates him. The women are still too far away to determine ages but there is an unmistakable mix of young and old. The younger ones -- Stephan guesses that some might be teenagers – are more playful and distracted. They are wearing gloves, probably to protect their fingers from the merciless bolls. One larger woman stands out like a scarecrow in a crowded corn field. She is not wearing a hat. Her coarse hair, streaked with grey, is cropped very close to her face. Even from a distance, he can see that her eyebrows are completely white. She stands in one spot swaying from side to side, refusing to move. Her large arms, the excess flesh jiggling below her elbows, are directing the rest of the group to fill open gaps in the picking line. He has never seen them before but assumes they are somehow connected to Clyde's helpers. Wives, sisters, cousins or daughters. *How hard it must be to see your child toil in the field like this.* They carry themselves in a way that tells him, regardless of their age, they know what they are doing. The women spread out and get to work immediately. Only twenty yards behind Stephan and his work detail, they are already closing fast. Just like the Negro men, their movement and pace are relentless. No question they will each pick more cotton than Stephan's fingers could hope to deliver on this cool November morning. The large woman is yelling. At first, he thinks she is shouting instructions to the others. It takes Stephan a few seconds to realize *he* is the object of her raised voice.

"Move, now. Go on. Move! You're burning daylight soldier!" He can't understand what she is saying but her body language provides the necessary translation. *Get back to work.* He has been standing and staring far too long. "Schnell!" This time the order comes from a different direction. Dobbs, the only American guard, is not to be outdone by a Negro woman picking cotton. Everyone carries a sense of urgency. Peter Bauer wants the job finished today. Stephan drops his lightly filled sack to the ground behind him and returns to work, makes his way down the row of plants, determined to stay ahead. He keeps moving and soon the extra weight tells him it's time to unload. He finally dares to turn around and sees the women have closed the gap.

As he approaches Clyde and the waiting scale, he notices one woman much further behind the rest. She moves oddly, less confidently. Her head is protected too but differently than the others. She is wearing a light-colored brimmed straw hat that swallows her head. A blood red scarf is pulled tightly around the hat and under her chin, making her face disappear even further into the cavernous headwear. The pale blue long sleeved shirt she wears is oversized, spilling over her hands. Rather than working a row of plants in a straight line, she is jumping from row to row plucking at random bolls that the pickers ahead have missed. It reminds Stephan of the sanitation workers combing the public squares in Vienna, poking at trash that barely touches the ground. This random pattern eventually brings her close to the service road where Stephan is standing, waiting for Clyde to return his empty sack. Stephan observes her odd movements more closely.

The first thing he notices are the eyeglasses hidden below the wide brim of her hat. Her white skin stands out against the red scarf. This is not a Negro. This is not a hired hand. *This is Rose.* He leaps back into the field almost forgetting to retrieve his sack from Clyde. Rose is oblivious. Her head is down, individually taped fingertips peek out from her shirtsleeves, picking renegade tufts of fiber with intensity. She doesn't notice Stephan who has leapt into the row next to her. She begins to repeat her erratic movements when he blurts out in German, "stay straight."

He startles Rose who straightens up. She recognizes the voice. *Your German is very good.* She wants to say something but just stares.

"I am sorry. I just meant that you can be much more efficient if you remain in one row."

Both hands rest on her hips. He can hardly make out her face. "I've been doing this a lot longer than you have, I think I know how to pick cotton."

"I'm sorry Rose." He realizes immediately that he should not have used her first name. She pounces on his social miscue. "How did you know my name?"

He is embarrassed. Tries to explain. "I'm sorry Miss Bauer, please forgive me. I remember your uncle using your name the day you lost the mail."

She softens her response. "That's okay. I remember you now." *I never forgot you.* "What is your name?" *God, just admit you know his name.*

He stands up straight and bows in her direction. "I'm Private Stephan Jurgen." She forgot how tall he was.

"Well private, I never properly thanked you for helping with the mail. So, consider yourself thanked."

"It was my pleasure to help you. This farm receives quite a lot of mail."

"No, actually I don't collect the mail frequently enough. It was my fault for not doing my chores properly."

Rose realizes they have been standing still too long. Clyde is watching them closely. She bends down and begins hunting for missed cotton. Stephan takes her lead and drops his empty sack to the ground. He eases his right arm under the thick strap and reacquaints himself with the row next to Rose. Their heads are both down, concentrating on their work. She changes the subject. "You seem to have learned how to harvest cotton very quickly."

"Thank you, Miss Bauer. I have done the chopping and now the picking. But I feel like there is more to learn. I am just curious about the harvesting we are doing here. What happens to the cotton we are picking today?" He points to the wagon just as Clyde reaches the top of the ladder and another sack of cotton disappears inside.

"You're not a Nazi spy, are you?" She winks, and Stephan feels himself relax.

"Oh no Miss Bauer. Just curious."

"Well, I'm not the expert on this farm but I can give you a pretty simple explanation. All the cotton goes to a gin a few miles from here, where it gets graded and weighed. That's where the cotton or lint is separated from what we call the trash." She stands up to show Stephan a piece of cotton that still has parts of the burr and plan stem sticking to it. "This is all trash. So, the cotton you see in that wagon has to be separated from the trash. That's what happens at the cotton gin."

"How much trash is removed?"

"Let's see, it takes about 1200 pounds of picked cotton to make a 500 pound bale after the trash is removed. Not sure how much that translates in kilos but there is a lot of waste." A shrill whistle interrupts their conversation. "That's Clyde. He's getting nervous. Better get back to work." They both return to their picking. Stephan is on his knees to give his back a break, so they are both at eye level, but the shrubs obscure their view of each other.

Rose continues, "Because all of our cotton is still handpicked that makes it cleaner, which brings higher prices."

"That's good for you and your family."

"We do have a good reputation. My uncle prides himself on that. But the truth is that the Great Depression interrupted any attempt to modernize and now a country mobilizing for war is placing far greater emphasis on planes, tanks, and ships instead of manufacturing cotton pickers. So it gets kind of complicated and that's where my lesson ends."

"Thank you, Miss Bauer." Stephan adds the observation, "Farming can be a demanding occupation."

"Are you a farmer back home in Germany?"

"Austria, Miss Bauer. I am Austrian. No, I am not a farmer. My family lives in Vienna. I helped my father. He is a watchmaker."

Rose stops. Stands upright. Tightens the scarf around her straw hat. "Really. Do you repair watches?"

Stephan is back on his feet, still moving. Now shouting back at Rose. "I was always fixing watches for the men in my platoon. My father taught me well."

Rose wants to know more. She holds back, continues picking the random cotton that still remains. They move at a steady pace, not looking at one another. Each carving their path through the endless row that lies ahead. There are extended periods of silence, but neither seems to care. As they reach the end of the section, Rose has filled her sack enough that it's time for a visit to Clyde. She breaks away, dragging the cotton behind her.

"Please, allow me." Stephan grabs the sack, but she pulls back. "No, um private. I can do it myself."

"Of course. I was just ready to have mine weighed as well"

"No. everyone here pulls their weight." Stephan looks confused at her comment. Rose realizes the expression about "pulling your weight" probably does not translate well for Stephan. She explains, "It is an English expression. To pull your weight means to do your share of the work. It would not be looked upon kindly by the other women working the fields today if you carried this for me. Besides, I'm perfectly capable."

"I understand. My mother would not forgive me, but I understand." *A gentleman. Your mother raised you well.*

They deliver their cotton sacks to Clyde, who takes care of Rose first. He returns the sack, commenting, "Here you go, Miss Rose. Thanks for helping out today. I hope you're not running into much trouble out there." He is nodding toward the patch of cotton, but his eyes never leave Stephan. His voice is extra deep. Rose is quick to put Clyde at ease, though she doubts he believes her. "Happy to help Clyde. And everything is fine out there. Everybody is minding their own business." She turns and heads back to the field, twirling her empty sack while adjusting her oversized hat and leaving Clyde with Stephan, who can feel the penetrating stare of the overseer. Clyde swings the loaded sack on to the scale and glares more deeply. "You are a little light here, STEPH," he says, exaggerating his name. "Better pay more attention to the cotton and less to Miss Rose." Stephan doesn't understand most of what Clyde says, but interprets the message regardless of the language barrier. He responds in English like the others taught him and surprises Clyde, "Okay boss."

Clyde groans and heads toward the ladder, beckoning Stephan to follow him. They reach the ladder and Clyde hands the sack to Stephan, pointing skyward. *Is this some sort of punishment?* Stephan has watched Clyde long enough that he knows what to do. But the effort is laughable. He slings the loaded sack over his shoulder and grabs the ladder with his free hand. His first step shifts his full weight against the wagon and it creaks defensively, defying him to keep moving. He accepts the challenge, moving very carefully, straining already to keep his cargo balanced. Clyde would have been up and down the ladder three times already and Stephan is barely a third of the way. Halfway up his breathing becomes labored. His calves are straining as he struggles to keep his balance. Each rung rejects him. *Don't look down. Keep moving.* The sack begins to slide backwards on his shoulder. He compensates by leaning forward more heavily. Every groan of the makeshift wagon exaggerates his pathetic pace. He is waiting for the sideboards to snap, sending him deep into a suffocating sea of white. Finally, he manages the last few rungs and reaches the top. His first instinct is to let go of the entire sack, but he knows better. Instead he slides it over the brim of the sideboard, then drapes both arms over, still clinging to the bag as it releases its cotton. Free of the weight and steadier on his feet he makes a normal descent down to earth.

Clyde is waiting impatiently, a much larger haul of cotton

balanced on his shoulder. As soon as Stephan touches ground, Clyde sweeps him aside and leaps onto the ladder, hoping to humble Stephan with every rung he quickly clears. Stephan could care less. He is searching for the wide brim hat with the blood-red scarf. But Clyde's little diversion has worked. Rose is a half-acre away, surrounded by bonnets of ivory and checked squares and calico. Stephan resumes picking. His rubber legs reminding him to keep his distance from Rose Bauer. He is again a solitary figure following another endless path.

Two hours later, their work is completed. Stephan is disheartened, knowing he must return to Camp Huntsville, feeling the emptiness that haunts him whenever he feels trapped by the reality of his incarceration. He has been a prisoner now for six months. He has been away from home for almost five years. He still feels the most fearful when he is among the men who wear the same uniform as his. Every time he thinks there is a way out, a path to survival, he is left breathless by the futility of it all. Yes, the men in Camp Huntsville may wear German uniforms, but they are Austrians, Poles, and Lithuanians. Some are decent men. But many are thugs, criminals, and Nazi zealots. For a very brief time, he thought he had friends with whom he could share a common goal: surviving and getting home. But it has become complicated again. And he's not sure the Americans can fix the problem.

Another reality disappoints him. His work at the Bauer Farm is probably over. Now that the cotton harvest has successfully ended there is little work left for his crew. He must leave the very place he feels the safest. Peter Bauer, who has been so kind. Clyde, his gruff but fair boss. The old woman on the porch, who makes him laugh though they have never spoken. And Rose. Of course, Rose. He knows how crazy it is to feel this way, but he wants to get to know her more. He can't be sure how she feels but there is only one path to finding out and that can't happen now. That chance will disappear as soon as he gets on the bus. His despair is deepened as they approach the work yard.

There on the porch, looming large and reminding him of his impending loss, are Uncle Pete, Rose, and the old woman. They are engaged in a serious conversation. Uncle Pete, his hands on the railing, is surveying Stephan's work detail. Oma is rocking comfortably in her chair, listening intently. Rose is removing her hat and scarf, shaking her golden curls and using the wide brim of her hat to dust lint off her work clothes. She props her hat on one of the rail posts then uses her scarf to clean her glasses. She puts the spectacles back on and Stephan imagines she is peering directly at him. He swallows hard and realizes that he actually feels breathless. *How can I let this go?*

Now it is Uncle Pete who makes eye contact with Stephan. *Am I imagining this?* He gestures toward the prisoner, beckoning him to come over. No one else is paying attention. His fellow prisoners are occupied in idle chatter. Dobbs is smoking a cigarette and checking his watch. The Negro workers are furthest away, indifferent to the scene that is playing out in front of Stephan. *It's not my imagination. He wants me to come over.* Stephan steps away, his legs feel like rubber again, but for a very different reason this time. His pace is timid at first, unsure if this is the right thing to do. Uncle Pete is still motioning, now more urgently as if to say, "yes you, hurry up." Stephan obliges. The picket fence slows his approach as he fumbles with the latched gate. One more step and then Dobbs explodes. "No! I mean nein. I, um, halt, halt, halt!" He races forward to intercept Stephan. Now, everyone is watching. Uncle Pete jumps off the porch and puts his hands up to slow down the advancing guard. He can't contain himself and starts laughing, "Easy soldier, it's okay. I asked him to come over." Dobbs is panting, grateful he won't have to explain to his superiors why he shot a prisoner dead in his tracks. Stephan wants to share in the embarrassment of Dobbs but thinks twice and simply acknowledges the guard. "Danke."

Uncle Pete invites Stephan up on the porch. He removes his hat and takes forever to clear the three simple steps. Rose watches him closely. Oma smiles warmly and holds out her hand. It is Rose who speaks. "Private Jurgen." And Oma who softly interrupts. "Now, Rose. You know the young man's name. We don't need to be so formal."

"Stephan, this is my grandmother, Mrs. Bauer." Oma rests comfortably in her rocking chair, a dull yellow shawl draped across her lap, the fringes brushing the scarred porch floor. He has seen her so many times from a distance. Stephan is surprised how different Oma looks as he gets close. He expects to see a face with the unavoidable lines and wrinkles that come with old age. But her complexion is smooth. And her blue eyes sparkle. Arthritis has not been as kind to the rest of her body, leaving her even more frail than he could discern from a distance. Oma takes his hand and squeezes it gently, soft and cool in Stephan's weathered grip. It feels wonderful. She doesn't loosen her hold and neither does he. He expects her voice to be equally fragile. Instead it is strong and vibrant. Bavaria still lingers in her dialect. "It's nice to finally meet you Stephan. I feel like we've been getting to know each other from afar. Your guards have provided all of us with some comic relief, but this dunce today is by far the funniest." Stephan smiles and glances sideways at Dobbs who has no idea what's being said about him. Oma continues, "Rose tells me that you are a watchmaker's son."

"Yes Mrs. Bauer. It was our family business."

"Did you work closely with your father, Stephan?"

"Oh, I helped him now and then around his shop. When he wasn't too busy he would let me practice on some of the old timepieces he had in his inventory." Another memory jars him. A recollection he thought he had buried.

"Any brothers or sisters?"

"No, just me." He looks at Rose. "I envy those who have the

gift of siblings. Of course, I cherished the time spent with my parents in their shop. Wonderful memories." He is fighting to remember the good times, but the dark memories of Vienna are aching to haunt him again. Oddly, he wants to share his pain with these strangers. Maybe it's because he wants them to see he isn't like the Nazis. Perhaps it's simpler than that. He needs to grieve.

"It was hard to find work at the end. Before I left, I mean. I didn't really work on anything of importance, until..."

"Until, what Stephan?" Oma is curious, slides further to the edge of her seat. Stephan hesitates at first, wringing the soft cap that had protected him all day in the afternoon sun. He glances toward the prisoners still gathered in the work yard. They are far enough away. They won't hear. Still he turns his back towards them, lowers his voice.

"Until it was a matter of life and death. Actually, my parents had gone away one weekend, checking on my aunt who lives in Salzburg. It was not a good time for my family. My parents were rather vocal in the community about their opposition to the Nazi annexation of our country, so the Germans were making things difficult for them and...I'm sorry you don't need to hear all of this. I'm afraid this is getting rather long-winded."

Rose and Oma are shocked when it is Uncle Pete who responds first, "Nonsense, continue your story, Stephan."

Stephan takes a deep breath, realizes how tense the muscles in his neck have become. "Very well. They had received threats from the Gestapo. Their friends had been told to stay away. Customers were being turned away from the shop. I was actually happy for them to get away for a few days. Well, I was in the shop cleaning up one Saturday afternoon when a Gestapo officer entered and asked for my father. I told him the truth, where my parents had gone, and he was not happy. He told me they were instructed not to leave the city.

I felt terrible, like I had put my parents in even greater danger."

The Bauers are riveted. Uncle Pete leans back against a railing, scratching his two-day old beard. Rose grabs a battered wicker chair, slides it next to Oma and sits down. She reaches across and holds her hand gently. Oma squeezes, but never takes her eyes off Stephan. "Go on young man."

"Yes, I felt terrible for them. The officer took out a pocket watch and told me he needed it repaired immediately. Of course, he already knew my father was not around, so I told him he would be back late Sunday night and could take care of it right away. And then he said to me, 'I can't wait until Sunday night. You will repair it for me by this afternoon. If, when I come back, it is not repaired, I will make sure your parents never return to this place.'"

"What did he mean?" asks Rose.

"He meant that they would be sent to a camp. That I would never see them again."

Rose grabs her head. "They would do that? Why would they do that? What did you do?"

Uncle Pete weighs in. "That son of a bitch."

And then Oma, "Hush, all of you please. Go on Stephan."

He glances sideways at the prisoners in the yard. Nobody is paying attention. "Yes, Mrs. Bauer. As soon as he left the shop, I tried everything my father had taught me, but nothing worked. I consulted his books. I replaced all the parts. I felt sick. My hands were shaking. It was all my fault. I should have lied to the officer. I had less than an hour remaining when I realized there was nothing left to do. I began thinking of ways I could warn them. Tell them to stay away. But there was no time." He paused. His anguished face surrendered to a subtle smile.

Rose asks what everyone is thinking. "My God, what happened, why are you smiling?"

"I finally lost my temper, angrier with myself than anything else. I slammed the watch down on the workbench. As soon as I did I regretted what it could mean. I thought I had cracked the crystal. Now what was I going to tell him when he returned? I remember being afraid that the door was going to open. I picked up the watch and that's when I realized it was ticking. It was keeping time. I checked it closely for fifteen minutes and it kept time perfectly. I cleaned it, placed it in our best gift box and waited for that swine to return. I'm sorry, but that was how I felt. I wasn't even sure if he would come back or even keep his word."

Oma and Rose almost spoke simultaneously, "Did he come back?"

"He did. And when he picked up his watch he told me to warn my parents never to leave Vienna again without his permission.

"I'll bet your father got his tail up when he heard that."

Stephan hesitates. Doesn't understand Uncle Pete's strange comment.

Rose senses his confusion. "It means angry Stephan. Your father was angry?"

"Oh, yes. I think he also felt terrible for what I went through."

"Have you been able to keep in touch with your family?"

"No, Mrs. Bauer. I entered the army shortly after that and haven't heard from my mother and father in nearly five years."

Rose knows how important it is for her to keep in touch with her brothers. She can't imagine the fear and uncertainty that comes with no communications from the people you love. "When was the last time you heard from them?"

"Well, I have tried on many occasions, but the letters have never been answered. The last thing I had that contained messages from my mother was a family bible she gave to me before

I left." There is sadness in his voice.

"It sounds like you don't have it anymore. You lost it?"

"Not exactly, it was taken from me. Just an unfortunate thing that happens when your army surrenders, and the captors want to collect some souvenirs."

Stephan continues, "It is not the bible so much as the little messages my mother left for me. They would inspire me when I would come upon them. Written in the margins. I cherished reading them." His voice trails off. "Especially the last words she wrote in the bible the night she gave it to me...before I left home."

Rose hesitates, chokes back tears but asks the question anyway. "Would it be too personal to ask you what she wrote."

Stephan smiles, the gesture alone makes Rose feel less guilty about asking. "No, of course not. It was very simple actually. Probably words that thousands of mothers have written to their sons." He realizes they are waiting, too embarrassed to ask again. The words come effortlessly. Memorized forever. "She wrote, *keep your faith and come home to me.*"

An awkward pause is followed by Oma's encouraging response. "And you will Stephan, you will go home. And don't stop trying to reach your parents. We find it very difficult to keep in touch with Rose's brothers. It can be very upsetting, I know."

"Thank you, Mrs. Bauer. The Red Cross is trying. Perhaps soon."

"I will pray that happens for you." She offers her hand again and Stephan squeezes it a bit tighter this time. Oma goes on. "And now I would like you to do something for me. One of the casualties of this war are the able-bodied men who you have been filling in for around here. That's why we are grateful for the work you and most of your fellow soldiers have done on our farm. But we have also lost craftsmen as well. And sometimes natural events take people away -- including the only watchmaker in Huntsville." She finally loosens her grip from Stephan's hands and retrieves a purple satin bag underneath her shawl. She hands the bag to Stephan. "Go ahead, open it."

He carefully pulls the strings and loosens the pouch, his fingers speculating about its contents. He opens his palm and a slender woman's watch slides into his hand. Well preserved, elegant, and simple. He cradles it tenderly and looks at the face of the watch. His eyes widen and Oma smiles. "You know this watch?"

"Of course, it is a Glashütte, the greatest of the Saxon watchmakers."

"It was a gift from my grandfather. I'd like you to repair it."

He reverently returns the watch to the pouch and tries to place it in her hands. "Oh no Mrs. Bauer, I am just an apprentice at best. I don't know anything about this watch. I am afraid I would do more damage than good. I am flattered but really, I don't think this is a good idea."

"Well, too bad Stephan. If you refuse, I'll have this dunce shoot you." She looks at Dobbs, smiles, and waves. The clueless guard smiles back.

Uncle Pete chimes in, restoring some sanity to the conversation. "Stephan, there is a watch repair shop in town that has been closed for six months. The owner, a widower himself, died without any family to call his own. We'll need to figure out how to make this work, but I can at least get you started with the proper tools and parts. Now, we would have to set you up at the camp because it would be impossible to have you work in town. But since Rose works at Camp Huntsville, maybe we can make those arrangements."

Stephan is shocked. "I did not know that you, ah Miss Bauer worked at the camp." He remembers the PA announcements the day of the prisoner exchange. The familiar voice. *It was Rose.* "I, I don't know what to say. I am still not sure how this will work."

Rose finally speaks. "I will make some inquiries Stephan and see what we are permitted to do. And then I will get back to you. How does that sound?"

Stephan's response is inaudible. He will see her again. There is still hope.

He finally leaves the porch to join his fellow prisoners for the trip back to Camp Huntsville, when Oma interrupts his departure. "Stephan, one more thing."

"Yes, Mrs. Bauer, what is it?"

"Your parents. What are their names?"

CHAPTER 30
P.O. Box 1142

Scruples

Ralph always relies on his German-American heritage as a negotiating advantage with a prisoner. "Natural instincts for an interrogating officer" is how instructors within the Military Intelligence Service put it. That was one of the reasons he earned a transfer to P.O. Box 1142, where better training and even more experience has created a healthy tension with prisoners he constantly uses to his advantage. His advanced courses at Camp Ritchie sharpened Ralph's natural instinct when dealing with men whose nationality provide an uncomfortable connection to his own heritage. It used to make him feel guilty. Now he leans heavily on lessons learned from numerous lectures, especially *Practical Instructions in Interrogating Prisoners.* He has memorized the words:

> *Some German POWs crumple when they realize that German-Americans have no use for Hitler's theories and are willing to prosecute the war against Germans as long as necessary to defeat the Nazi system.*

This notion was drilled into Ralph and others with strong German ancestry. POWs think that a German-American will be more understanding and supportive of the Nazi way and then are demoralized when they realize that the opposite is true – Nazis are despised.

Ralph reviews the substantial file of a hot-blooded artillery officer, Captain Klaus Becker. He is an ardent Nazi who survived Germany's defeat in North Africa but was redeployed and eventually captured during the Allies' dogged pursuit of German forces in the southern half of the Italian peninsula. Enough advanced intelligence has been done to satisfy the Allies that Becker may have information about the development of a new 88 mm anti-tank gun. A fierce loyalty to Hitler has sustained him over the last several weeks. He has been anything but cooperative with his captors – leaving previous interrogators in Italy frustrated and empty.

Ralph sets that tone early in an hour-long dialogue with Becker. It begins like most of Ralph's sessions. Becker is delivered from his two-man detention cell to a separate interrogation room where Ralph is waiting. The guards tap on the door, announcing the prisoner's arrival.

Becker is dressed comfortably in prison-issued overalls. He is cleanly shaven and appears well-rested. He looks a lot better than Ralph. Becker is hungry, not because his captors are subjecting him to brutal starvation. He is well-fed. But he is annoyed because his session with Ralph is taking place before breakfast, his favorite meal of the day. Ralph knows that already but asks the question anyway.

"Is there anything you need to make our session more agreeable?"

"No captain, your accommodations have been fine, but perhaps we can get through this efficiently, so I can join the others for breakfast."

"We won't be long this morning. May I call you Klaus or would you prefer to maintain military discipline?"

Becker answers through a sarcastic grin, "Ask your questions and I will provide the answers and let's leave names and titles out of it altogether."

"As you wish. I hope my German is good enough for you. Please let me know if you don't understand."

Becker escalates the sarcasm. "I understand completely. Your German is quite good. I am sure that is one of the reasons you are safely hiding here and not risking your life like many of your friends."

Ralph doesn't flinch. Not the first time he's heard that response. "I owe that to my German-born grandmother, who is still alive. She taught us well, insisted we learn the language."

"She is a wise woman." He offers his first and only sincere smile of the morning. "Understands the advantage of maintaining her connection to her homeland. It will be easier for her and you when we – well, your German brethren -- win this war and we destroy the Jews and communists."

Ralph's response is measured and confident. Almost matter of fact. Not a hint of anger. "Except that I am not a German. I am an American. I speak your language because it is one of the few things that still connects my grandmother to a place where today she would be a stranger."

Becker returns the stoic response. "Where is she from?"

"Bavaria."

"It would not be strange to her. It is still the same beautiful place."

"It could never be the same because of the Nazis. My grandmother, like all German-Americans, despises the Nazis for what they did to her precious homeland. It's why thousands of us have volunteered to fight the Nazis for as long as it takes. We are not brethren. We are embarrassed."

Becker is deflated by Ralph's comments. And Ralph has learned from experience that a prisoner less emboldened, less defiant tends to go through the motions and easily sends signals that he is not being truthful. So, he smartly shifts the session to the task at hand. Ralph understands intuitively that Becker, now hungry and frustrated, is astute enough to know that the Americans brought him to this mysterious destination because of his artillery expertise. Ralph is respectful, but still manages to remind Becker that the Germans are losing the war. They lost in North Africa. They are losing in Italy. And they are collapsing against the Soviets on the Eastern Front. But he plays with the German's ego. Marvels at his artillery expertise, especially his knowledge of ammunition. Becker deflects his line of questioning, saying only that he worked for the Goldschmidt chemical firm in Essen in 1939 when they were experimenting with various compositions of metal powder. That's the direction Ralph wants to go but deliberately steers far away, allowing Becker to believe he had evaded his interrogator. Instead, Ralph chooses another opportunity to pick away at Becker's battered Nazi psyche.

"Essen must have been a very exciting place when you worked there. It's a shame what the bombings have done to the city."

"Do you mean the innocent civilian lives your bombs have taken?"

Ralph refuses to take the bait. "No, I was speaking of the factories and industries that have been destroyed this past year. Perhaps you are not aware of the damage that has been done. It is significant. Just this past July the Krupps Works suffered from the most damaging raid of the war."

"Propaganda most likely. I have not heard of any damaging raids. In fact, we are producing new technology in anti-tank guns and shells. So, your attacks are clearly not working."

For the first time the prisoner has acknowledged advancements in technology. Ralph gets the subtle slip that he wanted. Deftly avoids direct questioning. "You are probably right. I marvel at how sophisticated your artillery has become over the last few years."

Becker knows he has probably said too much. He quickly

became uncooperative, complaining that he would like to be fed. Ralph trusts his instincts and brings the session to an end. He closes the file and thanks Becker for his cooperation.

The prisoner is brought to the mess hall and then returned to his two-man cell. There, he is reunited with his cell-mate, a quiet prisoner named Dorfmann, a doormat who mostly defers to the strong-willed Becker. Except when they talk about the Americans. Then the docile Dorfmann spits venom. And he leans on Becker for his guidance on how to beat their system and withhold cooperation. Becker's inflated ego cannot resist the opportunity to guide this timid excuse for a German soldier. It's never too late to help the cause so Dorfmann has become Becker's special project. Two other things about Dorfmann. First, he has a brother who is still working in Essen, which gives him a common connection to Becker. Second, he is a stool pigeon. This quiet prisoner Becker has taken under his wing is a fierce anti-Nazi who long ago sold his soul to the Allies. His only job is to make sure he feeds Ralph every shred of information that Becker shares. And he does his job splendidly.

After Becker is led back to his cell Ralph walks down the corridor with dull grey cinder block washed by incandescent bulbs dangling from exposed rafters every twenty feet. It is the only source of light for this entire section of the building that is underground. At the end of the hall he turns sharply left and runs immediately into two MPs who know him well but always behave like they've never laid eyes on him.

Their simultaneous salutes and rigid military protocol never get old for Ralph. He loves this place. And who wouldn't. On the other side of those doors behind these two brutes is Ralph's ultimate secret weapon. He's on the hunt and he can't wait to get inside. He returns a sharp salute, the MPs step aside, and Ralph enters the Monitoring Subsection. He knows the rules. Dead silence. He carefully makes his way past the rows of monitoring officers, all wearing earphones.

All intensely writing while they are listening. Mentally exhausting work. He places his hand on the shoulder of staff sergeant Cliff Rayburn, who turns and acknowledges Ralph with a simple thumbs up. It is understood. Becker has returned to his cell. Rayburn adjusts his earphones and slides Becker's file in front of him. To hell with scruples.

Two hours later, Ralph sits in one of the spartan interview rooms that barely accommodates two people. It is deliberately isolated and very quiet. He opens the Becker file that he patiently waited to get back from Rayburn. Each page gets better. This is one of his greatest achievements since arriving at P.O. Box 1142. Rayburn's report says it all:

- *The anti-tank shell 40 or 42 (POW was not sure of the number) has a soft lead nose which spreads on impact and clings to a metal surface before bursting. These shells will not ricochet from a tank even when they hit at an angle. POW thinks these shells contain thermite, he calls it "Thermite A."*
- *Referenced his work at the Goldschmidt Chemical Firm in Essen. Discussed tests that were being conducted on such thermite shells for use against tank and fortification armor plating. Said the Russians have protected their tanks against such shells by covering them with a coat of concrete to which the soft nose of the projectile will not adhere.*

Ralph would have been happy with that information alone, but there's more. *This guy couldn't shut up.*

- *POW claims that morale in Essen factories is very poor and has been further lowered by the presence of the volunteer Ukrainian Russians who were brought into the city shortly after the Germans overran the Ukraine and whose presence is very much resented by the German Workers.*
- *There has been a revolt of youth in Essen. The young*

people have had enough of the Hitler Youth and refuse to allow themselves to be herded around by its leaders. They now call themselves "Piraten" when they go out together on hikes without the supervision of the Hitler Youth leaders who are left to cool their heels at home.

- *On foreign workers in Essen: POW claims that 200,000 of the total population are now foreign laborers. Poles, Russians and Italians constitute the majority. The Italians represented a considerable problem when they were first imported because of difficulties that developed from changes in diet. The problem was quickly settled when the provisioning was taken over by Italian representatives. The volunteer Ukrainians worked harder than the Germans themselves, which accounts for the bad feeling which has grown up against them. The Ukrainians who are doing forced labor do not work well.*
- *POW states that part of the Krupp plant in Essen has been moved to the town of Berndorf, south of Vienna, where there is a famous, old Austrian metal plant the owner of which is related to Krupp.*

Reading this kind of intelligence makes all the hard work and preparation worthwhile. He is lucky to be part of this team. None of this comes together without the identification of high-value targets, extensive research and files built before the POW is ever interrogated, electronic monitoring day and night, and the effective work of stool pigeons like Dorfmann. There is a knock on the door. He closes the file, and shouts "enter." A guard opens the door slightly and in slips Dorfmann.

"Hello captain, are your pleased?'

"Not a bad day's work. You did really well. Your training has paid off."

"Thank you, captain. I shouldn't stay away from my cell too long. He'll want to hear about my session with you."

"Well of course tell him how well his mentoring has prepared you to deal with me. That you gave me nothing. All honor and glory for the Reich. Right, Dorfmann?"

"Absolutely captain. But I am hoping that when this war ends you will remember my true loyalty."

"You know sometimes I wonder if all your hard work is just a selfish way for you to save your own ass. I mean, if you were so against the Nazis, why didn't you just have the guts to stand up to them when you had a chance?"

"Walk in my shoes and then answer that question. If I had the guts to confront the Nazis, maybe they would have shot my parents for raising a traitor. Or maybe sent my sisters away to a labor camp. So, instead people like me choose to survive. Hope the right side wins and maybe we can come home to something that was worth all the lies and deception."

Ralph slides a pack of cigarettes across the table. "For your sake Dorfmann, I hope your hard work pays off."

"It really doesn't matter anymore captain. One day I lie to the Nazis so maybe my family gets to live. The next day I help steal information that will probably lead to your bombs dropping on innocent civilians like my parents. There are no honorable choices for me anymore. I have to live with that forever. Thank you for the cigarettes."

The door closes and Ralph stands to leave the tiny room. *I finally feel sorry for the guy. But my job is to help win this war as soon as possible. That means I need to find more Dorfmanns.* Strange how thoughts enter the mind of a man who is already distracted. But there it is, out of nowhere. An idea. No, it's a gift. Brilliant, actually. *What about Heller? The perfect stool pigeon. Anti-Nazi who owes me big-time. This place can be his penance. And he can help us crush the Nazis. Plus, it gives me another reason to get home to Huntsville.* Ralph is inside the interrogation center, pulling the file of his next prisoner. He's on top of the world.

CHAPTER 31
Camp Huntsville

Close

Just ten days removed from her family meeting on the porch with Stephan, Rose steps off the bus, wishes a good morning to Mr. Martin, and reports for work at the American garrison – arriving a little earlier than usual. There's a lot about today that gives her energy. For all the times she has tolerated the same old routine here at Camp Huntsville, today is going to be different. She digs into the pocket of her coat just to make sure it's still there. She can feel the satin bag, twists her finger around the drawstring for extra security. Squeezes her hands around the contents. Today, Oma's watch is finally getting repaired. It seems Rose can't remember to empty a mailbox or feed the dog, but in less than ten days she has managed to set Stephan's watch repair assignment in motion.

The easy part was convincing Colonel Warren who agreed that Stephan could set up shop in a spare room down the hall from the hospital waiting area. The logistics are simple. Each morning, after breakfast and roll call, Stephan will leave the prisoner compound and report to work, escorted by a guard who will unlock the door to his new shop. Because the workroom is located down the hall from the camp hospital, there is always a guard present. At the end of each workday, around 4:00 PM, the guard will lock the door and escort Stephan back to the prisoner compound.

Since Colonel Warren's only concern was too many people coming out to the prison to drop off and pick up watches, Rose and her family agreed that residents could drop off their repairs at the farm on Saturdays. Rose will bring them to work on Monday and customers can pick them up the following week back at the farm. Rose is grateful for Colonel Warren's cooperation, but her boss also made his intentions clear.

"Miss Bauer, I am agreeing to this because it fills a need for the community, creates goodwill with the prisoners, and helps with administrative costs. But, if there are any problems with this little business arrangement, I will shut it down immediately and Private Jurgen will be cleaning latrines."

He then handed Rose two watches, a stopwatch that hasn't worked since his West Point days and a government-issued Elgin A-11 wristwatch that has been running slow. She's grateful for his display of confidence and for giving Stephan some work to get started. But there is no question the first customer would be Oma, who made the toughest obstacle for this operation disappear by making one visit to the attorney for the estate of Mr. Wilder, the deceased watchmaker. In exchange for access to the shop's inventory, it was agreed that ten percent of the cost of Stephan's labor will be paid to the Wilder estate. Following strict POW wage guidelines, Stephan will receive 85 cents per hour for his services and the remaining profits will go towards administrative costs at Camp Huntsville.

The final hurdle was handled by Uncle Pete, with Clyde's help. In one weekend, they moved the necessary furniture, lighting and initial inventory of parts and tools from the shuttered shop to the American garrison, where guards monitored the set-up and secured the workspace for Stephan's first day on the job. It will be the first time Rose has seen him since they hatched their idea back at the farm. Now it is really happening. She's been nervous since last night and the anticipation is more intense now.

It is still early enough in the morning that the full staff has yet to arrive. Rose enters the building, removes her coat, carefully placing it over her arm so the right pocket remains upright, keeping Oma's watch secure. She smiles and waves at two guards, their friendly faces smiling back. She then turns left at the first hallway, a narrow passage that leads to the hospital waiting area. She is alone, the sound of her heels echoing loudly. At the end of the corridor, standing in front of the hospital doorway is a guard she doesn't recognize. She smiles but his neutral response is what you would expect from a stranger protecting his post. He is standing at-ease, his semi-automatic pistol protruding from a heavy brown leather holster. Rose's excitement is dampened, and she realizes the reality of the situation. For now, Stephan is a POW who will need to earn the trust of a lot of people around here. She decides to break the ice. Looks for the insignia on his right arm. He is wearing two inverted chevrons, silver-gray on dark blue.

"Good morning corporal. My name is Rose Bauer, I'm a prisoner liaison with Colonel Warren's staff."

"Yes ma'am, I know who you are."

She's not sure if that's good or bad. "Oh, okay. Well we have a prisoner who will be starting a new assignment here today and I'm here to make sure he has everything he needs."

"I can take care of that ma'am. I've been told to expect the prisoner and unlock the door for him." He holds a key up for Rose to see. "All set, ma'am."

Before Rose can respond she hears the sound of several footsteps coming closer from behind her. She turns and sees him. Stephan, deliberately suppressing a smile, nods to her in a very formal way, the kind of reaction you would expect from a prisoner in the presence of American guards. She knows Stephan's escort. Private Buddy Miles, a great kid who always has a smile on his face. Except this morning. *God, could everyone lighten up a bit?* Apparently, he doesn't know the corporal either. "Good morning, Miss Bauer."

"Good morning private."

Private Miles acknowledges the other guard. "Corporal, I am escorting this prisoner for his new assignment."

"Thanks, private, I'll take it from here."

"Have a nice day, Miss Bauer." Buddy turns and nods to Rose who lets the social protocol slip. "You too Buddy."

Both Stephan and the corporal catch the slip-up and glance at Rose. She looks at the corporal, shrugs her shoulders and touches her fingers to her lips, "Old friends."

"Yes, ma'am." His response is as stiff as his movements as he turns to the door and unlocks it, allows Stephan to enter the room and then steps in front of Rose. He turns on the light switch. Stephan stands awkwardly in the middle of the room, still a stranger to his new workplace. Rose remains in the hall, waiting for the inevitable. The corporal remains stoic as he addresses the prisoner, "I will be outside if you need me."

Stephan's response, in German, is one thing the guard is not expecting. For the first time, Stephan sees a crack in the corporal's emotionless behavior. "I um, you, ah, do you speak English?"

"Ich spreche kein englisch. "

The corporal has no idea what to do next. Rose comes to the threshold, looks at his name on his tunic. "Corporal... Burns, correct?"

"Uh, that's right ma'am."

"I speak German fluently. If you'd like I can translate for you."

"Yes ma'am, thank you ma'am. That would be great. I just want him to know that I'll be outside if he needs me."

"Of course, may I come in the room?"

"Oh, please, yes. Please"

Rose looks at Stephan and shows off her fluency in German for the guard.

"If you need assistance, the robot who has been assigned to watch you will be outside loosening his underwear." Then, she looks directly at the corporal, smiles and continues in German, "Don't worry he's harmless. He wouldn't bite a biscuit. And he's going to become our very good friend."

Corporal Burns, oblivious to the true banter, whispers "thank you."

Stephan hasn't bitten his tongue in a long time but does everything he can to keep from laughing. He wants to play along but knows that would be tempting fate. So, he just smiles at the guard and says, "Danke."

"So, Corporal Burns I'm going to give the prisoner a few watches to repair. Two of them belong to Colonel Warren.

"Yes, ma'am. I'll be outside if you need me. I'll just keep this door open"

Stephan is already adjusting the light over his workbench. Memories of his father's simple shop flood his mind. He is overwhelmed by thoughts of his parents and the peaceful life that was torn from them. It has been so long, and he's been through so much, but this is the first time he feels like crying. First, he wanted to laugh at Rose's joke about the guard and now he wants to cry for his parents. He pinches his tear ducts, tries to avoid any emotion in front of Rose. It's not working. He brushes a tear with the knuckle of his index finger. Turns away and wipes both cheeks with a work rag he picks up from the bench. It smells old and moldy. The nasty scent lingers on his fingertips as he discards the rag and brushes his hands down his prison overalls. From behind, Rose places her hand very gently on his shoulder, careful not to alarm him. "Are you okay, Stephan? What's wrong?"

He turns slowly, and her hand falls naturally down his arm. She doesn't move away. Instead she grabs a handful of his shirt-sleeve and holds tight. They are no more than five feet from the corridor. Stephan peers nervously past Rose towards the doorway, then glances directly into her eyes. They both know how dangerous this is. She lets go, steps away and looks to the hallway, relieved that nobody is watching them. Relieved but excited at the same time. Her heart is pounding in her throat. *Rose you need to leave now.*

Backing out of the workshop Rose instinctively looks for Corporal Burns. He's safely down the hallway, erect as a statue. *What was I thinking?* She tries to sound casual but can barely utter the words, "I'll come back later corporal to check on things." *Go!* She is clear of the workshop, when Stephan whispers, "Rose." Then again, a little louder, "Rose, the watches!" She stops, fumbles through her pockets then almost runs back into the room avoiding eye contact with him, her heart pounding wildly. She drops the watches on the table and hastens down the hallway. She feels terribly lightheaded, places her left hand against the wall, while her right hand is balled into a fist, as if she were still grasping his shirt. *What would have happened?*

Similar thoughts leave Stephan paralyzed. He is standing in the same spot where they came so close. Two watches and Oma's satin bags sit on the table. Reminders of why he is here. Right now, they mean nothing to him. Rose left no instructions. Just left him crestfallen. He opens the purple sack, removes Oma's watch and gently lays it on the workbench. Looks to the doorway, defying anyone to interrupt him and then slowly holds the soft material up to his nose. Stephan inhales slowly. The scent of Rose's perfume lingers.

CHAPTER 32
Camp Huntsville

Potatoes

The weather in Huntsville is beginning to turn for good. Cooler nights have finally arrived. While daytime temperatures no longer feel oppressive, the humidity is more stubborn, choosing to linger even as winter approaches. From Tunisia to Texas, most of these prisoners have known intolerable heat since they surrendered. Now, as November inches closer to the final month of the year, this milder climate is a welcome change to their daily routine. But for Heller, improving weather offers no relief from his confused confinement. Despite the grand plans he imagined, this shepherd remains displaced and disheartened. Everywhere he looks there are troubled souls who ignore his presence, plentiful sheep who barely tolerate his existence. He knows many want to follow, but sadly his willingness to serve them only heightens the danger. They have been warned: follow and you will be led to slaughter. Because of his rank, Heller is housed in a separate compound away from the enlisted men. His daily companions are other officers who speak openly of their loyalty to Hitler and mock his contrived role in their army. Confronting them is beyond fruitless, it is dangerous. One young captain told Heller that if they were ever to meet back home in Germany he would shoot him on the spot as a traitor. Another boasted to him about a convent he helped to raid in French Lorraine. Heller made the mistake of engaging this hardened Nazi, questioning why he took so much delight in ruining the lives of innocent women who meant no harm to him. Immediately he wanted to take the question back, realizing what a hypocrite he was for asking. After all, isn't that what he did to Sofia? Didn't he ruin the life of an innocent woman? But the chilling response from the Nazi revealed a far darker world, one that Heller's conscience has no capacity to consider.

"Meant no harm? Of course, they meant harm. They made silly vows to a God that has no role in our society. Their loyalties were displaced so I made them pay."

"What do you mean? You killed them?"

"No, that would have been far too easy." He paused, delighted with what he was about to share. "I made them beg for their lives. Made them get down on their knees and renounce their vows. If they did, I let them live and sent them off to work camps where they could do the Reich some good."

"Did any of them refuse to renounce their vows?"

"Most of them, of course." He shakes his head, shrugs his shoulders. "So stupid. A perfect waste of good labor." His cold, dark eyes are probing Heller's, inviting him to ask for more depraved details.

But Heller already knew the answer, knew he executed those nuns. He didn't want to give this monster the satisfaction of telling him. So, he walked away. These are the men who share his barracks, fellow prisoners who are supposed to be on the same side. Instead, Heller uses every chance he can to get away, spending as little time as possible with these twisted souls. Because he is a chaplain, he is given permission to move freely between compounds. Although he is mostly ignored, he takes advantage of any opportunity to be among the men, no matter how frustrating it may feel.

Now, far away from the officer compound, he stands inside

the walls of one of the least used buildings on these sprawling prison grounds – the chapel. It is a narrow space, twice as long as it is wide. A single-room building with three windows on each side that allow plenty of natural light. There are no curtains or blinds so outside eyes have free visibility into the room. Unopened boxes are stockpiled three or four high against one of the long walls. The opposite side is where folding chairs are stacked between each of the windows. Along the back of the chapel a couple of these chairs are randomly opened and facing each other. Centered in front of the room are two square folding tables arranged side-by-side and covered with a green canvas tarp. A wooden crucifix rests on top. It is a place of worship, but it feels like any other building in this complex.

The sound of Heller's footsteps bounces off the bare walls, the echo exaggerating the emptiness of the room. This is a place intended to bring the prison community together, yet it is ignored by Nazis or avoided by prisoners afraid to express their need for spiritual strength. When he first arrived at Camp Huntsville, still eager to pursue his ministry, the chaplain was given enthusiastic permission from the Americans to formalize a worship schedule and encourage prisoners to participate. Despite all the obstacles he faces, Heller still has not abandoned his hopes to make this happen. It may just take a little more time than he imagined. He moves respectfully around the room, envisioning this empty shell filled by men whom he can lead; hoping for a congregation he can grow. He approaches the simple altar where he can say Mass. Shakes a wobbly podium that can be the pulpit for his sermons of hope and salvation. He wants this to be a place where anyone, regardless of their religious beliefs, can feel safe in an environment that is far more threatening than Heller ever imagined.

He thinks he is alone but soon discovers a lone prisoner sweeping dust and debris from the seldom-used floors. It is Hugo, handling another one of his random chores that keep him camp-bound as his injuries continue to heal. It doesn't take long for the two men to find common ground. They speak candidly, both appreciating each other's difficult journey to this place. Hugo interrupts Heller at one point and asks him quite randomly if he likes jazz. Heller admits that he does, acknowledging another of Hitler's hypocrisies. Jazz has been banned in Germany. Hugo is elated. "Well now, if a man of God is willing to challenge the Fuhrer, then don't let me stand in his way." He limps to the rear of the chapel and pulls a tarp off a small table, revealing a battered, portable wind-up gramophone. Heller claps his hands and questions, "Where did that come from?"

"Believe it or not Father, it was always here, buried under all these boxes. But I did bring this." Hugo reaches down to the table and picks up a paper sleeve containing a brittle gramophone record. He carefully removes the record and places it on the playing device. "I play this while I am cleaning in here. Sometimes, I let my friends in to listen, for a small charge of course." He winks at Heller. "But it's free for you Father." He winds the gramophone and sets the needle down on the record. The scratchy sound of Glenn Miller's *In the Mood* begins to play. "Not my favorite but the beat helps me clean a little faster. Besides, it's the best I could do for three packs of cigarettes."

The gramophone is rewound several times as the two continue their dialogue. They move beyond the shallow conversation of two strangers searching for common ground. Warmed by the afternoon sun that slices through the windows, they search more deeply. Inevitably they turn to the pervading grip of the Nazis. Heller is the first to take a leap of faith. He shares a conversation he had with his American counterpart, a Baptist chaplain who has given up any hope of turning the "Hitlerites" away from their beliefs. "He actually told me that 'you might as well preach Christianity to a wall.' Can you imagine that? A Baptist preacher who has given up on saving souls? He told me the Nazis are 'treacherous, mad, and fanatical with their dogma.' And you know what Hugo? I can't disagree with him." Heller picks up a flimsy corrugated box of unused prayer books. "This is not what I imagined when I came here. I thought it would be different. I imagined these books getting a lot of use. This is supposed to be America where freedom of speech and freedom of religion are rights given to everyone. Why not us? We should be protected by the Geneva Convention and the Americans. Instead they look the other way while the intimidation continues."

Hugo leans on his broom, a small pile of sawdust and dirt at his feet. "I've been intimidated since I was forced to join the army. It's just more of the same in here. You know, the Gestapo keep lists, Father."

"Lists? Of what?" He removes a handful of prayer books from the box.

"You name it. They have a list. People who don't salute properly. People who talk too much to the guards. People who attend services here."

"Are you serious? That actually happens?"

"Why do you think this place doesn't get used?" He takes one of the prayer books from Heller's hand to make a point. "Never used. Hell, even the camp library has books that we are forbidden to read. They sit there, gathering dust. Just like these." He defiantly takes the prayer book and puts it in his back pocket. "Anyway, the Gestapo made it clear that anyone attending any type of religious service would be identified and their names would be sent back to Germany, where their families would be punished."

Heller shakes his head. "These poor men, no wonder they are so paranoid. I can't blame them for not showing up. Tell me Hugo, how many men do you think we could actually gather here for worship?"

"Well, Father. If you had asked me that question a few

weeks ago I would have been more optimistic. Now, I think the Nazis have an even heavier presence here after the botched transfers."

"Yes, I saw that first-hand the day I arrived. But I also know there are men like you who are brave enough to stand up to them."

Hugo points to the fading bruises on his face. "Brave or foolish? That depends on who you talk to. To tell you the truth, I'm not even sure any more about some of the anti-Nazis coming into the camp. Some of them are scoundrels. Convicted murderers and thieves. A few communists maybe. They hate Hitler and they make a lot of noise with the guards who actually have very little respect for them. The Americans view them as snitches and troublemakers. They'd rather have the Nazis running things and keeping order, so they don't have to bother with all the complaining." Hugo pushes the broom to the edge of the room and leans it against the wall. "It seems hopeless at times for men who just want to do their time and go home."

"Are you one of those men?"

"Well, I certainly would like to do my time in peace, Father. But I have no wish to go home. My parents worship Hitler and when Germany loses the war, I have no desire to go back to them or a country that will be torn apart by the Allies."

"If you had a choice of anywhere you could go, where would it be?"

"This country. Back to New York maybe to pick up the pieces of a career that was stolen from me. But all of that is just wishful thinking. I know I can't stay in America. And I sure as hell can't live among the Nazis." Hugo hesitates for a moment. He takes a deep thoughtful breath. "Father, the time may come when I may not have a choice. I may have to get away from here, escape I mean. You know we are encouraged to escape, don't you? It is our duty we are told."

"Since when were you interested in pleasing the Nazis? Escaping. That is quite a risk Hugo."

Hugo laughs. It is the most animated Heller has seen him since they began talking. "Well, now. If you run for the fences and ignore their commands to halt, the Americans will definitely shoot you." He mimics a soldier firing his rifle. Then he holds his fingers to his lips and whispers, "But, if you manage to quietly get out of here, there's very little risk once you are on the outside."

"Wishful thinking Hugo. There's always a risk."

"Father, all you have to do is surrender without a fight and they just bring you back, maybe reduce your rations for a few days and that's it. They can't punish you. It's not permitted. Did you hear about the boy scouts?"

Now, Heller is laughing too. "Tell me!"

"Two guys from another camp escaped and were picked up hitchhiking by a truck driver. He asked where they wanted to go, and they said Mexico." Hugo points to his own desert khakis. "He looked at them in these uniforms and asked why Mexico and they told him they were going to a boy scout convention. Can you believe it?"

Heller claps his hands in disbelief. "What happened?"

"The truck driver stopped at the next town and turned them over to the local police. And a few days later they were safely back in camp with no punishment."

"My God, Hugo where did you hear this story?"

"I have my sources. This one came from one of the guards. It's a true story."

"I believe you. Who could make up something like that?" Heller finally turns more serious. He grabs Hugo by both shoulders and offers a suggestion, "Listen, since you have so many good connections around here, can't you just ask to be transferred?"

"I tried that. Others have too, believe me. Instead the Americans thought it was a better idea to get the Nazis out of here and we know how well that turned out. Worse than before."

Heller unfolds two chairs stacked against the side of the narrow room. He opens both and invites Hugo to sit with him. "Do you have a plan?"

"Yes, I've been working on it since the day I got here. I've been scavenging and hoarding materials for months. And getting beat up has been a blessing in disguise with the odd jobs I've been assigned inside the camp. While most men are out on work details, I've been able to move around here during the day and put together a pretty good plan."

"Can you share it with me?"

Hugo smiles. "Sorry Father. It doesn't work that way around here."

Heller frowns. "I understand. I went too far. I apologize."

"Not so fast, chaplain. I didn't say I wouldn't tell you. I just need a favor in exchange."

"What is it?"

Hugo shakes his head and it is Heller who answers for him. "Okay, I get it. Doesn't work that way, right?"

"Pretty much. You promise the favor first before I share my secret."

"Looks like we are about to trust each other, Hugo." Heller leans in closer "I promise. Now, tell me."

In step-by-step fashion he calmly explains to Heller how he has prepared for his escape. Each ingredient of his master plan.

His only assignment outside of camp was working at a livestock farm. In the beginning the guards watched him closely. Eventually, they became lazy and paid little attention to his activity. That meant Hugo worked with little or no supervision. The owners trusted him and applauded his work ethic. The guards considered his tasks routine and harmless. Soon he was visiting the tool shed every day. Ultimately the reward was a pair of wire cutters.

After he was beaten and began working solely inside the camp, his inventory came from numerous sources. When he worked in the camp laundry detail, he collected small change from guards' pockets. When one guard was transferred and left without picking up his laundry, Hugo suddenly had a free pair of pants and a shirt. One of his prized possessions is an old army coat from a guard who thought he was donating a prop for a Christmas show that the prisoners are planning. In return, Hugo whittled a carving of a swastika of all things, but that's what the guard wanted, since it was the closest he would ever get to a real German artifact. So, Hugo gladly obliged and got his jacket in return. Using his ample supply of cigarettes, he bribed a guard for a piece of Camp Huntsville stationery, telling him he just wanted a souvenir of his time as a POW. That letterhead, along with salvaged cardboard, a discarded pen, and a piece of linoleum acquired from general scavenging were all the pieces his artistic skills would require in order to create false military documents that he researched in the library.

And then there were those sacks of potatoes. It was Hugo's greatest challenge. He kept having to go back and get more from his mess hall source, who bled him dry of his extra beer coupons. Not to mention the guards who required plenty of bribes to look the other way. It took a lot of practice, but Hugo eventually carved the equivalent of a rubber stamp, essential to the forging of his documents.

His time at the prison incinerator proved especially profitable, not for what he collected but what he discovered -- the most remote and ideal location to exit the camp with

So, if our little agreement is settled, I have a question for you." Heller says nothing just tilts his head in anticipation. "Do you have anything against the consumption of alcohol? I mean any kind of religious conviction. You know what I mean."

"I think I do. No, I am not opposed to drinking. In fact, I think the rationing of beer is a good thing for the men here. It can be healthy I suppose. But I don't condone excessive drinking. That would be gluttony."

"Ah yes, one of those seven cardinal sins. Never mind the mortal sins we are all preoccupied with, like killing innocent people."

"Well that's an entirely different conversation but that wasn't your question. You asked me if I objected to alcohol and the answer is no. And now my question to you, why is my tolerance of alcohol so important?"

Hugo takes a deep breath, pats his chest and looks around the room. "Let's just say that before I leave, I would like to repay your kindness with a plan to gather your flock, without the help of your hopeless Baptist preacher friend."

"Hugo, I've learned enough about you not to question your ingenuity. So while I have no idea what you're planning, in a strange way it already leaves me hopeful, something I haven't felt in a long time."

Outside the chapel, as the sun begins to fade, two men stand together peering through a middle window. One of them reaches inside his pocket and produces a piece of paper. One side features a printed mess hall menu from several weeks ago. The other side contains a handwritten list. He adds Heller's and Hugo's name.

CHAPTER 33
Camp Huntsville

Flirting

Within weeks, word is spreading quickly throughout the prison community about Stephan's watch repair services. Business for the young Austrian is exploding. After successfully fixing Colonel Warren's two watches, repair requests from his staff alone is keeping Stephan occupied. It doesn't take long for many of the civilians employed there to catch on as well. That means Colonel Warren's worst fear is happening with little or no control of the requests coming to Stephan. Staffers approach his workshop, unable to speak German, and dangle a watch or two that needs his attention. Ironically, it is Corporal Burns who rights the ship. He makes it clear that requests must come through him or the work won't get done. He sets up a system for receiving and filling each job, and he documents Stephan's hours and monitors his work schedule. Best of all, the corporal coordinates everything with the accounting office so receipts are properly kept, and Stephan's wages are accurately recorded. He quickly becomes Stephan's trusted aide with a wonderful side benefit to their frequent interaction: they begin to learn each other's language.

Noticeably absent from all of this is Rose, who can't bring herself to face Stephan. His good nature, friendly smile, and impeccable manners have made him a popular presence in the halls and offices that buzz with garrison personnel. Just like in the cotton fields they call him "Steph" during infrequent appearances outside his little workshop. He is permitted to share coffee and lunch breaks with them. So, it doesn't take long for Rose to notice the number of women in the office who are attracted to this tall, charming, and very handsome guest. She hears them giggling and sharing their fantasies about him and that upsets her even more. She has to admit the obvious. She is jealous. One woman in particular flirts with him whenever she gets the chance and Rose wants to strangle her. Her name is Brenda and she works in the typing pool. She's a nice enough person but suddenly Rose has decided she is completely annoying. That frustration comes to a head in the break room right after a morning staff meeting concludes. Rose is already getting her cup of coffee when she sees Stephan enter the room with Corporal Burns and get in line. Brenda notices him too and converges on the unsuspecting prisoner.

"Good morning Steph. Let me get you that cup of coffee." She raises an empty cup and mimics pouring into it. "A big strong man like you needs plenty of coffee to get going in the morning." Rose rolls her eyes. All Stephan understands is coffee, so he responds politely, "Kaffee, ja." That's good enough for Brenda. She nudges him out of line and ushers him to the front, while the others in line look as annoyed as Rose feels. She escorts him right up to the table where Rose is filling her cup at one of the urns. Brenda brushes Rose aside to fill Stephan's cup. It's the closest Rose has been to him since they were together in his workshop. Their eyes meet, and Stephan deliberately goes cross-eyed as Brenda babbles on. Rose giggles, and everything is okay again. Everything except Brenda who is now holding a cup of black coffee and looking up dreamily into Stephan's eyes. "Let me blow on this a little Steph. Or do you like it hot?" A few of Brenda's friends think she is hilarious, but Rose has had enough. She casually knocks a pitcher of milk off the table and it splatters on the floor then straight up Brenda's skirt. She shrieks, Stephan jumps, and Rose doesn't miss a beat. "Brenda, darling, I am so terribly sorry. Please forgive me. I've made a mess." Brenda is flustered and already heading for the door, but Rose's eyes are elsewhere. She picks up her cup of coffee, blows on it and quietly whispers in German, "Sei sehr vorsichtig. Flirten ist nicht erlaubt." *Be very careful. Flirting is not permitted.*

When Rose stops by the workshop later in the afternoon, she is still mimicking Brenda, making fun of the flirtatious typist, but also teasing Stephan at the same time. "Will you be coming by for coffee again tomorrow, Steph? I'll make sure it's just the right temperature."

"Please, Rose, don't hurt her feelings. She was just being kind."

"Oh, brother, you've got a lot to learn about these ladies."

"Brother, I don't understand?"

" 'Oh brother' is just another expression Stephan. Like 'Oh God' or 'sacré bleu.' A way to express surprise or exasperation."

He frowns. "You are exasperated with me."

"Oh, no. It's just that you are a little naïve, that's all."

"Well maybe you can help me with that, to understand women I mean. For example, how should I respond to a woman who felt comfortable to touch my arm and not let go?" Rose swallows hard but he isn't finished. "A woman who grabbed a handful of my shirt and looked in my eyes and ignored the danger of being found in that sensitive situation? Would it be naïve of me to think that woman is interested in me?"

Rose can't breathe. It's happening again. She can't feel or sense anything around her. Just him. Just her. Until a loud knock on the opened door startles them both. Corporal Burns fills the doorway. "Miss Bauer, could you translate for me, tell

Steph I've got to run this paperwork down to accounting or they'll be all over me in the morning." He smiles as his eyes settle on Rose. "And tell him not to go anywhere."

Rose obliges and relays the message to Stephan who salutes the corporal in jest and replies in English, "yes, sir."

Corporal Burns smiles and replies in German, *"sehr gut."* Nods to both of them, delivers his best attempt at *"danke"* and is off on his errand.

Rose is impressed. "Well, it looks like two boys are learning new language skills."

"He is a good man and it helps with the work around here if we can understand each other's language. Plus, I have been studying at the camp library whenever I get a chance."

"Every day, I learn something new about you."

"I hope you are not surprised or exasperated by what you have learned."

"No Stephan, but there's more I need to know. I need you to be honest with me."

"Of course I will. Please ask me."

Rose pulls up a chair and plops herself down. She removes her glasses and nervously fidgets with them. "Okay, forgive me for being so blunt, but have you killed anyone? Have you killed Americans?"

"No. Never."

"But you fought for Rommel. You've been fighting for three years Stephan."

Stephan shakes his head vehemently. "I did not fight. I was a mechanic. Since 1941 I served in one of the tank maintenance crews attached to the 21st Panzer Division."

"That still sounds deadly to me."

"I have no blood on my hands."

Rose slides her glasses back on and leans back in her chair.

"But you witnessed death and suffering?"

"For the better part of two years. I was in the middle of a mechanized war, Rose. Tanks at the epicenter of every great struggle with the Allies. We were constantly in motion, often repairing tanks during battle, or visiting the remnants of a battlefield... to witness..."

"What? Witness what?"

"The utter destruction of human life beyond anything you can comprehend." *I can't remember my mother's voice, but I can hear those screams.* "You asked me to be honest, Rose. When my unit was mobilized and sent to North Africa, our early victories were kind of a salve for my personal battle over right vs. wrong. I lived a double life, imitating the bravado among my friends while suppressing my contempt for the Nazis. If winning the war meant getting home, I remained willing to play the game. I'm embarrassed to say I looked the other way."

"We all look the other way Stephan. *I want to kill Bobby Ford.* We all leave innocent victims behind." *Clyde and Barbara deserve better.* "Listen, Stephan what happened the other day was my fault. I should never have put us in that situation. You could lose this job and I...." she searches for the right words, so Stephan finishes the thought for her.

"...would be embarrassed? You would not be able to face your family, especially your brothers? You would be a traitor, for befriending the enemy?" He remembers his mother's own words, *never do anything that would shame you or our family.*

Rose offers the truth and hates every word of it. "Stephan, this war has brought us together, but it is also the reason we will always be apart. We are casualties, too."

He knows everything she is saying is true. Millions of people are dying because of the Axis countries. Beyond his isolation in this small American town that has no watchmaker, there are innocent citizens like Rose and brave warriors like her brothers who are suffering mightily at the hands of a misguided army that wears his uniform. He knows she is right. He knows what is beyond his reach today. But he will not be a prisoner forever, so he clings to the hope of what might be. But that something he desires can only happen if she answers one question.

"Today, everything you say is true. But I need to know something. I need you to be honest with me. Do you think I am one of them? A Nazi?"

"No, no, no. I've been around here long enough to know what's going on. I've seen the evil within these camps and I understand how innocent people like you have no choice. I know you did not volunteer, that you were forced to join the German army for the safety of your family. And I know you miss them. I can't imagine what that must feel like." Stephan looks past her towards the doorway and Rose realizes that Corporal Burns is back. By the time she turns around he is already in the room, laying paperwork and another watch in the receiving bin he has set up for Stephan. "I'm back at my post if you need me."

Alone again, Stephan exhales deeply and acknowledges Rose's response. There is relief in his voice, "That means a lot to me. Another question and I promise this will be the last."

"Okay, what is it?

"If these were more innocent times, if our paths had crossed in a different way, could we have been friends?"

"We are friends."

"Could we have been more than friends?"

Rose knows what he is asking, and her answer is uncomplicated, because it is true. "Yes Stephan. I know we could be more than this."

"Then I will pray for more innocent times."

Rose feels the tears pooling at the rim of her glasses. She instinctively reaches for her mother's worn handkerchief and removes her spectacles. Stephan very calmly takes both from her hands. Rose offers no resistance. He wipes the glasses, hands her back the handkerchief as she dabs below her eyes. Then the glasses, which she adjusts as Stephan's smile comes into focus. Nothing more is necessary for now.

"Oh, I almost forgot, I have your grandmother's watch."

"You fixed it. She's going to be so happy."

Stephan wants to boast a bit but knows Rose won't appreciate the challenges he faced, fixing a premium timepiece with marginal parts. "I hope it will continue operating. I am not so confident yet about guaranteeing my work." He reaches inside a manila folder clearly labeled by his friend Corporal Burns. Pulling out the now-familiar satin bag he turns to Rose, takes her right hand and gently presses the sack into her open palm. Then he cups his fingers underneath and gently surrounds her petite hand, like a cocoon guarding a creation that someday will escape darkness and inspire others.

That was hours ago, but now it is the only thought that accompanies Stephan's walk back to his barracks. Corporal Burns escorts him to the compound gate and now he is alone, making his way along a path filled with the kind of thoughts he used to enjoy walking home from school in Vienna. About a girl he liked. Maybe a moment they had alone. An innocent laugh or funny joke they happened to share. Memories that made it a good day. He would return home and tell his mother, who would listen closely then remind him to be a gentleman at all times. Stephan wonders if his mother would approve of Rose. Yes, he knows she would. So too would his father.

Waiting for him as he enters the barracks are two men who are not part of his company. One is Schroeder, the Nazi who beat Hugo on the train and somehow escaped the prisoner transfer. The other man is almost as large as Schroeder, but his uniform is different than the faded desert khakis so common among the Afrika Korps. Maybe he's a more recent prisoner, probably surrendered in Italy. None of that matters. What Stephan is quite sure of without even asking is that he's another bully, another Nazi. That's the only company Schroeder keeps. Both of them are sitting on Stephan's top bunk, sagging under their weight. Schroeder jumps off the mattress and lands with a thud. His crony remains on the bunk, peering down at Stephan.

Schroeder, arms folded, is the only one who speaks. "Jurgen, we haven't seen much of each other. How is your friend Hugo?"

"I'm really not sure. We also don't see much of each other."

"That's right, you've got a new job now, spending plenty of time with the Americans, I hear."

Already, Stephan doesn't like where this is going. "It's a job, that's all."

"Just a job? In the American's headquarters? Surely, you have seen and heard things that would be of interest to us, haven't you?"

"I don't know what you mean."

Schroeder looks up at the other bully and sneers. "Well, let me tell you what I mean. There are a lot of people around here who are watching you closely. You've managed to get by so far without too much trouble although your friend has certainly paid the price." His words are a sharp reminder that Hugo's beating was in retaliation for Stephan's false bravado with Werner.

"What is it you want?"

"Information you fool. You spend all day with these people. Give us information that we can use."

"Use for what? I don't understand." Stephan sits down on a cot opposite his bunk and begins to unlace his boots. "I work in a repair shop all day."

"You mingle with them. You share coffee and lunch with

them. You are closer than any of us. Bring us something. Guard schedules. Notes or reports left around. Something. Or else you will have to pay the consequences. Or maybe it will be your friends who will suffer, maybe your attractive little American friend."

Stephan lies immediately. "I don't know what you are talking about. And who gives you the authority to threaten the Americans?"

"Authority? The Americans are our enemy. We are sworn to defeat them, even in here. Don't tell me about authority you weakling. Just give us something valuable or else you'll wish you were back in the desert repairing tanks. Do you understand?"

Stephan's weak reply reflects his total despair. "I will do what I can."

"Well, that's a start. We'll be back here in a week and see what you come up with." Schroeder turns to the other thug and motions with his head that they are leaving. The man jumps off the bunk and continues to stare at Stephan, who smiles grimly and adds sarcastically, "it was such a pleasure to meet you. Very charming"

He can hear them laughing outside as their vile voices fade away. Darkness again. People he must protect.

CHAPTER 34
Camp Huntsville

Requiem

It is late afternoon in Camp Huntsville and Hugo's plan to conceal his escape gear in the chapel is successfully completed. From mid-morning through lunch, he moved back and forth from the chapel to various locations throughout the compound where he had carefully secured most of his materials over the last several weeks. Because he doesn't trust any of the men in his company, none of it was stored in his barracks. Too much hard work and ingenuity was spent creating precious keys to his escape. It would only take one scoundrel to ruin it all. He knows his paranoia is getting the best of him.

The last few days he sensed even greater scrutiny, so he feels relief when the final items, his coveted army jacket and pants, are carefully folded into the box. There it is. Everything. He slides the box against the wall and stacks the rest of the cartons containing Heller's prayer books on top. This is real now. He's going to do this soon. He's narrowed down his escape window, giving serious consideration to the evening of Thanksgiving, when he knows the Americans will be preoccupied. That's less than a week away but Hugo is surprisingly calm. He's confident his plan will succeed. In the meantime, he has one more commitment to keep, the promise he made to Heller to recruit enough souls to fill this chapel. He pulls on a pair of soiled grey work gloves and heads toward the exit.

Sitting outside the building is a battered wheelbarrow used to carry materials down to the incinerator whenever he is on trash detail. It is a common sight to see Hugo pushing it between the compounds, collecting litter as he goes. It's as ordinary as watching rotation of the guards every few hours or the incinerator belch smoke every afternoon. So, there is nothing unusual about the sagging cart filled with a large amount of debris parked near the chapel path. Hugo tugs his gloves and gently lifts some of the trash from the top of the heap. He glances casually to see if anyone remains in the area and is relieved there are no guards and very little foot traffic. Then he reaches in and pulls out a burlap potato sack, placing one hand under its fragile contents as he lowers it to the ground. He then returns to the cart for a second sack, retrieves it with equal care and gingerly walks into the chapel, his gloved hand now firmly squeezing the gathered neck of the bag. Inside, the faint sound of clinking glass can be heard as he lowers the sack to the chapel floor. He wastes no time returning outside and gathering the remaining bag. A cool breeze sweeps him up the path that leads back to the chapel. It has already been a busy day, but he feels invigorated, like he's finally doing something about his life. He thinks of his disapproving parents and feels no guilt or remorse.

Once inside, Hugo again checks his surroundings. He walks by the windows on each side of the room to make sure nobody is watching. Satisfied, he returns to the two sacks and removes several large jars with dented lids that once held pickles but now contain a russet-colored liquid. He opens one of the jars, hesitates, then sticks his nose close to the rim and slowly inhales. He looks surprised and nods approvingly. Next, he brings the jar up to his chapped lips and carefully sips. Immediately, he begins to cough, trying to catch his breath as the liquid sears his throat and his eyes begin to water. He wipes his runny nose with the sleeve of his shirt and sips again. This time he coughs only briefly. He is satisfied. Hugo's first batch of Camp Huntsville moonshine is ready for consumption.

For months, he tinkered with his recipe, throwing out early batches and resuming his research in the library until he settled on the right ingredients. Scraps from oranges, and potatoes were plentiful. Apples were more elusive, but raisins were the hardest to secure. He often had to pluck them from the raisin bread served at breakfast. He saved his sugar rations and was able to bribe the prison baker for yeast by plying him with cigarettes. Hugo and a couple of his trusted friends from the Sunday kitchen detail would combine the ingredients and then take the jars back to their compounds where they would secretly let them ferment in the blazing Texas sun. It was no secret to the prisoners, regardless of their loyalties, what was going on. Alcohol has no special kinship with Nazis, communists, agnostics, or criminals. Most prisoners wanted to taste the result of this makeshift distilling process. The key was keeping it from the guards. After all his hard work the last thing Hugo wanted was to have his whiskey confiscated and consumed by some of the lazy Americans who already cleared out his cigarette inventory.

It is now close to 5:00 and dusk is quickly approaching. Most of the prisoners have returned from outside work details and will be enjoying some free time before heading to mess halls within their compounds. The door to the chapel squeaks loudly, announcing a visitor as it opens slowly. Hugo recognizes the ruddy complexion of Otto, a fellow jazz enthusiast and one of his kitchen cronies. He dispenses with the pleasantries and asks Hugo immediately, "Do you have it?"

"I do, and it is very passable I might add." Hugo picks up one of the sealed bottles. "Get this back to your compound without the guards seeing it and remember your promise."

"How many times are you going to remind me, Hugo?"

"Until I'm sure you're listening Otto. What is our agreement?"

"Before I share this finely distilled whiskey with trustworthy people, I will make them promise to come to the chapel on Sunday at 9:00 to get to know Heller."

"He's a priest Otto, for Christ's sake. Show him a little respect."

"Okay, Hugo, relax. I will invite them to meet *Father* Heller at 9:00 on Sunday. Is that better?"

"It's better only if they show up." Hugo removes the lid and sips his whiskey, this time allowing it to numb the inside of his mouth before swallowing. He clenches his teeth and says, "Let's hope enough people have some guts around here to take on the Nazis. It's time somebody grows some balls." He offers the jar to Otto, who takes a far more generous swig and pays for it.

Gasping, he says, "I thought you said this was passable."

"It's whiskey, Otto, not apple juice. Now get moving."

Hugo repeats the same instructions with several more of his friends who stop by the chapel to pick up their whiskey. He has also shared a sip with each of them. It is close to 7:00 by the time he finally exits the chapel. *You are going to pay for this in the morning.* He steadies himself, leaning against the tarpaper wall of the building and struggles to get his bearings. His head now spinning from the whiskey. *Which way are the barracks?* He shuffles slowly away and walks directly into the wheelbarrow, striking his left shin. Already off balance, he ends up on the ground. He's oblivious to the pain in his leg. The sun has already set so it is difficult to see his limp body curled up behind the wheelbarrow. He makes no effort to get to his feet.

Two hours later, Hugo is awakened by the sounds of men singing and laughing nearby. He sits up on the ground, buries his head in his knees, and smells the vomit immediately. *What a fool. Never again.* He can't remember what he did with the whiskey jar. Did he leave it in the chapel? Is it somewhere on the ground? At this moment he doesn't care. He needs to get back to the barracks and get some sleep. He's able to stand up, surprises himself that he can even walk. Begins to move slowly. Not sure of the time but figures it must be close to the 10:00 curfew. He veers away from the path and grabs the chain link fence that separates two of the prisoner compounds. He sags away from the fence, his fingertips barely holding him upright, and vomits again. The vile taste of fermented fruit lingers on his tongue. In the distance, a guard whistles softly in one of the towers. Hugo takes a deep breath and continues towards the barracks now only twenty yards away. He stumbles into his building, oblivious to the disdainful eyes of almost every man watching him. Cold, condemning eyes that follow him, the way a hunter stalks its prey. He collapses on his bunk, rolls over on his stomach, and is asleep in less than a minute. The men resume their conversation in hushed tones, not because they are polite or respectful. They are merely returning to the whispering campaign around Hugo that has been sustained far too long. His time is running out.

Midnight. The camp is quiet. Too late in the year now for the whining song of the cicadas. Instead there are hushed, agitated voices that dent the silence around Hugo's bed. His drunken stupor leaves him oblivious until a rag is shoved into his mouth and he is violently awakened and pulled to his feet. Still semi-conscious, he is dragged across the floor by his elbows towards the rear of the room where a black pot-belly stove blends into the darkened space. Off to the right is a narrow washroom with a single sink that rests unevenly on the wall – exposing the pipes below. A faulty faucet delivers a steady drip into a rust-stained basin.

Matches are struck, and several candles are lit within a small circle of prisoners surrounding an empty chair that is placed in front of the stove. Hugo is now fully awake, his eyes blazing with fear and confusion. He is dragged to the chair by two of the larger men in the group – one of them is Schroeder, who produces a 6-inch knife with a rusty serrated edge, and presses it into Hugo's throat, careful not to puncture the skin.

"I am going to take the rag out of your mouth. If you make any noise, I will slit your throat. Do you understand?"

Hugo closes his eyes and nods. Schroeder pulls the rag slowly from his mouth. Hugo gasps for air, begins panting and eases himself back into the chair, trying to collect his thoughts. "You are still a stupid piece of shit."

Schroeder raises his free hand, ready to strike a blow across Hugo's face. One of the others, a recent prisoner transfer who Hugo barely knows, grabs Schroeder's arm and spins him around. Barely inches from his face, he emphatically whispers, "No marks, remember? No marks."

Schroeder turns back to Hugo, who now understands what is happening. He tries to remain calm and keep his wits about him, but his knees are trembling. Schroeder begins wiping the knife on the rag, his voice more irritated than before. "Not a word out of you." Hugo can barely breathe let alone speak. He searches for a friendly face, already resigned to his core that none exists. The uneven light from the flickering candles reveals a chin or a forehead or the merciless eyes of the men surrounding him. They tighten the circle but say nothing. In the distance the high-pitched scream of a red fox pierces the silence. Finally, it is one of the senior officers, a recently arrived member of the Gestapo, who speaks.

"Private, from the moment you arrived here in this country you have abandoned your duty as a soldier of the Reich." His voice shows no emotion. "You fraternize with the American guards, speaking their language and trading information. You have shown little or no respect for your superiors and fellow prisoners." Hugo finds Schroeder and glares at him, the way a defendant in a trial would scowl at a witness who is lying. Schroeder attempts to stare back but quickly relents and looks briefly away. When he looks again, Hugo is still glaring, a satisfied sneer on his lips. The officer continues his assault on Hugo's character. "You have been conspiring to recruit prisoners to attend religious services, bribing them with liquor. You play jazz music and encourage others to listen, when you know it is the music of the Jews and Negroes. Above all, you have been accused of treason." He lets the words sink in, but Hugo offers no reaction other than to shake his head. Not in denial, but in utter contempt for such ludicrous charges. And then the verdict. "It is the decision of this committee that you have been expelled from the German community of fellowship."

Hugo bursts into laughter. He holds his hand up to his mouth, mocking his accusers, his eyes wild with disdain. "How can I be expelled from the German community when I barely even lived in Germany. I was raised here in America."

Before his accuser can respond the fox, so close now it feels like it could be in the same room, barks again. The sharp sound is more unnerving to Hugo than the words of the officer, "Silence, private! You are an embarrassment to your family."

"And I am embarrassed to wear this uniform." These are the last words Hugo will ever speak. Schroeder grabs his hair and pulls his head back forcing Hugo's mouth to open. He stuffs the rag deep into his throat. A belt is tightened around both his ankles while his hands are taped behind his back. He is dropped to the floor, unable to speak or move. They roll him on his belly. He is barely breathing through a broken nose that never healed properly. With his right cheek resting on the floor, he is conscious of Schroeder and the others moving silently behind him. He is eye level with one of the candles sitting on the floor. He focuses on the flame and feels a peculiar sense of calm. Maybe it's the whiskey. Or maybe he just wants it to be over.

It takes forever for Hugo to die. Three men lift him up and pass his head through a noose, already secured to a low-hanging rafter in the washroom. The noose is tightened around his neck and then he is released. If Hugo had been dropped from a greater height the speed of his descent and the distance traveled would have broken his neck, killing him immediately. But his executioners slowly suspend him from the ceiling. It is a cruel purposeful act, so he will die slowly from strangulation. Hugo's natural reaction is to reach for the noose and pry it away from his neck, but his hands are still bound behind his back. His dangling feet are inches from the floor, his toes desperately trying to reach something, anything that will support his body and let him breathe again. As Hugo slips away, the men who condemned him go about their business as if they are cleaning up after a party. The single chair is folded and stacked. Candles are snuffed out. The rag is rudely pulled from Hugo's mouth. The tape is ripped away from hands that no longer desire life. Finally, Schroeder removes the belt that secured Hugo's ankles and slips it back around his waist, carefully passing it through each loop, indifferent to the man whose barely beating heart is about to expire.

The light in the washroom is turned off. The men return routinely to their beds, left to reflect on behavior defined by their own inner voices. It is 1:30 AM. Four hours until roll call. No one speaks. The fox has retreated, and an almost reverent silence consumes the camp. Hugo is alone. The steady drip of the faucet his only requiem.

CHAPTER 35
Camp Huntsville

Quicksand

Hundreds of yards away in the furthest prisoner compound from the chapel, Stephan is feeling the effects of a fitful night's sleep. He digs his hands deep into the frayed pockets of his field coat. Schroeder's threats consume him. *You will have to pay the consequences*.

He turns to Franz, who shares each plodding step away from the mess hall as the two return to their barracks. He's been a sympathetic ear and Stephan needs someone to trust right now. It doesn't take long for Franz to understand Stephan's predicament with Schroeder.

"Steph, I wish I could make you feel better but these guys are ruthless. Look, I'm not stupid. I know it's just a matter of time before they move beyond the threats. Everything is calculated. Everything is about sending a message."

"Believe me Franz, I don't think Schroeder is bluffing. I'm scared for what he might do." *Maybe it will be your friends who will suffer.* Stephan points to a sentry tower, its long protracted shadow stretching across their path. "Don't you find it ridiculous that we have no protection from the threats? They will kill us if we try to leave but they can't safeguard us from one another."

"Can't or won't? In the end it doesn't really matter. This is our new life and death struggle, and it's not going to change." Most of their barrack mates are congregating outside on this lazy Sunday. At first Stephan doesn't notice a stranger within the ranks, but Franz spots him immediately. "What's he doing here?"

"Who?" Stephan is unsure where to even look.

"Over there. Near the gate. That's Heller, the chaplain. He must be desperate to find enough guys with the balls to attend Sunday services. I guess the whiskey didn't work."

"What are you talking about?"

"Boy you really are preoccupied. Your buddy Hugo cooked up a batch of whiskey and was peddling it in return for prisoners in the pews."

"Ha! That sounds like Hugo. So that's the toxic chaplain. I heard the crap they've been spewing about him too. Threatening us to stay away from him." Stephan smiles broadly. "So while most of them keep their distance like good little Nazis it doesn't surprise me a bit that Hugo is trying to help him."

As they get closer to the cluster of prisoners it's clear that Heller is looking for someone. A couple of the men talking to him scan the crowd then suddenly stop when they see Stephan and Franz approaching the group. Stephan notices the exchange.

"Are they pointing at us? They are. Look, he's coming over here. Not very friendly looking."

Heller slowly approaches, nervously twirling the crucifix hanging from his neck. "Which of you is Private Jurgen?"

Stephan salutes. "I'm Jurgen, sir"

"Could I speak to you privately?"

Stephan looks at Franz, who begins moving away. "I'll be inside if you need me Steph." He bows slightly to Heller. "Sir."

Heller never takes his eyes off Stephan. "I'm afraid I have

some bad news for you about Hugo."

"I was afraid of this. I just heard about the whiskey. Is he in some kind of trouble? Did he..."

"He died last night." Heller stares at the ground.

"Hugo? Dead?" Stephan drops to both knees as he sags against Heller. "Please. Not Hugo." He leans back on his heels looking up at Heller. Despair paralyzes him. "I, I don't..."

Heller squats down and whispers gently, "your friend hung himself. They found him this morning."

"No! Impossible. That's impossible. Who told you that? They are lying!" Stephan scratches the cool soil of a distant land that will soon claim the remains of a true friend.

"Come on, let's get you up." Heller tries to assist him but Stephan is shaking uncontrollably. The chaplain loosens his grip and instead sits next to him. "Hugo considered you a dear friend."

Stephan buries his head in open palms and sobs. He struggles to speak through his tears. "Not a friend. Just another coward he couldn't help. He was avoiding me and I didn't even try to reach out."

Heller leans in and whispers, " No, he was protecting you Stephan. He was looking out for you. Listen, I am going to have our Sunday service in about an hour. I don't know how many of the men will show up, but that doesn't matter." Heller stands and offers his hand. "Let's show these people that Hugo's life mattered. That's the least we can do for him."

Stephan grabs Heller's hand firmly and pulls himself up. "Thank you, Father. I'd like that."

"Good. Come with me now. It's early but you can help me set up."

Stephan wipes his face, runs both hands through his hair. He feels unsteady on his feet but wills himself to take that first step. He thinks of Hugo's parents – wondering how long it will take to get word to them. Worse still, will they even care? *Of course. He was their only son.* Then he remembers his conversation with Hugo after the football match and he's not so sure. *They would disown me if they knew how I was behaving.* Stephan can't imagine losing the love of his parents. But the person he most wants to see right now is Rose.

Franz' voice breaks through. "Stephan, I am so sorry."

"It was just a matter of time Franz. That life and death struggle you were just talking about. Now it's real for us."

"Well, for some of us. Most of these bastards don't care. Why should they? To them, men like Hugo...and us. We are weak and useless."

"Not any more Franz." Stephan points to Heller waiting by the open gate to the compound. "Right now I'm going to say a proper farewell to a courageous friend. Why don't you join me?"

Franz' answer is not what Stephan expects. "I can't. I know I should but I just can't." He looks away, unwilling to face Stephan's disappointment.

Stephan joins Heller and they begin their journey toward the chapel. Heller is silent, allowing Stephan to grieve. Within minutes, Stephan is talking.

"I'm angry but I blame myself."

"This is a bitter pill to swallow. Don't be so hard on yourself."

"Easy for you to say, Father. You don't know what it's like to carry this guilt."

Stephan is not expecting Heller's passionate response.

"Listen to me! Stop feeling sorry for yourself. Do you think you are the only with a guilty conscience in this war?" They reach the narrow path that leads to the chapel. Heller stops walking but his passion intensifies. "Evil people have put us in this quicksand. Evil people tore us away from all that is good.

Millions of people are doing things they regret in this war. None of us are innocent." Heller's voice trails off and he almost whispers, "none of us."

"Even you Father?"

Heller exhales deeply. "Even me Stephan. You are here because of surrender. I am here because I betrayed an innocent Red Cross worker, an innocent girl whose fate was in my hands. But I lied so I could come to America, escape the Nazis, and survive until the end of the war."

"I'm not sure I understand."

"Of course not, how could you. Sometimes I have a hard time understanding it myself."

"But you are doing good work here."

Heller laughs. "Am I? Sometimes I wonder."

"You are helping me right now. You and I are not evil people. We are doing the best we can."

Heller slaps Stephan on the back. "Who's helping who here? Let's make a promise to each other that we can only live our lives moving forward and we will make the most of each opportunity, starting with today."

"For Hugo."

"Yes, for Hugo."

"And for...What is her name, the Red Cross worker?"

"Sofia, my sacrificial lamb."

Stephan actually laughs at the chaplain. "What happened with the new start. You've already broken your promise!"

"No, no. Every day I already beg God to protect her. I can only hope she has forgiven me and is praying for my blemished soul. For now, that has to be enough."

CHAPTER 36
Washington, DC

Home of the Brave

Ralph flows through the great hall of Union Station. Part of a muted kaleidoscope of military dress that dominates the landscape of travelers carving their way through caverns of marble, granite, and gold. It is impossible to stand still as the wave of passengers surges towards crowded train platforms or escapes to the congested USO canteen that looms ahead. Ralph has been told that over 200,000 people pass through here on a single day. Today, he thinks that figure could easily double. High above, hanging from one of the massive arches is a floating banner that reminds these wartime travelers of their mission. "Americans will always fight for liberty" is displayed at the bottom of the banner that also features split images of colonial soldiers and today's warriors in full battle gear.

Very few people are paying attention to this display of patriotism. Just like Ralph, most are hoping to get home in time for a rare Thanksgiving reprieve. Huntsville. His sister. Oma and Uncle Pete. Clyde, of course. He knows that his brother Henry is still far away and won't be coming home anytime soon. That's what it always comes down to these days. Duty first.

That reminds him of the paperwork he carries. The good news he was hoping for. Ralph has signed orders for the transfer of Heller from Camp Huntsville, Texas, to Fort Meade, Maryland, the official destination that provides cover for Ralph's top secret work at P.O. Box 1142. He has mixed emotions about seeing Heller again. In one sense he is an adversary who got the best of Ralph and should be punished for his actions. On the other hand, Ralph now has a chance to secure an ideal stool pigeon who could serve him well for the duration of the war. He decides it's worth the tradeoff. Now on the platform, Ralph double checks the departure board and confirms he's in the right place. He puffs smoke from another cigarette and watches a steam locomotive belching its way to a full stop while conductors continue to announce its arrival. Soon, he'll be on his way, the first leg of his journey taking him to Atlanta, where he'll have an extended layover. Then finally on to Houston, where Uncle Pete will hopefully be waiting for a brief ride home to Huntsville. There's a last call for passengers to board his train. He flips the cigarette onto the tracks and looks at his watch. It is 10:00 AM.

That means in Camp Huntsville it is 9:00 AM Central Time. The hour for Heller's Sunday Service that Hugo was determined to organize. Outside the chapel, the wheelbarrow lies on its side, trash and debris long ago scattered by the wind. Stephan watches as Heller grabs both handles and returns the empty cart to its original spot. He spies the bottle of whiskey, its amber contents reflecting the morning sun. Stephan picks up the jar, unscrews the lid and turns it upside down, letting the whiskey disappear into the earth. He tosses the empty container into the wheelbarrow and pushes it down the path toward the chapel. By now, the news of Hugo's death has gripped the camp. The Americans have already concluded that Hugo hung himself sometime last night, his body discovered when he was absent for this morning's roll call. The thoughtless conclusion was predictable, and it sickens Stephan. *Evil people have torn us away from all that is good.* His guilt is marginalized. And grief is tempered by too many years of war. Now, it is anger that remains.

His mood is darker than char from a grasslands wildfire. Despite all the ugliness that he has witnessed in this conflict -- killing and suffering and needless sacrifice -- nothing compares to this cowardly act of men who wear the German uniform. None of the usual excuses apply here: A soldier's duty? Self-defense? Kill or be killed? None of it. Hugo is gone because he was murdered. The conclusion of suicide is preposterous. His anger surges. He hears the chapel door open, revealing a poignant and unexpected diversion.

Prisoners. At first, perhaps a handful, then so many more. Scores of them maybe, and yet still they come. Faces he recognizes along with strangers. All with somber expressions, hands holding caps in mourning and in reverence to this place of prayer. Some just nod. Others greet Heller, "Hello Father." Otto, approaches Heller and whispers softly, "Father, we'd like to have a memorial service for Hugo but we're not sure how to go about that."

Stephan sees a change in Heller's demeanor. He is serene yet empowered by this bold display of friendship and unbridled courage to publicly defy the threat of Nazi reprisals. "Of course, son." He points to the walls where the chairs are stacked. Let's set these up ten across." The men immediately respond. They will need more than a hundred chairs. Heller opens one of the boxes containing prayer books, pages through the paperback and easily finds what he needs. "Yes, this will do nicely." The prisoners again follow his lead and open the other boxes, placing a book on each chair. Otto reaches for the last unopened box but Heller gently intercepts him. "Different materials in there, for a different occasion." He carries the box to the front of the room and slides it underneath the makeshift altar.

For the next 30 minutes, Heller's true vocation commands the room. He leads the group through formal prayers and the men respond in earnest. Outwardly, there is a conviction and strength to his voice. Somehow for Stephan it quenches his thirst to do the right thing. *Maybe this will show them that more brave men cannot be silenced.* Heller offers the opportunity for any man to say a few words about their friend. There is nothing powerful or eloquent offered. Just the sincere observations about someone who will be missed. Most of the comments elicit smiles and strong nods of approval or affirmation. "He was always making trouble." "He made me laugh." "He wouldn't back down from anything or anybody." "He had more beer coupons and cigarettes than anybody else in this camp." Stephan finally stands and looks at the men around him. His words offer more than just an observation about Hugo. They express profound guilt. "We behaved like cowards compared to our brave friend."

Otto eases the tension, adding, "I hope he's listening to Dizzy Gillespie in heaven right now." That sparks Heller, who steps away from the podium and moves around the rows of chairs that occupy the front half of the chapel. He reaches the back of the room and raises a phonograph cover. He lifts up a record, blows the dust away and settles it back on the gramophone. Heller smiles as he winds the machine, explaining, "This wasn't his favorite, but he liked the beat." The Glen Miller selection begins to play, bringing a smile to every man as weathered boots tap the chapel floor. Stephan feels better for the first time in hours. *Hugo couldn't have asked for a finer farewell.*

THREE DAYS BEFORE THANKSGIVING

* * *

CHAPTER 37
Camp Huntsville

Choices

The national holiday is less than three days away. FDR has already issued a national proclamation setting November aside as Food Fights for Freedom Month. To the citizens of Huntsville, there is stoic preparation for a day of mixed blessings from the scattered farms to the tree-lined neighborhoods within the city limits. Food is purchased, but with utmost respect for saving and storing more for the troops than for their own tables. It is a time of thanks tempered by grief and loss and separation.

To the Americans charged with oversight of Camp Huntsville there is a heightened sense of foreboding. Nothing is normal within the prisoner compounds. The suspicious suicide of Hugo, combined with several beatings of anti-Nazis over the past weekend, has everyone on full alert. American guards are less approachable. Nazis are emboldened by the escalating terror. For Stephan the agitation is undeniable. He also knows his own life is at risk if he doesn't deliver information to Schroeder. He knows he is living on borrowed time. Yesterday was a sure sign of that. After the service for Hugo, Stephan made his way to the barracks, wishing the day would race by, so he could see Rose again. As he got closer to his quarters, he saw Schroeder along with the man who visited him just a few days ago. He knows his name now. Captain Siegel. Rotten teeth and an even darker soul. Trouble since he arrived here during the bungled transfers. The fact that he has bonded with Schroeder says it all. Stephan averted their gaze as they chose to walk toward him. He finally had the courage to look up as they were passing so Schroeder's message was in his face. "Time is running out Jurgen." Stephan went straight to his barracks unable to think clearly and unable to sleep. *Why is this happening to me? What would father tell me to do?*

Knowing that sleep would never arrive, he laid on top of the single wool blanket that covered his cot. He tried to close his eyes, but fear ruled over fatigue. His discomfort was aggravated by something in the small of his back. Something under the covers. He stood up and looked at a small mound in the middle of the cot He didn't notice it before. Now he recalled not only recognizing the shape but smelling it. Slowly, he peeled the covers back and the odor of a chicken carcass hit his nostrils. Bones stuck to the sheet. Congealed gizzards clumped to the mattress like spitballs to a blackboard. It was a warning. Usually the last message delivered before the Holy Ghost visits. *Time is truly running out.* Stephan walked the barracks most of the night, but he survived.

Now, without any breakfast in his stomach, he stands at the final chain link fence that separates the prisoner compounds from the American garrison. It is more than just a physical boundary. It marks the difference between an ideology sustained by terror versus a way of life built on free will. Stephan knows it is not perfect in America. But he also knows that Americans are free to express their opinions and to change things they don't like with their voice and their vote. On the other side, waiting for him is Corporal Burns. "Guten morgen." Stephan returns his new friend's authentic greeting with a distracted smile. How ironic, he is leaving a group of men who are supposed to be his comrades, his safety net, and instead he feels less threatened and more welcomed by people who don't even speak his language. Burns escorts him toward the workshop, more like two friends wandering through the park than guard and prisoner. Burns is unaware of Stephan's grief or his connection to Hugo. For the American it's a simple fact. A prisoner hung himself over the weekend. It's happened before. It will probably happen again. The depth of the event and the terror it has unleashed is lost on him.

Waiting for them outside Stephan's workshop is Rose. Despite his mounting fears, everything slows down when Stephan sees her. He can't help but think back to their time together in the cotton fields. That was just a few weeks ago but now everything seems out of control. She is holding a small wooden box containing the most recent watch repairs that were dropped off at her farm. Stephan immediately notices the purple satin bag sitting on top. It stands out like a lone sapphire protruding from a sea of colorless gems. Oma is making a return. He hopes he hasn't let her down. Corporal Burns acknowledges Rose and the box filled with watches and says, "Stephan, many repairs for you today." Rose begins to translate but Stephan politely interrupts in English, "I understand. Repairs. Thank you corporal." The German word for "repairs" is *reparaturen*, close enough for Stephan to comprehend. He repeats for Rose, "I understand."

"Wunderbar, Stephan. Wunderbar!" Corporal Burns is clapping his hands, applauding, and sharing one of the few new words he has mastered in a limited attempt to expand his German vocabulary. Stephan again smiles politely but he is distant. Rose senses that something is wrong. "Okay corporal, I think that's enough for our language exchange this morning, let's allow the private to get to work."

"Yes, ma'am." He remains in the room.

"I'm going to go over these orders with him, but I'll be speaking German, corporal."

"Understood ma'am." His feet are still cemented to the floor.

Finally, it is a nurse from the hospital who leans in the doorway and pries him loose. "Corporal, we need you right away. We've got a couple prisoners coming in who were pretty badly beaten last night. Looks like there may be more on the way. The hospital is on high alert. Come on corporal, move it please."

Corporal Burns is not even out the door, but Stephan already recognizes what is happening. His lips are pronouncing what his mind has already sorted through. "*Der Heilige Geist.*" The Holy Ghost. "What do you mean Stephan? What are you talking about?" Rose carelessly tosses the box of watches onto the worktable and presses him "What is going on over there?"

Without dramatic flair, Stephan explains as if reading a definition from a dictionary. "A pillowcase is thrown over a man's head and he is beaten by assailants he can never identify. Beaten so violently he may never survive or wish he hadn't."

"Oh my God. That's horrible."

"It is not a pleasant experience."

The way he says this. The far-away look in his eyes. Rose deciphers his body language and raises her hands to her lips. "Oh my God this happened to you, didn't it?"

"It was a long time ago. It made a coward out of me."

"I, I don't understand. You are not a coward."

"Rose, did you hear about the prisoner who committed suicide over the weekend?"

"That's all they were talking about in the break room this morning. You knew him?"

Stephan's voice cracks, "He was my best friend and he had more courage than I will ever have." There is more activity in the hallway now. The hospital entrance has become a focal point, mostly for the curious. Corporal Burns' voice can be heard above the din, instructing personnel to get back to work and to keep the hallways clear. Rose tries to bring Stephan back from his pain.

"What was his name, your friend?"

"Hugo."

"Why did Hugo take his life?"

"He didn't kill himself Rose. He was murdered. His fate was sealed by a kangaroo court." He scoffs, "They call it a court of honor. But they have no honor."

She nods toward the hallway and the hospital beyond. "And these victims this morning, they were beaten by these same men?"

Stephan pulls himself up on to the worktable, his long legs almost touching the floor. "I'm just guessing but they probably were singled out because they attended a memorial service for Hugo." *And I'm probably next.*

"Did you attend the service?"

"Yes, I...."

"Oh, God. You...You're in danger too? Rose's concern for Stephan is real. It cuts through the sadness and chaos. Stephan feels it too. He wants to tell her the truth. Wants her to know that his time is limited too. That very soon they will grow impatient with his unwillingness to spy on the Americans. Laughable but true. He could share it all, so she can worry even more. But he wouldn't do that to her. He realizes that he also cares. Perhaps too much. So, he lies. "Don't worry, I am not at risk. I'll be safe."

Her relief is undeniable. And then that moment is upon them. When two people connect at precisely the same time. A shared sensation that requires no explanation. Seconds pass. The hallway is silent, void of people banished to their offices. Corporal Burns is yards away but committed to guarding his post. He won't be visiting any time soon. Time doesn't matter now, it's as meaningless as the broken watches that wait for Stephan. He slides off the table and walks to the doorway. Rose watches as he peers into the hallway. She wants that hallway to stay empty. Stephan slowly pushes the door shut. It clicks into place. His palm is still on the cool surface of the door. Everything else is white hot. He is not afraid.

* * *

The afternoon is now pressing toward dusk. Rose is bewildered and overwrought by the day's events. *Who am I supposed to care about? Have I crossed the line?* She ambles by Colonel Warren's office -- watching him carefully. Everyone knows his strategy to eliminate Nazi elements within the camp has failed catastrophically. The problem today is greater than ever. She sees the paperwork so she also knows that manpower demands of the war abroad continue to challenge his ability to adequately guard the prisoners and maintain a semblance of order within their ranks. Once again, his best option is to leave the Nazis in charge -- a choice that now troubles Rose in a very different way . The upcoming holiday also means juggling guard assignments and stretching his men way too thin. Rose watches him shuffle papers on his uncluttered desk. Regardless of the chaos surrounding him, his work pace is always the same. Organized and tidy. A battered leather desk pad that has traveled with him since his West Point days is perfectly centered on the work surface. A plain black government-issued inbox for his mail is perched on the top left corner of his desk. On the far right is a telephone with a long cord that drops off the side and snakes its way to a single phone jack affixed to a pine strip that passes as a baseboard.

Finally, she knocks and enters his office. "Colonel, here are the non-military staff assignments for the holiday weekend."

"Thank you, Miss Bauer."

Rose deposits them on his desk and can't help but notice the framed picture that smiles back at him. His son Todd, who was an early casualty of Operation Torch in North Africa. He was the only child of Warren and his wife, Mary. Rose has never met her but she imagines a brave woman alone at home. Shattered. Warren reaches across the desk pad for his pocket watch that was recently repaired by Stephan. Her boss has gone out of his way to acknowledge that it is now keeping perfect time. On more than one occasion Warren has also referred to his newly repaired timepiece as "one of the few things around here that is working smoothly." He flips open the brass casing of the watch. Rose exits his office and glances at the hallway clock. It is almost 3:00.

At that moment, not far from Warren's office, Corporal Burns stands with Stephan in his workshop reviewing the day's accomplishments. This now-predictable routine means categorizing repairs that have been completed. The amount of time required to finish each job is noted and documented by the American. This will be forwarded to the accounting department, so an invoice can be created, and Stephan's compensation properly recorded. Not once has Stephan given any thought to how much he is earning for his services. Since this morning, his only consideration right now is Rose and his passionate desire to stay alive for her. He regrets not sharing more earlier today when they were together. He also feels guilty that his thoughts lately have focused on Rose more than his parents. He desperately hopes they are safe, wants them to know he is okay, but his driving desire is to be with her. At the rate things are going, he's worried he's not going to be around for anyone on any continent.

His thoughts are interrupted by Corporal Burns who slides a stack of empty envelopes over to him. Stephan, knows the routine. Each repaired watch is slipped into an envelope and placed on the gray steel shelving perpendicular to his worktable. The rest of the unrepaired watches remain in the box that Rose supplied this morning. Oma's returned watch is still in the unrepaired group. The corporal exits the room to run his paperwork over to the accounting department, leaving Stephan alone in his cramped workshop.

Stephan waits a few minutes just to be certain he is alone. He picks up the purple bag containing Oma's watch and loosens the drawstring. Carefully he opens the sack and reaches in with his thumb and index finger. He has no intention of removing the watch. In fact, he's confident the timepiece is working perfectly. Instead, he carefully draws out a piece of paper that has been meticulously folded. He turns to his right to confirm no one is watching. Then, he carefully unfolds the paper and stares intently at the few words carefully written in German. His eyes widen. Perhaps hope has returned to this room after all. He refolds the paper, unbuttons his left breast pocket and tucks it inside. He feels motivated, adrenaline fuels a surge to survive. A heightened sense of urgency overwhelms him.

He checks the time. It is 3:30. He has thirty minutes before he heads back to the prisoner compound. His heart sinks. Right now, he doesn't see a way out. Doesn't have an answer. He needs more time to fend off Schroeder until he can come up with a plan. Every option seems fruitless except one. His only hope now is Rose. His brain is racing as he instinctively upends the box of unrepaired watches. He pushes them carelessly to the side of the table, except for Oma's watch, which he slides into his right trouser pocket. He turns to the shelves and begins to pluck each of the envelopes containing finished repairs, attempting to stack them neatly in the box. His fingers are trembling as he races the clock. He has trouble handling the parcels and finally drops one to the floor. He can hear the crystal shatter inside the envelope as it strikes the leg of the steel table and spins away. He doesn't even bother to pick it up, instead uses his boot to sweep it under the shelving. He gathers the filled box and steps into the hallway.

No sign of Corporal Burns. Probably still at the accounting department. He does something he has never attempted before. Without a guard escorting him he begins to move down the narrow hallway, away from the heavily guarded hospital entrance towards the lobby. The first person he sees is Brenda, his flirtatious friend from the typing pool. She is carrying a stack of folders and deliberately lets the top one drop to the floor as soon as she sees him. Stephan understands the game and knows he must play. He shifts the box of watches to one arm and with his other free hand plucks the folder from the floor and returns it to Brenda, using his very best English, "Miss Brenda."

"Well now, look at you, carrying on a conversation in English." He understands half of what she is saying. He just smiles and nods but keeps moving. Brenda continues in the opposite direction but not before she makes it clear, "don't be a stranger Steph. Come and visit." But Stephan is already in the lobby where he turns sharply to the left and sees a guard ahead whom he recognizes only as a friend of Corporal Burns. The soldier is standing erect, his back against the wall. Stephan decides to approach the guard instead of avoiding him. The guard seems surprised that Stephan is alone. Again, in English Stephan says, "Um, good day. I wish to be with Colonel Warren, okay?"

The guard seems at ease, but replies, "Why isn't Corporal Burns with you?" Stephan understands the question and give a cryptic response. "The accountants office?"

"You mean the accounting department. So, why do you need to see the Colonel?"

"No, no. The office. Miss Bauer?" Stephan holds up the box of watches. "Miss Bauer. For her and the corporal."

"Well why didn't you just say so." He gestures for Stephan to follow. "Come on. This way." Stephan's heart is pounding. *So far, so good.* "You know you really shouldn't be walking alone around here. Next time wait for Corporal Burns, okay?"

Stephan glances at a wall clock. 3:45. "Okay, yes. Thank

you for this. Okay." They head down a broad corridor, twice the width of the hallway that leads to Stephan's makeshift workshop. There are more people working here than Stephan thought, far more than the smattering of employees he sees during a coffee break. He hears Corporal Burns' voice and then laughter as he enjoys a pleasant exchange with one of the younger secretaries in the accounting department. They sweep past and Burns' voice fades quickly. *Almost there.*

"What are you doing back here?" Rose's surprised voice means only one thing to Stephan. His plan still has a chance. Now he needs a little luck. "Says he was looking for you. I think he wants to give you these watches."

Stephan begins speaking German and his words are tumbling out quickly. "Tell him that I was worried I wouldn't get these to you before the holiday. Tell him I need to review these orders with you. Please. I don't have much time."

Rose is having difficulty with her response. She looks at Stephan who swallows hard. She turns to the confused guard. "It's okay private. The prisoner was worried that he would be unable to get his repairs back to me for the weekly pickup at my family's farm. He thought the Thanksgiving holiday might interfere with our normal schedule. He wants to get paid for his work."

The guard rolls his eyes. "In case he didn't understand me, tell him not to wander these halls by himself. And make sure Corporal Burns escorts him out."

"Of course, I'll tell him. His English isn't very good."

"No kidding. I need to get back to my post."

Now they are alone. Stephan is no longer motivated by passion, but sheer survival. He speaks quickly and succinctly. "I should have told you sooner. My life is in danger. Unless I can show that I am willing to spy on the Americans, the Holy Ghost may be visiting me soon, maybe even tonight. I don't want to jeopardize your job, but I also want to find a way to be with you some day. I, I don't know who else to ask." He looks at his watch. 3:55. "Burns will be coming for me soon."

Rose wants to help but feels trapped. She wants to embrace him, share his anguish but knows that is madness. "What kind of information do you need?" Just asking the questions feels wrong.

"Something that you would consider harmless, maybe. Information that I can prove is authentic. I am sorry to do this......"

Rose interrupts. "Corporal, we were looking for you." Corporal Burns walks up to them both. "The prisoner was concerned that these watches would not get back to his customers promptly because of the Thanksgiving holiday. Turns out he was right."

Stephan's expression changes. *What is she talking about?*

"I just heard myself. Looks like Colonel Warren is ordering a shutdown on prisoner activity until after the weekend, so you better take those with you tonight."

"Yes, I was just about to explain to him, do you mind?"

"Not at all, let's see how good my German is."

Rose smiles and fires away, knowing Burns will be unable to understand.

"Stephan, you have to find a way to stall him. I need some time. Take him back to your workshop and stall him."

"How can I stall him? I can barely communicate with him. My English is weak, and his German is embarrassing." Stephan suddenly thinks of a way to sidetrack Burns. He explains it to Rose, since she will have to set it up if it has any chance of working.

Corporal Burns is standing by, waiting for their extended German dialogue to end. "My God, they have such long words for everything. No wonder they are losing the war, it takes so long to give an order. Ha!" He is very amused with himself.

Rose is half-listening, hoping to give Stephan a chance to make this plan work. "Corporal, the prisoner is concerned that he is missing one of the watches I am supposed to be returning. He is embarrassed to tell you. He knows how hard you have worked to make his paperwork so efficient, but there is definitely a watch missing. Could you go back and check his workshop. And please take him with you. I don't want to get reprimanded for letting him walk the halls alone."

Burns looks at his watch and his eyes widen. "Yes ma'am. But we've got to make it fast. I'm already late getting the prisoner back." He turns and grabs Stephan by the elbow. "Come on Steph. Let's go find that watch."

As soon as they leave the area, Rose gets to work. She guesses the safest piece of information she can share without violating any security concerns is the guard rotation. It doesn't give away any secrets. It certainly won't compromise security. The prisoners already know what time the shifts change. What does it matter if we tell them who is going where? A guard is a guard. At least Stephan can show that he got his hands on something. He can buy some time. She thinks she knows where the guard rotations are typed and filed for tomorrow. For the first time she realizes there is silence. She looks at the clock. It is 4:15. *No wonder, everyone has left for the day...and I've got 15 minutes to catch the bus.* For some reason, the silence weighs more heavily on her. It makes her feel sneaky. *Am I doing anything really wrong here? Or just trying to save someone's life. This is for Stephan. I trust him.*

Rose opens the door to the typing pool. She hesitates as her fingers brush the light switch then pull back. She decides to work in darkness. She knows she's in the right room because she can smell Brenda's cheap perfume. It's nauseating. The "outbound" file is stacked high with orders for tomorrow. Her eyes are already adjusting to the dim light. It takes her less than a minute to find the guard rotation. She hurriedly returns the rest of the papers to the stack and quietly closes the door.

Standing in the hallway she takes a closer look at the schedule and realizes immediately there is a problem. The rotations are very different. Guard assignments have been thinned out. Some gates are more heavily guarded than others. These orders reveal a weakness in the system. *I can't share this information. It could be dangerous.* Her back is still toward the hallway. As she turns around, she is startled by Colonel Warren. "Miss Bauer, would you care to explain what you are doing?"

* * *

Stephan and Corporal Burns reach the workshop. The American wastes little time beginning his search for the missing watch. He's speaking to Stephan as if he can understand him. "Okay, Steph let's not waste any time. I'm already behind schedule here." But wasting time is exactly what Stephan is doing. That's the plan. Give Rose a chance to find something she can pass on to Stephan without committing treason. He keeps glancing toward the doorway. Hopes he will hear the sound of Rose heading this way. Instead, the reality of what he has done sets in. He has asked Rose to take a big risk. She is putting everything on the line for a coward. For him. Burns is no longer speaking, too busy searching. The hallway is quiet, and the void is filled with too many memories that shout cowardice. Accepting the annexation of Austria so his belly could be full. The German officer in his parents' workshop, intimidating Stephan with a death grip he has never shaken. Compromising his scruples during basic training, doing anything to escape the Holy Ghost. Never coming to Hugo's defense on the train as Schroeder pummeled him. Standing up to Werner, only because he was intoxicated by a silly crush on an American girl, then retreating meekly when Werner exacted his revenge on Hugo. Then sadly never trying to stay close to Hugo, rationalizing his friend's growing detachment as the safe thing to do. And now he has put Rose at risk, using the excuse that he wants to be alive for her.

"Found it!" Corporal Burns is holding the envelope high above his head, shaking it in triumph. "Okay let's go find Miss Bauer so you can get back to camp."

What if we go back there and he catches Rose doing something she shouldn't? I can't let that happen. He takes a deep breath "*Nein, mein freund.*"

"What do you mean no, Steph? This is the missing watch isn't it. We have to go, now." He tries to emphasize his point using his limited German vocabulary. "*Schnell!*"

Stephan pulls the envelope from Burns' hand and begins shaking it. Burns is surprised by Stephan's odd behavior then hears fragments of the shattered crystal inside the envelope. He doesn't waver. "No, we don't have any more time." Then a greater sense of urgency. "*Schnell!*" This is no longer a request. It is an order from a guard to a prisoner. The line is drawn, and Stephan decides to cross it. Defiantly, he reaches for the parts bin on his worktable, slides it toward himself while searching for a replacement crystal. He is waiting for Burns to bark more commands but instead hears the clatter of footsteps in the hallway. Urgent and fast. *Rose?*

Yes. And Colonel Warren. *She's been caught. It's all my fault.* Corporal Burns snaps to attention and salutes.

"At ease corporal." Warren crosses the threshold into the tiny room and approaches Stephan, who is looking over the colonel's shoulder directly at Rose, trying to apologize with his eyes. It is Warren who speaks, "Private, Miss Bauer here tells me you have been working late to keep up with all these repairs. Sounds like you've got a profitable business going." Warren realizes that Stephan is struggling to understand. Rose steps in and translates. "*Danke Oberst*" is Stephan's crisp reply and Colonel Warren comprehends. "*Thank you, Colonel*" He removes his own pocket watch and holds it up with his right hand. With his left hand he offers a thumbs up, while he says, "I know firsthand the quality of your work. I'd like to give you a letter of recommendation for your file. Miss Bauer will file the original but here's a copy that you can keep if you'd like, just in case you need it to *convince someone that you can be trusted.*" He slides the letter into a brown, flat manila envelope as Rose translates for Stephan. She emphasizes for Stephan, "convince someone that you can be trusted." Stephan peeks inside the envelope and understands fully. Warren and Rose are working together. Inside the envelope are two blank pieces of Warren's personalized stationery. This is golden. Stephan has his ticket. And then Rose fills in the missing piece, right in front of the oblivious Corporal Burns. *"Im Gegenzug werden Sie die Nazis ausspionieren."* Stephan stares at Warren but does not respond. Rose repeats the order, but Stephan understood the first time, *"In return, you will spy on the Nazis."*

Stephan nods yes. "Warren's reply confirms the transaction, "*gut.*" "*Good.*"

* * *

Stephan has certainly been more physically challenged since his arrival at Camp Huntsville. The long days in the cotton fields during the summer are testament to that. But he has never felt so mentally drained as he does right now. This day has provided every kind of emotion that could tax his resolve. Passion. Fear. Despair. Hope. He is seated at the end of one of the longest tables in the mess hall. Three prisoners are huddled together in the middle of the table, too immersed in an argument about football to even notice him. His spoon is playing with the turkey noodle soup that will never touch his lips. He has no appetite. He is only here because he got the word as soon as he re-entered the camp that Schroeder wanted to meet with him. Despite the unknown reason for this meeting, Stephan feels little if any anxiety. More than anything he wants to know he can crawl into his bed and finally sleep through the night without fear of a beating or worse. *I just need some rest. Need to clear my head.*

He feels a grip on his shoulder and tightens immediately. That fast he is back in his parents' shop frightened by a German officer whose sole purpose was to terrorize him. Now it is Schroeder who relishes that role. *Hugo was right. He truly is a swine.*

"Jurgen, your soup is getting cold."

Stephan's tone is flat. "I'm not hungry. They said you wanted to see me?" The three men nearby grab their trays in unison and timidly move to another table.

Schroeder slides into the seat closest to Stephan's right-hand side. He pulls the soup bowl away, picks it up and begins to slurp, deliberately drinking until he finishes. He sucks noodles from the bottom of the bowl, making Stephan shudder. Schroeder wipes broth from his chin and lips with a worn sleeve. He deliberately tosses the bowl on the table, so it will annoy him even more. The bowl lands loudly, wobbles for a few seconds then quickly stops. "You have something for me?"

"As a matter of fact, I do." Stephan looks around to see if anyone is watching, playing up the drama of the moment for Schroeder. He slides a manila envelope across to Schroeder who asks, "Where did you get this?"

"I stole it from the office of the camp commander. It contains a copy of his personalized stationery." *You don't need to know I kept the extra copy for myself.* "I thought that some of our men who are planning escapes could use this to their advantage. I hope it is helpful."

"Why the sudden cooperation private? Don't you like sleeping with a chicken carcass?"

Stephan remains composed, his tone unemotional. "None of that was necessary. I told you before I just needed some time to earn their trust and now, I have."

"Apparently so. I'm looking forward to seeing what else this trust can deliver for us."

"Listen, this takes time. I can't produce something overnight. It doesn't work that way." Schroeder doesn't answer, creating an awkward silence. Finally, a line of questioning Stephan doesn't expect.

"The chaplain, Major Heller, what do you know about him?"

"Why are you asking me? You already know the answer."

Schroeder picks up the spoon and begins tapping it on the table. "Your friend Hugo knew him very well, it seems."

Stephan remains calm, even though he wants to get away from this scum. *Why did he have to bring up Hugo?* "I met him for the first time on Sunday. He told me about Hugo's death. Now, can I go? I'm exhausted."

Schroeder raises his eyebrows and feigns interest. "Are you looking forward to a restful sleep tonight?

"As a matter of fact, I am," For the first time he sounds defiant. He taps emphatically on the manila envelope and says, "I took a big risk getting this for you. And I can get more. But right now, I'm tired."

"What do you have in mind for tomorrow? What kind of risk are you willing to take?"

"Look, I already explained that getting these things takes time. And besides, there is a shutdown tomorrow. No outside work details and no prisoners over at the American side." *You just said too much.*

"When were you planning on telling me that? Why were you holding back?"

Stay calm. "I just found out when I was getting escorted back to camp this afternoon. I really didn't think it was that important. Thought the officers here were already informed."

Schroeder pulls himself even closer to Stephan. "You tell me everything you see or hear. I will decide if it is important. Understood?" Schroeder is already getting up and moving away.

Stephan replies "understood." But Schroeder is already gone. Stephan slowly exhales and remains seated. A solitary figure alone with his thoughts. A young man his age should not be consumed by the conflicts he faces, but the conclusion he is finally reaching defies his youth. Instead it reflects a wisdom well beyond his years. For too long he has used this war and the suffering it produces as an excuse. He has chosen to be a victim of the carnage. He has ignored the examples of others who have chosen a different path. His parents. Hugo. And now today, Rose. The pain of this war is out of his control. But he has a choice and finally he has a path. *I am not a victim. I can make a difference.* He almost forgets another person who has touched his life, a quiet light who wants to make a difference. He unbuttons his shirt pocket and pulls out that folded piece of paper he read earlier in the day; a message cleverly concealed in the purple satin bag. He remembers what it says but he wants to read it again. Stephan carefully unfolds the thin parchment and smooths it out on the table. The perfect penmanship of a gentle soul. Direct and powerful.

"Ich will helfen." "I want to help"

"Ich brauche die Adresse deiner Eltern." "I need the address of your parents."

The note is signed *"O."*

TWO DAYS BEFORE THANKSGIVING

CHAPTER 38
Huntsville, Texas

Carsick

Rose sits in Uncle Pete's truck, peering intently at the piece of paper Oma gave her minutes earlier. "Oh God, it's bad enough I can't understand her writing. But I swear I'm gonna barf if I read this while we're driving."

"Please, Miss Rose, don't get sick now." To her left is Clyde, nervously handling the steering wheel, trying to watch her while paying attention to the road.

"Clyde, you okay?"

"Fine Miss Rose. You know I don't like to drive much, especially Mr. Bauer's truck."

"I get it Clyde, but you know my uncle is tied up and you certainly don't want to see me driving!" She puts the paper on her lap. "We can both blame Oma's Thanksgiving shopping list. Forcing you to drive today and making me.....oh my God, I'm going to..."

"Please no, Miss Rose, please..."

Rose starts clapping and squealing. "Gotcha Clyde. Gotcha good!"

"That's not funny Miss Rose, but I'm glad you were kidding." He laughs heartily and sighs. "Mighty glad. Don't know how I would explain that to your uncle." Then unexpectedly,

"Oh no, we got trouble."

"What's the matter, Clyde?" She turns and sees the flashing lights of a police cruiser. Clyde is already pulling over.

"Miss Rose, I'm not sure why we're being stopped."

"Oh I've got a pretty good idea" Bobby Ford is already rolling out of his car, hitching up his pants and reaching back inside to retrieve his wide brimmed hat. He pulls it on his head then uses his window as a mirror, making sure it's straight. He walks down Rose's side of the truck and reaches the cab. His night stick is out and he presses it against her closed window. Tap. Tap. Tap. Rose rolls her eyes and slowly lowers the window.

Rose looks at the club. "Don't you think that's overkill?"

The deputy ignores Clyde and looks only at Rose.

"Good morning, folks. Seem to be in quite a hurry. You in a hurry Clyde?"

"No deputy, just driving Miss Rose here on some errands. I don't...."

Still looking only at Rose. "Well now, that doesn't excuse breaking the speed limit and running a stop sign."

"Oh come on Bobby, we did no such thing."

He finally raises his eyes toward Clyde. "Is she calling me a liar, Clyde?"

Clyde looks straight ahead.

"You better look at me when I'm talking to you."

Rose reaches across the seat and gently touches his arm. "Don't say anything to him Clyde."

"Memory serves me correct this isn't the first time you've been caught speeding around here."

Rose pushes her spectacles up her nose and blows straight up, her blonde curls lifting and settling back on her forehead. "Okay Bobby this is ridiculous and you know it."

"Time for warnings are over Clyde. You'll have to answer to a judge. He takes out his citation booklet. "Let me see your license." Clyde hesitates, turns to Rose and whispers. "Miss Rose, I don't have it. I got caught off guard about driving and I just forgot." A smirk appear on the deputy's face.

"So driving without a license, too. What were you thinking Clyde?"

"No sir, just an honest mistake."

"I don't like your attitude now. Not one bit. Don't start giving me lip. Or I'll have to arrest you for disrespecting this badge."

Rose explodes, "Stop now. Stop! We've done nothing wrong. He's done nothing wrong. And he certainly is not giving you lip. You want to hear some lip just keep it up you moron." The deputy's grip tightens on the night stick. Rose can feel the pressure as he reaches across and pokes her left shoulder.

"Clyde, maybe you can help Miss Rose out here. She doesn't have her big brothers around to protect her. Maybe you can protect her?"

Tears are streaming down Rose's cheeks. She looks at Clyde and can see the anger in his eyes, muscles tightening in his neck, the death grip on the steering wheel. She shakes her head. *Don't do it Clyde. Don't move.*

Rose exhales, sits up straight. She grabs the nightstick and calmly pulls it away from her shoulder. Then turns defiantly toward Bobby Ford. "Either you back off right now or arrest us you coward."

ONE DAY BEFORE THANKSGIVING

* * *

CHAPTER 39
Houston, Texas

Fuel

"Arrested? What the hell, Uncle Pete?" This is not the welcome Ralph imagined after the final leg of his train ride. He is standing near the doorway of the crowded Houston train station. Uncle Pete's truck is parked by the curb with the engine running. Outside, a cold snap has delivered temperatures in the teens and the heater in his truck is barely keeping pace.

"Oh, it's true. You can bet the farm on it. I spent the whole day yesterday scrambling to find a lawyer willing to take the heat on this. Not exactly a popular cause in Huntsville. Anyway, the two of them are bailed out and home. So, Happy Thanksgiving Ralph. Here, let me get these for you." He reaches for Ralph's oversized duffel bag, but his nephew declines. He wants more information.

"What was she thinking?"

Uncle Pete moves toward the exit and Ralph reluctantly follows. "It's not the first time Bobby Ford has gone out of his way to make things uncomfortable for Clyde. Let's face it, around these parts a law-abiding Negro driving a vehicle alone is reason enough to get pulled over. But this one is a head scratcher. Your sister's got something else bugging her about deputy do-nothing but I frankly don't have the time to figure it out."

"Can't say I blame her. That guy is a creep."

"Seems like everybody agrees on that."

They are outside the train station now and Ralph stiffens. "Well I'm grateful to see you Uncle Pete, but this is not how I expected to start Thanksgiving. My sister was in jail yesterday and now this freezing weather. Got any more surprises for me?" He places his bag in the rear bed of the truck, reaches into his pocket and pulls out a pack of cigarettes. He flicks his wrist and offers them to his uncle, who gladly pulls a cigarette from the pack. Ralph lights it for him and does the same for himself. They both inhale quickly, hastened by the stiff wind.

Their thoughts are interrupted by a police officer who politely approaches them. "Sorry to move you along boys, but we've got a lot of people traveling through here today."

Ralph flicks his cigarette to the curb. "No problem, officer. Stay warm out here."

"Thank you, captain. Enjoy your time home with your family."

Ralph looks at his uncle and they both start laughing. Uncle Pete holds out the keys. "Why don't you drive, if you still know the way."

Ralph takes the keys. "First gear still stubborn?"

"As stubborn as your sister." Uncle Pete takes the last draw on his cigarette and climbs inside. Ralph lurches into gear, grimacing as the clutch fails to respond. Uncle Pete whistles in jest, but his nephew quickly settles into the parking lot traffic, then smoothly pulls onto the highway for the 90-minute drive to the Bauer Farm. Home. The sun is quickly falling and there is barely an hour of sunlight left in the day. The city of Houston fades from the rearview mirror and the familiar rural highway that leads to Huntsville opens up in front of Ralph. Without thinking, he accelerates quickly, and the truck soon reaches a speed of 50 miles per hour. Uncle Pete pounds the dashboard. "Whoa, fella. Slow it down there. Speed limit is 35."

"Since when?"

"Been almost a year, Ralph. Slower speeds mean less wear on tires. Gotta save rubber for the war effort. You know, do our part. In most places they even stopped making bicycles. Rationing is serious business around here."

"I didn't realize."

"It's not just tires. Fuel too." Uncle Pete points to a sticker on the windshield to the left of Ralph. It displays the letter "B."

"See that sticker there. It means we get 8 gallons a week. We got lucky because Rose is considered a war worker now that she's employed at Camp Huntsville. Otherwise, we'd be rationed at just 2 gallons a week. Still, she takes the bus every day to work."

"Now, I'm feeling guilty. I should have taken the bus from the train station."

"That's nonsense. I've got this trip planned down to the last drop of gas. Got here just fine with plenty to get us back. May take us a little longer with the lower speed limit but it'll give us plenty of time to catch up."

True to his word, Uncle Pete fills the gap easily. The first thing they discuss is Henry. Although Ralph can't divulge his intelligence sources, he is able to tell Uncle Pete that the USS Midway is not in active duty yet. The ship is currently in its second shakedown cruise, which means Ralph's brother is safe. That's welcome news for Uncle Pete. "Well getting that update about your brother along with a hug from you will do your grandmother a world of good, that's for sure. Maybe you can even tell her a little bit about what you've been doing since you've been back in the states."

"Nothing to tell, really. Just routine stuff."

"Routine, huh? Ralph, you're slicker than a slop jar. I know your job is anything but routine." Ralph winds down the window, partly to get a little fresh air but mostly to drown out his uncle. A blast of cold air reminds him of the rare weather that has welcomed him home. He quickly raises the window just in time to hear Uncle Pete shouting, "But that's okay, I'm also happy as a hog in mud to see you, so I won't be asking any more questions." Ralph's *heard-that-before* expression brings a stronger response. "I'm serious Ralph. No more questions."

Ralph smiles and cranks the window closed. "Great, that means I get to do all the asking. So, tell me about my sister."

"Sure, what do you want to know?"

"Is she dating? Anybody I should know about?"

"Well now you picked a complicated subject."

"Not sure I like the sound of that. What's so complicated?"

“”Well, for starters, she's got a more than average interest in a POW. Innocent now, don't get me wrong. Guy started off chopping cotton and now he's repairing watches at the camp – with a little help from...."

"Well, go ahead. With a little help from...?

"Me, Rose, Oma. Basically our entire family. Sounds even more crazy when I say it out loud."

"Well I agree with the crazy part."

"Okay, I'm done talking about this. Ask your sister if you're looking for more. Just be careful, though, cause she has no patience these days for other people's bullshit. Just ask Bobby Ford if you don't believe me."

"I hear you loud and clear, but now you need to hear the same thing I'll say to my sister. Falling for a German prisoner is a bad idea."

"Funny thing is, the guy isn't even German. He's Austrian."

"Yeah, we saw that a lot when I was stationed in North

Africa. Plenty of Austrians were conscripted into the Wehrmacht." *I am not a Nazi. I was drafted.*

"Well, he hates the Nazis. And he's one hell of a watch repair man. Even Clyde likes the guy, and that's saying something. Told me he's one of the best workers he's ever had in the fields. I gotta tell you Ralph, if these were different times, I think you would like this guy."

"Okay Uncle Pete. So, he's a nice guy and a hard worker. He still doesn't have to hang around my sister." Ralph looks at the gas gauge. "Looks like we might need a refill before we reach Huntsville."

Uncle Pete leans over to peer at the gauge, then dismisses Ralph quickly. "Nope. We'll make it. Trust me. Plenty of fuel to get us home." He flops back into his seat and continues the conversation. "I'm not gonna lie to you Ralph. I'm grateful his work detail was assigned to our farm. Some of the Nazis made it difficult but men like him made it worthwhile."

"Wow, I never expected to hear this coming from you."

Listen, nobody was more against this whole POW camp than me. Thought it was a horrible idea. Couldn't imagine treating these prisoners better than our own guys. But I get it. Rules are rules to help protect our boys who end up in Kraut prisons."

"You're talking about the Geneva Convention?"

"Right, right. Whatever they call it. Yeah, we got the message loud and clear from the camp commander, Warren's his name. Rose's boss." Ralph recognizes the name immediately. He's the one who will sign the orders to release Heller into his custody.

"Well, I've got a little business to take care of at the prison before I head back this weekend so maybe I'll check this guy out for myself."

"That might be a little tricky. Seems the Nazi problem is

getting worse at the camp. They've had a couple ugly incidents with some of the prisoners and Rose says they are locking down the place. No work details going out and prisoners strictly confined to their barracks. At least until after Thanksgiving."

That news takes Ralph's mind off anything but Heller. *I hope I won't have a problem getting him back to Virginia. I need him, and he owes me.* They are ten miles outside of Huntsville. Despite the fading daylight, Ralph recognizes the familiar terrain. One of the well-known landmarks is a Texaco station on his right. It forces him to look at the gas gauge. He turns on the truck's lights and squints at the dashboard. The needle is squarely on E. Uncle Pete knows what Ralph is thinking but won't have any of it. He points his right hand forward. "Keep going. We'll be fine." As they crawl past the station, its elderly owner, Bob Elliott recognizes the truck and waves casually. Until he realizes Ralph is driving. He breaks into a big grin and flaps his arms emphatically over his head. Ralph lowers the window and quickly pokes his arm out in reply. It is now dusk, and the station's lights are turned on. He can't help but notice the billboard nestled in the pine trees, its rationing message reminding him that things are very different back home, too.

"Millions of troops are on the move.

Is your trip necessary?"

He's grateful his trip, no matter how brief and unseasonably cold, has finally brought him home. Maybe not under the best of circumstances, but there's no place he'd rather be right now. Rose may have tilted the world upside down but so what? He's seen and heard too many ugly things not to appreciate the time he's going to spend with his family. In a couple days he'll have to be a soldier again, with orders to follow. That means getting to Camp Huntsville, making Heller's transfer official, and then getting him on a train heading north. By Sunday they should be back in Virginia where his prized stool pigeon will get to work immediately. The truck is moving through the main street of Huntsville. More familiar faces and places only make him realize just how homesick he is.

At the northern edge of town, he slows down for the last traffic light between here and home. For all the emotions he has felt in the last few years, he is surprised how excited he feels. The truck climbs the last subtle incline before the road levels out all the way to the Bauer Farm. He is tempted to hit the gas pedal and race the final few miles. He looks at Uncle Pete, who is somewhere else right now. Staring out the window, probably thinking about all the problems that just a few years ago he and Ralph used to solve together. The truck sputters and Uncle Pete is brought back to reality. Ralph presses hard on the accelerator but the only response is a belch from under the hood. He lets the truck coast a few more yards as he steers it toward the shoulder of the road. He applies the brake, turns and stares at the side of Uncle Pete's anguished face. They are still 2 miles away from home. And they are out of gas.

"Hell, Ralph, I'm sure you've been in tighter spots than this. Let's start walking and somebody we know will come along."

"Maybe even Bobby Ford." He winks at his uncle.

"If that son-of-a-bitch comes within ten feet of me I'll shove that shiny club of his right up his fat ass."

Ralph reaches into the truck bed and grabs his duffel bag, slinging it over his good shoulder. He hands his attaché to his uncle. "That would make running out of gas worth it!" They both laugh and head down the road. Within five minutes, they hear the sound of a large vehicle approaching. The road vibrates and Ralph instinctively moves over. *I've had it with big trucks getting too close.* The vehicle slows considerably, and Ralph realizes that it might be stopping to help. He turns his head slowly to see who might be lending a hand. It isn't a truck. It's a bus. A large drab gray bus. It pulls over to the side of the road after passing them. Clouds of condensation erupt from its tail pipe, surrounding the back of the bus; the red glare of its rear lights softened by the billowing exhaust. The noxious combination of burning oil and carburetor fumes fills Ralph's nostrils.

"Told you Ralph, I knew it wouldn't take long." Ralph hears the relief in Uncle Pete's voice.

"This bus looks familiar."

"Well, partner, things are about to get even more familiar." Ralph follows Uncle Pete along the thin stretch of road remaining between the bus and the shoulder. It is dark inside. When they reach the door, Uncle Pete taps politely, and the panels squeak open grudgingly. Uncle Pete deliberately steps aside so Ralph can get a full view of Mr. Martin, looking a whole lot older and skinnier but still offering the same sour expression he glimpsed years ago from the safety of the pine trees while his sister got a scolding. The old man looks directly at Ralph. "I hope you ain't expecting a ride from me, son."

Ralph is speechless, unable to think of an appropriate answer. *Boy this guy really holds a grudge.* He hopes Uncle Pete will set things right. They are freezing, and he can feel inviting warmth pouring out of the bus. Then Mr. Martin turns to Uncle Pete and they simultaneously break into contagious laughter. Ralph wants to join in, but he is too confused.

"Ralph, you can thank your sister Rose for the ride I'm about to give you. Welcome home son. Looks like your visit is off to a rough start."

"Thank you, sir. Much appreciated. Glad to hear you and Rose patched things up. I'll be sure to thank her."

****

Rose is waiting by the kitchen door. Still no sign of Uncle

Pete's truck. Finally, she hears voices on the porch and recognizes Ralph's laugh. The door opens and the reunion is chaotic. Rose is squealing. Ginny is leaping. And Uncle Pete is still on the porch, unable to break through the tangle of arms and paws. Rose is crying and hugging her brother tightly. Each has the same unspoken observation about the other. A sibling who looks older than remembered and far more exhausted than each imagined. Finally, a brief conversation that portrays young lives interrupted by war.

"Wow sis, that hug was worth an 18-month absence. You look beautiful."

"And you're too skinny. But still handsome as ever in this uniform. Oh Ralph, we missed you."

"Hey, where's Oma?

"I just checked on her. She's asleep. She was hoping to see you tonight but..."

"It's okay Rose. I'm glad she's resting." He smiles at Uncle Pete, who is finally closing the door. "Sorry. We got a bit delayed, right Uncle Pete?"

"Okay, you two, the important thing is we're here. No need to waste any more time on that subject."

By early evening Rose and Ralph are catching up. Very soon the war will separate these siblings again. But tonight they are just a brother and sister back in their kitchen. Sitting at a table carved by a man who never shared the memories they made in this room. Each nurses a glass of Uncle Pete's prized batch of bourbon. Rose toasts her brother and asks, "do you remember the last time we opened this bottle?"

"Of course, it was the night before Henry and I shipped out. The rest of it is kind of a blur. Hey, here's to Henry."

"To Henry, my favorite brother."

"To Rose, who can't stay out of trouble."

"I knew it wouldn't take you long to go there. That's a sore subject brother. Bobby Ford crossed the line. I swear Clyde wanted to kill him."

"Wait a minute. Did he touch you?"

Rose swirls the bourbon in the glass then places it back on the table without drinking it. "Sort of. With his night stick, yeah. He didn't hit me. I swear he was doing it more to tease Clyde."

"He's a cowboy Rose, trying to throw his weight around. The guy is 4-F. Needs to prove himself."

"Ralph, he stopped us for bullshit traffic violations. Clyde didn't do anything wrong."

"Well it's one thing for Clyde to get stopped. That's gonna happen around here. He knows that. But it's another thing for Bobby Ford to intimidate you."

"Hold on. Are you saying it's okay for that horse's ass to pull Clyde over for no good reason?"

"Well, Uncle Pete said Clyde didn't have his license so..."

Rose slams her fist on the table, startling Ralph.

"Take it easy, okay. I know it's complicated."

"Do you Ralph? Do you really understand? Or are you just as willing to look the other way because it's more convenient. Because you know a kind man like Clyde won't speak up on his own so it's okay to just accept unacceptable behavior."

"Like I said. It's complicated."

Rose ignores his comment. "You know what I just heard on the radio earlier today? One of our ships, I don't remember the name of it, but it was an escort carrier just like Henry's. It was sunk by a Jap submarine. Hundreds of sailors were killed. Do you know who was on that ship Ralph?"

Her brother shakes his head no.

"His name was Doris Miller. Ship's Cook Third Class. Nobody special to you and me but he was a hero. I've heard Clyde and his men talk about him in the fields. At Pearl Harbor, he manned an anti-aircraft gun and helped the wounded on his ship. He was eventually awarded the Navy Cross, the first black man to receive that honor."

Rose can see the compassion in her brother's eyes. But, also the confusion. He is not sure where she is going with this story.

"Ralph, that boy – he was only 24 – was from Waco, just a few hour's drive from here. A real American hero. And now he's gone. A citizen who gave his life for this country. Are you telling me that his family – also American citizens -- are supposed to just expect to get pulled over by cowards like Bobby Ford for no good reason.? Tell me what's right about that?"

"It's not right Rose, but it's going to take time."

"No, it's going to take people like you and me to stop looking the other way. It's not Clyde's responsibility. It's ours Ralph. It's ours." She folds her arms defiantly and leans back in her chair. "So, if you think you're going to give me a lecture about how complicated things are and how it's just going to take time, you better think twice. Because I'm not going to have any of it. Not from you and certainly not from Bobby Ford. So be forewarned, if you think I can't stay out of trouble well you and deputy dickhead ain't seen nothing yet."

Ralph drains his bourbon and reaches for the bottle. "You know what I'm thinking right now? I'm thinking that our parents would be mighty proud of you. It takes a lot of guts for you to say all these things and I'm proud of you too."

"Thanks brother, but right now it's just words. I have to do something" She slides her empty glass across the table. Ralph carefully pours another ounce for each of them. Rose closes her eyes and brings the glass up to her nose, slowly inhales the sweet aroma of vanilla and caramel.

"So Rose, speaking of doing something. Since I'm only here for a couple days do you want me to kick Bobby Ford's ass or should I leave that to you."

"Oh no, he's mine." *He's in more trouble than you'll ever know.*

"Understood loud and clear. Then, I need to switch gears on you and talk a little business. Are you familiar with a prisoner, Major Heller?"

"Heller, sure. He's a chaplain, right?"

"That's him. Well, I'll be taking him back with me when I leave this weekend."

Rose sips her bourbon, allowing it to rest on her tongue, just the way Uncle Pete taught her. She gently swallows and smiles teasingly, "where are you taking him?"

Ralph plays along. "Oh, it's all in the paperwork Colonel Warren will need to sign. It's really no mystery Rose, he's going to a POW camp in Maryland. Now don't ask me anything else or I'll be forced to lie to my sister."

"God you are brutal Ralph. You've been gone forever and don't share anything with your only sister. Meanwhile, I'm sitting here babbling, baring my soul, and telling you everything."

"Everything? Are you sure?"

"What's that supposed to mean?

"How's the watch repair business?"

Rose stares blankly at her brother.

"Seriously Rose, what's going on?"

She wipes her finger around the inside of the empty glass. "I can explain it to you Ralph, but I can't understand it for you...."

THANKSGIVING DAY

* * *

CHAPTER 40
Huntsville, Texas

Unraveling

Ralph wakes up in his bedroom for the first time in nearly two years. *Too much bourbon.* The cold, raw weather outside makes it even more inviting to stay under the covers. He hears Ginny scratching at the door. It used to be annoying. Now he misses that dog's loyal companionship and promises himself he will never take it for granted. He tosses away the heavy comforter and his shoulder immediately reminds him that all is not healed. He lets out a soft grunt, springs out of bed and heads for the door. He rubs his shoulder hard and wonders if he'll ever share with his family the story of how an Austrian soldier saved his life. Maybe later. When the war is over. He can hear Ginny panting on the other side of the door and decides to tease her. He whispers her name. She stops scratching, then hurls her body against the door just as Ralph opens it. The beagle is all over him before he can react. Tugging at his pajama pants, then tearing down the hallway at full speed. He almost forgot her playfulness but remembers just as quickly that she's not finished with him. Sure enough, with a full head of steam in her trim 20-pound frame she is back in the room, then on the bed, then out the door again without ever breaking stride. Ralph laughs out loud. Thanksgiving Day is off to a good start.

He heads down the hallway to the bathroom, intercepting the dog one more time and planting a kiss on her forehead. He's not sure what time it is, but he's grateful for the extra sleep he got. He pees a lot, grateful for indoor plumbing. Then fills the basin and begins to shave. His hangover reminds him of the intense conversation he had with Rose last night.

Back in his room he finishes getting dressed. It feels odd wearing civilian clothes. A lot of things feel odd this morning. He can smell the coffee brewing downstairs. *I wonder how much they sacrificed the last few weeks just to have enough for me this morning.* He hears Ginny padding down the hallway again but is startled when he turns to see Rose standing in the doorway.

"Good morning, brother."

"Hey, Rose. I was just on my way down. Does your head hurt as much as mine?"

"I have no idea what you're talking about. I feel fine." She smiles and leans against the door frame. "Listen, Oma is having a rough start this morning. That's pretty common these days. I was going to bring a breakfast tray to her room but thought you might want to do it instead."

"Of course. Yes. Yes. I will."

"Okay, I'm going down now to get everything ready. It won't take long."

Ralph hesitates. "Sure thing. I'll be right behind you." Rose watches him retrieve his attaché from the corner of the room and place it on the bed. She turns and walks away. Ginny's head swivels back and forth, not sure where she should go. Finally, she chooses Rose and brushes by her as she makes her way toward the rear staircase. Ralph carefully removes the bible, still wrapped in the extra packing he added before departing Washington. He cradles it under his right arm and turns for the doorway. For some reason he hesitates, steps back and returns to the bed. He gently returns the bible to the empty slot in his attaché, leaves his room and walks toward the inviting aroma of coffee.

* * *

Camp Huntsville

Stephan brings a steaming mug of coffee to his lips. For the first time since his arrival in Texas, he yearns for the warm weather. He presses his palms against the side of the mug. He thinks about his response to Oma. Neatly printing his Vienna address on a small slip of paper and inserting it into their private "messenger pouch." Hopefully, Rose has returned the pouch and watch to Oma, not knowing that she has become the unwitting courier. Stephan feels guilty that Rose is unaware but tells himself that Oma should be the one to tell her not him. He's grateful for Oma's assistance yet can't imagine how this frail woman, isolated in her home, is going to help. But it doesn't matter. It gives him hope and that makes him feel better, a fleeting emotion that is shattered by the sight of Schroder approaching. Stephan scratches his scalp, squeezes the back of his neck and exhales slowly. *These visits are never good.*

"Jurgen, I need to talk to you."

"Okay, then talk."

"Nice to see you in such a pleasant mood this morning." He sits down opposite him, arrogantly grabs the mug and starts sliding it back and forth between his open palms, oblivious to the precious liquid splashing onto the table. Stephan wants to pull it back and hurl coffee in his face. He remains quiet, waiting for the Nazi's inevitable orders that will be difficult to stomach. Schroeder does not disappoint.

"Today is an American holiday."

"Yes, Thanksgiving."

"A stupid concept. Giving thanks to the Almighty for what?"

Stephan just stares at him, pulls the mug back and sips his coffee.

"Not in much of a talking mood are you Jurgen?"

"Too excited to hear what you have to share, that's all." Even Stephan surprises himself with the sarcasm he is dishing out. Schroeder is not amused.

"Well, since there is this petty holiday, and we have a temporary shutdown around here, we thought you might be able to help us out with a little assignment this evening."

"Go on." Stephan tries to sound detached, but he is visibly worried what's coming next. Like a lion that smells its wounded prey, Schroeder is not about to back off.

"You still have a lot to prove to us, Jurgen. The material you got was a good start but it's time to get your hands dirty. Demonstrate your true loyalty."

"What do you want me to do?"

"The Holy Ghost is going to make a visit tonight and you'll be part of the team."

Stephan's voice is quivering. "Visiting who? What team?"

"So many questions. I thought you would be excited to finally prove to your friends how loyal you are to the Fuhrer."

"I already stole information for you. What more do you want?"

Schroeder's smile sickens him. "Well Stephan, my friend, this is what *we* want. You are going to help us with your new friend, the chaplain..."

"What? The chaplain? I barely know the man. This doesn't make sense."

"Actually, it makes perfect sense. He wouldn't trust a word we say, but he'll certainly trust you."

"Why would he trust me? The coffee is tearing a hole in Stephan's stomach.

"You both knew that lazy dog who killed himself."

"Hugo?"

"Was that his name, Hugo? Such a loss. Well, you are going to visit Heller at the chapel later tonight, after they feed us their Thanksgiving slop. Tell him you have some things that your friend left behind for him. Maybe more of those putrid jazz recordings they listened to...."

Stephan stands up abruptly and accidently knocks his coffee mug onto the floor. It doesn't shatter but skids and spins away, stopping at the foot of the adjoining table where a more light-hearted conversation is taking place. "That won't work. He won't believe me."

"Well then you better start practicing being believable. Once you get to the chapel, we'll create a diversion, so the guards will be distracted. Then we'll join you and your new friend, and you'll help us teach him that his anti-Reich rhetoric has gone too far."

"He's a priest for God's sake!"

"Exactly why he needs to be reminded that his religion has no place here or anywhere else. Don't you agree?"

"Hugo was right. You are a swine." Stephan turns to leave.

"We have people inside the American garrison who could make things very uncomfortable for your American girlfriend."

"Don't even think about laying a finger on her, do you hear me?" Never has Stephan wanted to kill a man more than right now. He isn't even afraid. Knows he could choke him to death with his bare hands. It would be easy. Shut him up once and for all. But he wants to protect Rose more than he wants to end this Nazi's life. He has no choice. Must bide his time. Has to figure out a way to warn her. He turns to Schroeder, stunned at the words coming out, "Just tell me where I have to be and what I have to do."

"That's more like it. Simple really, even for an imbecile like you Jurgen. Spend time with him at dinner to soften him up -- and so we can keep an eye on you. Then visit him at the chapel later for all the fun."

* * *

The Bauer Farm

Ralph steadies the breakfast tray on his right palm and taps gently on Oma's door. Her soothing voice replies, "It's open Rose, come in." She is surprised to see Ralph but not disappointed. Ralph's first impression is how tired she looks.

"Good morning, stranger. What a nice surprise. I'm so sorry I couldn't wait up for you dear. Seems I need more of my beauty sleep than ever before."

"Well it must be working because you look more beautiful than ever."

"Bullenscheiße."

Ralph smiles. *Bullshit. One of the first curse words she taught me.* He carefully balances the tray and closes the door. Oma notices her breakfast is covered with a pale yellow linen napkin.

"What surprise did you bring from Frau Bauer's kitchen?"

"To be honest Oma, I have no clue. Rose just said to keep it covered and not to trip going up the stairs. Just following orders, so....so far, so good." He places the tray on a small end table beside Oma's chair. "Is this okay?"

"That's perfect. Now come here so I can give you a big hug." Ralph embraces her warmly before he is smothered with kisses. She points to the bed, already made up, the familiar flowered pillow shams tucked into place. "Here, sit down, I want to hear everything you are able to share with me without committing treason."

Ralph eases on to the bed and points to her tray. "Plenty of time for that but eat your breakfast first." Oma lifts the napkin and squeals with laughter. Her Bavarian brotzeit, It's all there: bread, cheese, a pretzel, sausage with mustard. Even a small glass of beer. Ralph recognizes the meal immediately and enjoys Oma's reaction. "Well, looks like Rose delivered your second breakfast a little early."

Oma is already sipping her beer.

"Okay, Captain Bauer, let's move on. How has this war been treating you, hmm?" She drops her napkin and it slides off the tray, settling at Ralph's feet. He leans over and stretches to pick it up, but his ailing shoulder limits his reach. He instinctively groans catches himself, then reaches for the napkin with his good arm. Oma is carefully following every movement as he snaps the napkin and places it back on her tray.

"Thank you, Ralph. Did you injure yourself?

He is silent. His eyes pleading, *"don't ask me."*

"Ralph, you know we have very little time to be with each other. It's better for you to shed those silly little secrets. You can trust me. As long as I don't have a second glass of beer."

"Oma, I missed your sense of humor. There are things I can't talk about. I swore an oath."

"Sounds so mysterious and exciting."

"Not really. But it is important to the war effort."

She hands her tray to Ralph. "Does that include the triple top secret file that explains how you hurt your shoulder?"

He places the tray on the bed. Then he slides down on the floor, pulls his knees up to his chest and settles his body against her chair. It's a spot he's occupied hundreds of times before. At the feet of his grandmother as she patiently taught him a language that has given him a purpose in this war.

"What happened Ralph?"

He tells her everything, sparing no detail. When he is finished, Oma is silent.

"Did I upset you Oma? I probably said too much."

"No Ralph, I'm actually wondering how you feel, now that you've finally shared this story?"

Ralph, still sitting on the floor, exhales and leans backward. "To be honest, I feel much better. I'm glad I told you."

"And I'm glad you shared it with me. I'm curious, did you tell Rose any of this?"

"Nope. You're the first. To be honest, Rose has been doing most of the talking since I got home."

"Well now it's time for her to listen. Would you mind sharing it at dinner?"

* * *

Camp Huntsville

Back in his barracks, Stephan is dreading the next few hours. He's been on the receiving end of the "Holy Ghost" and knows he will be unable to inflict that kind of suffering. While concerned about Rose, he weighs Schroeder's threat against her, and lets common sense prevail. *It's just a toothless threat.* Heller is a different story. His life is truly at risk. *How can I warn him?* Stephan is alone in the barracks and begins pacing, the floorboards squeaking under his weight. He feels the pressure of time passing with no solution in sight. He peers out the window and focuses on the cross-hatch pattern of the chain link fence that separates each of the prisoner compounds. Beyond his focal point is the first of two 10-foot high barbed wire fences that surround the entire camp. *Rose is safe out there. Heller is at risk in here.*

He pauses then moves with purpose away from the window. Motivated by a sudden thought, he returns to his cot, still tidy despite the chaos in his life. He reaches underneath for a large rectangular-sized wooden vegetable carton with flimsy sides that barely hold its contents. It wobbles as he pulls it out and lifts it onto the cot. Inside is the usual collection of junk and personal items any prisoner would keep. From the bottom, he carefully removes a piece of paper that has been folded enough times that it is one-fourth its original size. He surveys the room to make sure he is still alone. He smooths the paper out on his cot. It is an extra copy of Colonel Warren's blank stationery. Retrieving a pen from the box, he hesitates, searching for the right words. Squeezing the pen, he quickly scribbles a message in German.

You are in danger. Leave the chapel.
I will try to warn the Americans, but it may be too late.
Protect yourself and destroy this note.

He re-folds the paper, this time placing it in the breast pocket of his tunic.

Outside, framed by the barracks window, Stephan sees a familiar figure in the distance. Corporal Burns. They haven't seen each other since the day Stephan pushed him to the limit and defied his orders to leave his workshop. *You don't have time to waste. Go.* Stephan quickens his pace and finds himself well past the barracks and heading toward the closest thing he has to a friend. Burns is strolling along the inside fence, his rifle strapped over his shoulder. *What do I tell him? What can he possibly do?* Stephan remembers the sentry towers. He slows considerably and looks to his right, following the base of the tower twenty feet straight up to the now-familiar sight of an armed guard. They've been warned repeatedly not to get too close to the barbed wire, an imaginary line ten feet out that should not be crossed. The Americans call it the deadline and they will shoot without warning. It's already happened to a couple prisoners. One poor guy was just chasing a soccer ball. Now he's a statistic.

Stephan waits until Burns makes his turn and heads back toward him. *This is my chance.* Burns finally sees him and smiles immediately. Stephan waves and walks parallel to the fence, careful not to alarm the sentry. He looks up at the tower and realizes the guard is following his movements, his rifle trained on him. Corporal Burns sees the interaction and understands Stephan's hesitation. He raises his fingers to his lips and delivers a shrill whistle. He gets the attention of his counterpart in the tower. He motions to Stephan then to himself as if to say, "let him approach." Stephan looks up again and can see that the sentry has backed away. Stephan acknowledges him, then slowly approaches the warning line, still a considerable distance from where Burns is standing. *I'll just tell him the truth. I can make a difference.*

Burns' expression changes to bewilderment as he looks past Stephan, who can sense someone approaching from behind. Before he can even turn around, Schroeder wraps his arm around him in a seemingly friendly gesture. Schroeder waves to Burns and mutters through a fake smile, "just keep walking with me and don't look back." Schroeder is holding Stephan's elbow tightly, steering him toward the barracks. Corporal Burns resumes walking but remains curious. He looks back once as they disappear into the barracks. Inside, Schroeder immediately shoves Stephan, who tries to break his fall. He ends up flat on his back looking up at the enraged Nazi. Before Stephan can even get back to his feet, they are joined by Captain Siegel, who does all of the talking.

"Jurgen, the next time I see you it better be with Heller. And whatever warning you thought you were delivering to the Americans, don't ever think about doing that again. Or you won't live through the night. Is there any part of that you don't understand?"

"The misunderstanding is all yours. You idiot."

Siegel's rotted teeth are on full display as he laughs at Stephan's response. "I have to hand it to you, Jurgen, you've got balls. I never saw that in you."

"Well I always knew that both of you were morons." Stephan points to Schroeder, who is straddling the doorway, with one foot outside the barracks. "And what he just did proves it." Schroeder surges forward and grabs Stephan. He lifts him up by his shirt collar, but Stephan is so tall he clumsily releases him. Siegel pushes Schroeder away.

"Stop. Leave him alone. What did you mean, Jurgen? What did he do?"

"He stopped me from talking to the American guard, Burns. That's one of my sources." Stephan watches their expressions as he lies to them. *Keep going.* They each look at one another in confusion so Stephan continues the deception.

"I was going to ask about the guard rotations tonight, so your little plan could actually work, but thanks to Schroeder that never happened. You want me to help but you don't trust me. You want me to prove my worth, but you threaten me. You even threaten the welfare of the American girl, but you don't realize that she is also one of my sources. How am I supposed to serve the cause when you make every effort to sabotage me?"

Siegel starts clapping his hands very slowly, mocking Stephan with false applause. "Bravo, Jurgen. Bravo. Such a brave soldier. Well, we still don't trust you. In fact, we'll be watching you in the mess hall, just to be sure you don't change your mind. Isn't that right corporal?" Siegel turns to Schroeder, who just shakes his head and steps completely outside the barracks, leaving Stephan alone with Siegel. Stephan stares at the vacated doorway, then slowly turns back to Siegel. "When we get back home captain, that man will end up in a real prison. This war has given him a license to hurt people and he enjoys it."

"You mistake his loyalty to the Nazi Party as a defect in his character. It's men like him that will allow us to win this war. He's doing his duty, just like you, right Jurgen?"

Stephan swallows hard and continues the ruse. "Let me show you something." He returns to the cluttered box under his cot. He slides it away from the bed, then reaches in with two hands and delicately pulls a phonograph record from the pile. He pushes the box back under the bed with his foot. A thin brown wrapper covers the record with a hole in the middle that exposes the record's label. Stephan blows on the wrapper, then wipes it with his sleeve. He walks back to Siegel. "I plan on giving this to Heller in the mess hall and telling him I'll be bringing more over to the chapel later. I'll say they are a gift from Hugo. That will make it personal for him. He can't refuse."

"Let me see that."

"Careful, it's fragile."

"Like I give a shit Jurgen." Siegel roughly inspects the record and sleeve. He seems satisfied and nods his approval. He bends down and violently rips a pillowcase away from its pillow and tosses it at Stephan. "Of course, we'll be expecting you to lead the way. In the meantime, we'll be watching and waiting."

Stephan does not reply. He slips the phonograph record under his right arm. Once outside he heads toward the mess hall. As the barracks fade in the distance, he finally turns around to see if he is being followed by Schroeder. For now, he is alone. Without stopping he shifts the record envelope to his left hand. With his free right hand, he reaches inside his breast pocket and removes the note he had scrawled earlier. He slides it carefully inside the record envelope, picks up his pace and heads toward the mess hall. The sun is beginning to set, and he feels a considerable drop in the already unseasonably cold temperature. He turns his collar up to deflect the wind and realizes that it is practically torn away from his shirt. It's a reminder of Schroeder and his violent tactics. Stephan realizes that he has the chance to stop him -- to save a man's life. He wonders if he'll ever see home again.

* * *

The Bauer Farm

Ralph tosses a log onto brilliant embers in the seldom-used fireplace just off the kitchen. It easily warms a living room that once seemed too small to contain the boundless energy of the Bauer siblings. On the wall opposite the fireplace sits a polished mahogany radio cabinet and a single overstuffed chair used by Uncle Pete whenever he listens to the President's fireside chats. Ralph uses a poker to gently encourage a new flame to rise. The heat presses his face as he slides the fireplace screen back into position. Ginny refuses to move, her tail thumping softly as Ralph maneuvers around her. The fire's warm glow and the gentle flicker of candles Rose has placed on the table in the kitchen soften the harsh edges on this cold Thanksgiving evening. Uncle Pete, Oma and Rose are waiting for Ralph to join them. Ralph reaches his chair on one side of the long table, enormously satisfied that a plate of Oma's biscuits serves as a centerpiece. His mouth waters as he anticipates the gravy he's about to ladle on top of them. "Oma, forget the turkey, this is all I need to make my meal complete. You don't know how many times I've dreamt of these."

"Flattery will get you everywhere, Ralph. You better fill up because our traditional dinner is somewhat lacking this year."

Rose, wearing a muted yellow dress that hung in her closet for nearly a year, laughs. Her right hand caresses an earring that belonged to her mother as she adds a little detail. "Rationing, combined with the fact that one of the cooks was briefly incarcerated while Uncle Pete was searching for a courageous lawyer and the result is...biscuits!"

The mood is lighthearted, so Uncle Pete doesn't hold back. "And the two men of the house provided no support last night because...."

"Because why Uncle Pete? You can say it. Why were we late?" Everyone is laughing but Ralph wants an answer. "Come on. I want to hear you say it."

"Say what?"

"Let me help you. We ran out of...?"

"Money. That's right, money. We ran out of money because I had to bail out your sister, and poor Clyde." The mention of Clyde dampens Rose's mood quickly. She moves her napkin to her lap. "I just wish he could have joined us tonight. But he wanted no part of it."

Uncle Pete offers a reason. "Maybe he was a little embarrassed and felt uncomfortable being here."

No one is surprised by Oma's sympathetic response, "He has no reason to be embarrassed."

Ralph tries to lighten the mood again. "Actually, Uncle Pete is more embarrassed that he ran out of gas."

"You had to get that in, didn't you? No respect for your old uncle. And, as I remember, you were the one driving."

"You're right about that Uncle Pete."

Rose senses her brother's attempt to make the most of their limited time together, adding, "Okay boys enough bickering. Let's blame it on the weather. It's cold as hell with the furnace out. Ralph, how about another log on that fire?"

Ralph obliges. When he returns to the table, he is carrying the bible he's protected for so many months. He sits down. Rose, unaware of what her brother is holding, asks, "Are you going to read us a story?"

"No actually, it's an extra piece to a story I've decided to share with you...with Oma's encouragement. She and I spoke about it earlier this morning and of course she wants me to bare my soul and release my demons."

Rose wrinkles her nose. "Sounds ominous."

"Nothing like that. Kind of embarrassing, actually. A POW saved my life last year while I was interrogating him."

Rose reaches across the table for her brother's hand. "Oh my God Ralph. What happened? Why didn't you tell us?"

"Hard to believe but a runaway truck was about to flatten me when this guy pulled me out of the way. As for the reason I never told you, quite frankly I was embarrassed that an enemy prisoner saved my life far away from any battlefield. Pretty pathetic."

Uncle Pete raises his voice, "Nothing about surviving war is pathetic, Ralph."

"Sure, I understand that." He looks at his pen pal, Rose. "Still, it's not exactly the kind of thing you write home about. Anyway, the guy lost this bible." He places it carefully on the table. "And because I've now gone from angry to grateful, I'm on a mission to find him, thank him and return it." He rubs the gold lettering. "Which, by the way, has not been easy."

Rose is becoming increasingly attentive, fidgeting in her seat. She asks, "do you ever wonder what happened to him?"

"All the time Rose." He moves the bible toward Oma. "Not just to return it. But because I never said, 'thank you.' I could have done it as soon as it happened, but my pride got in the way. And then it was too late. He was shipped off to a POW camp here in the states and I was left with...."

"This." Oma finishes his thought and delicately rubs the bible. She opens the book and smiles. "It is in German. At least he was a man of faith."

Uncle Pete adds, "If he was carrying a bible, he sure wasn't a Nazi. We learned the difference real fast working with the

Krauts in the fields."

"No," Ralph explains, "he wasn't even German. He was Austrian."

Rose nervously twirls her earring.

Ralph continues. "We saw a lot of that when we were processing the Axis prisoners. They may have been wearing a German army uniform, but they could have been from other countries – Austria, especially."

Rose is now fully engaged. "Ralph, we were told that most of the prisoners who came here last Spring were from North Africa, is that true?"

"Oh yeah. Camp Huntsville was one of the first camps, that's a fact."

"I'm curious. It was such a traumatic event for you, this prisoner saving your life. With all the interrogations you were doing, would you remember what this guy looked like?"

"I would recognize him immediately. You never forget the face of your guardian angel, right?" He smiles but Rose escalates her line of questioning.

"So, could you describe him for me? Your guardian angel?" She glances sideways at Oma who is following every probing question.

"Well, for starters he was tall, unusually tall. I had to look up at the guy when I spoke to him."

Rose grabs her napkin with trembling hands. Ralph sees she is distressed. It confuses him. "Hey are you alright?"

"Blond hair? Hazel eyes?" Her voice is quivering.

Ralph just laughs. "Sure, him and every other member of their master race."

Rose gets oddly defensive. "He's Austrian. Not German. He's not a Nazi." Now Ralph is completely perplexed. He looks to Oma, who has an expression similar to Rose.

Uncle Pete intervenes. "Ralph is there anything else you can tell us about this guy. Starting with his name. Do you remember his name?"

"I don't. But I'm working on it. Would anyone care to tell me why you are interrogating me like this. What's going on?"

Oma opens to the front of the bible and begins carefully scanning the first few pages. She stops abruptly, her fingers noticing the ragged remnants of a missing page. "There's a page gone."

"Um, yeah. I have it."

Rose stands up. She begins walking around the table toward her brother. "What do you mean? Where is it?"

"Easy now. That's another long story for another time. It had a note written on the page."

"What kind of note?"

"Jesus, Rose. Calm down. It was a note from his mother."

"What did it say?"

"Why in God's name would you care what it said?"

"What did it say?!" The question comes from Oma, Rose, and even Uncle Pete, almost in unison.

Ralph looks around the table. The words come so easily. "Keep your faith and come home to me."

Rose barely whispers, "Stephan." She reaches out her arms to Oma, who stands to embrace her. Rose buries her head in Oma's shoulder and begins to sob. Oma fixes her eyes on Ralph who looks to Uncle Pete for something, anything to help him understand what just happened.

"Wait. What? Who the hell is Stephan?"

Uncle Pete leans back on his chair, shakes his head and smiles broadly. "Ralph, I don't know what I'm enjoying more. The bewilderment on your face. Or those two ladies happy as a hog in mud. Remember I told you yesterday that I think you're gonna like this POW who's taken an interest in our family? Well it seems you may have met this young man before the three of us ever set eyes on him. Looks like your guardian angel is living over in Camp Huntsville."

* * *

Camp Huntsville

Stephan enters the mess hall and reluctantly joins the long line. He is struggling to follow a normal routine, but nothing about this evening is ordinary. He grabs a tray to receive generous portions of a traditional Thanksgiving dinner he has no intention of eating. His appetite abandoned him hours ago. He is indifferent to the food being placed on his tray as he manages the assembly line offering of turkey, stuffing, sweet potatoes, green beans, and cranberry relish. He is numb to the prisoners around him complaining about this traditional American meal that leaves them terribly disappointed. He scans the long tables throughout the room, searching for Heller. He clings to the foolish hope that if the chaplain fails to appear it would somehow relieve him of any responsibility for a hateful act he must avoid at any cost. The only test is how much courage Stephan can muster to do the right thing. Finally, he notices Heller on the far side of the room leaving the food line and searching for an empty place at one of the tables. Stephan realizes what a solitary life Heller must lead. He is scorned by the Nazis and avoided by the prisoners who don't want to incur the wrath of men like Schroeder. That's playing out right in front of him as Heller struggles to find a seat.

Stephan instinctively loads his tray with utensils, knowing they won't be needed. He scans the crowd again and stops on the large frame of Schroeder filling one of the aisles. He can tell immediately that Schroeder already sees him. *He's prob-*

ably been watching me since I got here. Stephan follows him as he walks up the narrow aisle with long picnic-style tables on each side. Near the end of the aisle Schroeder slows considerably and turns toward Stephan, who understands what is happening. Schroeder is serving as a spotter and the subject is Heller. Sure enough, three feet away from where Schroeder planted himself, Stephan spots the chaplain. He is seated at the end of a table where the prisoners around him have left a buffer of two or three spots to isolate themselves. Stephan begins his journey toward Heller and their uncertain fate, his wobbly knees reminding him what his heart already knows: this is a life or death situation. As he gets close to the table, approaching Heller from the rear, he notices that Schroeder has positioned himself one table away on a bench seat that is within earshot of where Stephan will be sitting. Stephan refuses to make eye contact. Instead, he takes several deep breaths and tries to calm himself, but he's out of time.

"Major Heller, sir?"

The chaplain looks up from his dinner. His eyes widen at the sight of a familiar face. Schroeder is seated on the opposite aisle with his back to Stephan and Heller. His head is turned sideways, hoping to pick up their conversation.

"Excuse me, sir. May I sit down?"

"Good evening Stephan. What gives you the courage to sit with me, hmm?"

You deserve to live, and I'm going to help you.

"I wanted to thank you again for our little memorial service for Hugo. He was a special person. Troubled but special."

"Troubled? No more than any of us."

Schroeder is craning his neck to hear their exchange. But he cannot see their faces. Stephan turns to Heller. Facing him, he moves only his eyes sideways toward Schroeder and speaks softly, without any emotion. "Hugo was extreme. He always felt people were watching him. Perhaps he overreacted a bit."

Heller follows Stephan's eyes. The sight of Schroeder changes his demeanor. *He is playing along.* "Hugo could be a little paranoid at times. So perhaps we can agree that's what made him special."

Stephan awkwardly changes the subject. His voice begins to shake. "I remembered that both of you enjoyed jazz and played it frequently in the chapel."

Despite the tension, Heller manages a genuine laugh. "Not the kind of music you'd expect from the chapel, but it helped us relax."

A prisoner walking behind them drops his tray and the noise is jarring. Stephan cringes. Heller remains calm and composed. Schroeder is visibly annoyed by the distraction but remains in his seat, whispering urgently to the man who spilled his meal.

"How about you Stephan, do you enjoy jazz?"

"Since I have been in the army, I have not listened to that type of music."

"Ah, loyal to the Fuhrer I see."

Stephan is reassured by Heller's calm demeanor and responds, "Intimidated more than loyal would be the honest answer. Regardless, I brought this for you." From underneath his tray he pulls out the record envelope. With two hands he lifts it up and delicately hands it to Heller. The chaplain takes it and watches Stephan's eyes very carefully. "Hugo would want you to have this. I know it will have a *special meaning* for you."

"Thank you, Stephan. That is very kind."

Then Stephan raises his voice a little, just enough for Heller to notice and for Schroeder to hear. "If you don't mind, I can come by the chapel a little later and drop off a few more records that Hugo saved. I won't have any use for them."

"Alright, Stephan. when can I expect you?"

"I'll be there within the hour."

Heller stands and picks up his tray. He winks at Stephan. "I look forward to seeing you." The charade is finished.

Heller strolls casually away, deliberately avoiding any contact with Schroeder. His gait is casual. showing no sign of urgency and fear. He even takes a moment to engage with two other men who seem unafraid to approach the chaplain. One of them is Otto. Their conversation is brief and then Heller finally breaks away. He reaches the sanitation station and empties the remnants of his tray into an overflowing trash receptacle.

Stephan remains seated and watches Heller leave the mess hall, noticing for the first time that Siegel is standing near the doorway. His evil eyes darting left, then right. Stephan turns to Schroeder, who is in his face. "No time to delay Jurgen. Your job is just beginning!"

"Relax, corporal. He trusts me." Stephan pushes Schroeder aside. "That's why you picked me for this so let me do my job."

Schroeder grabs Stephan by the arm. "You're staying with me for the rest of this night. Let's go." He pushes Stephan ahead. As they near the mess hall exit Stephan senses a larger than usual gathering of prisoners outside. They are agitated and loud. *The diversion. Where's Heller?* He turns to speak to Schroeder who has been joined by Siegel.

"So, Jurgen, are you ready to prove your worth?" Siegel is shouting to be heard above the crowd. Stephan doesn't have the energy for a sarcastic response. He is scared. Siegel is holding a three-foot section of lumber. Stephan recognizes it immediately. It's a floorboard from one of the barracks. For the first time he hears the agitated voices of American guards behind him, but he can't see them. There are too many prisoners blocking the streets of the compound. Many of them have clubs as well. Pieces of furniture. Handles of garden tools. More floorboards. This is not a crowd. It is a mob.

Schroeder shoves Stephan. "Let's go. Now."

"No, I won't do it!" Stephan tries to maneuver away from them, but he is trapped, surrounded by Nazis wielding weapons. *You need to buy some time.*

"You coward. You worthless pig." Siegel steps forward and slaps Stephan's cheek with the back of his hand. Without hesitating, Stephan lunges at Siegel and tries to disarm him. Siegel pushes him away and Stephan is immediately struck on the side of the head by Schroeder's fist. He staggers, drops to his knees and gropes for anything to keep him from falling. Siegel raises his boot to Stephan's chest and pushes him backward into the crowd. *I'm going to be trampled alive.* Siegel reaches down, grabs his leg and drags him to a clearing several yards away from the mob. Schroeder joins them and gets his instructions from Siegel, "Take him with us to the chapel. He's going to do what he was ordered to do. Heller is going to die at his hands."

Schroeder lifts Stephan to his feet. Another Nazi pulls out a rag, shoves it between Stephan's teeth and ties it tightly behind his head. It reeks of mold and Stephan almost vomits. Still dazed, he stumbles forward with Schroeder's grip tightening. On the ground he sees a man being beaten and kicked. It is Otto. *Heller is next.*

Siegel and his band move quickly through dimly lit paths toward the chapel. Stephan resists, but his legs are weak. The floodlights that surround the prison are in a fixed position, so pockets of darkness allow the group to move freely and quietly toward their destination and Heller. When they arrive at the chapel, Siegel stations men at every conceivable exit. He takes two of the larger prisoners with him and bursts through the front door hoping to overpower Heller quickly. They are met immediately by an unexpected sound. Music. Glenn Miller's *In the Mood* is playing loudly. It bounces off the walls of the empty hall. Siegel searches half-heartedly. "He can't hide forever. We'll find him before the night is over and he will pay the price."

Stephan is dazed, his heart pounding. *Maybe he got away.* Siegel is interrupted by one of his men standing near the altar. "Captain, you should see this." Folded neatly on the altar is Heller's uniform. Laying on top of it is his chaplain's armband. One of the candles is smoldering. The wax is still warm. Below the candle holder lay the ashes of something that was just burned. The record reaches its conclusion, the exhausted needle on the turntable has nowhere to go. It produces a light scratching sound, reminding them that the man who started the music is not returning. Siegel looks angry and confused. He turns to see Stephan smiling through the rag in his mouth. He pulls Stephan away and pummels his face with a closed fist. Stephan can feel the bones of his nose move. Blood soaks the rag. "You won't be laughing when this night is over. Corporal, take him back to his barracks and don't lay a finger on him. I want the pleasure of watching him die."

Stephan and Schroeder are half-way back to the barracks when they hear a muffled order to "halt" from one of the sentry towers. Then, gunshots startle them. Schroeder keeps repeating "they shot somebody, they shot somebody." Despite his heightened anxiety, he has not loosened his grip on Stephan, who is being forcibly dragged by his collar. More shots ring out, this time without warning and Schroeder instinctively crouches low, momentarily losing his grip on Stephan as the collar rips off. Stephan immediately sprints away, tearing the gag from his mouth. He sucks in air. Stumbles briefly. Regains his footing and can now see the entrance gate to his compound less than twenty yards away. He can hear Schroeder panting heavily and gaining ground. There is a heavy presence of Americans along the other side of the chain link fence that separates the compounds. For Stephan it is the wrong side. He is close enough now to realize he is in trouble. The gate has been locked and a group of Nazis are rapidly filling the space between the Americans and him. *No way out.* Schroeder tackles him from behind. Stephan hits the ground hard, his face smashing the gravel first. His eyes burn, and more blood fills his mouth. Schroeder calls for help and the mob responds immediately. Stephan is still on the ground, but he knows he is surrounded by vultures. A violent kick to the groin leaves him breathless. Someone grabs his hair and raises his head from the ground. *They don't even know who I am. Don't even know why they are beating me.* The next blow comes from a flat object that crushes the side of his head. His body goes completely limp. He can't move but still hears muffled voices. Schroeder isn't finished. He barks at the men, ordering them to drag Stephan to a nearby latrine. "Dump him in with the shit and piss where he belongs." He spits at Stephan's bloody face as the men move his body.

Like savage dogs, still hoping to fill their bloated bellies one more time, the rest of the mob moves away looking for their next victim. As they clear the area, the American guards can finally see Schroeder and his gang dragging Stephan's body toward the latrine. The gate opens, and three guards slip through with pistols drawn, barking orders to stop. One of the guards is Corporal Burns. All of the Nazis abandon Schroeder, leaving him standing alone over Stephan. Schroeder has no place to run. He picks up a club and slides into the latrine. Burns is the first to arrive. He almost doesn't recognize Stephan, his face is so badly bruised, but he has spent so much time with him he knows by his height alone he is the watchmaker's son. "Jesus, Steph. Jesus."

Burns composes himself. "Get him to the hospital now and move your asses." He grabs a flashlight from his service belt and shines it at the latrine. Six doors. He cocks his revolver, releases the safety, and approaches the first door on the left. The excrement is already overpowering. He kicks the door in while shining the powerful light inside. Nothing. Second door. Schroeder pounces before Burns has a chance to react, knocking him backwards. The flashlight drops to the ground but Burns manages to keep his feet. Schroeder's club hits him squarely on the left shoulder. Burns winces but still remains standing. The beam from the flashlight on the ground throws enough light that Burns sees the second swing coming. He steps back and feels the club miss his face by inches. Schroeder is now vulnerable, and Burns doesn't miss the shot. A single bullet pierces the Nazi's shoulder and drops him backward into the latrine, his twisted body lodged between the commode and the half-closed door. Burns picks up the flashlight. He approaches the latrine door, looks around to see if anyone else is in the area, and with his boot shoves Schroeder's face deeper into the hole of the commode.

THE DAY AFTER THANKSGIVING

* * *

CHAPTER 41
Huntsville, Texas

Empty-Handed

Ralph turns the ignition in Uncle Pete's truck and immediately checks the gas gauge as the needle settles on half-filled. Good to go. Ralph was supposed to be meeting with Colonel Warren this morning to finalize the orders to pick up Heller. Now, it's also become a surreal journey to thank the prisoner who saved his life and happens to be infatuated with his sister. He looks over at Rose, who is more intense than he anticipated. He gives her shoulder a gentle reassuring squeeze. "Hey, it's going to be okay. I'm a little edgy, too."

"No kidding Ralph, you've been up since four this morning. I heard you outside with the dog. What were you doing?"

Just trying to get my head on straight. Let's face it Rose, this is beyond coincidental. It, it..."

"Was meant to be?"

"That's not what I was going to say. I still can't get past the fact that out of more than a quarter million prisoners who surrendered in North Africa, one guy – the one who also happened to save my life – not only gets shipped to Huntsville but has been working on our farm for the last six months. I mean, that's just not possible..."

"Unless it was meant to be."

"I don't even know what that is supposed to mean Rose. Seriously, what do you want me to say?"

She is looking out the closed window. "Say that you understand he is a good person. That he's not a Nazi. That he has parents who raised him with the right values. That if he wasn't wearing a German uniform, we wouldn't even be having this conversation."

"It's hard for me okay? I saw what the Germans did to our guys. What their tanks did on the battlefield. Tanks by the way that *your friend* repaired so they could go back into battle and kill more Americans."

Now she turns directly to her brother, jabbing the air with her finger. "His name is Stephan and he saved your life."

Ralph ignores the truth and presses on. "All I'm saying is he could have refused to serve. He could have followed his conscience and stood up to the Germans. Instead he took the easy way out."

Now Rose is fed up and the dashboard feels her anger. "I can't believe those words are coming out of your mouth. The easy way out? Do you understand they would have killed his parents or sent them off to a camp if he refused to serve? You understand right? Mr. high and mighty. You're all gurgle and no guts." Rose removes her glasses and cleans them even though they are not dirty. She places them back on her nose, folds her arms and stares straight ahead.

"Whoa sister, now you're questioning my courage?"

She continues to stare straight ahead. "Would you have had the courage to stand up for Clyde or would you have walked away? Or as you like to say, 'take the easy way out.' I think we both know the answer to that."

Ralph knows he is whipped. "Okay, look. Can we call a truce here?" Rose's only response is silence, which is good enough for Ralph. She continues to stare ahead as the truck heads down the final stretch of highway towards Camp Huntsville.

Three miles later, Rose speaks for the first time. "This is strange. I've never seen it like this before. Why all the guards and trucks out here by the road?"

"Beats me, but we're about to find out." Ralph rolls his window down as he slows the truck to a crawl, then finally stops at a checkpoint staffed by two MPs. "Do you know these guys?"

"No. What the hell is going on?"

One of the guards approaches Ralph's side of the truck and stiffens a bit when he sees the uniform. "Good morning sir. Ma'am. What's the reason for your visit today sir?"

Ralph starts to reply but Rose is already leaning across his chest to interrogate the guard. "What's going on here? Did something happen? Why are you stopping us?"

The guard looks to Ralph for help as Rose slumps back into her seat. "My sister actually works here. Colonel Warren's staff. And I've also got an appointment with the colonel this morning."

The guard asks for their names, then produces a clipboard that verifies Rose's employment and Ralph's appointment. "Okay sir. Sorry for the inconvenience, ma'am. I'm sure you know the way from here." He steps back from the truck and signals for them to pass. Before pulling away, Ralph asks what his sister is already thinking. "Is there a reason for all the security this morning?"

"All I can tell you is they had some prisoner unrest last night. It was pretty crazy, but they got it under control quickly. I'm sure Colonel Warren can fill in the details. Thanks again for your patience, sir."

Within minutes the truck is parked, and Ralph hustles to keep up with Rose as she bolts through the lobby on her way to Colonel Warren's office. The guards – all familiar faces – let her pass. The mood is somber. She can feel it. Halfway down the final hallway, Rose sees Brenda from the typing pool rushing to intercept her. *Oh God not now.* Before Rose can brush her aside, Brenda blurts out, "Oh Rose, I'm sorry. I'm so sorry."

Ralph finally catches up just in time to hear his sister's quizzical reply. "Sorry about what? What are you talking about?"

Brenda is sobbing, trying to catch her breath. "I thought you knew. That you heard."

"Jesus Christ, Brenda heard what?!"

"It's Stephan, he was attacked last night. Beaten badly."

Stephan's voice explodes in her brain. Their conversation just a few days ago. *My life is in danger.*

"Where is he? Where did they take him?"

"He's right here. In the hospital." *The Holy Ghost may be visiting me soon.*

Once again, Ralph is in pursuit as Rose hurries back to the lobby and veers down the hallway toward the hospital. She can see Corporal Burns at his usual post. She barely notices that his left arm is in a sling. The sight of him releases uncontrollable sobbing. She stumbles, and her left shoe slides off her foot, causing her to veer into the wall. She balances herself and continues toward Burns, with no intention of retrieving her shoe.

"I want to see him."

Burns tries to be as gentle with Rose as he can. "Miss Bauer, I can't. That's not my call. I've got strict orders."

"He needs to see me, please?" Ralph is now standing beside his sister, her shoe dangles from his fingertips.

"Corporal, I'm Rose, um Miss Bauer's brother. Is there any more information you can give us? Anything?"

"Sorry captain. I wish I could."

"Rose are you okay?" It is the voice of Colonel Warren and it is the only time she has ever heard him use her first name. She turns, further surprised by his appearance. His eyes are bloodshot. His tie hangs from a loosened collar at an awkward angle. His broad shoulders sag ever so slightly. "Colonel, I just found out what happened. When we....I'm sorry colonel, this is my brother.... "

"Captain Ralph Bauer, sir." Ralph salutes and Colonel Warren responds briskly. "Listen, why don't we sit down, and I'll explain everything I can. Give you a chance to get that shoe back on your foot." He motions to the first room he sees, which ironically is Stephan's small workshop. Rose and Ralph take the only two seats while Colonel Warren leans against Stephan's workbench. He wastes no time. "Last night there was a riot staged by the Nazi prisoners in our camp. Pretty damn organized. In addition to defying authority it was used to create a diversion."

Rose probes. "A diversion from what?

"While the guards were trying to restore order, many of the Nazis were attacking prisoners because of their anti-Hitler sentiments. These targets were not random. Each was ambushed on purpose. One of those men assaulted was Private Jurgen."

"Is he going to be alright?"

"Rose, it does no good for me to mislead you. He was beaten pretty badly. His right leg was broken. So was his collarbone."

Ralph squeezes his sister's hand.

"And he took a few vicious blows to the head, the usual approach when these thugs carry out one of their attacks. However, the doctors seem pretty confident that his head injuries are manageable. No skull fractures and no sign of brain injury. He's just heavily sedated."

This time it is Ralph who speaks up. "So, we won't be able to speak with him?"

"Not today, that's for sure. But he's not going anywhere for a while. He's got a lot of mending to do before we transfer him."

Rose shoots out of her seat. "Transfer? Why are you transferring him? He didn't do anything wrong!"

"Okay, young lady you need to calm down. We are transferring the prisoner to protect him. That's our responsibility. All of the men who were attacked need to go to a safer place. And God knows he deserves it. He's been a model prisoner. If I had five thousand Private Jurgens I could have run this place in my sleep."

Ralph feels sorry for Rose. Plus, plenty of guilt about the things he said this morning about Stephan. *Obviously, he was courageous enough to stand up to the Nazis. Look where it landed him.* Another realization finally settles in -- once again he will not have the opportunity to thank Stephan. Once again, he'll be denied closure. What he says next surprises Rose. "Are the men who did this going to be punished? Can he at least get justice?"

"We're doing the best we can Captain. Most of the troublemakers will just be transferred. The ones we can actually pin these assaults on will face stiffer penalties, maybe even court-martials, hopefully hard labor for some of them."

Rose interjects. "Do you know who attacked Stephan?"

"He was attacked by a mob, so we really can't identify most of them. But we do know the ringleader." He turns to the doorway and nods in the direction of Corporal Burns. "In fact, the only reason Jurgen is still alive is because that individual was stopped -- shot actually by Corporal Burns." Rose eyes widen. She grabs her brother's arm. "The guard we were just talking to. That's Burns. They worked closely together. In here. This was his workshop. Oh my God." For the first time

Ralph notices the trays of watch parts stacked behind them.

Colonel Warren continues to explain. "The corporal took a pretty good blow to his shoulder, but he managed to fight back and stop the attack. The Nazi was shot once in his arm, so he'll survive. A better result for him than some of the others who broke for the fences. Two were shot. One didn't survive. So, we've still got a lot to sort out. Plenty of tough decisions to make and to be honest, I don't know if I'll be making all of them."

Ralph understands the army well enough to know what Colonel Warren means, but Rose is confused. "Why? Who is going to decide?"

"Well, Rose, it's very possible that I might be moving on as well. When something like this happens, the responsibility falls to the man in charge. As it should. So, there could be some consequences for me and more changes coming here."

"But Colonel, you stopped the attacks, didn't you?"

"Well, I appreciate your support Rose, but some won't see it that way. Despite the warnings, things still escalated pretty quickly, and they may want fresh blood in here." He takes a deep breath. "Also, there's one more piece of information that complicates things." There is a prolonged silence. Neither Rose nor Ralph respond. They are just waiting. "One of the prisoners managed to escape last night. Not that it hasn't happened before. They almost always get recaptured. Most of them actually come back on their own when they realize how good they have it in here."

Ralph leans in. "So, what's the complication?"

"Well, unfortunately, it's complicated for you captain."

"For me, sir?" And then it hits Ralph before Colonel Warren even explains. He sags in his chair and bows his head. *He's done it to me again.* Colonel Warren confirms it. "The chaplain, Heller, is gone. Looks like he cut through the fence down by the incinerator. Took advantage of all the diversions." Ralph actually chuckles to himself. "So, colonel, it appears that I'll be leaving here empty handed."

CHAPTER 42
Huntsville, Texas

Favors

Before Ralph returns to Virginia, Oma has some unfinished business with him. Uncle Pete is waiting outside, his truck ready for the ride back to the Houston train station. He promised Ralph it will be an uneventful journey and vigorously rebuffed his nephew's attempts to arrange for a return by bus instead. Now Uncle Pete leans against his truck, half-listening to Clyde's smooth voice talk about winter projects but more interested in what Oma and his nephew are discussing in her bedroom perched directly above them.

"Ralph, nobody is going to believe what you experienced these last few days. Not exactly the peaceful, relaxing break you were hoping for I'm sure." She is fidgety. Her breakfast tray sits on her bed, untouched.

"It's been the most unique Thanksgiving of my life Oma, that's for sure. I wish I could spend more time with you. I hate to even say it but duty calls."

"Well before you head off to your secret war, I hope you've taken care of business here at home."

Ralph is not sure what she means. His whole life right now is filled with unfinished business. She can see the perplexed look and doesn't hesitate to clarify. "You and your sister. I trust you are parting on good terms."

He hugs his grandmother who is standing near the window. She hasn't been able to sit down since Ralph entered the room. She walks stiffly to her dresser, picks up a brush and labors to work it through her healthy head of silver hair. Barely gripping her brush, she uses it to punctuate the air as she lectures her nephew. "Do not leave here with any ill feelings toward your sister. She may not be brave like you or Stephan, but she has the kind of courage you've never been asked to summon. A special courage. The kind this country is going to need. You should be very proud of her."

"Of course, I'm proud of her. I just hope she and Clyde don't end up in jail."

"Oh, don't you worry. By Christmas that will all be resolved. And some heads will roll too." Ralph knows better not to ask, preferring instead to offer a heart-felt compliment. "Well, Oma maybe your granddaughter learned to be courageous because she had a very special teacher. Did you ever think of that?"

"All the time Ralph. I hope your mom and dad are satisfied with the job Uncle Pete and I did for all of you kids. We tried our best. I know it wasn't easy for you, but we loved you every step of the way. And God knows we are proud of all of you."

She's talking like she's never going to see me again. "Okay, that's enough emotion for this Thanksgiving. Let me get moving here before Uncle Pete forgets he's driving me to the station." He hugs her extra long. Oma holds on to his shoulders then slides her right hand down to the chest of his crisp military tunic that Rose pressed for him. She taps his chest lightly, looks him directly in his eyes then closes her own. "Oma, what's wrong?"

"Nothing dear, nothing. I just need a little favor."

"Just a little favor? No offense Oma, but there has been nothing little about anything since I've been home." Her eyes are twinkling, and he melts. "Okay tell me what you need."

She pulls her top dresser drawer open and gently removes a small piece of paper. She hands it to Ralph. "This is the address of Stephan's home in Vienna. I want you to find his parents."

Ralph stares at the paper, now in his right hand. "How did you get this?"

"You think you're the only one with clandestine schemes?" He starts to object but his grandmother places her cool fingers on his lips. "Now Ralph, you just told me earlier that duty calls. And God knows, not even once, have I asked you what's so hush-hush about what you do up there in Washington. I'm not even going to ask you now. But I want you to look me in the eyes and tell me you can't help me with this." She barely touches the paper. "Just tell me it's not possible, and I'll take that back."

Ralph slips the paper into his breast pocket. She smiles. He kisses both her hands softly and turns to the door. As he descends down into the kitchen, she shouts in German, *don't lose that paper, it's my only copy!*

As soon as he steps onto the porch, Uncle Pete cranks the ignition. The passenger side door is already open. Ralph notices Clyde coming out of the tool shed and flashes him the V for victory sign. Clyde smiles and tips his cap. Ralph throws his gear in the back of the pickup and climbs into the cab. The truck is moving before he even closes the door. He nods to Uncle Pete and closes his eyes, then slides down enough so he can rest his head against the narrow ledge between the rear window and the back of his seat. He is leaving his home in a far different state than he ever imagined. Nothing is settled. Pieces of everyone's lives still need to be sifted and sorted. He smiles again when he thinks about the favor for Oma that needs his attention. *There might be a way.* He feels surprisingly calm. His mind wanders away from the farm to a final conversation he had with Colonel Warren. Alone. Ralph did most of the talking. When it was over, he had secured a very big promise from the colonel. *Oma isn't the only one who knows how to drum up a favor.* They've only been on the road a few minutes, but Ralph feels drowsy and knows sleep is coming. It's a sleep he welcomes.

DECEMBER 1943

✽ ✽ ✽

CHAPTER 43
Huntsville, Texas

Images

Inside the Bauer kitchen, Rose presses a warm mug of tea to her cheek. With her thumb, she erases a hint of frost from a single windowpane. She peeks outside and shakes her head. *I can't believe she wants to do this.* Oma sits on the porch. Her rocking chair positioned to take full advantage of a brilliant early December sun that washes the eastern side of the house and bathes her fully. She wears a seldom-used taupe winter coat. Wool mittens, reeking of moth balls, protect her hands. Her favorite yellow shawl is wrapped around brittle shoulders for added protection from a gentle breeze that rustles the small needles of the loblolly pines. She faces the dormant fields and barren work yard that will remain lifeless until the next growing season.

Uncle Pete wraps his arm around Rose's shoulder. She grabs his hand and squeezes it tightly. "She's one of the bravest people I know."

"Rosie, she'd charge hell with a bucket of ice water. But we'll be right here if she needs us."

"Maybe Uncle Pete, but I need to hear what's going on. Will you crack that window please?"

"Sure thing." As he slides the window upward, he asks, "any updates on Stephan?"

"Still not able to see him but Corporal Burns is keeping me updated. He's healing slowly but the doctors say he will be well enough to be transferred by the end of the year, maybe early Spring if we're lucky."

"The rest is out of your control Rosie. For now you better focus on this disorderly conduct charge."

"Oh don't you worry Uncle Pete, that's exactly what we're doing."

"You and your grandmother are thick as fleas on a farm dog. I hope you know what you're doing cause that toothless lawyer I found you is worthless. And Judge Tyler is not about to back down. Tough as they come. And not about to go soft on Clyde with an election coming up. You're foolish if you think you can convince him otherwise."

"You've got it all wrong. We're not going to convince him. He is." Rose points beyond the porch.

Gravel churns in the driveway. Oma instinctively consults her beautiful timepiece that Stephan repaired. A police cruiser pulls into the work yard, moving way too fast and kicking up hardened mud as its driver slams the brakes. The car comes to an ungainly stop inches from the picket fence. Soon, the pudgy frame of Bobby Ford fumbles with the gate then rushes toward the porch. He's not wearing a coat. Rose smiles. *Good.* He lands heavily on the first step that creaks stubbornly under his weight. Before he can reach the third and final step, Oma's clear, defiant voice is punctuated by an open mitten that establishes an immediate boundary. "That's far enough deputy. Far enough."

The deputy is startled to see her. "Mrs. Bauer, I didn't expect to meet with you out here. Why don't we take the conversation inside? I'm sure you would be more comfortable." He is already shivering.

"No thank you. I'm quite comfortable right here. Would you care to move away from the door?" Rose pulls Uncle Pete away from the window.

The deputy steps back and blows on his hands. “If I had known we were meeting out here I would have dressed a little differently.”

“Don’t trouble yourself. I’m sure this conversation won’t take very long.”

“Fine by me Mrs. Bauer. You asked to see me so what’s on your mind this morning?”

Oma takes her time. Just stares and rocks. Rose giggles and whispers to Uncle Pete, “I believe his lips are turning blue.” Uncle Pete is fixed on the porch. He steps closer to the window to hear Oma.

“Well deputy, it’s no secret the hearing for Rose and Clyde will be coming up very soon and I was hoping we could reach an understanding before we waste too much of that nice judge’s time.”

“Reach an understanding? I’m not sure I follow Mrs. Bauer. That’s between their lawyer and the court. In fact, we shouldn’t really be talking about it. Best to keep me out of it.”

“Oh, I disagree deputy. After all, it seems you’ve had a lot to say about this case to a lot of people since you arrested my granddaughter and Mr. Turner. Not exactly an example of impartiality, do you think?”

“I have no idea what you are talking about. The facts are pretty straightforward.”

“Oh now deputy we both know there was no crime committed.”

“We’ll let the judge decide that. Seriously, Mrs. Bauer I have better things to do with my time than debate this. I guess I’ll see you at the hearing.” He backs away from Oma and grabs for the railing. Before he can turn away, Oma offers a single word. “Barbara.”

“Beg your pardon, who?”

"Barbara Turner. Clyde's daughter. You remember her?"

"Yeah, sure. Did some domestic work for me and my wife a while back."

"That's right. Bright young woman. A good worker, was she?"

He responds as he moves down the steps. "You'd have to ask my wife about that, Mrs. Bauer. What's this got to do with the hearing? Or with anything for that matter?"

"You take one step off this porch and I will be having the rest of this conversation with your wife." *She is so strong.* Her threatening tone also has the deputy's attention. He remains frozen on the step. "What kind of conversation? What's going on?"

"So, why don't you tell me why Barbara Turner's services were no longer needed. Or would you prefer I ask your wife?"

"There you go again with my blasted wife. What are you getting at?"

Oma begins rocking smoothly in her chair. Every creak of the porch seems to underscore her command of the conversation. "Again, tell me why you let her go."

"I've had enough."

"No, seems to me it was your wife who had enough. It was bad enough she had to struggle with her suspicions. But when she walked in on you trying to assault that poor young girl, she finally did have enough."

"I never touched that little bitch."

"Her name is Barbara. And yes, you did touch her. In fact, every time you had a chance you laid those fat appendages all over her."

"So, what do you intend to do here, Mrs. Bauer? Go off to Chicago or wherever the hell she took her black ass and drag her back to Huntsville? Have her make false accusations against me? Her word against mine?"

"Not just her word deputy. I don't think you realize how many enemies you have in this town. Seems like you've spent too much of your career intimidating people and stepping all over them. The only thing that's saved your sorry white ass is your poor wife. But that's about to change, especially if she learns that Barbara Turner is *only one* of your many indiscretions."

"Old woman. You are overdrawn at the memory bank. You need to get inside and thaw out."

"I'm touched that you are concerned about my well-being, but I'd be more concerned about how you're going to explain to Judge Tyler how you and his sorry excuse for a wife decided to share some private moments..."

The wind increases along with the shrill pitch of Bobby Ford's irritated voice. "That's bullshit. You're a liar!" The front door opens a crack. Uncle Pete is clearly visible with Rose right behind him. "Everything okay out here?" He looks directly at the deputy. Oma waves him away, "We're fine. Just catching up. Deputy Ford was just warning me about Judge Tyler. Says he's tough as stewed skunk."

The door closes, Rose giggles and takes up her post again at the window.

"Look, it's cold as a frosted frog out here. Can we take this conversation inside and try to sort out whatever's bothering you?"

"First of all, deputy, you will never set foot inside my house as long as I'm alive." She nods to the window and the bespectacled eyes of Rose peering above the curtains. "And I'm pretty sure that order will stand long after I'm dead. Beside you'll be long gone by then."

"Are you threatening me?"

"Heavens no. Certainly not the way you threatened Barbara. The way you warned her if she ever said anything to her father you would make sure he never held another job in Huntsville again. And on top of that you forced that poor girl to leave town, just so you didn't have to deal with her 'black ass.' Terrible language, especially considering how fond you were of her company when your wife wasn't around."

Oma has shredded his bravado. "What do you want from me?"

"I understand your daddy has a lot of political connections in New Orleans. Word has it that he's been after you for years to move, get a fresh start. Maybe you should take him up on that offer, rather than tarnish his ambitions with unsavory rumors."

He laughs nervously. "You're telling me to move?"

"Oh, my no, deputy. It's merely one of many *suggestions* I have for you today."

"Many suggestions?"

Oma tightens the shawl around her shoulders and rocks a little more emphatically. "That's right. Drop the charges. Tell the judge that you don't want to waste his time with such a trivial case that's not nearly as important as his re-election. Then go home and tell your sweet wife that you're ready for that new start. I'm sure Louisiana law enforcement is a little short-handed with all our brave boys serving overseas. Maybe your daddy can help find a suitable job for his big...brave... boy."

"I've had enough."

"Oh, no, no deputy, there's more." Oma removes her shawl, revealing what first appears to be a small leather box on her lap. "Do you know what this is?"

He swallows hard. Just nods.

"Well of course you do. Who doesn't recognize a Kodak Brownie, right? It's a wonderful way for people to take photographs of all sorts of things. Sometimes they could be embarrassing photographs of things we don't want people to see. Things that could even ruin a person's career. Did you know that Barbara was an aspiring photographer? She used to take amazing pictures of all sorts of things. Very inconspicuous. Had a real knack for capturing images of people when they least expected it. We happened to stumble upon some of those pictures."

He stammers, "I n-never saw her take a picture."

"Well of course you didn't deputy. You were too busy trying to get inside her panties. Barbara didn't take them when she was with you. She took them when you got careless with the others. You remember *all* the others, don't you? Let's see, I can name at least three...."

He is half-way to his car before Oma can get herself out of the rocking chair. She is leaning on the sun-blistered railing, her stiff joints having surrendered to the cool air hours ago. "Deputy?"

He doesn't look back. Doesn't respond. His car moves slowly away from the house before braking abruptly. Deputy Bobby Ford pounds the dashboard violently, unable to drive through the rage of a cornered dog. From inside the car, muffled curses incoherent and raw finally subside. The brake lights flicker off and the car moves down the driveway. Oma removes her mittens and waves goodbye forever.

Rose turns to Uncle Pete. "She'd charge hell with a bucket of ice water."

TWELVE DAYS BEFORE CHRISTMAS

* * *

CHAPTER 44
Huntsville, Texas

Bittersweet

Rose has been thinking about this day for a fortnight. Now it has arrived, and the bitter-sweetness of the moment is intense. She's grateful that she will finally be able to see Stephan. But that also means he's well enough to be transferred. This visit is a parting gift from Colonel Warren, who is being replaced -- another bittersweet reality of the last eight months. Rose is grateful for the time she served on his team. Understands more than many just how hard he worked and the personal sacrifices he made. Yet the army can discard him without a single measure of appreciation simply because they can. She will miss him. When he granted this favor, he made it clear this is not a social visit to an old friend. "You are still meeting with a prisoner of war, Rose. Don't forget it." How can she forget it? She will be escorted at all times. She will never be left alone.

Still, the beginning of her visit is off to an encouraging start. Her escort is Corporal Burns. Already, she feels better. He searches the leather satchel she is carrying without incident. Then invites her to follow him into the hospital. Rose has never been inside the camp hospital and she is surprised at how bright and cheerful it feels. It helps that a large Christmas tree, brilliantly lit and decorated with care, greets her as she passes the nurses station. Aside from a few rooms set aside for emergencies, the rest of the facility is wide open with beds aligned side by side. Privacy is not a priority. Only about half of the beds are occupied so the room feels less crowded. Corporal Burns glides quickly down a narrow aisle and heads towards a far corner of the room. *He's made this trip before.* She follows him closely but most of her attention is focused on locating Stephan. Finally, she sees him at the very end of the row closest to the windows. It is nearly evening so little daylight is available, but she sees the smile of recognition and a gentle wave. Corporal Burns stops and allows her to pass, staying as far back as possible. He whispers gently, "please remember the rules, Miss Bauer."

Stephan is sitting upright. His back against a pillow that cushions him from the railed, half-moon headboard of the government-issued bed. He is smiling broadly as she approaches. "Merry Christmas, Rose." He is speaking English.

"Fröhliche Weihnachten." She wishes him Merry Christmas in German and continues to speak his language. "Stephan you look so healthy. How do you feel?"

"I feel very good. The Americans have taken such good care of me. I am very grateful." He looks at Corporal Burns and says in English, "I am grateful for that American, too." Corporal Burns winks at them both but manages to maintain the look of a guard watching his prisoner.

Again, in German Rose responds, "I missed you Stephan."

Understanding why Rose wants to speak in his native language, he responds in kind, "I have thought about us a lot over the last month."

"Good thoughts I hope." She sits on the unoccupied bed closest to his. He swings his long frame around to face her. "All good thoughts Rose, but...."

"Ah, we've already gotten to 'but.' Let me down easy."

Thirty days-worth of soul searching pours out of Stephan.

"What do you imagine for us Rose? Honestly. With this war. With our situation. What do you truly imagine?"

"I imagine that we will tie Corporal Burns hand and foot, leap through that window where Clyde is waiting on the other side with Uncle Pete's truck and we'll drive to Mexico to start our life together."

He laughs. "Now, I feel better. That is exactly what I was thinking."

"Seriously, you could have died. You should have died. But you didn't. You survived for a reason. For me. For your parents."

"Do you know how many men on both sides of this struggle pray for the same outcome? I am not special Rose. I'm just lucky."

"What about me? Is that just luck?"

"I don't want to hurt you."

"Oh, please Stephan, don't use that line. Just tell me there is no future."

He reaches out for her hands only to hear Corporal Burns deliberately clear his throat. Rose reminds him, "apparently we are off limits to each other."

"You see. Exactly. That's what they've already decided. We are off limits. Neither of us has any say in what happens next. I am going to be transferred. The war will end God knows when. They'll ship me back to Europe and I will never see you again."

"But do you *want* to see me again?

"Of course, I do. That's all I've thought about this last month."

"Stephan, do you believe in fate? That if something is meant to be, nothing can stop it from happening, even a world war?"

"More than anything, I want to believe that."

Rose turns to Corporal Burns. "May I give him something? A small gift?"

The corporal rolls his eyes. "Yes, ma'am."

Rose reaches inside her satchel and pulls out the bible. She treats it with reverence as she holds the book in both hands and leans in toward Stephan.

"What is that? Why are you giving it to me?"

"Take it."

Stephan's hands are trembling. He has been separated from his mother's bible for more than six months and he knows immediately what Rose is holding. Tossed into the Tunisian desert by a bored souvenir hunter. His tears come quickly. "I don't understand. I, I, how is this possible?"

"Take it."

He finally lets the book slip into his hands. Rose is tempted to hold onto him and never let go but she simply releases her fingers. And the bible is home. Instinctively, Stephan opens to the front. Rose knows what he's looking for.

"That page is missing but it's safe."

"Safe? You have it. You took it?"

"No, my brother has it."

Stephan wipes his tears with one hand, holding the bible with the other. He takes a deep breath. Exhales. "Rose, forgive me but I am so confused."

She can't help but laugh, soaking in the joy and confusion and complexity of it all.

No one is more confused than Corporal Burns, watching this game of emotions over a little black book. He struggles to understand what they are saying as Rose begins moving around Stephan's bed, careful to keep her distance, her arms and hands in motion, her voice more animated now. *She's telling him a story.*

"Stephan, when you were taken prisoner, you were being interrogated by an American and something unusual happened."

"Yes, that's right. But I never told you about it."

"No, you didn't. But my brother did."

"Your brother? How does he know?"

"Fate, Stephan, do you believe in fate?"

Gripping the bible tightly, he repeats, "how does your brother know?"

"His name is Captain Ralph Bauer, and before you were sent to Huntsville Texas you saved his life."

In English, Stephan blurts out, "Holy Shit!" It startles Corporal Burns whose eyes widen. Stephan tries to apologize in English, "I'm sorry. That was told to me by Boss Clyde's friends when we were picking the cotton."

Corporal Burns adds, "well, they'll be happy to know you put it to good use."

Stephan has a special bond with Corporal Burns but right now he's not interested in a friendly exchange. There's too much he needs to learn from Rose. She is now standing at the foot of his bed, her hands wrapped around the white rails. Stephan turns slowly in his bed to face her. His sore ribs, a reminder of Schroeder's brutality, slow his movement. "Rose, where is your brother? I still don't understand."

"It's a long story Stephan. He wanted to meet you in person but after you were assaulted that was out of the question. He is gone now but assures me he has the missing page. But don't ask me. I have no idea how it got separated from your mother's bible."

"I am so grateful for this Rose. Thank you. Perhaps someday I will get to repay your brother."

"It's the other way around Stephan. My brother wants to

repay you. Right now, he is doing everything he can to reach your family and let them know you are safe."

"That's admirable Rose but nobody has been able to reach my family. The Red Cross has been trying for years."

"If anyone can do it Ralph can."

"Miss Bauer. I'm sorry. But we are way over the time we were given. We've got to wrap this up." Corporal Burns' words have a greater sense of urgency. Stephan remembers hearing that agitated voice before.

Rose feels weak in the knees. Her thighs are trembling. "Stephan, I don't know what to do. How to say goodbye."

"Then we won't say goodbye to each other. Instead, let me give you a gift as well." He stands up and walks to the foot of the bed. They are only inches away from each other, far too close for Corporal Burns' liking. Stephan offers the bible back to her.

"What are you doing?"

"I am doing what my mother would want me to do. I am giving this to you for safekeeping, just as she gave it to me. Someday, I will come back for it. This is our bond. It made me want to survive for my family. Now, it makes me want to survive for you. So, you must promise me that you will keep it safe for me Rose."

She nods but says nothing.

"Rose, do you believe in fate?"

She laughs through the tears. "You know I do."

"Then promise me you will keep it safe until we see each other again."

"I promise, Stephan."

"We are leaving Miss Bauer." Corporal Burns turns abruptly toward the front of the room and barely begins to walk away. "Follow me, please."

Stephan offers the bible and Rose allows it to rest in her hands. He vividly remembers the exchange with his mother too many years ago. Like her, he does not let go of the book but instead slides his hands over Rose's. He gently kisses her on the forehead. She leans into his lips.

"Don't make me turn around Miss Bauer!"

Bittersweet.

CHRISTMAS DAY

CHAPTER 45
Huntsville, Texas

Red Tail

The unseasonably cool weather around Thanksgiving has given way to more normal conditions for Huntsville as Christmas Day delivers sunny skies and the thermometer threatens to break 70°. Church services were heavily attended throughout the area and now the fleeting daylight of winter beckons people home to celebrate the remaining hours of their holiday. Inside the Bauer home, a freshly cut pine tree stands in the living room in the spot normally occupied by Uncle Pete's favorite chair. For now, his overstuffed throne has been exiled to the far corner of the room. This way, the tree can be easily seen by visitors entering the home from the rear kitchen door. The shortleaf pine is Oma's favorite. Its clusters of short needles and a pyramid shaped crown provide the perfect frame for simple strands of tinsel that hang freely from its stubby limbs. There are no lights on the tree. Not because Oma is opposed to them. The lighting sets that Uncle Pete tried to nurse through another season have finally surrendered. No electric lighting sets are being made during the war, so the tinsel and home-made ornaments reflect the type of simple Christmas decorations that most American families are content to display during these more somber times. The only exception is the illuminated tree top angel that Rose ordered for her grandmother in

1941, several weeks before Pearl Harbor. Uncle Pete thinks it's gaudy. Oma calls it "inspirational." The box containing the angel proclaims, "She's New! She's Beautiful!" As Christmas day gives way to dusk, the gentle light from the angel reflects off the tinsel and casts a warm glow for two visitors standing nervously with Rose in the living room.

There is a gentle knock on the kitchen door.

Uncle Pete almost runs to open it. "Let me get that." Rose remembers a time not so long ago when her uncle was hesitant to welcome the same visitor into their home. *Trust me, sweetheart, he'll sort this out.* Clyde's melodious voice fills the room. "Merry Christmas, Mr. Bauer."

"Same to you Clyde, same to you." Uncle Pete shakes his hand immediately, almost pulling Clyde across the threshold.

"Well, thank you Mr. Bauer. Thank you for inviting me."

"Clyde, we are so happy you are joining us." Oma, entering from the kitchen, embraces him and kisses his cheek. The back door is still open blocking their view of the living room. "As usual Mrs. Bauer it sure smells good in here."

"Thank you, Clyde. Please come in." Uncle Pete shuts the door and Clyde steps into the kitchen, unsure where he should go next. He's waiting for his hosts to guide him, but they are both silent, looking at one another. Then he hears *her* voice. "Hello, daddy."

Barbara rushes toward him and throws both arms around his neck. He gently embraces her and begins to sob, burying his head deep into her shoulder. She steps away, barely able to speak. She laughs briefly, begins to cry, and uses her thumbs to wipe away tears from her father's cheeks. "Merry Christmas."

"You're so beautiful. And so grown up."

Oma adds. "She looks more than ever like her mother."

"Thank God for that" is Clyde's reply. They all laugh, and Clyde feels himself starting to relax, just in time for Barbara's next surprise. "Daddy, there's someone I'd like you to meet." She turns back toward the living room and Clyde follows her eyes to the tree. Standing there is a Negro soldier. Rose watches Clyde, whose face still registers surprise. "Daddy, this is Lieutenant Earl Spencer."

"It's an honor to finally meet you sir, Barbara has told me so much about you."

"All good, I hope."

"Yes sir, your reputation is intact." Clyde just smiles. Rose can see his fatherly instincts take over. "Well, good, good, that's fine. You're in the army son?" Barbara glances sideways at Oma and smiles.

"Yes sir." But Barbara quickly interrupts. "Air force. Army air force," she says proudly. Earl clarifies further, "I'm with the 332nd Fighter Group."

"You're a Red Tail."

"I am indeed sir."

"You're a pilot?"

"Just got my wings, sir. So, I can officially say I am a pilot."

"God bless you son. God bless you." He turns to Barbara, "How did you..."

She leaves her father's side and stands next to Earl, holding his hand. "I've been doing some photo assignments as a stringer for local newspapers. There was a story being done about the Tuskegee Airmen and I got the assignment. That's when we met."

"So, you aren't in Chicago?"

"It's a long story daddy. I went where the work took me and that eventually led to Alabama. I didn't want you to worry. I just wanted to get settled first."

He looks at both of them smiling and winks, "are you settled?"

Earl looks at Barbara. "I can answer that sir. It looks like I'll be shipping out soon. Could be gone for a while. So, I guess *unsettled* is probably a better way to describe things. I – we – were hoping that maybe Barbara could come back to Huntsville while I'm away and then, God willing, we could try to make things more permanent when the war is over."

Oma claps her hands and raises them to her face. She is giddy, and so is Clyde who sincerely adds, "this is always home, as long as she needs it to be." He hesitates. "Things have changed around here. The war has changed a lot of things."

"Things are changing everywhere daddy. Faster than ever. Maybe we can figure out how to handle some of those things together." Then she adds with a sarcastic grin, "if you promise me you can stay out of jail."

Uncle Pete finally weighs in. "Well, I'm sure you heard those charges have been dropped against your father...and the other instigator. Seems the arresting officer convinced the judge it wasn't worth it. And then before I could even digest that news, the rumors start flying that Deputy Ford has decided to pursue another law enforcement opportunity in Louisiana."

"Shocking" is Oma's one-word reply. Barbara turns to Rose, "why do I have this strong feeling that your grandmother is the least shocked person in this room?"

Oma puts her arm around Barbara. "Honey, everyone knows that man was about as welcome around here as a skunk at a lawn party. Good riddance is all I have to say. And God bless his poor wife. Now why don't we let this young pilot get off his feet and enjoy a simple Texas Christmas dinner?"

FEBRUARY 1944

* * *

CHAPTER 46
Maryland

Fate

Stephan sits in a comfortable armchair in a small well-lit holding area outside the administrative offices of his new home, Fort Meade, Maryland. A square metal folding table in the middle of the room holds reading material, most of it written in German. A black radiator sits between two large windows, each covered with bent venetian blinds. The radiator hisses and clanks as it stubbornly generates heat for Stephan and the dozen other prisoners contemplating the next step at their new destination. It is late February but the temperature outside is still below freezing. Light flurries provide a stark contrast to the subtropical climate of Huntsville. They are 1500 miles north of Stephan's previous camp. His transfer from Huntsville has been far more complicated than he imagined. He thought he would be moved to a nearby camp in Texas but a visit from a Red Cross volunteer changed all that. Just days after Christmas, she visited him in the hospital with the news that his final destination would be Fort Meade, a small POW camp half-way between Baltimore and Washington, D.C. She repeated several times that he would be safe there, free from Nazi radicals. He felt she was trying to convince herself more than him. In the days following the visit, he worried about the length of the journey. Wondering if he was healthy enough to keep up. In retrospect, the week-long trip was a blessing.

It meant that he got to spend a little more time with Corporal Burns, who escorted his prisoner until they arrived in Atlanta. He knows he will probably never again look into the eyes of the man who saved his life, yet Stephan takes comfort from the few days they got to spend together. He'll cherish his American friend's final words. He spoke to Stephan in German. It was obvious that Corporal Burns had rehearsed the phrase diligently, wanting to desperately get it right. *Ich werde dich niemals vergessen.* "I will never forget you."

He thought a lot about the Bauers, grateful for the American family that redefined his life. Oma, the courageous quiet light who understood him before they ever spoke a word to each other. A woman who appreciated -- like few others -- the indescribable connection of a son to his mother. Who lost part of that connection in her own life yet still wanted it for him, a perfect stranger on the wrong side of a war that neither of them asked for. Uncle Pete. Full of bravado and wit, but the kindest man he's known since he said goodbye to his father in Vienna. He reflects grimly as he thinks of the weighty Texas expression Uncle Pete taught him. "He's not worth spit." He used it first to refer to Werner, one of Schroeder's lazy cronies who never broke a sweat chopping cotton. But Stephan can think of a lot of people who deserve that description. Hitler is at the top of his list. The Gestapo agent who threatened his family. Schroeder of course. The cowards who contributed to Hugo's murder. The Nazis who looked the other way while innocent people suffered. *Not worth spit.*

His thoughts are interrupted by the order to fall in line with newly delivered paperwork in hand. They move quickly beyond the waiting area then outside again. The cold air reminds him they are no longer in Texas. He quickly puts on the heavy winter jacket he was given during his brief session with the Red Cross when he first arrived here. He expects to be led to his barracks, but instead the group is diverted to a bus with blackened windows. Unsure of the layout of the camp, he assumes the drive to the barracks is further than he imagined.

He is one of the last in line to board the idling bus. It's very warm inside so he quickly removes his coat as he looks for a seat. The guards have spread the small group out, so nobody is sitting together. Stephan doesn't mind. *I'll get to know them soon enough.* His thoughts turn to Rose. He closes his eyes and pictures her during their last visit together. Avoiding goodbye. Believing in fate. Making promises. For all the terrible people not worth spit, there will always be his Rose. His hope. The bus begins to move. It doesn't take long for him to realize they are not being shuttled a short distance. He can't see outside but he knows they are on a highway, moving quickly. He reaches inside his coat and retrieves an envelope that has been opened and closed frequently over the last few weeks. He remembers the first time he held it in his hands.

It was early February, the new year 1944 was now a month old and he was still awaiting his transfer, unsure of the next steps in his life. Just another prisoner being moved to another camp. He can't remember the day exactly. The middle of the week. Maybe a Wednesday or Thursday. Stephan had finished breakfast and was keeping busy. He was exercising his legs, strolling up and down the rows of beds, stopping periodically with some of the prisoners whom he'd gotten to know over the previous month. Most, like him, were survivors of the Nazi assaults. Almost daily he would think about the chaplain, Heller. Word around the hospital was that he managed to escape. Still not found. If that was true -- if Heller managed to avoid the Nazis -- then Stephan would feel even more fulfilled. Knowing he had helped save a man's life. As he rounded the last row of beds and headed back to his own private corner, he heard his name being called by one of the day nurses. She was a volunteer from the local civilian hospital. A woman of few words but very caring. "Private Jurgen!"

"Yes ma'am."

"This is for you. Arrived in yesterday's mail." He wasn't really paying attention nor fully understanding her thick Texas drawl. He was more focused on what she was holding. An envelope. When was the last time he received an envelope? He couldn't remember. Didn't care. He wanted this one. He took it in his hands. *Danke.*

"You're welcome private."

The first thing he looked at was the return address. Saint Gallen. Switzerland. *I know this town. Right across the Austrian border!* Stephan raced to his bed carefully opening the envelope. Afraid to damage its contents. It was thin, but it definitely contained a letter. He stood by his bed, unable to sit. He ignored the body of the letter and looked first at the signature on the small delicate stationery. *Your loving mother.* He sat on the bed. His face grew pale and his hands trembled. He read it from the beginning.

Now he reads it again as the bus speeds away from Fort Meade. He's lost count how many times. He really doesn't need to read the words. They are committed to memory. But he wants to see the handwriting. His mother's words.

24 December 1943

My Dearest Son,

Blessed Christmas greetings to you. I have so much to share and so little time. We are moving again at the end of this day and I am unsure where we will go next. The most important thing you need to know is that your father and I are safe. It has not been without sacrifice and sadness, but we are still together and doing fine. I am so sorry that you have not heard from us until now. We have been hiding from the Gestapo and finally are safe in Switzerland because of the kindness of strangers. I know you are safe because of the American family that has been protecting you. They have been kind enough to share information with us. I feel like I already know Oma as a sister. For so long we knew nothing, but she has given us hope. She is my Christmas angel. Your father sends his love and wants me to tell you how proud he is of you. I promise to write again and share a more permanent address. Until then, Merry Christmas.

As always, keep your faith and come home to me.

Your Loving Mother

Beyond his mother's precious words, Stephan can't ignore the peculiar timing of the letter. It starts with the date. Christmas Eve. It was delivered to him in the hospital six weeks later. Switzerland to Texas in six weeks? Possible but highly unlikely. It often took months for letters to reach his friends in Camp Huntsville. Then the envelope. No stamps. At first, he questioned whether it was real. *Of course it's real. I know my mother's handwriting.* He looks at the envelope again. Pristine. Almost new. Not an envelope that traveled over 5,000 miles. Unless it was delivered in a different way. *My brother wants to repay you.* He never asked Rose what her brother did now for the United States. *Right now, he is doing everything he can to reach your family and let them know you are safe.*

The bus slows down, makes a series of turns and finally rolls to a stop. The guard is on his feet barking instructions. "This is the final stop. Take all your gear. If you leave anything behind you will never see it again." Stephan carefully stores his letter in his pocket. "On your feet. Have your paperwork ready." Stephan is one of the first to exit the bus. Immediately he is directed toward the entrance of a building that looks no different than the ones he used to frequent at Camp Huntsville. An MP greets him and gestures for his paperwork. He surveys the document and escorts Stephan down a brightly lit hallway toward a small room that can be viewed through a large plate glass window. There is nobody inside. The MP opens the door and waits for Stephan to enter. He closes the door and plants himself outside in the hallway. Stephan suddenly misses Corporal Burns. The only furniture in the room are two chairs facing each other across a small narrow table. Outside he hears the distinct sound of boots on tile. Definitely coming closer. The footsteps stop outside the door. Muffled conversation between two people. The door creaks open slowly, and Ralph enters the room. Stephan is paralyzed. He remembers the face. Cannot believe how much he looks like Rose. *Do you believe in fate?* Ralph closes the door behind him, taking forever to release his hand from the knob. He folds his arms and stares at his new unsuspecting stool pigeon. "Private Stephan Jurgen?"

"Yes, sir."

Ralph begins speaking in German. "Sit, please."

Stephan forces his body into the chair. His heart is pounding mercilessly. *If anyone can do it Ralph can.*

Ralph slowly draws his chair away from the table. He drops a thick file down and plops his body into the seat. He stares at Stephan, folds his hands on the table and leans in toward the man who saved his life. A silly grin comes next. "We have a lot of catching up to do."

Outside the room, the MP stands at ease guarding the door. He's done this a hundred times with Captain Bauer, the toughest I/O at P.O. Box 1142. A man who always gets his answers. He hears laughter, subtle at first. They are speaking in German and the conversation is animated. Then, in plain English, he hears the prisoner loud and clear. "Holy Shit."

SPRING 1947

* * *

CHAPTER 47
Huntsville, Texas

Quiet Light

Uncle Pete has been gone way too long and Rose is getting worried. She knows his bravado and quick wit can only sustain him for so long. He has to be hurting more than he's letting on. Oma's sudden death took them all by surprise. They knew her frail body was losing the battle with arthritis, but her sharp mind and positive outlook helped them ignore the inevitable. She never complained. Never hinted she was near the end. That morning ten days ago when Rose backed into Oma's room carrying her breakfast tray she knew it would be a different day. No greeting. The empty chair. Her sweet grandmother still in bed, asleep forever. When Rose didn't return to the kitchen, Uncle Pete knew, too. Then, it was just the two of them together, surrounding Oma's bed. The way it was supposed to be. Quiet tears for their quiet light.

Rose wears a modest lightweight black dress with mid-calf pleating. Her hair is longer now, with brushed out curls in soft waves that almost reach her shoulders. She wears no jewelry, with the exception of Oma's slender Glashütte wristwatch. Her fingers linger on the watch. *He repaired this for her.* She looks for her brothers in the crowd of neighbors and friends who quietly fill the living room and now spill into the open kitchen. It took almost two days to reach Henry and Ralph after Oma's death. And several more before they returned to Huntsville. The war ended nearly two years ago but her siblings remain far removed from the Bauer Farm. Ralph's military career is over but he still works for the government in a world that remains top secret. Henry surprised everyone when he announced he was going to stay in the navy and make it a career. He was one of the lucky survivors after his ship was sunk by a kamikaze strike during the Battle of Leyte Gulf. Rose hoped that would be enough for him to leave the Navy behind as soon as the war ended. But Uncle Pete saw it differently. "The two of them are at it again, Rose. Everyone is in awe of Ralph and his hush hush heroics so his brother's not going to rest until he's a goddamn admiral."

Rose smiles at the unspoken competition between her siblings. *It's gotten a lot more complicated than tossing pinecones.* She's grateful they are together to mourn the loss of Oma. She still can't find either of them among the visitors, whose muffled voices remind her of the school library. Whispers are occasionally interrupted. Sometimes by laughter. Or a raised voice that accompanies a renewed acquaintance. Rose doesn't mind. Oma wouldn't either. She is more concerned about Uncle Pete's absence and finding her brothers. She makes her way around the kitchen table. It's covered by a blanket of food that will yield days of leftovers. Ginny, older and whiter, hesitates to follow her, deciding instead to camp under the table and wait for treats from generous guests. Rose reaches the rear kitchen door and is surprised by the number of well-wishers mingling outside on the porch. She's grateful for the pleasant Spring day and the fresh air that frees them from the congested house. She steps onto the porch and passes Oma's rocking chair. It is unoccupied. Her yellow shawl draped reverently over the back. Finally she sees Henry, so handsome in his Navy dress blues, mingling comfortably in the yard with many of the Negro workers whom Oma treated so kindly. Henry is laughing and animated. Such a contrast to the stoic figure who delivered an unexpected eulogy at the cemetery. What touched people most was his eloquent description of Oma as a quiet soul who made a difference in so many people's lives. Her humility, Henry said, was beyond compare. But Rose knows Oma's legacy will be her courage. She always taught them that courage is not the absence of fear. It's doing the right thing in spite of the fear. Those weren't hollow words. Oma lived them. That's why so many people are here today. *But somebody she touched profoundly is missing.*

"Miss Rose?" Her thoughts are interrupted by Barbara, standing beside Clyde. "Sorry to interrupt Miss Rose but we have to get going or we'll miss our train."

"Barbara, Clyde. Oh I feel like I've hardly spoken to you since the service. I'm so sorry."

Clyde gently takes her hands but Rose squeezes his tightly. "Miss Rose, you know how much your grandmother did for us. We both want you to know we will never forget her."

Barbara rubs a small bump in her belly and adds, "I want my child to know about her. To understand what it means to do the right thing, even when it's a difficult choice."

"I knew it. I told the boys I thought you were pregnant. I'm so happy for you and your husband. And for the expectant grandfather of course." She gives Clyde a playful shove. "This will keep you busy in retirement Clyde."

"Not exactly retired Miss Rose but slowing down for sure. Little odd jobs here and there you know." He winks at Barbara. "Gotta pay my landlord."

"Do you have a ride?"

"We sure do. Daddy's got a lot of friends over there all willing to help." Barbara reaches out to shake Rose's hand but Rose hugs her instead. "Take care of yourself and keep us posted on that baby. Clyde, sure you don't want to hang around to chop some cotton?"

"Easiest question I've been asked all day. No thank you ma'am. I'll say my goodbyes to Henry and we'll be on our way. Please tell Ralph and Mr. Bauer that I said goodbye."

Rose scans the crowd again. "I know my uncle is missing. Didn't realize Ralph disappeared too."

"Wouldn't worry too much Miss Rose. You can count on those two."

Clyde takes his daughter's hand and leaves the porch to find Henry. Rose follows down the steps then turns sharply left, keeping close to the side of the house. She reaches the corner and feels the wind pick up, sweeping down the fields from the north across the young cotton plants. She knows this will be the last crop of hand-picked Bauer cotton. This time next year, one of those big corporations will swallow up this place, letting Uncle Pete keep just enough land to raise some livestock and maintain the house. The rest will be gone, just like Clyde and Ralph and Henry. Rose suddenly feels cold, thinks about the shawl. Desperately wants to wrap it around her shoulders the way Oma kept her safe and warm and protected. She turns toward the house and her guests. From behind she hears the sound of Uncle Pete's truck and that stubborn transmission. *Thank God!*

Rose turns and sees the truck with Uncle Pete driving and Ralph occupying the passenger seat. Both of them have shed jackets and ties worn at the funeral. Their sleeves are rolled up with arms dangling out opened windows. A cigarette hangs from Ralph's mouth. He sees his sister first and smiles broadly, his hand tapping the door. Directly behind the truck is a Huntsville taxi, mustard yellow and kicking up gravel. She doesn't recognize the driver. Three passengers are seated in the back. *Where are all these people coming from?*

The truck comes to a stop but neither Uncle Pete nor Ralph move from their seats. Both back doors of the taxi open simultaneously. From one side a middle-aged woman emerges wearing a simple black dress. Her silver hair is braided and clipped, barely reaching her neck. The man, seemingly older, is wearing a beautiful black suit that perhaps at one time fit him perfectly. Today, it hangs from his gaunt frame. He moves slowly around the taxi toward the passenger side where the woman waits patiently for him. They find each other and hold hands. The woman acknowledges Rose from a distance and smiles warmly. She is a stranger but Rose knows that smile. She could never forget it. *Stephan's smile.* The couple look inside the back seat, inviting their passenger to join them. Rose drops to her knees, gently sobbing, unable to move. Stephan emerges, healthier and more handsome than she ever remembers. Ralph finally leaves the truck and approaches his sister. He takes her elbow and gently helps her to her feet. "Hey sis, listen I know this is kind of overwhelming but I busted my ass and called in every favor from the last four years. So get over there and give the guy a proper hello, please? You're making me look bad."

"Ralph, I don't think I can move." They both laugh.

"Well, let me help you. It's the least I can do for the girlfriend of the guy who saved my life."

"How?"

He starts guiding her toward the taxi. "Not now Rose. Trust me. It's complicated. And Oma's fingerprints are all over this."

Stephan meets her half-way and she falls into his arms. She is sobbing again but manages her first words to him in four years. "You got taller."

He laughs and in perfect English responds, "and you are more beautiful than ever." He leads her to his mother and father. Down the same path where four years earlier he first saw the old woman on the porch. A place that brought him happiness and hope. Where the seed of courage was planted and dared him to dream of a day like today. Stephan's father kisses her softly on both cheeks. No words are spoken yet their bond is beyond question. Rose turns and embraces his mother for the first time. Still no words necessary between two women whose stories are deeply fused.

Ralph's tender touch is on her shoulder. He is holding the bible, safeguarded by Oma since that December day Rose made her promise to Stephan. She rests her head on her brother's strong shoulder. Stephan is behind his parents, his long arms cradling their war-torn bodies. Rose finally speaks to them. "We have something for you. I promised your son I would keep it safe until I saw him again."

His mother's trembling hands gently take the book from Rose. A single tear traces its way down his father's cheek. She opens the bible to the missing page that launched Stephan's journey. Inviting eyes, full of life, meet her son, who is already holding a carefully folded leaf of paper. He opens it and returns it to its rightful place. His mother reads her own faded words. She closes the bible then brings it to her lips, kissing it as tenderly as she kissed her son's forehead too many years ago.

THE END

EPILOGUE

* * *

1948
Basel, Switzerland

Heller sips his second cup of espresso. Strong and dark, he savors every drop. He is seated alone inside a quiet café near the Rhine River in the Old Town section of Basel. It has been five years since his escape from Camp Huntsville, but old habits are hard to break. Inside not outside. Never frequent the same establishment. No close friends or permanent relationships. Keep moving. He has never lost the instinct of a man being hunted. Perhaps he gives himself too much credit. The war has been over for three years. The Americans could care less about his whereabouts. His country has been partitioned among the Soviets, Americans, French, and British. Reeling economically and socially from the ravages of a war they initiated, the whereabouts of a rogue Catholic priest is an insignificant priority of a divided Germany. In many ways he is still a prisoner. Not one confined by fences or barbed wire. But a man who has no place to call home. A priest without a parish. Time has not been kind. Unable to purchase new clothing, the threadbare garments he wears hang loosely from a body that is considerably thinner. His face, unshaven for a few days, is grey and gaunt. His eyes are sunken and lifeless.

Since the night he freed himself from Camp Huntsville, peace has evaded Heller. The escape itself was easy. Hugo had seen to that. Heller donned the uniform Hugo had cobbled together. That allowed him to move more freely through the camp, using the diversion of the Nazi attacks to make his way toward the weakest link in the camp and ultimate escape. After he cut his way through the fence near the incinerator, Heller was able to string together enough lies to execute Hugo's plan. He easily hitchhiked his way into Huntsville, telling the motorist who stopped that he was trying to catch up with an army buddy who invited him to join his family for Thanksgiving. That got him close enough to the bus station for the last bus heading south towards Mexico. Hugo's meticulous fake credentials and the loose change he saved was all Heller needed. The rest was challenging but uneventful. Work as a laborer in Mexico for several months. The most fulfilling job, helping a local pastor in central Mexico where he actually celebrated Mass and visited the sick. He ultimately bribed his pastor and found stowage on a less than seaworthy ship carrying hemp to Canada. From there, it was a series of odd jobs and misadventures that carried him across the continent and ultimately to Europe as part of a relief mission. By then, he was openly wearing his collar and taking advantage of the good will and generosity of anyone who would help his cause: get to Switzerland. Not to eventually get home to Germany. Not to start a new life in a neutral country. Not to escape the past. Just one reason. The only goal he's ever embraced since he cut through that chain link fence and barbed wire. To find her. Sofia.

For all the good he has tried to do since his errant ways in North Africa, Heller cannot rest knowing the danger he placed her in. Not to mention the damage to her reputation. All the vile and despicable people who crossed his path got away with acts of pure evil while this innocent woman wanted nothing more than to do something meaningful with her life –

and he took that away. A selfish act to protect himself.

Slowly, he has connected the dots. He has spoken to more Red Cross officials then he'll ever remember. Wearing his collar often helped. One scrupulous official in Bern began asking too many questions of him. That made him nervous, so he backed off for several months. This time he thinks he has found her. This time, his burden may be lifted.

He pays for his espresso and steps outside into the bright sunshine. It is such a beautiful day. He should walk. But time is of the essence. He ignores the opportunity to cross the Rhine via a nearby pedestrian bridge. Instead he times his walk perfectly and arrives minutes before the ferry is scheduled to leave. He ambles to the side rails. The craft is lightly filled. Soon he is on the opposite bank and heading up a steep cobblestone street toward a heavily populated residential area. He is surrounded by one spectacular architectural specimen after another. Fifteenth century buildings that defy time just as they escaped the Allied bombs less than six years ago. He consults the slip of paper he's been holding in his hand since he left the café. The ink has run slightly from sweat on his palms. It doesn't matter. He has memorized the address. He stops an errant soccer ball that comes his way. Kicks it back to a group of children who follow it like a mouse to cheese. The apartment building seems out of place among the historic buildings that dot the wide avenue leading up from the river. It's easy enough to gain entry to the courtyard and soon he is scanning the signs for the correct number. Apartment C-23. The sign points toward a narrow set of steps on the east side of the building. His heart is fluttering. That second cup of espresso isn't helping. He removes the light raincoat he's been wearing. Underneath he is dressed in black. His tattered Roman Collar, on full display, appears far too large for his shrunken neck. Inside, he can hear the sounds of children. Mixed with adult voices. Her voice. For a brief moment, he considers coming back later. Perhaps that's enough for today. That's the cowardly thing to do. Today, he is courageous. He raps lightly on the door. The animated sounds continue inside, oblivious to his gentle approach. The next time he pounds harder with the side of his fist. A flurry of feet approach the door. It opens freely, and Heller is face to face with a man he has never seen before. He is holding a young girl, no more than two years old. He can't stop looking at her sad eyes. Like her mother. Finally, this is the right place. At his feet are two boys. Heller is pretty certain they are twins. Four years old perhaps. Their father smiles. "Good morning, Father. Can I help you?"

"Yes, perhaps this is not a good time. I was looking for someone who I thought might live here?"

"Who are you looking for Father?" The little girl is squirming out of her father's arms.

"I see you have your hands full. I will come back later."

"Father Heller?"

It is Sofia. She looks exactly as Heller remembers. Her sad eyes. Her gentle smile. She is not angry. She is standing behind her husband but now comes around him to greet Heller. She is pregnant.

"How did you find us? Why are you here? Oh, I'm sorry, Father. This is my husband Kurt." She explains to her husband. "Father and I worked together in North Africa. He was a chaplain."

"For the Germans?" Kurt's confused expression says it all.

Heller laughs nervously. "Yes, I know. A contradiction I am unequipped to explain."

"Everything about the war is hard to explain, Father."

"That's for sure. Sofia, I was wondering if I could have a word with you. If this is not a good time, I can come back."

"No of course. Kurt, do you mind?"

"Why don't you talk out here. I'll keep the chaos contained

inside. He moves the twins away from the door. Come on you two, inside. Nice to have met you Father."

"You as well, Kurt. Thank you."

They are standing on the landing outside the apartment. High enough that small slices of the Rhine can be seen down the narrow streets that intersect the river. Heller abandons any additional small talk. "Sofia, I came here to apologize to you."

"To me? For what, Father? What did you do?"

"You can't be serious. You must remember?"

"No, I really don't."

"Do you remember the rumors about a Nazi spy within the ICRC?"

She leans over the railing, watching children playing in the courtyard below. "Of course. From the day I started working there. We all heard the rumors. But nobody ever proved it. Nobody turned anybody in."

"But Sofia, I did. I told the Allies you were a spy. I sacrificed you in exchange for a way out of North Africa. I ruined your career."

"Father, the Allies interrogated everybody. Not just me. Most of my friends were under suspicion. Kurt was detained for a week. They were looking for a scapegoat but couldn't get any evidence no matter where they turned. You poor man. You have been beating yourself up about this for four years."

"Nearly five." Heller sags against the railing.

"So for five years you have been searching for me just to apologize. That humbles me Father. You are so kind. And now you are free of all that guilt."

His sunken eyes brighten. "I must admit. A great weight has been lifted."

Sofia reaches out to hug him, but he is reluctant to embrace a pregnant woman.

"Oh Father." She gently kisses his cheek. He blushes.

"Now, let's agree that all of this nonsense is behind us, okay?"

Heller sighs heavily. "Yes, yes, I agree." His relief is palpable.

"In fact, Father I know you came here to talk to me. But now I want you to leave with me having the final word." She rubs her belly gently. "Our baby is due in five months. Promise me you'll stay in Basel. And when the baby arrives you can perform the Baptism, how does that sound?"

"It would be an honor Sofia."

"Good. Then it's settled. Come back again and let us know where we can reach you, so we can stay in touch. Now, I really should be getting back. Kurt has his hands full."

She remains on the landing and watches Heller descend into the courtyard. She can see the burden lifted. The carefree gait. No sense of urgency. He even stops to talk to some of the mothers in the courtyard. Playfully teases some of the children. His soul is clear.

She steps back into the apartment. "Sorry that took so long Kurt."

Their daughter is sleeping in his arms, her head draped across his shoulder. "Is that really him?"

"Sure is. After all these years of doubting my suspicions, I was right all along. That's the bastard who nearly got me arrested. The Allies were closer than they ever realized."

"You were too smart for them, Sofia. They never had a chance. But why did you let him get away like that? He needs to pay for his disloyalty to the Reich."

"Don't worry. He'll be hanging around long enough to baptize our baby." She stretches her arm and takes their daughter from Kurt.

“Don’t you ever get tired of the hypocrisy? Going to confession. Getting the kids baptized.”

“Not really. It’s the only way to avoid suspicion and keep them believing we’re one of them. Besides, what’s one more baptism? It keeps him close for a few weeks. By then, the right people will know about his disloyalty. By the time they’re finished with him, he’ll wish he never escaped America.”

She steps back outside and looks below. Heller is gone. The sun has vanished and a fine drizzle begins to fall. She strokes the hair of her still-sleeping daughter. Scans the distant boulevard and glimpses him crossing the busy street as he struggles with his raincoat. He is heading back toward the river. A foolish man with a clean conscience.

ACKNOWLEDGEMENT

While years of independent research delivered a solid foundation for my historical novel, I want to single out a few authors and their scholarly contributions to the subject. The late Arnold Krammer's *Nazi Prisoners of War in America* gives a sweeping account of the topic while *The Enemy Within Never Did Without*, by Jeffrey L. Littlejohn and Charles H. Ford, delivers a peek inside Camp Huntsville, Texas. I am grateful for the context and clarity these books provided.

But all of the research that helps define the backdrop of *When Courage Comes* fails to trace the true journey of this first-time novelist.

It begins with my beautiful wife and forever friend, Judy. How many guys get to say that every choice, decision, and dream in their lives was met by those same soothing words -- "I believe in you." Well, thanks for believing one more time and letting me escape to write without burdens or limitations. I love you. And thanks to our amazing daughters, Moira and Megan. You are the reason I get to say that being a father is the greatest job in the world.

Maybe I feel that way too because of my special parents, to whom this book is dedicated. Their love story and the sacrifices they made in World War II nurtured this tale. I am forever grateful to them and to my siblings who share our priceless bond -- the special gift of parents who never asked for war then never complained about its unforeseen consequences.

Today, my extended family and loyal friends deepen the

immeasurable support I have received. One person in the Fleming family tree deserves a special nod. To my niece Kristen I am so thankful for your insights and encouragement at a time when I naively thought my book was complete. Not realizing that another year would pass while your gentle influence led me to personalities in the publishing world who provided a nurturing spirit that fortified me.

One of those people is Beth Jusino, a Seattle-based publishing consultant whose professional evaluation of my early manuscript left me both humbled and more excited than ever about my journey. Thank you Beth for delivering on your promise of helping me tell a better story.

Similar gratification comes courtesy of my countless early readers who enthusiastically embraced their roles. Too numerous to mention, each of you brought an objective eye to every page of my book. I will never be able to repay you for your willingness to read early manuscripts, deliver incredible insights about developing characters and honestly critique the evolving plot of *When Courage Comes*. Your candid observations helped shape this story. Your unsolicited encouragement provided fuel. My gratitude is boundless.

Finding amazing talent to market my book meant searching no further than the savvy young hotshots who surround me every day. They made the difference, giving *When Courage Comes* the identity it deserves. Shout outs to Kiersten Hepler and Derek Evanosky for sacrificing early mornings and priceless personal time to deliver a website, search campaign, and social media strategies that embraced Kiersten's merciful message to me, "Paul you need to be a little less humble." And the book's beautiful cover art and design? It belongs to Aaron Baksa who nailed the assignment while finding time to polish my website. How cool that so many readers will get to see his work.

If you haven't figured it out yet, I have been blessed in so many ways. *When Courage Comes* is certainly the realization of a personal dream. But it's wrapped around a compelling reminder that something bigger made this happen. That writing a book draws so many wonderful people into your path and humbles you at every turn. And that's what makes the journey remarkable.

Paul M. Fleming

August 10, 2020

Hugo returns the folded chairs to the tilted stack "You have a dream to serve the men in an army that ignores religion. I have a dream to return to New York. Stephan dreams of a better world beyond this war with someone that God put into his life. So, who is to judge the foolishness of our dreams?"

"You are cunning and wise my friend. Will you at least promise me that before you do anything foolish, you'll talk to me?"

"Ah, that's why we still need to discuss the favor you now owe me."

Heller raises his eyebrows and smiles. "I was actually beginning to think you forgot. Now, I don't think I'm going to like this favor."

"Actually, this is a pretty easy one. I need to hide the materials I've been gathering. It's getting too dangerous to keep them in my barracks."

"I'd like to help but my living quarters are not exactly the safest option either. They watch me rather closely, too."

Hugo walks over to the stack of prayer books. "Actually, that's not where I was thinking of hiding my things."

"I don't like the look on your face."

Hugo leans over the partially empty box that Heller had been unpacking. He empties the rest, placing them gently on the floor. He turns to the chaplain and looks inside the empty box then up at Heller. "I was thinking right in here."

"And then where would you put the box?"

Hugo places the empty box against the wall. He then grabs another unopened box filled with prayer books and places it on top. Then stacks another on top of that one. He smiles and shrugs, "Perfect, yes?"

"When will you fill that empty box before it collapses?"

"I think it's better if you don't know that answer Father.

limited exposure. The easiest find was a local bus schedule left on the library counter. It not only provided an essential map for the direction of his escape, but it established an accurate schedule that would help with the timing of his departure. And if he is lucky enough to make it to a bus, he will have plenty of American currency to pay the fare, courtesy of his laundry detail.

"Brilliant Hugo. I have just met you but it appears this battered man whom the guards consider a lazy hustler and the Nazis use as a punching bag has fooled them all." Heller stands up, walks behind Hugo and grips his shoulders. "So it is not a question of *if* but *when* for you."

"Correct, preacher."

"This is dangerous Hugo. You are sure no one else knows?"

Hugo stands, folds his chair and leans on it. "There is one person who deserves to know but I want to protect him."

"From what?"

"Himself."

"I don't understand. "

Hugo points to Heller's chair. The chaplain folds it and Hugo takes it from him.

"His name is Stephan Jurgen, an innocent Austrian conscript.

"Very few of us are innocent of wrongdoing in this war."

"Perhaps. But this guy is as close as you are going to get."

"And why the desire to protect him?"

"If Stephan knew and was somehow implicated, he would not be harmed by the Americans, but his activities might be curtailed. And that would mean precious time away from a young woman he fancies."

"How romantic. And maybe foolish on your friend's part. That doesn't sound like it will have a happy ending."

Hugo returns the folded chairs to the tilted stack "You have a dream to serve the men in an army that ignores religion. I have a dream to return to New York. Stephan dreams of a better world beyond this war with someone that God put into his life. So, who is to judge the foolishness of our dreams?"

"You are cunning and wise my friend. Will you at least promise me that before you do anything foolish, you'll talk to me?"

"Ah, that's why we still need to discuss the favor you now owe me."

Heller raises his eyebrows and smiles. "I was actually beginning to think you forgot. Now, I don't think I'm going to like this favor."

"Actually, this is a pretty easy one. I need to hide the materials I've been gathering. It's getting too dangerous to keep them in my barracks."

"I'd like to help but my living quarters are not exactly the safest option either. They watch me rather closely, too."

Hugo walks over to the stack of prayer books. "Actually, that's not where I was thinking of hiding my things."

"I don't like the look on your face."

Hugo leans over the partially empty box that Heller had been unpacking. He empties the rest, placing them gently on the floor. He turns to the chaplain and looks inside the empty box then up at Heller. "I was thinking right in here."

"And then where would you put the box?"

Hugo places the empty box against the wall. He then grabs another unopened box filled with prayer books and places it on top. Then stacks another on top of that one. He smiles and shrugs, "Perfect, yes?"

"When will you fill that empty box before it collapses?"

"I think it's better if you don't know that answer Father.

limited exposure. The easiest find was a local bus schedule left on the library counter. It not only provided an essential map for the direction of his escape, but it established an accurate schedule that would help with the timing of his departure. And if he is lucky enough to make it to a bus, he will have plenty of American currency to pay the fare, courtesy of his laundry detail.

"Brilliant Hugo. I have just met you but it appears this battered man whom the guards consider a lazy hustler and the Nazis use as a punching bag has fooled them all." Heller stands up, walks behind Hugo and grips his shoulders. "So it is not a question of *if* but *when* for you."

"Correct, preacher."

"This is dangerous Hugo. You are sure no one else knows?"

Hugo stands, folds his chair and leans on it. "There is one person who deserves to know but I want to protect him."

"From what?"

"Himself."

"I don't understand. "

Hugo points to Heller's chair. The chaplain folds it and Hugo takes it from him.

"His name is Stephan Jurgen, an innocent Austrian conscript.

"Very few of us are innocent of wrongdoing in this war."

"Perhaps. But this guy is as close as you are going to get."

"And why the desire to protect him?"

"If Stephan knew and was somehow implicated, he would not be harmed by the Americans, but his activities might be curtailed. And that would mean precious time away from a young woman he fancies."

"How romantic. And maybe foolish on your friend's part. That doesn't sound like it will have a happy ending."

ABOUT THE AUTHOR

Paul M. Fleming

Paul is a restless baby-boomer who finally ran out of excuses for writing his first novel. A Philly-born entrepreneur who started his own advertising agency over 3 decades ago, he built an award-winning business, raised a beautiful family with his wife Judy, and never lost his passion for storytelling. For years he delivered polished writing that motivated, inspired, and educated audiences for lots of grateful clients. Now with his breakout novel, When Courage Comes, Paul combines his research skills and fondness for history with a startling story he's been itching to tell the world. This ultimate optimist with a wickedly dry sense of humor is already nurturing more unexpected tales -- usually inspired during long walks on the beach at the Jersey shore.

Made in the USA
Monee, IL
02 April 2022

93981634R00225